Awards, Select Reviews, & American Editions of *The Kommandant's Mistress*

Awards

• The University of Rochester's *Janet Heidinger Kafka Award* for "the outstanding book of prose fiction written by an American woman" (1994)
• Selected as one of *The New York Times Book Review's* "Top 100 Books" (1993)
• Talmadge McKinney Award for Research Excellence (Central State University, OH) 1993

Select Reviews

• "A fictional work of tortured brilliance and power... Devastating... Riveting... Remarkable." — Patrick McGrath, *New York Times Book Review*
• "Szeman's uncompromising realism and superb use of stream-of-consciousness technique make this a chilling study of evil, erotic obsession, and the will to survive." — *Publishers Weekly* (starred review, "denoting a work of exceptional worth & merit"), © 1993 Reed Business Information
• "Daring... Intoxicating... Addictive." — *The New Yorker*
• "Szeman has created a novel that announces her arrival as a major talent." — Geoffrey Stokes, *Boston Sunday Globe*
• "Szeman never shrinks from the terrible truths of her dark theme... By choosing such a disturbing subject, and treating it in original and uncompromising ways, Szeman has added her voice to this essential literature of recent history." — Hilma Wolitzer, *New York Newsday*
• "Riveting... A stunning achievement." — Andy Solomon, *San Francisco Chronicle*
• "A novel of considerable power. Szeman's sense of character, place, and history is unerring, and her mastery of her narrative strategy is remarkable." — Emily Wright, *Atlanta Journal Constitution*

American Editions

• First Edition published by HarperCollins 1993 (Hardcover/Cloth, 5 printings), HarperPerennial 1994 (Trade Paper, 4 printings);
• Second edition (including translations of Verdi's opera *La Traviata*) by Arcade Publishing 2000 (Trade Paper, 6 printings);
• Revised & Expanded, 20th Anniversary Edition, Trade Paper (2013) & e-Book (2012) by RockWay Press 2012-2013

Other Books by Alexandria Constantinova Szeman

Novels

• *Only with the Heart,* Revised & Expanded, Legally & Medically Updated, 12th Anniversary Edition

• *No Feet in Heaven*

• *The Kommandant's Mistress* (1st Edition: HarperCollins 1993, 5 printings; HarperPerennial 1994, 4 printings; 2nd Edition [with translations of Verdi's opera *La Traviata*]: Arcade 2000, 6 printings), (formerly writing as "Sherri")

• *Only with the Heart* (1st Edition: Arcade 2000, 8 printings), (formerly writing as "Sherri")

Short Stories

• *Naked, with Glasses*

Poems

• *Love in the Time of Dinosaurs*

• *Where Lightning Strikes: Poems on the Holocaust*

Creative Writing
Non-fiction

• *Mastering Point of View: Using POV & Fiction Elements to Create Conflict, Develop Characters, Revise Your Work, & Improve Your Craft;* Revised, Updated, & Expanded; 12th Anniversary Edition

• *Mastering Point of View: How to Control POV to Create Conflict, Depth, & Suspense* (1st Edition: Story Press 2001, 8 printings), (formerly writing as "Sherri")

About *The Kommandant's Mistress*

The rumors spread by the Camp's inmates, other Nazi officers, and the Kommandant's own family insist that she was his "mistress", but was she, voluntarily? Told from three different perspectives — that of the formerly idealistic Kommandant, the young Jewish inmate who captivates him, and the ostensibly objective historical biographies of the protagonists — this novel examines one troubling moral question over and over: if your staying alive was the only "good" during the War, if your survival was your sole purpose in this horrific world of the Concentration Camps — whether you were Nazi or Jewish — what, exactly, would you do to survive? Would you lie, cheat, steal, kill, submit?

Flashing back and forth through the narrators' memories as they recall their time before, during, and after the War, and leading, inevitably, to their ultimate, shocking confrontation, "Szeman's uncompromising realism and superb use of stream-of-consciousness technique make [this novel] a chilling study of evil, erotic obsession, and the will to survive" (*Publishers Weekly*).

Winner of the University of Rochester's Kafka Prize for "the outstanding book of prose fiction by an American woman" ('94) and chosen as one of the *New York Times Book Review*'s "Top 100 Books of the Year" ('93), the tales told by the Kommandant, his "mistress", and their "biographer" will mesmerize and stun you, leaving you wondering, at the conclusion, which, if any, is telling the complete truth about what happened between them.

This Revised & Expanded, 20th Anniversary Edition contains new material, including the author's original "story" and "poem" which formed the inspiration for the book, a Chapter-by-Chapter Scene Index, as well as Discussion Questions for teachers, students, and book groups.

About the writing style of The Kommandant's Mistress

The writing style of Szeman's novels is highly unusual, moving as it does from past to present to a further-back-past and to present again, seemingly without warning. It imitates how the mind works, especially with respect to memory, where everything always appears to be happening in the present.

In the mind, especially in memory, thoughts, sounds, smells, feelings, and words lead to memories which then lead to other thoughts, feelings, etc. and to other memories associatively.

Sometimes the switch between scenes in *The Kommandant's Mistress* is triggered by words in the narrator's memory; at other times, the switch is triggered symbolically by something in the previous scene(s).

For dialogue tags, only "s/he said" is used, even for questions (as William Faulkner does in his books & stories) so that the reader can interpret for himself how the character is saying the lines.

The Kommandant's Mistress

a novel

Revised & Expanded
20th Anniversary Edition

Alexandria Constantinova Szeman
(formerly writing as "Sherri")

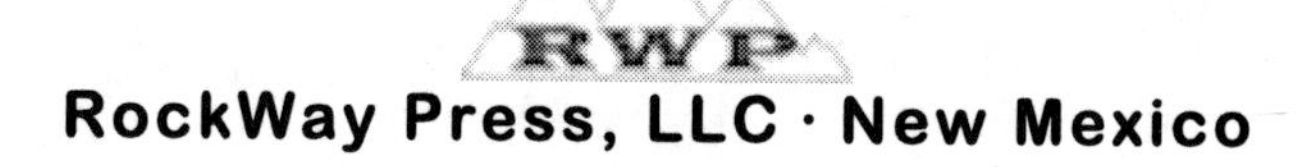

RockWay Press, LLC · New Mexico

Permissions & Publication Acknowledgments

• Excerpts from *Eichmann Interrogated: Transcripts from the Archives of the Israeli Police,* edited by Jochen von Lang. Translation © 1983 by Farrar, Straus & Giroux, Inc. Reprinted by permission of Farrar, Straus & Giroux, LLC.

• Excerpts from *Einsatz* instructions, *Waldsee* postcard, and C. H. Kori letter (about ovens) from *The Rise and Fall of the Third Reich* by William Shirer, © 1959, 1960 by William L. Shirer; © renewed 1987, 1988 by William L. Shirer. Reprinted with the permission of Simon & Schuster.

• Excerpts from the official documents, orders, anecdotes, speeches, and language from *The Destruction of the European Jews* (revised and definitive edition), © 1985 by Raul Hilberg. Used with gracious permission of author, his agent Raines & Raines, and publisher.

• Excerpts from teletype messages 4 May 1943 and 13 May 1943 from *The Stroop Report: A Facsimile Edition and Translation of the Official Nazi Report on the Destruction of the Warsaw Ghetto,* translated by Sybil Milton, © 1979 by Random House, Inc. Reprinted by permission of Pantheon Books, a division of Random House, Inc.

• Excerpts of Verdi's *La Traviata,* © 1853-1865. Used with permission.

• A small portion of this work appeared (in altered form, as a poem entitled "The Kommandant" under the name "Sherri" Szeman) in the following journals: *MSS, Red Cedar Review, Sidewinder.*

• The poem "The Kommandant" was published under the name "Sherri" Szeman in the Ph.D. creative writing dissertation of original poems, *Survivor: One Who Survives* (University of Cincinnati, 1986).

• The original poems "Cutthroat: A Player Who Plays for Himself" and "First Day of German Class" originally appeared, in their entirety, under the name "Sherri" Szeman, in *Hawaii Review* and *Ohio Journal,* respectively.

Library of Congress Cataloging-in-Publication Data

The Kommandant's Mistress, a novel: Alexandria Constantinova Szeman (formerly writing as Sherri Szeman).

1. Holocaust, Jewish (1939-1945) — Fiction. 2. Nazi Concentration Camps — Fiction. 3. Jewish women — Fiction. 4. World War II — Fiction. 5. Political Studies — Fiction. 6. Psychological Studies — Fiction. 7. Women's Studies — Fiction.
PS3569.Z39 K66 2000
811'.54—dc210055840

American Editions

• 1st Edition published by HarperCollins 1993, ISBN 0060170115 (Cloth/Hardcover, 5 Printings), & by HarperPerennial 1994, ISBN 0060924977 (Trade Paper, 4 Printings).
• 2nd Edition (including translation of lyrics to Verdi's Opera *La Traviata*) published by Arcade Publishing 2000, ISBN 1559705426 (Trade Paper, 6 Printings).
• Revised & Expanded, 20th Anniversary Edition (including Author's Note, Original Story & Poem, Chapter-by-Chapter Scene Index, and Discussion Questions) published by RockWay Press, LLC, 2012.

Revised & Expanded, 20th Anniversary Edition

RockWay Press Trade Paper ISBN 9780976819653
LCCN 2011963579
E-Book ISBN 9780976819615

Visit our Web site at RockWayPress.com

For **Tom,**

Here's [my hand],
with my heart in it.

William Shakespeare
The Tempest 3:3:89

For **Becky Keller,**
il miglior fabbro

Gladly wolde he lerne,
and gladly teche.

Geoffrey Chaucer
The Canterbury Tales
Prologue: 308

For **Sharon Brown,**

Thy word is a lamp unto my feet,
and a light to my path.

Psalms 119:105

Acknowledgments

Grateful acknowledgment is made to Dr. Terrence Glass, my colleague-poet and friend, who patiently read the manuscript of my first novel in draft and provided invaluable criticism.

To Dr. Gerd Fricke, who provided the German translations, always in context of the scenes, and always with keen interest in the characters' natures.

To Christopher Williams, belovèd "son", who reads everything I write, gives honest & insightful critiques, makes me laugh every time we talk, and who makes me happy and proud of him every day.

To my dissertation advisor, Michael Atkinson, who read the original story (which was undeniably dreadful) and advised me to "stick to poetry". His advice changed a bad story into an award-winning poem, which eventually yearned to become this novel. Thank you, Michael, for your loving yet frank honesty (and, no, you didn't hurt my feelings, even thirty years ago).

To Evelyn Schott, my friend who saved the story all those years and then sent it to me, long after the novel had been published and won critical acclaim as well as awards, cautioning me, in advance, that the original story was "really bad". And to Evelyn's husband, Greg, both of whom came to every single reading I ever did in Cincinnati, though they must have had the book memorized by the tenth time or so. Love to you both, always.

To my Uncle Paul, retired police officer/detective, for teaching me all about guns and shooting for the scenes between Max & Rachel. To the Wright Patterson Air Force Museum Special Collections Director, who trusted me alone in a room with an SS-Officer's uniform and weapon. Bless both of you for taking an interest in a writer's first novel.

To my agents, Geri Thoma, of the Markson Thoma Agency, who originally sold the novel to HarperCollins; and to Jennifer Hengen, formerly of Sterling Lord Literistic, who sold it to Arcade. Thank you for your efforts on my behalf.

To Brenda Segel, Senior Vice-President & Director of Rights at HarperCollins, who came up with the much improved title, suggesting the change from my original *The Kommandant* to *The Kommandant's Mistress,* based on the "rumors about Rachel" in Part Three of the novel as well as on John Fowles' famed *The French Lieutenant's Woman.* Thank you, Brenda, for putting Urgency in my title, and helping to sell the book not only here in the US, but all over the UK, Europe, and Asia.

To Spike, Zoë, Vinnie, Hannah, Zeke, and Mosie: though you were taken from us far too soon, you're with us still. I thank you for your unconditional love as well as for lying on my desk and computer every single day while I wrote. I miss you more than I could ever say. You are in my heart forever.

To Shooter Tov, Mr. Eli, Trixie, Ling, Sascha, Sophie, and Sadie-Doggie: without having rescued you and brought you into our lives, my own happiness would be lessened. Thanks for letting me use my office, desk, printers, computer keyboard, and chairs when it doesn't inconvenience you too much.

To Grandpa and Grandma Hirsch, who gave me my first chess-set when I was 8-years-old, spoke Yiddish at home, faithfully honored the Jewish Sabbath by closing Grandpa's neighborhood/corner grocery every Saturday (and opening it on Sundays despite living in the era of "Blue Laws"), had *Shabbas* every Friday at sun-down, and instructed me on "being Jewish" when I was a little girl.

"Grandpa, how did you know all I wanted in the world was a chess-set?"
"A little angel sitting on my shoulder told me."
"Aren't we Jewish?" I said. "Do Jews believe in angels?"
"Such a smart little girl we have," said Grandpa Hirsch, patting me on the head.
"Who's a smart little girl?" said Grandma, behind me. "Because she plays chess?"
"Because she just asked if we were Jewish."
Grandma Hirsch knelt down, took me by the arms, and whispered.
"If anyone asks if you're Jewish, you must say, 'I was baptized & I go to Catholic schools'. You understand?"
I nodded.
"Are you Jewish?"
"Yes."
"No," she said, still holding onto me, shaking her head. "Are you Jewish?"
"I was baptized… and I go to Catholic schools."
"Good girl," she said, kissing me on the cheek and hugging me.
"You see?" said Grandpa Hirsch, mussing my hair. "I told you she was smart."

To you, Grandpa and Grandma Hirsch, who thought your family name would die with the baby boy you lost & other family members killed in the Holocaust; because you had to hide our ethnicity and heritage; because you sent all your daughters, grandchildren, and great-grandchildren to Catholic schools "to keep us safe" from anti-Semitism — *Yom HaShoah* — I've never forgotten.

To all the family members I lost during the Holocaust, though I didn't learn about you until after I wrote this novel and did a genealogical search on Grandpa and Grandma Hirsch's family in Germany.

To Great-Aunt Z, who escaped Russia and came to America, alone, without knowing any English, when she was only 12-years-old, between 1903-1906, the last time Czar Nicholas permitted any Jews to freely leave his country to escape the government-organized *pogroms*. Your stories and love are still with me.

And special acknowledgment to my dear friend Dr. Anna Brunn Ornstein, who survived Auschwitz; who, along with her husband Paul, welcomed me into their home, hearts, and lives; and who, over the years, has told me the sort of details that could never be found in any books: *köszönöm, edesem Anna.*

Table Of Contents

Part One: Max 1
Chapter One 3
Chapter Two 12
Chapter Three 21
Chapter Four 34
Chapter Five 43
Chapter Six 52
Chapter Seven 58
Chapter Eight 66
Chapter Nine 74
Chapter Ten 86

Part Two: Rachel 93
Chapter One 95
Chapter Two 107
Chapter Three 118
Chapter Four 129
Chapter Five 138
Chapter Six 146
Chapter Seven 156
Chapter Eight 167
Chapter Nine 177
Chapter Ten 186

Part Three: Biographical Encyclopedia Entries 193
Maximilian Ernst von Walther 195
Leah Sarah Abramson 199

Additions to 20th Anniversary Edition

Chapter-by-Chapter Scene Index 203
Discussion Questions 210
The Characters & Their Relationships 212
Epigraphs 213
Max's Six-Pointed Star 213

The Three Different Endings ... 214
Max's Ending ... 214
Rachel's Ending ... 215
Additional Questions: Max's and Rachel's Endings ... 215
The Biographies of Part Three ... 216
Questions About Endings in Biographical Entries ... 217
The Biographer of Part Three ... 218
Additional Questions on the Three Endings ... 219
Rachel as the Kommandant's "Mistress" ... 220
The Theme of Parents & Their Children ... 221
Rachel & The Underground ... 224
Select Sources for *The Kommandant's Mistress,* 1st edition ... 226
Author's Note on *The Kommandant's Mistress,* 20th Anniv Ed ... 228
My Start as a Poet ... 228
Writing my First Novel ... 229
Publishing *The Kommandant's Mistress* ... 235
On My Name ... 238
Special Notes to Readers about *The Kommandant's Mistress* ... 239
On the Three Different Endings ... 239
On Rachel as the Kommandant's "Mistress" ... 241
On Rachel's Poems & Books ... 242
On the Camp's Underground ... 243
Additions to the 20th Anniversary Edition ... 243
Revisions to the 20th Anniversary Edition ... 245
Original Story and Poem: "The Kommandant" ... 252
Original Story ... 253
Original Poem ... 259

Author BIO, Photo, Amazon Page, Web-site, Twitter, Blog, & Contact Information

Photo ... 266
About Alexandria ... 266
Alexandria's Amazon Author Central Page ... 268
Alexandria's Web-site ... 268
Alexandria's Blog: The Alexandria Papers ... 268
Alexandria's Twitter: @Alexandria_SZ ... 268
Contact Alexandria ... 268

The Kommandant's Mistress

Part One

For who can make straight
that which He hath made crooked?

Ecclesiastes 7:13

Chapter One

Then I saw her. There she stood, in the village store, her hair in a long braid down the center of her back, her skin white in the sunlight, and my hand went to my hip, seeking the weight of my gun. As the girl spoke, I stumbled back against one of the shelves, my fingers tightening at the leather around my waist. While the shopkeeper arranged the food in the bag, the morning sun glinted on the storefront windows, illuminating the girl. The wooden shelves pressed into my shoulders and back. Sweat dampened my forehead and ribs. Another shopper spoke, frowned, pushed aside my arm to reach a jar on the shelf behind me, but I didn't move. My hand slid down over my hip and leg. No, I'd forgotten that I no longer wore my gun.

There she stood. The first time my adjutant brought her to my office, she seemed frailer than in the yard: the faded grey dress hung loosely from her thinned shoulders. A red scarf was on her head. After my adjutant addressed me, I put down my pen and rose from my desk. I dismissed my adjutant and approached the girl. Her cheekbones were sharp under the skin, and the hollows around her eyes were faintly shadowed, but her lips were full, and the light grey gown fluttered over her small, firm breasts. I nodded as I slowly moved around her, my baton brushing her belly, hips, thighs. She didn't move away. I stroked my hand down the center of her back: she wore nothing beneath the thin gown. I smiled to myself as my fingers dragged themselves around her slender body until the girl and I faced each other. When my baton lifted her chin, she didn't look away.

"*Ja*," I said, returning her stare. "*Ja*.

I didn't look away. I've never looked away. Even in the beginning, I faced it all, without blinking. I stared up at the speakers' platform and I nodded. All around me, eager young men wore black uniforms, like mine, under the clear night sky. We gazed up at the speakers' platform, at the small man in wire-framed glasses. He was only a name to us then, his face outlined by the flames of the torches surrounding the platform, surrounding us. Our chests swelled under the black wool. Our breath sounded in each other's ears as we leaned toward the podium to catch his words. In the dark, the speaker's glasses reflected the torchlight: bright flames burned in place of his eyes.

"We are the pure of this nation," he said. "We are the noble. We are the good. We are the hope of our country."

All of us officer candidates nodded.

"We don't fear to shed our own blood for our cause," he said. "More important, we don't fear to shed others' blood."

No, we'd never been afraid of sacrifice. We applauded until he raised his hand for silence.

"You have pledged your honor and duty, but I expect you to do more than your duty," said his voice from the flames. "I expect you to save our country. Save our country. Save our Fatherland."

The crowd roared. I gripped the butt of my pistol with one hand and raised my other hand in salute. It's difficult to explain to someone who wasn't there. The speaker, high on a platform above us, his arms raised to the dark of the night. The glow of the flames, the warmth of the uniforms, the smell of excitement. The glare of the light in our eyes. And all around me, my companions' voices, chanting, like a prayer.

"*Meine Ehre heisst treue,*" I said. "My honor is my loyalty."

The glare of the light stung my eyes. The pistol was heavy in my hand, but comfortable. Warm. It was trembling. I gripped the top of the weapon and readied it for firing, pulling up and back on the two circles of metal at its top: *snap, click*. I raised the gun. My hand lowered. I took another drink of whiskey, set the glass on the back of the sink. I clenched my teeth, closed my eyes, and lifted the weapon again. Its muzzle pressed against cold flesh.

"Do it," I said. "Do it."

When I opened my eyes, the image of myself in the bathroom mirror fixed me: the muzzle gouged the skin at my right temple. My hair was like an animal's. My eyes like an inmate's. My stomach and throat heaved. I bent over the sink until the gagging stopped, gripping the cold basin with my free hand. It seemed so easy to think of it: put the gun against bone. Pull the trigger. I'd fired the weapon so many times I could've used it in my sleep. I splashed my face with cold water. I stood. I held my breath and pressed the weapon tighter against my skull. Tighter. Tighter. Steel against bone. Bone against steel. Tighter. Tighter. Until my head hurt. No, I wasn't afraid: I wasn't strong enough.

"My head hurts, Daddy," said Ilse.

She slumped in her chair at the dinner table, grimacing as she rested her chin in her palm.

"From the gas," she said.

"Gas?" I said, my knife scraping against my plate. "I don't smell any gas."

"Maybe the stove needs to be checked," said Marta.

She wiped her hands on her apron after she set her own dinner plate on the table and leaned over the stove, squinting and sniffing near the burners.

"Maybe one of the pilots blew out," she said.

"Not that gas," said Ilse.

"What gas?" I said, putting down my fork and wiping my mouth with my napkin.

"The Jew-gas," said Ilse, leaning more into her hand.

"Jew-gas?" said Marta, standing up from the stove. "What are you talking about, Ilse?"

"The Jew-gas, the Jew-gas. The gas that kills the Jews."

"Max," said Marta, looking at me.

"You can't smell that gas, Ilse," I said.

"Yes, I can."

"No, you can't."

"It's giving me a headache."

"If you could smell that gas, you wouldn't be alive right now."

I broke apart a piece of dark bread. Ilse shoved away her plate. At the other end of the dinner table, Hans knocked his spoon off the tray of his highchair. He kicked his feet and leaned over the side of his chair, reaching for the spoon. I put more potatoes on my plate.

"I can smell the Jew-gas," said Ilse. "It's making me sick."

"You can't smell it. If you smelled it, you'd be dead."

"Max, please."

Hans squealed and kicked the tray of his highchair. I cut another piece of meat as Marta sat down. Ilse pushed away her silverware. Hans kicked the edge of the dinner table. Marta reached for the baby's spoon, lying on the floor beside his highchair.

"Eat, Ilse," I said. "You can't smell that gas."

"It's giving me a headache anyway."

Marta never liked it when I discussed work at the dinner table. Even if the children were already in bed. Even when I spoke with Dieter. I don't think women understand men's work. They're so intent on family, they don't see that the family couldn't exist without everything that we men do, without our work. But men understand each other, without having to talk about it. Dieter and I almost always understood each other. Whenever Dieter had the time to join me for a few hours, I had the cook serve us lunch in my office, so Dieter and I could really talk. I raised my glass of wine and stared at it before draining the goblet. The aroma of garlic and spices filled my office as Dieter and I sat ourselves down at the table.

"Caviar," said Dieter, scooping some of the glistening black beads onto toasted bread. "How did you pull that off?"

"I'm the Kommandant," I said.

I lifted my glass toward Dieter's.

"To the greater glory of Germany," I said.

"To our *Führer,*" said Dieter, clicking his glass' rim against mine.

We drained our glasses. As I lifted the bottle of Burgundy and refilled the glasses, Dieter spread another crisp of bread with caviar. He closed his eyes as he put it into his mouth, and he made appreciative noises as he chewed.

"Delicious," said Dieter.

"To the everlasting Third Reich," I said, raising my glass.

"To the wealth of the Jews," said Dieter.

Our glasses clinked. The light from the windows glinted as the goblets were emptied and refilled. The music of violas, violins, and cellos swelled around the walls of my office as Dieter lifted the cover of one of the chafing dishes and inhaled.

"To us, my old friend," I said.

"To us," said Dieter, replacing the lid.

He drank his glass of wine and lifted more food covers.

"I envy you, Max, being here instead of at the Front, or in Berlin."

"I deserve it," I said.

"So do I, but I don't have it."

"You like being at the Front. You like the excitement."

"Sometimes," said Dieter. "But here: no bullets whizzing by your face in your sleep, no one hanging over your shoulder, memorizing every movement, writing down every word to put in a file on you."

"Sometimes the stench is unbearable," I said, twisting the corkscrew, releasing the cork from the wine bottle. "Marta complains all the time."

"And you have such a beautiful Jewess," said Dieter, his mouth full of pâté.

We both looked over at the girl. She sat, motionless, on the floor in the corner, her legs drawn to her chest, her arms wrapped around her legs. She wore no scarf, and her short hair looked white. She gazed steadily in front of her, at the windows darkened by storm clouds.

"Such an extraordinary face," said Dieter, "even now."

"Yes."

"And Marta doesn't..."

"Marta isn't permitted in my office."

"Wives complain about everything," said Dieter, filling his plate with roasted meat.

"Yes."

"Rudi had to send his Jewess off," said Dieter, pouring gravy over his meat and sighing.

"He did?"

"And the son."

"When?" I said, leaning forward.

"Last month."

"Why didn't you tell me?"

"I thought I did," said Dieter.

"He sent her to the gas?"

"Maybe he shot her," said Dieter, his mouth full. "I'm not sure. I'll ask around."

"So, the rumors were true," I said, and Dieter nodded. "Owl-eyes had him."

"If he didn't, the Blond Beast did," said Dieter. "Delicious goose."

"Done just right," I said. "Just the way I like it."

"How will you take care of the girl?" he said.

"What do you mean, how will I take care of the girl?"

"You heard me," said Marta. "How will you take care of the girl?"

When I looked up, Marta slapped a book down on the coffee table in front of me.

"What are you talking about?" I said.

"You should've taken care of her before," said Marta, "when I told you to. Now look what she's done."

On the coffee table lay a slim book, dark red, with black lettering: *The Dead Bodies That Line the Streets.* When I stretched out my hand to pick up the book, Marta snatched it away, opening it as she stood there, frowning at me, tapping her foot.

"Do you want to hear? Do you want to hear what that Jewish whore wrote about you?"

"She didn't write anything about me," I said, standing, the newspaper sliding from my lap to the floor. "That's impossible."

"You want to hear 'impossible'?" said Marta, flipping the pages. "Listen to this: 'First Day of German Class'."

"Give me the book," I said, and Marta stepped back.

"'The German sweeps in: he wears a blue-grey uniform and a halo of sunlight'."

"Let me see it."

"'He trembles, and I know that he, too, has been longing to play this part'."

"Give it to me," I said.

"And this," said Marta, slapping my hands with the book when I reached for it. "This: 'In the Bedroom of the Kommandant'."

"What?"

"You took her to our bedroom," said Marta, shaking the book at me. "A whore. A Jewess. In our bedroom. In my bed."

"Marta, let me see the book."

"You didn't tell her that you loved her, did you, Max?"

"Give me the book."

"Even you couldn't love a Jew, could you, Max?"

"Let me see the book."

"You lied to me," said Marta, slamming me on the arm with the closed book.

"It's all a lie," I said. "All of it."

"And the things you said to her."

"I didn't say anything to her."

"'She's just a Jew,' you told me, over and over," said Marta. "Isn't that what you said?"

"She is just a Jew."

"She's a Jew who understands German," said Marta.

"She didn't understand German."

"It's all here," said Marta, her forefinger stabbing the book's cover.

"She didn't understand. Not even the simplest things."

"You stupid, stupid man. She understood everything."

"No."

"She put it all down."

"No."

"Names. Dates. Places."

"She didn't understand," I said, shaking my head and reaching for the book again.

"Everything you ever said around her."

"She couldn't..."

"You're the one who doesn't understand, Max."

"It's a lie."

"It's an indictment. She wouldn't even need to be called as a witness. She's already testified. Here. In these pages."

"It's a mistake."

Marta threw the book across the room.

"It's every mistake you ever made, Max."

I stared at the thin book.

"You should've taken care of her when you said you would. You shouldn't have lied to me, Max."

I crossed the room and stood, looking down at the book.

"If she testifies, they'll hang you. What will I do then? And the children, what about them?"

I knelt.

"Didn't you think of us? Don't you ever think of anyone but yourself?"

Marta paced, her hands clenched. I picked up *The Dead Bodies.*

"There must be some mistake," I said.

"A Jewess," said Marta, "In my bed."

"There's been a mistake," I said. "You're not a Jew."

The young girl who had just alighted from the train stared up at me. The spotlights glowed on her hair, and her skin was translucent. An elderly man and woman clung to the girl's arms as she stood there amidst the jumbled luggage. The guards with their rifles and their barking dogs swarmed around, crushing the resettled families together on the night platform.

"Are you a Jew?" I said.

The girl looked silently at me. When the *Sonderkommando* dragged themselves nearer, with their black-and-white striped uniforms and their shaved heads, the elderly couple shrank against the girl.

"Josef," I said, and my adjutant came over to stand beside me.

"Kommandant?"

"Find out what language she speaks," I said.

He spoke to the girl. She answered.

"Hungarian," he said.

"Are you a Jew?" I said.

The girl looked at me while the adjutant translated. The girl nodded.

"You don't look like a Jew."

After the girl glanced down at the six-pointed gold patch stitched securely over her left breast, her fingers brushed its edges.

"She says she's a Jew."

"Are both of your parents Jews?" I said.

"These are her parents."

The two old people clinging to her arms nodded.

"Do you have any ancestors who were not Jews?"

The girl shook her head. I stared at her a moment before walking away.

"I wish I could help you, but there's nothing I can do."

"There's nothing you can do now," said the young man in the hotel dining room as he hit his fists against my table, jostling my wineglass. His face and eyes were wild.

"Have we met?" I said, putting down my newspaper.

"I know who you are," said the young man. "I know what you've done."

"Waiter," I said.

"You killed my father," said the young man.

"Can I help you, sir?" said the waiter, looking at the young man.

"Get away from me. My business is with him."

"*Herr* Hoffmann is one of our guests. I must ask that you..."

"This isn't your business."

"This young man is disturbing me," I said. "And I doubt that he's a guest here."

"Come away," said the waiter as he took hold of the young man's arm.

"You killed my mother," said the young man. "Did you think I would forget you? Did you think any of us would forget you?"

"I'll notify the desk," said the waiter, waving one of his colleagues from another station.

A second waiter joined the first, and several diners turned to view the commotion. The boy bumped the table, spilling the water and the wine.

"You won't get away so easily this time," said the young man. "I'm not alone."

"Come along," said the first waiter.

"Don't disturb our guests," said the second.

"I know you, von Walther," said the young man.

"You've mistaken me for someone else," I said, and I stood as the young man twisted his body in the waiters' grip.

"We'll call the police," said the waiters as they tugged him toward the doorway. "Come away. Don't cause trouble."

"He killed my sister," said the young man.

The desk clerk picked up the telephone. I straightened my jacket and glanced around the room. The other diners looked down at their food. I reseated myself at the table as the two waiters struggled with the young man, dragging him toward the lobby. Several diners leaned toward each other over their tables and whispered. My bread had fallen onto my plate and was lying there, reddened, beside the steak. A third waiter righted my wineglass and filled it.

"We're sorry for the disturbance, *Herr* Hoffmann," said a fourth waiter as he dabbed at the spilled wine with towels.

"Do you want to hear what we're going to do to you?" said the young man from the lobby.

"Most embarrassing, sir," said one of the waiters as he removed the soaked newspaper. "We do apologize."

"It's not your fault," I said, reaching for my wineglass.

The glass trembled when I touched it. I left the glass on the table.

"Do you want to hear your future, von Walther?" said the young man as he strained against the grip of the waiters and the hotel's guard.

"We do apologize, sir," said the waiter as I picked up my knife and fork.

"Do you want to hear?"

"Yes, tell me," I said. "Tell me what happened."

"'In my life I have been a prophet, and tonight'," said Dieter, "'I want to be a prophet once more'."

"Did he really say that?" I said. "During dinner?"

"Between the soup and vegetable course," said Dieter, nodding. "He said..."

"How did you get invited?" I said, leaning back into the cushions of the couch. "I've never been to dinner with him."

"I told you," said Dieter as he lit his cigar. "My sister-in-law's cousin's husband. Do you want to hear what he said or not?"

"Of course," I said. "Tell me."

"Between the soup and the vegetable course he said, 'We will annihilate the Jews in Europe'."

"Yes. What else?"

"'We will save Germany'," said Dieter as Marta brought in the tray with coffee and cake.

"Chocolate cake," said Marta. "And real coffee."

"Marta," said Dieter, swooning toward her. "I'm in love. Will you marry me?"

Marta laughed as she sliced the cake with its thick caramel icing.

"Was he really wearing a tie that didn't match his jacket?" said Marta.

"Unfortunately," said Dieter, spooning sugar into his coffee.

"Was she there?" said Marta. "What's she like?"

"The *Führer* says we'll save Germany," I said, and Marta looked at me.

"How does it feel to be a Saviour?" said Dieter.

"Save Germany?" said Marta.

"Yes," I said. "Save..."

"Save Germany? We have to save ourselves," said Marta, "and the children. We can't think of anything else right now."

"Are you sure it's a warrant for my arrest?" I said, tying the belt on my robe.

"As soon as I heard your name, I grabbed my coat and rushed out," said the boy. "If they're not on their way now, they'll be here first thing in the morning."

"For my arrest?"

"Go," said Marta to the boy.

He clutched his cap, and rushed back into the night. Marta went to the stairs.

"Max, the trunks are in the upstairs closet."

"They're going to arrest me?"

"Max, we have to move quickly."

"Arrest me? On what charges?"

"Max," said Marta.

She hurried over to me, her fingers digging into my forearm.

"What did I do? Name one thing."

"Go wake the children," said Marta.

Chapter Two

"Is this the place?" I said.

"Am Grossen Wannsee No. 56."

"That's what I'm looking for."

"Come in."

"Am I late?" I said.

"No, it's just noon. Go on in."

"I was delayed. Is everyone here?"

"Not yet," one of them said as the dark-uniformed men glanced around their group. "Reinhard isn't here."

"And we certainly can't start without him," said a man with a long nose and a thin face. "You're von Walther, aren't you?"

"Yes."

"I'm..."

"Yes, I know," I said, and he smiled.

We shook hands.

"I'm flattered that you recommended me."

"We've heard a lot about you, von Walther. You seem like a man we could use."

"I hope so, *Herr...*"

"Call me Adolf. I was named after our *Führer,* you know," said the thin-nosed man, and the other men laughed. He gripped my arm and steered me toward the main conference room. "My invitation said 'followed by luncheon,' but let's see if we can get ourselves a drink now. I'll introduce you to the others."

"Reinhard's arrived," said one of the others, and the rest of the men strolled into the main room after us.

"Now we're in for some fun," said Adolf.

He leaned closer to me as Reinhard swept into the room, nodding at all of us. Adolf continued talking to me in a low voice as we seated ourselves at the oval table.

"I hear the *Führer* has switched policies: from emigration to annihilation," said Adolf.

"Yes," I said, lifting my briefcase, laying it on the table.

I opened the leather satchel.

"I was asked to do some research."

"You interviewed Rudi, didn't you?" said Adolf.

"Yes," I said.

"And what about the *Kazett* sites?"

"We'll pick *Kazett* sites that are secluded but which have access to local railroad lines."

"Bullets or gas?" said Adolf as the conference leader opened a thick folder and motioned for a glass of iced water.

"Gas," I said.

"How long did Rudi say it takes?" said Adolf as he poised his pen to take the meeting's notes.

"Three to fifteen minutes," I said, repositioning my pistol more comfortably, "depending on climatic conditions."

"Gas," said Adolf, nodding. "Gas is good."

"Bullets or gas?" I said as I unbuckled my holster and laid it on my desk. "Bullets. Yes, bullets. I'm no coward."

I hauled my chair to the other side of the desk, scooting closer to the girl until our knees collided. After I slipped my pistol from its holster, I leaned forward, displaying the elegant dark of the weapon to the girl. She didn't move when I laid the gun in her lap.

"*Freiheit,*" I said.

She didn't move. I opened the third bottle of champagne, to give her courage, and the pale liquid foamed over my hands and wrists. The girl's glass was full. I urged it toward her mouth. She sipped the liquor and returned the glass to the desktop. I drank from the bottle.

"*Du. Freiheit,*" I said, nudging the gun up the girl's thighs with one hand while I raised the champagne bottle to my mouth with the other.

She stayed still.

"*Freiheit. Freiheit.*"

I snapped the two small circles atop the gun up and back, urging the butt toward her hand.

"*Du. Freiheit.*"

I pointed to the silver Wound Badge pinned over my left breast, to show her I wasn't afraid. She stared at the silver oval: two swords crossed behind a steel helmet. I motioned toward the gun and aimed it just beside the Wound Badge. I took a deep breath and straightened my shoulders. I looked at her and nodded. Smoke from the cigarettes in the ashtray drifted upward. When she didn't lift the weapon, I gripped her wrist and the gun, pulling her to her feet along with me. I pressed the warm metal into her hands and folded her limp fingers around it, fixing her hand there with both of my palms.

"*Du. Freiheit,*" I said.

I pulled gun and hands until the muzzle butted my chest, the pressure keeping the girl's elbow rigid.

"*Feuer.*"

The girl blinked several times before she looked at the gun. She looked up at me, back at the gun. Her brow furrowed.

"*Ja,*" I said, lifting my chin as I released her hands. "*Freiheit.*"

Her arm lowered.

"*Nein, nein,*" I said. "*Feuer.* "

The weapon thudded to the floor between us. She didn't understand me, and German was the only language I knew then. I tried to make her see, to make her understand, and that wasn't the first time, but it was hopeless.

"No, no," I said. "You don't understand. I told you I can't remember her name."

"How can I help you find her, if you don't know her name?" said the Red Cross worker, frowning.

"She wrote this book," I said, setting it on the table.

The woman picked up *The Dead Bodies.* She opened the book. I glanced around the auditorium. Weeping, ragged people filled the main hall. They pressed insistently against each other as they waited in the long lines. A few of the refugees sat on worn pieces of luggage, but most had no possessions. A woman wailed and collapsed against one of the others, disturbing the lines as she crumpled to the floor. Workers from two of the tables rushed over to the fallen woman. The refugees looked at her. Rain pounded on the windows.

"There's no name," said the Red Cross worker.

"But she wrote it," I said.

"There's no name.

"I know that," I said.

She pushed *The Dead Bodies* back at me.

"You were sweethearts," she said, staring at me, "but you don't know her name?"

"I was injured. I told you that. My... my memory was damaged."

"Do you remember your own name?" said the worker, her crisp, white uniform rustling as she picked up a pen.

"Of course, I do, but what..."

"We could write to the publisher."

"What good would that do?"

"We could ask for the author's address. Of course, if there's no name on it, I don't see that we're going to get very far."

"How far do you think we could get?"

"Far away," said Marta. "As far away as possible. We've got to get far away from here, Max. You could write to my aunt's husband. Maybe he could help us."

"Help us what?" I said.

"Help us get out of this dreadful place," said Marta.

I slipped out of my evening dress jacket. I sat on the bed and took off my shoes. Marta removed the pearls from her ears, and brushed her hair. I unbuttoned my vest and removed my cuff links.

"Aren't you going to do something?"

"How many times do I have to tell you?"

"Tell me what?"

"This job was a promotion."

"I don't understand why I should be penalized when you get a promotion."

I sighed loudly as I stood, closing my eyes a moment before I went to the closet.

"I don't want to have this discussion again."

"We're so isolated here. There's no one to see."

"Not again."

"You told me I can't invite any of my friends here."

"You can go visit them."

"My place is with you. You're my husband."

"Then there's no problem."

"But why do I have to suffer? Can't I have a good life, too?"

"Would you rather I be at the Front?"

"Don't raise your voice. The children are asleep."

"Would you rather I risk my life in battle?"

"You always change the topic."

She stopped brushing her hair and frowned at me in the mirror.

"I don't understand why you can't get a job in Berlin."

"We've been over this and over this. I can't get promoted in Berlin."

"You could get promoted. Just not quickly enough to suit you. So the children and I have to suffer for your ambition."

"You call this suffering?"

"Keep your voice down. You'll wake the children."

"A housekeeper?"

"A Polish inmate," said Marta.

"A gardener?"

"Not a very good gardener."

"A tutor for Ilse?"

"A tutor who doesn't speak French."

I went over to the jewelry box sitting in front of Marta, and scooped out some of the jewels.

"Pearl necklaces? Diamond earrings?"

"I'm not talking about material things."

"If this is what you call suffering, then I'd better get promoted, and sooner than I thought."

"You never listen."

"I'd better become the next *Führer*."

"I hate it when you do this."

"Maybe you do want me in the fighting."

"It's pointless talking to you."

"Another wound like the last one and you'd be a war widow. A hero's widow. Maybe that's what you want."

"You don't even try to understand my point of view," said Marta as I laid my cufflinks on the bureau. "The smell makes me sick."

"Everything makes you sick."

"The stench is bad enough, but the smoke from the chimneys gets grime on everything: on my hair, on my clothes, on the children."

"Stay indoors. Then the chimneys won't bother you."

"There's a problem with the chimneys," said my adjutant.

I looked up from the paperwork on my desk. Outside, the dogs barked incessantly, and inmates' wails punctuated the guards' shouts.

"There's a problem with the ovens, Kommandant."

"Again?"

"Yes, sir."

"What is it this time?"

"The firebricks of the inner lining are crumbling," he said. "The chimney might collapse."

"Are the ovens being overloaded again?"

"I passed your instructions on to the *Kapos,"* said the adjutant.

"Then what's the problem?"

"The company representative says we need a new, square chimney, with a double lining of firebricks, if we're going to use it around the clock."

"They like to give advice."

"Yes, Kommandant."

"I'll never get all the transports dispatched on schedule if we keep having technical difficulty with their products. By the way, Josef, have you seen my letter opener?"

"No, sir. Do you want to see their response to your last letter?" said the adjutant as he opened the file folder he was holding and shuffled through its pages.

"How many times have I written them already?"

"Three," said the adjutant, passing me a letter.

"'We guarantee the effectiveness of the cremation ovens as well as their durability'," I said, reading aloud. "'We guarantee the best material and our faultless workmanship.' Best material. Faultless workmanship."

"Probably a Jew made it," said the adjutant.

"'Don't buy anything from a filthy Jew'," said Ilse as she read to Hans from one of his storybooks. "'Remember, my child, what Mother has told you'."

Sitting next to Ilse on the living room couch, Hans clapped.

"Did you like that, Hans?" said Ilse, hugging him.

"You read very well, Ilse," I said, smiling at her over my glass of Cognac. "Doesn't she read well, Marta?"

"Yes," she said, knitting. "Read Daddy the first part, Ilse, the part you read to me while I was fixing dinner."

Ilse flipped through the pages, a pensive look on her face. The Christmas wreaths filled the room with the scent of pine. The shiny paper of the wrapped packages piled under the tree reflected the fire's light. The red sweater Marta was making covered her knees, and she rested her hands atop it. Hans, wearing his pajamas, waited patiently beside Ilse, his small hands folded on his legs. Ilse stopped turning the pages and smiled.

The German is a proud man,
A worker and a fighter.
The German is a proud man,
Beautiful and brave.

The German is a proud man
Who hates the dirty Jew.
And here is a Jew, as all can see.
The vilest man that'll ever be.

"That's very good, Ilse," I said.

"She didn't understand what 'vile' was," said Marta, "until I explained it to her."

"Do you want to see the picture, Hans?"

Ilse leaned toward him and held the open book in front of him.

"Here's the beautiful German."

Hans clapped his hands.

"And here's the filthy Jew."

"What's that filthy Jewess doing here?" said Marta, and I looked up from my desk. "What's she doing in your office?"

"I've asked you to knock before you come in, Marta. This is my office. I'm working."

"And I'm your wife. This is my home."

She pointed at the girl, who was sitting in the corner.

"What is that whore doing in here?"

"Marta, I have a great deal of work to do."

"Answer me, Max."

"Not now, Marta. I'm working."

"What's she doing here?"

"I'm busy, Marta."

"Busy doing what? Sleeping with Jews?"

"How dare you," I said.

"What are you going to do?" said Marta. "Hit me?"

"Have you gone mad? When have I ever hit you?"

"*Schmutzige Hure*," said Marta to the girl. "*Schmutzige Hure*."

I took Marta's arm, turning her toward the doorway.

"So you sleep with Jews now?"

"How dare you insult me in that way," I said, holding Marta's arm. "I'm a German."

"Max, let go."

"I'm not only a German, but an officer."

"Max, you're hurting me."

"I'd never hurt a woman," I said.

"German officers don't assault women," said Dieter. "Not even Jewish women."

"So your brother-in-law was reprimanded?" I said.

"Not reprimanded. Expelled from the Party," said Dieter.

He stared at the girl while I put on my duty-overcoat. The wind pelted rain against the office windows. The Camp was a mass of clay and mud. Guards and inmates alike slipped and slid in the mire. Dieter stared out the windows at them. Then he looked over at me.

"It's quite cold out," he said.

"Yes, I have my gloves. They didn't charge you with any excesses, did they?"

"I didn't rape anybody," said Dieter. "I'm not a Russian."

"I didn't say that."

"I only executed a few Jews."

"I know that, but they keep changing the definition of 'excessive'..."

"I'd never rape a woman," said Dieter. "Not even a Jew."

"I never said..."

"I'm not a Kommandant."

I looked at him. We stared at each other in silence until he glanced away. My adjutant entered to hand me several documents. I accepted them without taking my eyes from Dieter. My adjutant left, closing the door. Dieter shrugged.

"I told my sister she never should've married him," he said.

"Were you completely exonerated?"

"Of course," said Dieter. "I didn't act on any baser instincts."

"No. You were carried away by your love for Germany."

"Yes. By my love for Germany. Don't forget the documents, Max. The papers."

"Oh, yes, the papers," I said.

"I need those papers, Josef," I said. "They're private."

"What papers?" said my adjutant.

"My private papers."

My adjutant only looked at me.

"There were papers on my desk, Josef."

He glanced down at the cluttered desktop, covered with documents, files, and folders.

"What kind of papers, Kommandant?"

"Personal papers."

"Personal papers?"

"Handwritten papers. On my personal stationery."

As I shuffled through the mound of documents on my desk, my adjutant glanced at the girl. She sat in her usual corner, arms wrapped around her legs, head against the wall, staring at nothing. Upstairs in the house, Hans was crying. Marta was in the garden, calling Ilse to lunch. I lifted some of the folders and papers on my desk, sifting through them. Hans continued crying. I dropped the papers I was holding back onto the desk. My adjutant blinked at me.

"Josef, where are those papers?"

"I'd be happy to help you find them, sir, if you'll tell me what I'm looking for."

"I am looking for my personal papers. They were right here on the desk."

"Perhaps you should lock up your personal papers, sir," he said, glancing again at the girl, "to keep them safe when you're not here."

"I put some papers for you in the safe," said the hotel clerk as I passed the desk on my way to the elevator.

"Papers?" I said. "What papers?"

The hotel clerk glanced around at the lobby; then he leaned toward me.

"Some letters came for you," said the clerk in a hushed voice. "The postmark made me think you'd like them..."

"Like them what?"

"Kept safe," he said. "Private. Just a moment. Let me get them for you."

One of the bellboys helped an elderly gentleman to the front doors. A young woman in a fur coat straightened the collar on the coat of her small son. Her husband stood near, scanning the train schedule. I looked at my watch. The clerk was taking a long time. I looked through some of the papers on the front desk.

"*Herr* Hoffmann? *Herr* Hoffmann?"

I released the papers. The clerk had returned. He had a small bundle: three letters, their stamps and postmarks foreign. He held them out to me, a hesitant smile on his face.

"Oh, yes," I said. "My letters."

"Did I do the right thing?" he said, his hands clutched together, his eyes blinking. "Putting them in the safe, was that all right?"

"Yes," I said, reaching into my pocket, then placing my hand, palm down, on the desk. "Thank you."

"Oh, thank you, sir," he said, smiling and swiping his hand over the money. "Thank you. Any time. I'll be happy to look out for you. Always happy to look out after one of our own. Always..."

The elevator doors slid shut. A young couple surreptitiously held hands, blushing and smiling. I closed my eyes, folding the letters. The couple whispered to each other. Giggled. The elevator opened. In my room, I tossed aside Marta's letters, and read the other.

Dear Daddy,

We miss you and wish you were here.

Mommy cries and Hans is a bad boy all the time.

He won't eat his vegetables and he won't learn Spanish.

Why don't you come live with us in our new house?

Can't Uncle Ricardo get a new name for you too?

Chapter Three

I'm a new man," I said, pushing open the door with my shoulders and back, my arms full of clinking bottles and white bags.

"What?" said Marta, coming from the kitchen. "What happened? You're so late, I was worried. What's all that?"

"For the celebration," I said.

"You got the promotion."

"You may now address me as *Herr Obersturmbannführer*."

"Oh, Darling," she said, throwing her arms around my neck and hugging me, crushing the bags between us. "Congratulations."

"I got some champagne. And some special food, to celebrate."

"Champagne? Where did you find it? How did you get it?"

"I have friends in the right places."

I displayed the bags' contents on the living room coffee table: caviar, pâté, bittersweet chocolate.

"Your husband is an important man, you know."

"Two bottles of champagne. Can we afford it?"

"I got promoted. Not only in rank, but in position. And salary. I have a new post."

"A new post?"

"In the East."

"The east?"

"We can afford anything we want."

"I'm so proud of you. But where in the east? Coffee? Is that..."

"Yes, real coffee. And another one of your favorites. Truffles."

"I'll get the glasses," said Marta, smiling at me. "And some plates."

"Where's Ilse?"

I bent over the wicker bassinet in the corner near the fireplace. Hans was asleep.

"She's in bed. It is after eight o'clock."

"I'm going to wake her."

"Wake her? Why?"

"So she can help us celebrate."

"But she's too small. She won't understand what it's all about."

"She doesn't have to understand it." I stroked Hans' cheek and tucked in the blanket. "She'll remember when she's older."

"She won't remember," said Marta as she came over beside me and untucked the blanket.

"Yes, she will," I said, and I went upstairs.

"Max, she's too little."

"Mommy's right here," I said as I came down the stairs, carrying a sleepy Ilse.

She rubbed her eyes and frowned.

"Mommy says it's all right for you to get back up. We're having a party."

"A birthday party?" said Ilse.

"A promotion party," I said as Marta took Ilse from my arms.

"Daddy got promoted," said Marta.

"Is that like a birthday?" said Ilse.

"I'll get the glasses," I said.

"Bring Ilse some apple juice," said Marta.

Ilse yawned as I came back into the room, glasses clinking.

"I was dreaming," said Ilse, resting her head on Marta's breast and closing her eyes. "Daddy woke me."

"I know, Darling," said Marta.

"Glasses for Mommy and Daddy, and apple juice for my baby girl. What will Hans have?"

"He's a baby, Max. Besides, he's asleep," said Marta, laughing.

I opened the first bottle of champagne and filled two glasses. I handed Marta one of them.

"To us."

"To my wonderful husband. And to his new job."

We drank, then I took the glass from her and swept Marta and Ilse into my arms.

"I love you."

"And I love you."

"You're the best wife a man could ever have. And I love you, Ilse."

"I'm sleepy," said Ilse, burying her face against Marta's throat when I tried to kiss her.

"Put her on the couch," I said.

"Let's put her back to bed."

"No."

"Why not?" said Marta.

"She'll miss the celebration."

"Max."

I took Ilse from Marta's arms and laid her on the couch. Ilse pulled her legs up tight against her body. Her eyes closed. I removed my jacket and covered her with it. I turned back to Marta. She'd lost the weight from the baby, and curled her hair. She looked beautiful. Exciting. She smiled at me.

"I'm so proud of you."

"Great things are in store for me," I said, pulling her into my arms and dancing her around the room. "And I have you to thank for it."

"Me? I haven't done anything," she said, but she smiled again.

"You stayed by me, and supported me."

"Any wife would've done as much."

"But I haven't always been such a good husband."

"Max," she said, glancing over at the couch.

Ilse was asleep.

"That'll be different now," I said, holding Marta tightly. "I'll be a good husband. You'll see."

"You're a good father to the children," said Marta. "And you're a fine husband except when you..."

"Never again," I said. "I swear it. I'll be a good husband. I'll be a good man. I swear it."

"You are a good man."

"I'll be an even better one."

I meant it. I've never said anything I didn't mean. I've always told the truth, even when it was a hard truth. But sometimes other people misunderstand, and the explanations make things worse. I am a good man. We were all good men. Bad men couldn't have saved Germany. Bad men couldn't have done what we did.

"You are good men," said Heinrich behind his wire-framed glasses, and we nodded. "You are the elite of our country."

The colonnaded reviewing stand was ablaze with light, and all around the field, the spotlights shone upward, forming pillars of light, a cathedral of light, towering against the dark. Later, we heard that the glow of the lights could be seen at Frankfurt, almost two hundred kilometers away. And I was there. The crowd swayed closer. Thousands and thousands of uniforms made the night denser.

"You are the pure. You are the purest of the pure," he said. "And only the purest of the pure can do what needs to be done."

There was nothing but the pillars of light rising from the darkness. Nothing but the sound of his voice in our ears. Nothing but the cathedral of light in our eyes. Nothing but the love of Germany in our hearts.

"This house must be Jew-pure," I said, but the old couple just blinked at me. "Jew-pure. Jew-pure. You must leave. Go."

"But we've no place to go, *Herr Hauptsturmführer,*" said the old man. "My shop is downstairs."

"Not anymore," I said. "It's the law. Now go."

"Where?"

"If you don't go, I'll have to take you into Protective Custody."

"You're going to arrest us?" said the old woman. "What for?"

"Papa, Papa," said a young girl who came rushing into the room. "The synagogue's burning."

"No," said the old man as he went to the window.

"You're breaking the law. You must go."

"No," said the old man as he stared out the window. "No."

"Then I'll have to take you into custody."

"No," said the old man, and tears dropped from his chin onto his nightshirt.

"Herschel," said the old woman, tugging at his arm. "Herschel."

"No," said the old man, pushing her away. He ran toward the door.

"Stop," I said.

The old man rushed down to the street. He shoved aside one of my men who was painting *Jude* on the sidewalk in front of one of the shops. The torches were reflected in the shop windows. The old man stumbled down the street toward the burning building, hitting and pushing my men as he scrambled past them.

"Halt."

"Herschel."

"Papa."

"Halt," I said.

My men's batons shattered the windows of the shops. Two of my junior officers grabbed the old man and dragged him back to me. He stretched his arms toward the sky, muttering in their incomprehensible language. Up and down the street, broken glass crashed onto the sidewalks.

"Take him into custody."

"Please, *Herr Hauptsturmführer,* " said his wife, kneeling and throwing her arms around my legs while their daughter sobbed. "Don't."

"Let go of me. Let go."

"Please," said their daughter, imitating her mother by kneeling on the sidewalk and clutching my thighs.

"You're breaking curfew. I'll have to arrest you."

"Don't hurt him," they said. "Please, don't."

My men stood, waiting for my orders. The broken glass glittered on the sidewalk. The smell of smoke filled the air. The women wailed, their mouths open against my trousers. I pushed at them, but they wouldn't release my legs until my weapon convinced them. The old man fell onto his knees beside his wife and daughter. I cursed at the damp spots on my trousers. I shook my head. It was a new uniform.

"We'll have to change uniforms. Change names. Change faces," said Dieter. "But it won't make any difference."

"What are you talking about?" I said.

"A thousand years will pass," said Dieter, "but Germany's guilt will never be erased."

"Guilt? What guilt? What are you talking about?"

Dieter stared into the fire, the glass of Cognac held close to his chest.

"Is there anything else you two boys need," said Marta, "before I go to bed?"

"Absolution," said Dieter.

"What?" said Marta, frowning.

"Abso..."

"Nothing," I said. "Good-night, Marta."

"Is everything all right?"

Dieter smiled and drained his glass.

"Ask Max."

"Good-night, Marta."

"Good-night," she said.

She stood a moment longer, her hand on the doorframe, before she turned on the hall light. Dieter smiled as she slowly went up the stairs.

"What's wrong with you, Dieter?" I said.

"Guilt."

"Whose guilt?"

"Mine."

"What have you done?"

"Yours. Germany's."

"I haven't done anything," I said.

"Our guilt will never be erased," said Dieter. "We'll never be free of it."

"I've done nothing wrong."

"No," said Dieter as he stood, moving unsteadily toward the liquor. "You never do."

"You're drunk."

"Not yet. Or at least, not enough."

"What's wrong with you tonight?"

"The same thing that's wrong with you, Max, with all of us."

"You've been saying cryptic things all evening."

"All the directives are very clear," said Dieter as he refilled his glass at the sideboard. "All the directives end with the same phrase: 'Avoidable cruelties are to be avoided'."

"Yes? Yes?" I said. "And?"

"And I've done things that ought not to have been done."

"No," I said, and he looked at me. "We've done what we had to do."

"It's always so easy for you, Max."

"We gave our pledge," I said, and he smiled. "We took an oath."

Dieter closed his eyes.

"That's one of your virtues, Max. Absolute, unswerving loyalty. And honesty."

"You are drunk."

"I wish I could be more like you, Max. Honest. Loyal. Obedient. Trustworthy."

"You're in no condition to drive. You'd better sleep over."

"I can't sleep here. I can't bear the smell of this place."

"The windows are closed. I don't smell anything."

"Marta's right," said Dieter. "The stench here is unbearable."

I wasn't drunk. I'm never drunk. Not that way. Except maybe once. After I saw her. She was buying vegetables in the market and I saw her. My heart started pounding even before she looked up. There she was. There were so many people, most of them refugees, begging for money, trying to pilfer some food. She was at one of the tables, a filled basket on her arm, handing the vendor some coins. I pushed the people around me, shoving their bony limbs aside. Their fingers scraped at me as they tried to stop me. Their voices were faint beneath the calls of the vendors and the clatter of coins. I had to reach her. I stretched out my hand. Call to her? What name would I have used?

"*Warte*," I said. "*Bitte. Warte.*"

"Stop," said one of the scarecrows dressed in rags. "Stop pushing."

"*Bitte.*"

"Stop."

"Stop with this girl," said Marta at the breakfast table.

I looked up from my paper. She wasn't dressed yet: she was wearing her dressing gown, and her hair was uncombed and tangled. Her eyes were red, puffy. Her bottom lip was bruised and swollen, from where she kept biting at it. She was clenching and unclenching her fists as she stood there, breathing heavily. I turned back to the paper.

"There's only so much I can ignore," said Marta.

"Mommy, my porridge's too hot," said Ilse.

"I must think of my position," said Marta.

"Mama," said Hans.

"Mommy, Hans spilled his milk."

"The children are calling you."

I buttered my toast while I scanned the front page. I spread some jam on my toast. Ilse dipped her spoon in and out of her porridge. Hans rolled his emptied glass across his highchair's tray. I looked up.

"Children, that's enough," I said.

Marta yanked the paper out from under my hand.

"Yes, it is enough. This has to stop, Max."

"Don't tell me what to do."

"This time you've gone too far."

Ilse raised a spoonful of porridge to her mouth. After she touched her tongue to it, she dropped the spoon, dripping porridge onto the table. Hans splashed his hands in the milk on his tray.

"Mommy."

"Give me the paper, and tend to the children."

"Mommy."

"I've had enough," said Marta.

"Enough of what?"

"Enough of your lies."

"I don't lie. You know about her. That's not lying."

"You always say that. As if it makes any difference."

Hans pushed at the spilled milk until it washed over the edges of his highchair's tray, dripping onto the floor. He leaned over to look at it. Ilse put another spoonful of porridge on the table, beside the first.

"Hans, Ilse, stop that," I said.

"You said you'd stop, Max."

"I'll stop when I'm ready, not when you tell me to stop. Don't let Hans..."

"I'll complain to someone if you don't stop."

"Complain?"

"My aunt's husband still has influence."

Hans slapped his hands in the spilled milk. Ilse dripped her porridge onto the tabletop. My hand on Marta's wrist freed the paper. I snapped the paper straight, and turned the page. Marta stood, holding her wrist. Ilse began to cry. Hans stopped splashing and joined in the crying.

"Tend to the children," I said.

I took a bite of my toast, a sip of my coffee. Marta rubbed her wrist.

"I hate you, Max. I hate you."

She ran up the stairs and slammed the bedroom door. When I looked at the children over the top of the newspaper, their sobs increased.

"Ilse, Hans," I said. "Stop. Please."

They cried louder.

She never cried. Not once in all those years. She never showed any weakness. She looked at everything absolutely unflinchingly. They weren't all like that. In fact, none of the rest was like that. Not even their men. I looked at the whimpering boy over the top of the paper he held out to me: a letter. He stood right next to her, next to the girl. This was the second time I'd seen her in less than an hour. She wore a fur coat, but no hat. Her parents weren't with her any longer. She had no letter. This whimpering boy stood beside her. He rattled the letter in my face.

"It's a Protective Custody letter," he said. "It certifies that I'm essential to the economy."

"I know how to read," I said, pushing aside his arm with my baton.

"The country needs me. I'm an engineer."

"You're a Jew," I said, and ended the discussion.

The page drifted to the crowded platform. I turned toward the girl. Behind her, in the unopened boxcars, other essential members of the economy pounded on the wooden door with their fists. She stared right at me, without blinking, with no emotion on her face. The dogs strained on their leashes as the guards herded the inmates toward the doctor at the end of the ramp. The spotlights passed rhythmically over the Camp, cutting the dark in a predictable pattern. In the boxcars, the pounding of fists and boots on wood continued. I touched the girl's face.

"You can't be a Jew," I said, though there was no translator near.

The pounding continued. Pounding, pounding, until it seemed it was in my head. As I opened my eyes, my hand slipped under the pillow for my pistol. It was still night. The knocking continued. I pulled on my pants in the dark and crept to the door. By the light of the hall, I glimpsed the young man who had accosted me in the hotel dining room.

"Let me in, von Walther, or everyone on the floor will hear what I have to say."

I leaned against the door.

"I can talk to you just as well from here, von Walther."

I tucked the pistol inside my belt, at my back. I opened the door.

"Turn on a light," he said.

I did. He glanced anxiously about the room before he entered, and again when I closed the door. He was very thin, and he coughed almost constantly. His eyes and chin were weak.

"Leave the door open," he said.

"What do you want?"

"Is there anyone else here? Show me your hands."

"You don't tell me what to do, Boy."

"Let me see your hands. I don't trust you."

"What do you want?" I said, crossing my arms over my chest. "Money?"

He coughed for several seconds before he was able to answer me.

"Money? You make me sick. You killed my family."

"Not that again."

"You killed them."

"The war killed them. Many people lost their families in the war. I lost mine."

"Not in the war. In the Camps."

His coughing bent him over.

"In your Camp."

"I was a soldier in the war."

"You were the Kommandant."

"No."

"Kommandant of..."

"As I told you in the dining room, you've mistaken me for someone else. My name is…"

"Von Walther."

"Hoffmann," I said.

He shook his head. He pulled a stained handkerchief from his pocket and pressed it to his mouth. This fit of coughing made him sweat and turn pale. A blotch of red spattered the cloth as he wiped his mouth. His voice was weaker after that.

"You shot my sister."

"I'd never shoot a woman."

"She was screaming. And crying. When we got off the train. You told her not to be frightened. Not to frighten the others."

"No."

"You told her she was upsetting everyone else. Some of the babies started to cry."

"I served in the east. I was wounded in battle."

"You told your guards to pull her out of the group. The other women and children were going to the showers. You had them pull her out. You walked with her around the side of the building. She was crying. The babies were crying."

"I'm afraid I'll have to ask you to leave now."

I went to the door and put my hand on the knob. He was coughing too much to speak.

"I'm not the man you think I am," I said.

He stopped coughing. He shook his head.

"You put your left hand on her shoulder. Like you were really talking to her. Telling her to calm down. Not to upset the others. 'Think of the children,' you said. Then you put your pistol to the back of her head. You pulled the trigger."

"An officer wouldn't shoot a woman. I've never shot a woman."

"You pulled the trigger. I saw you do it."

I shook my head.

"I saw you do it. I saw it all."

"No. You didn't see anything. There was nothing to be seen."

"I've been looking for you ever since. Ever since you ran away from the Camp."

I stood with my hand on the knob of the opened door. Out in the hall, a drunken woman guided a more drunken man to their room. When they bumped into the wall, the man grabbed wildly for the woman, calling her name. She hushed him as she pulled him toward their room. The boy in my room coughed and coughed. As I turned to look at the boy, I pushed the door of my room closed. The boy blinked, swallowed convulsively, coughed.

"You ran away," he said, "when the Russians were coming."

"I've never run away from anything in my entire life."

"You ran."

"Never."

"You didn't even go with your wife. Your adjutant took her and the children away. You were already gone."

"Liar."

"I was there. I saw it."

"Get out."

"I'll make you pay for your crime," he said. "I'll kill you myself."

"Who do you think you're talking to, Boy?"

I grabbed his shirtfront and shook him as if he were a puppy. When I pushed him from me, he stumbled back, hitting a table, knocking off the phone's receiver. I looked at him, and he threw himself at me, knocking me and the phone over the low table. When our bodies hit the floor, my pistol gouged my back. Our legs bashed into the small table and chairs as we scrambled against each other. His boots battered my shins, and his broken nails scraped at my chest and throat. His head banged against the foot of the bed, and he dragged off the bedclothes, trying to shove them into my face. I pushed him from me, and rolled away. I yanked one of the cushions from the chair and crushed it over his face. I reached behind me for my gun. He kicked and clawed. One shot from my weapon stopped him.

Breathing heavily, I disentangled myself from him. He lay still. I looked down at him, then grabbed the bedspread and sheets and laid them on the floor beside him. I kicked away the chair cushion and rolled the body onto the bedclothes. His eyes were open. I wrapped the spread around him, covering his staring face. I opened the closet door, pulled out my clothes and luggage. I dragged his body across the floor and shoved it into the closet. His shoulders and back thumped loudly against the back of the closet. I stood motionless, holding my breath, listening for any sound from the adjoining room, or from the hall. I bent his legs and shoved them into the closet. There was no movement. I forced the door closed.

I grabbed my luggage and pulled out my wallet and papers. I dressed quickly, layering several changes of clothes under my greatcoat. I shoved the remaining clothes into the dumbwaiter, pushed the empty luggage under the bed, and locked and chained the door to the hallway. I yanked the phone wire out of the wall. When I opened the window, the night air hit me coldly in the face, but I forced myself through the narrow window onto the fire escape. Few lights were on in the hotel windows. Night sounds swarmed around me as I crept down the metal stairs, dropping the last few feet to the sidewalk. I stood a moment against the building, watching the street. No one was around.

I made my way to my car, unlocked it, but I didn't turn on the lights until I was far from the hotel, until I was speeding away as fast as I could. No, that wasn't running away. That was saving myself. Anyone else would have done the same. We have to watch out for ourselves. No one else will.

"Can you do something for me?" I said to Dieter.

"Of course. Anything. What do you want?"

"Cyanide."

"Cyanide? Zyklon B?"

"No, not for them. Cyanide tablets."

"For the girl?"

"No."

"Just shoot her," said Dieter. "It'll be quicker."

"Not for the girl. For me."

"You're not serious, Max. What on earth for?"

"I don't think I can bear what's going to come after."

"You can bear it, Max. We all can."

I shook my head. Dieter emptied the wine bottle, then drained his glass.

"Will you?"

"Max."

"Dieter, I've never asked anything of you before."

"You're just stressed, Max, with Hans' illness. And the probation. And the Front moving so close."

"It's not those things."

"I'm not surprised you feel this way. I don't know what I'd do if they used the file on me. But it won't be as bad as you think. It never is."

"You don't understand. You're not listening."

"It won't be that bad, Max. You'll get through it. We all will."

"Can you get them for me? From your cousin?"

"There are other ways."

"Three should be enough."

"Max, we'll get through this."

"Listen. Can you get me at least three?"

"Why don't you go to South America?" said Dieter. "That's what everyone else is going to do."

"Listen. This is important. Are you listening to me?" said Ilse. "Are you?"

"Yes, yes," said Marta, wiping Hans' face and lifting him from the bath. "Get into the tub."

"First, listen."

"Get into the tub."

"Listen."

Marta frowned as she wrapped Hans in the heavy towel and handed him to me.

"What?" she said. "What is it now?"

"Is this soap Jew-soap?" said Ilse.

"Is it what?" said Marta.

"Is it Jew-soap?"

"Jew-soap? No Jew's been in my bathroom to use my soap."

"No," said Ilse. "Is it Jew-soap? Is it the soap made from the dead Jews?"

"Max, what's she talking about?"

"I never heard it before," I said.

I shifted Hans so my shirt wouldn't get wet. He bounced up and down in my arms. Ilse stood, naked, her hands on her hips, next to the bath.

"I don't know where she gets these ideas," I said.

"Who told you such a thing?" said Marta.

"The housekeeper."

"When?"

"This morning, when she was mopping," said Ilse. "She said..."

"That housekeeper has to go, Max."

"She's a good housekeeper."

"I don't like her around the children."

"Ilse probably misunderstood what she was saying."

"No, I didn't. She said..."

"I want a housekeeper who's not an inmate."

"What did she say about the soap, Ilse?"

"She said the fat from the dead Jews was being boiled into soap."

"Oh, my God, Max. That's it. I want that Jew out of my house."

"She's not a Jew. She's a Pole."

"I don't care what she is."

"And then she said..."

"I want a housekeeper from Berlin."

"You know that's not possible. I'll get another girl in her place."

"Not an inmate."

"Who else am I supposed to get?"

"Not an inmate. I've had enough of them."

"I'll take care of it."

"Not a Jew."

"I said I'll take care of it."
"But is this Jew-soap or not?" said Ilse.

Chapter Four

"We have something that needs to be taken care of, sir," said the hotel manager.

"Yes?" I said. "If it's about the bill..."

"Oh, no, sir, not about the bill," he said. "That's been taken care of, just as you said. It's about a gentleman, sir."

"A gentleman?"

"A gentleman has been inquiring after you, sir. A rather, shall we say, 'unsavory gentleman'."

"Unsavory?"

"Not our kind at all, sir," said the hotel manager.

"Looking for me?"

"Most persistently. He's been in every few hours for the past several days. He keeps asking the desk clerk if you're still registered."

"Is he here now?"

"He was just asking after you again, sir. He's at the desk."

"Fine," I said, standing. "Let's take care of it now."

The manager nodded, walking briskly beside me to the lobby. No one was at the desk. The manager approached the clerk and spoke to him. The clerk pointed to the door of the dining room. The manager said something else. The clerk shook his head. Several young guests, dressed in white, came in from the tennis courts. Laughing and poking each other with their racquets, they went into the dining room. The manager came back over to me.

"He seems to have left, Mr. Hoffmann. Apparently, he looked into the dining room after I went in to speak with you, then he left. I apologize if I erred in coming to you while he was here."

"Thank you for telling me about him," I said, looking out the wide glass doors that fronted the busy street.

"The clerk says he left in a hurry."

"It doesn't matter. I was checking out this morning anyway."

"I am sorry to hear that, Mr. Hoffmann; I hope there's no problem."

"Business."

"Oh, that's fine, sir. We hope you've enjoyed your stay with us. If you're ever in this area again..."

"Of course, your hotel will be my first choice," I said, and he smiled. "Send a boy up to my room for the luggage. My business is rather urgent. I'd better hurry."

"We're never hurried. It's always very leisurely," said Dieter. "This last time, most of us stayed till four in the morning."

"He spent that entire time with you?"

"Yes," said Dieter. "He was very generous with his time. And in a very good humor. Very entertaining."

"Ilse, go ask Mommy to bring us another bottle of wine," I said, and she ran toward the house.

A few moments later, Ilse came running back to us.

"Mommy's already coming," she said.

Marta came down the path through the garden and handed me the bottle and corkscrew.

"I anticipated your asking," she said.

Dieter picked Hans up from his blanket on the grass. Ilse plucked flowers and made tiny bouquets for each of her dolls, sitting in a row in the grass. I twisted the cork free from the wine bottle as Dieter sat Hans on his lap. Hans fingered Dieter's uniform buttons, and cooed at his medals. I laid the cork on the table as I handed Marta the bottle. After she filled our glasses with wine, she cut the plum cake.

"I've never thought of him as entertaining," I said.

"Oh, yes, he told all sorts of amusing anecdotes," said Dieter, dangling his Iron Cross in front of Hans. "Especially after the film."

"What film did you watch?" said Marta.

"Oh, some American thing, a comedy," said Dieter. "I was more interested in what he was saying."

"Yes," I said, "so would I have been."

Ilse leaned against my legs and spilled handfuls of Saint-John's-Wort in my lap.

"Oh, what pretty flowers," said Marta.

"Look, Daddy," said Ilse.

"A most fascinating man," said Dieter, while Hans grasped the shining cross. "Quite charming. Quite impressive."

Marta put another piece of cake on Dieter's plate.

"Look, Daddy," said Ilse.

"Daddy, didn't Ilse bring you lovely flowers?" said Marta.

"Beautiful," I said, patting Ilse on the head. "Beautiful flowers from my beautiful little girl."

"I wouldn't mind at all if I ended up like him," said Dieter.

"He has the requisite hardness," I said.

"Yes," said Dieter. "He has heart."

"Uncle Dieter," said Marta, lifting Hans from his lap, "Ilse's brought you some flowers, too."

"Thank you, Sweetheart," said Dieter.

"This is Angel... Angel...," said Ilse.

"Angelica," said Marta.

"Angelica," said Ilse.

"How pretty," said Dieter as Marta took the Iron Cross from Hans' mouth and wiped it with her apron.

"See, Daddy?" said Ilse.

"Pretty."

"He said, 'We should have no pity for those destined to perish'," said Dieter, smiling up at Marta when she handed him his medal. "What an incredible man he is."

"I hope one day to meet him personally," I said, "and spend time with him, as you have."

"Yes," said Dieter. "It's quite a moving experience."

"They are destined to perish," I said. "Do you understand that?"

"Yes, Kommandant," said the guards.

"Apparently, you don't. It's rumored that you continue to maintain friendly relations with them."

The guards gathered before me in my office stared rigidly ahead, their hands fixed on their weapons, their legs stiff. Their faces were round, and unshaved. Two of them had missing uniform buttons. One smelled distinctly of alcohol. I flipped through the papers in my hands.

"Three of you have been reprimanded before."

They said nothing.

"This is a most unsatisfactory situation."

My adjutant took the papers when I held out the folder. I'd dealt with this kind so many times before: narrow eyes, narrow wallets, narrow minds. Conscripts probably. I shook my head as I paced in front of the guards.

"I understand that the temptation is strong," I said, my baton in my hand as I walked. "These are wealthy prisoners of the state. But we must be strong."

They nodded their empty heads.

"We must rise above our ordinary human selves. We must be greater than we seem."

They nodded again.

"If this behavior continues, I shall be forced to assume that you are incapable of understanding the most elementary principles of National Socialism."

A few of them glanced at me. The one who stank of liquor wiped his mouth and nose with the back of his bare hand.

"I would be forced to regard your behavior as disrespectful to the measures of the State."

Several of them blinked as they stared at the windows. The drunken guard's eyes drifted closed, then jerked open. He swayed slightly on his feet. After I returned to my desk, my adjutant closed the folder over the papers he held.

"If this behavior continues, I'll have to take you into Protective Custody. Temporarily. For educational purposes. Have I made myself clear?"

"Yes, Kommandant," said the guards in unison.

"Dismissed."

"Kommandant. Kommandant," said the girl. "Kommandant."

I ran down the stairs to my office.

"Kommandant," said the girl. "Kommandant."

"What's going on here?" I said as I entered the office area.

My adjutant saluted me. Two guards held the girl by the arms. My adjutant picked up some papers from his desk. The guards tightened their grip on the girl. She winced as she struggled against them.

"Josef, what's this about?" I said. "Release her."

After the guards released the girl, she ran over and crouched behind me. The guards stood at attention. My adjutant held something out to me.

"I was just trying to carry out your orders, sir."

"What are you doing with the girl?"

"As I said, sir."

"What's this?"

"It was on my desk this morning, sir, marked 'Priority'."

The girl crept toward my office door, huddling near its frame.

"I assumed you put it there, sir."

Release for Annihilation of Life Without Value.
On this date. By my hand.
Kommandant

"What is this? I didn't issue this order."

"It's dated, sir. And stamped."

"It's not signed."

"You never sign them."

"It's unsigned." I held the paper in front of his face. "There's no signature. Do you see a signature?"

"No, sir."

"Since when do these Releases go through without my signature?"

"There are rarely any signatures, sir."

"That is inefficiency," I said, crushing the page. "From now on, these orders require my signature."

"All of them?"

"Yes."

"Even if they're dated and stamped?"

"Even if they're written out entirely in my handwriting. Is that clear?"

"Yes, sir."

"I won't have this Camp running without my direct supervision."

"No, sir."

"Dismissed."

The guards saluted. They turned, and left for the Camp's yard through the back door. I passed the adjutant and thrust open my office door. The girl rushed inside. No, it was more than just trying to disrupt or subvert the operation of the Camp. Someone was trying to destroy me. To destroy my character. My reputation. If I'd failed at the Camp, nothing could have saved me. I kept a tighter rein on the Camp's business after that. I closed my office door, locked it, put the key in my pants pocket. I buttoned my jacket.

"What shall I do about the order, sir?"

I held out my hand. My adjutant reached into the wire basket on the corner of his desk and pulled out the carbons. After he handed them to me, I realigned them with the crumpled original. I tore the order in half. In quarters. I tossed the fragments into the wastebasket.

"What order?"

"Do you want Daddy to give you an order, Ilse?" said Marta.

"I want to read the story one more time."

"Max," said Marta, "do something with the children."

"Hans wants me to read it again, too. Don't you, Hans?"

"Book," said Hans.

"Max, I can't do anything with them."

"Daddy wants to hear it one more time, too," said Ilse.

Hans squealed and slapped the book's cover.

"Max, it's past the children's bedtime. They were playing outside in the snow all day. They're so tired, they're being disagreeable. Tell them to go to bed."

"No. Tell us to read the story again."

"Book," said Hans as he pulled at it, trying to turn its pages.

"Max, what's wrong with you tonight? You're not listening."

"Please, Mommy. Daddy wants us to read the story again."

"Max, what's wrong? Are you all right? What did you do to your hand?"

"Please, Mommy, please."

"All right, Ilse," said Marta with a loud sigh. "But this is absolutely the last time."

"Yes," said Ilse, nodding.

"Then it's straight up to bed," said Marta.
"Yes," said Ilse, and Hans nodded.

> Listen, the boys are singing a song!
> Listen to the sound of the drums!

Marta stared at me, her sewing in her lap. I sat with my legs stretched out, my chin on my chest. Beneath its white gauze bandages, my hand throbbed. The fire spat, throwing sparks against the screen.

"What's wrong with you, Max? And what happened to your hand?"

I closed my eyes, and lifted my glass. Hans clapped as Ilse turned the page.

> Look at the boys, marching in step,
> Marching in rows of three.
> Look at the boys, saluting the flag.
> Saluting our beloved *Führer*.
> Listen, the boys are singing their song!
> Listen to the sound of the drums!

The Cognac burned its way down my throat. The fire was warm.

> Look at the boys: handsome and brave!
> Listen to the sound of the drums!

"What's wrong? Why aren't you going with us, Max?"

I opened the bureau drawer and took out my shirts.

"We've been over this, Marta."

"It's her, isn't it? It is."

"Don't be ridiculous. Is that all you ever think about?"

"Why aren't you coming with us?" said Marta.

"I'll join you later. I've told you that already."

I placed the folded shirts into my open suitcase. Marta stood at the foot of the bed, watching me as I opened another bureau drawer. She twisted a damp handkerchief. She'd been crying, and her eyes were red and swollen. I closed the bureau and went to the closet.

"It's her. I know it is," said Marta. "You'll never see me or the children again."

"Marta, you're my wife. You're the mother of my children."

"She's a Jew. Why are you going to her?"

"I never said..."

"She hates you."

I stood there, my uniform in my hand. Marta crumpled her handkerchief into a ball. She looked me in the face.

"She hates you, Max."

"I know that."

"Then why aren't you coming with us?"

"I'm telling you this for the last time, Marta. You and the children will go first..."

"You love her."

"Don't be ridiculous."

"You're in love with a Jew."

"Marta..."

"Why won't you go with us? You said you'd never leave me. You promised. Even when you fell in love with that one from Munich."

"I'm not leaving you. You're the mother of my children."

"You promised. You swore." Marta put the damp cloth to her eyes as she began to cry again. "You said, 'Till death do us part'."

I threw down my uniform jacket, and shoved my hands into the luggage. I yanked out my pistol, cocked it, forced it into Marta's hands.

"Yes, yes, till death do us part," I said. "Kill me."

She would never have shot me. I gave the girl my gun. Several times. And I always wore my service dagger. Yet she never even wanted to harm me. She was so different from Marta. She came to me when I needed her, and she didn't demand anything of me in return.

She took the gun from my hands, her fingers stroking its warm barrel, and she laid it on the desk. Her fingers were white against the dark of the gun, against the black of my uniform. She unbuttoned my jacket, and her hands stroked the front of my shirt. Then she unbuttoned my shirt. When she undid my belt, I closed my eyes. Her hands drifted over my body, and her skin was cool on mine. Then warm. Insistent. I leaned back in the chair. I let her push my legs apart and kneel between them.

The adjutant knocked on the door, but I didn't answer. When the girl bent her head over me, I pushed away the papers on the desktop. I heard the guards calling to each other from outside my window, but while her mouth moved, all words eluded me. The adjutant's phone rang. Once. Twice. Three times. The girl stretched one hand out to touch my face, and the other to stroke my legs. Her mouth was warm and wet and soft on me. All around me was the paper and leather and metal of my life, but when I closed my eyes and she touched me, it all drifted away.

"I always close my eyes when I drink a fine Cognac," said Adolf, his long nose poised over the glass of amber liquid.

"That's the best way," I said, nodding.

"Your wife knows how fond I am of liquor," he said. "She always has a bottle ready."

"She's always happy to have you visit. It's an honor for us."

"She's a lovely woman, von Walther."

"Thank you."

"A fine cook. A gracious hostess," he said. "A faithful wife."

"Yes, she's a good wife."

The others drifted into the living room, settling themselves around the dessert table.

"What's this?" said one of the officers' girls, her black dress shimmery and tight.

"Champagne cocktail," said Marta.

"No, the music."

"Beethoven's Seventh," said one.

"Second Movement," said another.

"Are you sure it's not Mozart?" said the girl, and everyone laughed.

"Have some strudel," said Marta.

She passed them the filled plates. The silver clinked against the china, and their voices blended with the music. One of the young officers leaned near Marta and said something to her. She blushed, glancing quickly in my direction, but she smiled. When he kissed her hand, she laughed, gently pushing him away. He smiled at her again before drinking his champagne. Marta stood and, carrying the decanter, came over to me and Adolf.

"It must give you extraordinary satisfaction," said Adolf. "All that you've accomplished. The life you've made for yourself. Your wife. Your family. Your home."

"And my work," I said.

"That's understood," he said.

"Would you like coffee with your Cognac?" said Marta.

Adolf shook his head, smiling up at her as she refilled his liquor glass. When the young officer leaned near the girl in the tight black dress, her fiancé crossed the room and sat on the couch between them. The young officer laughed, and slapped his colleague on the back.

"Without my work, the rest wouldn't be as rewarding," I said.

"Of course," Adolf said, nodding. "Having millions of Jews on my conscience gives me such extraordinary satisfaction that I could jump into my grave laughing."

"I can understand that," I said, accepting coffee and cake from Marta. "Work makes us greater than we are."

"Sometimes, I feel like God himself," said Adolf, and he leaned forward, his face suddenly intent. "God can't possibly be as small as in the Bible stories, can he?"

Whose God? Theirs? I never believed in God. I didn't need Him. Besides, He'd already betrayed me. No, long before the end. At the end, shells were exploding outside the Camp. The building shook with each explosion. Planes whined overhead, and machine guns rattled. The girl sat huddled in my desk chair. On my desk lay three blue-white capsules.

"Kommandant, Kommandant," said my adjutant, knocking on the office door. "The car is waiting."

I pulled the girl's hand up. She looked at me. Her hand was cold. I pressed a lone capsule into it.

"Hurry, Kommandant," said my adjutant, his knocking more insistent, more like pounding.

I closed the girl's fingers around the capsule, my hands around hers. Her body trembled, but not from fear. Another shell exploded, rocking the ground beneath us, dashing books and weapons from my cabinets and shelves. Shouts and screams filled the air of the Camp.

"Kommandant," said my adjutant. "Kommandant."

"*Du. Freiheit*," I said to the girl.

Then I left her there.

"Commander. Commander."

The knocking on the door imitated the pounding in my head.

"I know you're in there, Commander."

I jerked awake.

"Let me in, Commander. Open up."

I crept out of the bed and peered through the security hole. An unshaven, obese man stood outside the door. In the glare of the motel's lights, his suit looked rumpled, cheap. He pulled a handkerchief from his pants pocket and mopped his face. He began knocking again.

"Wake up, Commander. Let me in."

I was already dressed. I'd been sleeping in my clothes for weeks. I checked my pockets, shoved my gun behind my belt, and grabbed the books.

"I know who you are," he said. "I know what you did."

My keys and change jingled slightly as I climbed onto the bathroom sink, and eased open the window above it. He knocked louder.

"I have a business proposition for you," he said.

A nail in the ledge caught my trousers, scraping my skin.

"Damn."

I wrestled my trousers free and slipped to the ground. He was still at the motel door. I went to the car, unlocked the door, and slipped inside.

"I know who you are. I have a solution to your problem," he said, still knocking. "I've come to save you."

Chapter Five

"We have a solution," said Reinhard after we had settled ourselves at the conference table.

We all looked at him.

"You gentlemen have been specifically chosen," he said, "based on your service to the Party, to help implement this solution."

It was a small group. I was proud to be among them. In the distance, an approaching train blew its whistle. I sat up straighter, to hear everything that was going to be said.

"We have to settle the Jewish question in all the territories under our protection," he said.

We nodded.

"This has always been one of the Party's primary concerns, and its importance has increased with each of our conquests."

The officers murmured in agreement.

"Now that our territory has expanded significantly eastward, our problem has become more urgent."

He looked around the table. Several of the others leaned forward. My own heart pounded. This was what we'd been waiting for. We held our breath.

"Gentlemen, I have been instructed to carry out preparations with regard to the Solution of the Jewish Question."

We applauded. He nodded. The sun from the windows was bright in the room, and it shone all around him. He smiled. We continued clapping. He held up his hand. We kept clapping. Outside, the train roared by, its smoke billowing up into the clear sky, its whistle ringing in our ears. Reinhard smiled, holding up both hands, for silence, but nothing could stop us. We clapped until our palms stung. Until our hands hurt.

My forearm ached. It was still tender. Each time I moved and my sleeve touched the skin, I could feel the cut. I pulled off my boots, and lowered myself until I knelt before the girl, till I sat on my heels before her. I could feel the cold of the floor through my pants. I unbuttoned my uniform jacket and removed it, laying it on the floor beside me, next to the boots. With deliberate movements I rolled up my left shirtsleeve. The girl watched me in silence. My fingers got tangled in the cloth. My arm was aching, but I didn't let my face show it. Eventually I managed to fold up enough material to expose my forearm. I held out my arm to the girl.

There, on my inner left forearm, red and inflamed, still swollen from the cutting: a triangle atop an inverted triangle, her six-pointed star.

There was no more blood. Just the red welts of the cutting. I couldn't have been too drunk: the lines were too straight, the angles too sharp. With my service dagger. On my inner left forearm. No, that other was just a cigarette burn, from another time. No, no numbers. Just her name.

"*Jetzt bin ich ein Jude,*" I said.

Her mouth opened as if she were going to speak. Finally, we might understand each other. Finally, we might be able to touch each other. Her brow furrowed, and she trembled. I nodded, and stroked her thigh. I moved closer to her, to see her better. I took her hand and placed her fingers on my forearm, on the scar. She raised her head. Her eyes, when she looked at me, were like nothing I'd ever seen.

"*Jetzt bin ich ein Jude.*"

She slapped me.

"Now you're one of us," said the officer as he shook my hand, then he turned to the small, thin gentleman with wire-framed glasses. "This is von Walther."

"Von Walther," Heinrich said, nodding. "Welcome. What did you think of the rally?"

"Excellent, sir. And your speech was very inspiring."

He smiled, nodding to several other men after they hailed him.

"Von Walther. That name sounds familiar."

"I've mentioned him to you before," said my sponsor, and his hand on my back urged me forward.

"Have you?"

"Not only does von Walther have his baptismal certificate and those of his parents and grandparents, but he's proven his non-Jewish descent from 1750."

"Do we have an officer candidate?" said Heinrich.

"I hope so, sir," I said.

Heinrich stepped closer, peering up at me from behind his glasses. When he motioned with his hand, I leaned nearer.

"This is a page of glory in our history which has never been written. It may never be written," Heinrich said. "Do you have the strength for that? The hardness? Do you have enough heart?"

"'He has the requisite hardness'," I wrote, and the office door opened.

"Kommandant, there's a problem with..."

"Josef, I asked you to knock before you come in."

"I thought that was only when..."

"Whenever you come in," I said, "if you don't mind."

He glanced around the office for the girl. She lay on the cot, covered with a thin blanket.

"Of course not, sir. I didn't realize I was disturbing you."

He came over to the desk and held out a letter to me.

"There's a problem with the shipment, sir."

When I accepted the letter, he looked down at what I'd been writing. I rested my forearms on my papers. I folded the letter he'd given me and laid it aside.

"It's important, sir."

"I'll take care of it."

"It's urgent, sir."

"Yes, I'll take care of it."

My adjutant stared at my papers. I shuffled the handwritten pages into a stack.

"Is there anything you need me to help you with, sir?"

"No, thank you."

"Shall I type up some of this extra work?"

"No, thank you, Josef," I said, stopping his hand when he reached for some of the pages. "That will be all."

"I'll be at my desk when you're ready to answer the letter, sir."

"Thank you, Josef."

"Sorry for disturbing you, sir."

I nodded.

"I'll be sure to knock in the future, sir."

"Yes."

"After I knock, shall I wait for you to answer before I..."

"Yes. Yes. Dismissed."

He saluted. I picked up the letter and glanced at it until he closed the door. I was always being interrupted, if not by the Camp's routine or its problems, then by Marta or the children. I often got up in the middle of the night, just to have some time to myself, to be free of the constant demands. As soon as my adjutant closed my office door, I put the letter aside, and spread out my papers. Then I returned to my writing.

Ilse spread some papers in my lap after dinner.

"Look, Daddy," she said. "Mommy made me some dolls out of paper."

"That's nice."

"Some boy dolls. And some girl dolls," said Ilse.

She reached over the newspaper I was reading to show me. I nodded at them.

"Yes. Very nice."

"And they can play with my real dolls. Even though they're only paper."

"That's nice, Ilse. Now let Daddy read."

"Not so close to the fire, Ilse," said Marta, and Ilse settled herself at my feet. "It's almost bedtime."

"I know," said Ilse.

"Say 'good-night' to your brother," said Marta.

"Good-night, Hans."

Marta held Hans down in front of my newspaper.

"Say 'good-night' to Hans, Daddy."

"Good-night, Hans."

"Good-night, Daddy," said Marta.

She touched the baby's wet mouth to my cheek, then went upstairs. Ilse leaned against my legs as she arranged her dolls into two groups. I drank some of my coffee, and turned the newspaper page.

Ilse's stuffed doll knocked aside one of the paper dolls.

"Out of my way, Jew," said Ilse in a deep voice.

Several of the other paper dolls scrambled to my feet. They hopped onto my shoes. They slipped off. The stuffed dolls formed themselves into a straight line at the side of the chair, then marched closer to my legs.

"We've got a problem, sir," said Ilse in her play-voice. "What? An escape. How many? Two or three. How? Cut the wire. Call out the dogs. Yes, sir."

Ilse barked softly as the little paper dolls jumped onto my legs, as they climbed up my trousers, as they hid themselves behind my knees and under my thighs. The fire hissed and sparked as I turned the pages of the newspaper.

"*Bang. Bang,*" said Ilse.

Several of the paper dolls fell, screaming, from my legs to the wooden floor. The stuffed dolls rushed over and stamped on the fallen paper dolls.

"There's another one. Don't let him go. Get that Jew with the baby. *Bang. Bang.*"

When the paper dolls crashed into my newspaper, I shifted it away. I drank the last of my coffee. The paper dolls bumped into my newspaper again. I crossed my legs, crushing several of the paper dolls who were in hiding.

"Oh, no, the Kommandant," said Ilse. "Help us. Help us. Too late for you Jews. *Bang. Bang.*"

The paper dolls bashed into my legs. They bumped into the newspaper, making me lose my place. I started the article over.

"Oh, no. Save us. Save us, Kommandant."

The paper dolls threw themselves over the newspaper, landing in my lap.

"That's enough, Ilse," I said.

I gathered up the dolls that had jumped the paper and handed them to her.

"It's time for bed."

"But we didn't get all the escaped Jews back yet."

I extricated paper dolls from around my legs and from beside the chair cushions. I passed them to her.

"Yes, you did. Bedtime."

Ilse gathered up the scattered paper dolls. There were faint cries as she crumpled some of them, as the stuffed dolls marched over and punched some of the paper dolls, as the rest of the paper dolls crashed to the floor.

"That's enough now, Ilse. Bedtime."

She knelt in front of the fire screen, and tossed the paper dolls into the fire.

"Into the gas with you," she said.

"Time for bed, Ilse," said Marta, coming downstairs.

The paper dolls, screaming faintly, blackened and curled in the flames.

"Kiss Daddy good-night."

The papers in my office were scattered on the floor. I dropped my briefcase and rushed over to my desk, without closing the door. I looked over at the girl. She sat in the corner. She was chewing a crust of bread. Her breathing wasn't heavy. Her cheeks weren't flushed. But the papers were all over the floor. I knelt and gathered them up.

"Josef," I said, and my adjutant entered. "Has anyone been in my office?"

"I don't know, sir. I was with you."

"I mean earlier."

"Not that I'm aware of, sir. Is there a problem?"

"No. No problem. Just some disarrayed papers."

"I'll help you, sir."

"No, that's all right. I'll get them myself."

"Shall I close the windows, sir?"

"No. That's all right."

"Are you sure you don't want me to straighten the papers for you?"

"No. That won't be necessary. I'll take care of it."

"Yes, sir. Anything else?"

"No. Thank you, Josef."

My adjutant righted my briefcase and moved it slightly so he could shut the office door. I looked at the girl. She didn't move. I looked at the papers. I must've forgotten to put them away. Without going through them, I arranged them into a stack and put them into my desk drawers. I turned the key. I tugged at the locked center drawer. It didn't open. The girl bit another corner of the dark crust and chewed steadily, watching me as I moved to the window. I put my hand on the wooden frame and closed it.

I closed the window and pulled the drapes. I locked the motel door and put on the chain. I pushed the chair to the door and shoved its back under the handle. Not that it made any difference. My hand was trembling when I turned on the bedside lamp. The room stank of cigarette smoke. There were holes burnt in the carpet. The wall next to the bathroom door was stained, and the wallpaper beside the bed was peeling. When I sat on the bed, the mattress sagged. In the next room, the couple started their nightly argument. I turned the envelope over and over in my hands: it was from the publisher. Her publisher. Holding my breath, I opened the envelope. As slowly and carefully as possible, I opened the letter.

> We have received your recent inquiry and thank you for your interest in *The Dead Bodies That Line the Streets.* It is our policy, however, not to distribute authors' addresses. All correspondence to our authors may be sent care of this address...

I let myself fall back onto the bed. Outside, traffic roared by. The couple in the next room yelled at each other. One of them threw something heavy against the wall, and the light beside my bed flickered. I looked at the letter again.

> We are sorry that we are unable to help you with your request, but have enclosed an announcement of this author's other book, *Survivor: One Who Survives.*

The man next door shouted. The door slammed. The woman began to cry. I crushed the letter in my hand.

"If I don't have those letters right here, Josef, in my hands, they might as well not be done."

"I put them on your desk, sir," said my adjutant. "In a folder."

"I don't even see any folder, Josef, let alone the letters and the documents I asked you for."

My adjutant clenched his teeth. He stood. He marched into my office, looking pointedly at the girl. She sat on the cot in the corner.

"I put all the documents in a folder. And I put the folder right here. On top. So you'd be sure to see it."

I walked over to the desk, crossing my arms in front of my chest.

"Do you see it there now?"

"It was there. I put it there myself."

"I don't see it."

"I know how important those documents were. I was very careful with them."

"Not careful enough, Josef."

"I'm not the only one in this office."

"Just what is that supposed to mean?"

"Exactly what I said, sir."

"One of your responsibilities is to ensure that no one else does enter. Who else has been in here?"

"No one else comes in," he said.

"That leaves only the two of us."

"There are other people in this office, sir."

"My children? My wife? You. Me. No one else. But those papers are gone."

He stared at me. His breathing was heavy.

"What did they do, Josef? Get up and walk away?"

"Obviously not."

"I don't think I like your tone of voice, Josef."

"I'll redo the documents, sir."

"Those originals need to be found. They can't be floating around anywhere."

"I'll keep looking for them, sir."

"Find them, Josef. Replacements won't do."

"I'm not the one who lost them. Sir."

I looked at him, with a hard look.

"We'll talk about your attitude later. Right now, you find those documents. Including the letters."

It wasn't the first time important things of mine had disappeared in the Camp. At first I thought I was being careless, or forgetful. Weapons, documents, files, even my service dagger disappeared, but I found that a few days later, in the bedroom, on the floor by the bureau. But I knew someone was trying to sabotage me, to ruin my credibility with the Party. It started right after I took over the Camp, and it worsened toward the end. But I showed them. None of them could ever defeat me. None of them. Not Reinhard, not Ernst, not the Jews. But things continued to get lost.

"She's lost," said Ilse.

"You didn't find your baby?" said Marta.

"No. Hans lost her."

"No, he didn't."

"Yes, he did."

Hans shook his head.

"You did, too. You lost my favorite baby."

"Hans didn't lose her, Ilse."

"He was playing with her."

"You took her down to Daddy's office. Remember? Maybe you left her down there."

"Daddy, is my baby in your office? Daddy?"

"Max, Ilse's asking you a question. Max?"

"I'm sorry, Marta."

"That's all right. Ilse's asking you if..."

"I'm sorry. For the way things have been. It's all my fault."

Marta sat down abruptly at the table, the pan of porridge still in her hand. Her hair was pulled back, away from her face. She'd lost too much weight, and she looked tired. The steam from the porridge drifted up toward her.

"It's all my fault," I said.

"I didn't get any porridge yet," said Ilse.

"All the problems we've been having, they're all my fault," I said.

"Hans lost my baby. I know he did."

"No," said Hans.

"I just hope I can make it up to you, Marta."

"I want some porridge, Mommy," said Ilse. "You gave Hans some. I'm hungry, too."

"I love you, Marta."

"Max, what's brought all this..."

"You're the best wife a man could ever have. I've been so blind. Why are you crying?"

"It's been so long."

I went to Marta, and hugged her to me. She sobbed.

"What's the matter, Mommy?" said Ilse.

"I'm sorry, Marta. I'm so sorry. I do love you. And I need you."

I stroked the back of her head as she wept, and she let go of the pan to put her arms around my waist. Her tears wet my uniform jacket, but I didn't mind. Her body shook.

"See what you did, Hans?" said Ilse. "You bad boy. Daddy should send you to the gas."

"Gas? Of course, I'll pay for the gas. And for your time," I said. "It's nothing bad. I just want you to find her for me."

"I ain't getting messed up in no funny business."

"This isn't funny business. I assure you," I said. "Besides, I take responsibility for all my own behavior."

"What you want with this here girl, anyway? What's she to you?"

"I merely want you to find her for me."

"She done something bad?"

"No."

"You want to do something bad to her."

"No. I swear. It's nothing like that. Nothing like that at all."

I held out the two thin books of poetry.

"Look. She wrote these. I want to find her. I want you to help me find her."

"What for?"

"It's personal."

"It's bad."

"She knows me," I said.

"It's bad business."

"It's personal. I just want to find her."

"You ain't going to hurt her?"

"No. I swear it."

"If she knows you, how come you can't find her yourself?"

"She doesn't know I'm looking for her," I said.

"Maybe she don't want you to find her."

I looked down at the two books. His secretary came into the office and poured fresh coffee into his cup. Mine was full. She wore bright red lipstick, and had red nails. She was chewing gum. She stared at me brazenly before she went back out. Her employer took one of the books from me.

"*Survivor: One Who Survives.* What's that mean?"

"She was in the war."

"You in the war?"

"Yes. I was wounded. Several times."

"Which side?"

"I was hit by German fire, by German weapons."

He nodded as he flipped through the pages, not pausing long enough to read any of them. The secretary's typewriter clicked erratically in the outer office. The office was very small, and very cluttered: books and papers were stacked all around the room, on the tables, on the chairs, on the floor, on the windowsills. The windows were grimy. The office smelled of smoke. He put down the first book and picked up the other. He stared a long time at *The Dead Bodies*, but he didn't open it.

"She might not know that I'm looking for her," I said. "She might think... We were separated. At the end. She may not realize..."

He leaned forward and handed the books back to me.

"You ain't going to hurt her? You swear?"

"I'd never hurt her," I said. "I saved her."

Chapter Six

"A sworn oath isn't enough."

We knew that. We'd known it from the beginning. We didn't mind his saying it, but we wanted his speech to be over so we could be sworn in, so we could parade in front of our leader, so we could take our place in history. We'd save Germany. We'd shape history in our own image. It was each man's dream, and we wanted him to finish so history could start.

"It is essential that every man be committed to the very roots of his being."

We knew that, too. That was why he wanted family men: husbands, fathers, sons. Men who understood the value of commitment. Men who knew loyalty, honor, love. We were those men.

"By putting on these uniforms, you are casting off your former selves. By swearing this oath, you are newly baptized. Into a new faith. A faith of blood. A faith that requires sacrifice, commitment, courage, strength, hardness."

The flames from the torches glittered in his glasses, but we were the ones who burned. We strained to see beyond him, beyond the darkness, to glimpse the man behind him, to see our Saviour. Our *Führer.*

"Reach down into yourselves. Pluck out your very hearts. Look at yourselves. Do you have heart enough? Give yourselves to Germany. Give yourselves to our *Führer.*"

It was more than the torches and our uniforms that kept us warm that night. More than the thousands of voices chanting in our ears. More than the drums matching the rhythm of my heart. We leapt to our feet, our right arms extended in salute.

"We swear to you loyalty and bravery, even unto death, as God is our witness."

Nothing could have swayed me from that path. It was my destiny. By the time I became a husband, a father, nothing was more important to me than my family, than Germany. At night, when I watched Marta with the baby, I understood all of it: my purpose in life, my role. I would have done anything to keep my family safe, to secure the world for my children.

"Max, you're staring at me," said Marta.

"You look so beautiful."

Marta smiled and glanced down at the baby. Her hair fell to one side of her head, over her shoulder, like a veil, and the lamp's light glowed on the white of her cheek, her throat, her gown. The baby lay sleeping in her arms, his mouth open at her breast, his hands in tiny fists. I went over to the rocking chair and knelt before them. My fingers stroked the baby's head. Marta smiled.

"He's such a good baby."

"You're a good mother."

"He looks like you, Max."

"No, he's beautiful."

"He'll grow up to be a fine man," said Marta, and she touched my cheek. "Like his father."

"My son."

"Your firstborn."

"My son."

"He'll make you proud, Max. He'll be the best that any man can be."

"Oh, Marta, I never dreamed I'd be so happy."

I was happy. I thought it would always be that way. My son would grow up to be strong and healthy and beautiful. He would be the best in the country. In the world. Like us. We were the best in Germany. That's what we were told, over and over. The best. The bravest. The most beautiful. Again and again. Until we believed it.

"There has been a terrible decline in human heredity during the past century," Heinrich said, and his glasses caught the light. "But you officers are the treasury of the best human material. You are the hope of mankind. You hold the future in your hands."

"And I hold the soul of the German people in my hands," said the Doctor.

He stood at the podium next to Heinrich. We all turned our heads toward the Doctor.

"I tell you," he said, "the soul of the German people is as soft as wax. Waiting for us to mold it. For you to mold it. To shape it. To harden it into its destiny."

"Are you men enough to do it?" said Heinrich, and we leapt to our feet, cheering.

"I have seen the future," said the Doctor, "and I am here to tell you what Germany wants. Do you want to hear?"

"Yes. Yes."

"*Ein Volk, ein Reich, ein Führer.*"

We shouted. We stomped our feet. Clapped. Cheered.

"*Ein Volk, ein Reich, ein Führer.*"

"My *Führer*?" said the heavyset man woken from his sleep in the prison. "You're from the *Führer*? I don't understand."

"No one's asking you to understand," said the officer. "It's enough that I tell you I come from the *Führer* himself."

One of our men pounded on the cell doors as they were unlocked. Five other partially dressed men left their prison cells and joined the first. They pulled up their suspenders, rubbed their eyes, looked anxiously at one another, at us.

"Sepp, my friend," said one of them, with a bewildered smile. "What on earth's happening?"

"You have been condemned to death by the *Führer,*" said our squad leader, clicking his heels, and raising his arm in salute. "*Heil* Hitler."

"My *Führer.* My *Führer.*"

The shots rang out in the stone corridor. The bodies collapsed. One twitched as he lay there on the stained floor. He moaned.

"Von Walther, how could you have missed at such close range?"

"I didn't miss."

"You're supposed to be one of the best shots."

"I am."

"Finish him off. I don't want any mess. That's why you're here. Understand?"

I did. One mistake, and it was over. I had no intention of making a mistake. Any mistake. The Party was my life. My destiny. Nothing was going to ruin it for me. Nothing was going to get me out of the Party. Not malfunctioning ovens or crumbling chimneys or sniper's bullets or stolen grenades tossed at my car. Nothing. No one.

"So your brother-in-law was reinstated in the Party? How did he manage that?"

"I couldn't stand my sister's begging anymore," said Dieter, pouring himself more champagne. "I called in a favor."

"But he's doing Ghetto-clearing."

"What's wrong with that?"

"It's a degrading job."

"I didn't know you'd ever done it."

"Once," I said. "Not a good job."

"Why?"

"The men were like savage animals descending on the Ghetto with hatchets and bayonets. That was enough for me."

"My brother-in-law gets an official ration for doing it: half a pint of Brandy. Every day."

"Not worth it."

"No?"

"Not for me anyway."

"I'd do it for that," said Dieter. "I'd do it for less than that."

"I can't do it now, Ilse. Daddy's busy. Too busy to play."

"But Mommy told us to come down," said Ilse.

She was wearing her nightgown and slippers. She held her doll with one hand and Hans' hand with the other.

"Mommy says we're getting in the way of the party."

"What does Mommy want me to do?"

Ilse shrugged.

"She said, 'Go play with Daddy'."

"Daddy can't play right now. Daddy has too much work to do."

"Mommy told us to."

"All right. Here. You come play with Hans and your baby over here, by my desk."

"Are you going to play?"

"No. I have to work. But you can play right next to me while I'm working. That'll be almost the same thing."

Ilse dragged her doll and Hans over to my side. Hans took his thumb out of his mouth to take a bite of his cookie.

"Yes. Right there. That's good. Now you and Hans and your baby play right there while Daddy finishes his work. Yes. There."

"What kind of party is it?" said Ilse, leaning on the arm of my chair.

"A dinner party."

"What kind of dinner party?" said Ilse. "A birthday dinner party?"

"No. Just a dinner party."

"Why aren't children allowed to come?"

"Because it'll be past your bedtime. Hans, come away from there."

"I'm not sleepy," said Ilse. "I'm big enough to stay up late. I'm bigger than Hans. Why can't I come to the dinner party?"

"Hans, come away from there. It's a grownup dinner party, Ilse, and you're not a grownup."

"You let me stay up when..."

"Hans," I said.

I got up from my desk. He was standing in front of the girl. I picked him up.

"Ilse, you'll have to go back upstairs."

"But Mommy said..."

"Tell Mommy that Daddy's too busy to play."

"But..."

"Go on. Daddy's working."

I was always working. Often late into the night. Early into the morning. Actually that was a good time to work because no one interrupted me. I sat at my desk, with only a few lights on, and worked. Sometimes all night.

When the words wouldn't come, I pulled off my ring, the silver band with the Death's-Head and the *heil* rune, and turned it over and over in my left hand while I worked. I stared at the signature inside the ring. I touched the tip of my pen to the hollows of the Death's-Head's eyes and nose. The gold nib touched the indentation of the crossed bones behind its grin. It touched the asterisk rune. The words came. I slipped the ring back on. I saw the girl, watching me.

"Speaking of women," said Dieter, looking at the girl. "I haven't heard you talk about Dianne in a long time. What happened to her?"

"She got married," I said.

"Married? Are you serious?"

"Yes."

"When did she do that?"

"February. Just before the air raid."

"She got married? After all you did for her? After all the wage deductions to *Lebensborn*?"

"She said she needed someone."

"You didn't try to stop her?"

I shrugged.

"I didn't know until it was too late. Besides, she said if I did anything, she'd tell Marta."

"And she would tell Marta," said Dieter. "I thought she said she loved you."

"Things change."

"That's not your fault."

I looked at him.

"I hate women," said Dieter.

I've never hated women, but I've never understood them. Any of them. Now matter how hard I tried. Not even Marta. She was so gentle with the children. And she could be gentle with me, at times. But when I found the girl, after dinner, she was huddled in the corner. Her bottom lip was split, and crusted with blood. Her left cheekbone was bruised, her eyes swollen closed. Welts and bruises darkened her arms, her collarbone, her neck. When I touched her side, she cried out. When I moved closer to her, turning her face to me, my boot hit a piece of wood: Marta's wooden hairbrush.

I ran into the kitchen, the abandoned brush clenched in my fist. Marta jumped, clutching the dishtowel to her breast. I hurled the wooden brush at the small window over the sink, but its falling glass fragments were soundless beneath my rage. I grabbed the china and crystal she'd been drying and shattered them against the wall. Marta stumbled to the table, twisting, untwisting, twisting the white dishtowel. It wasn't enough. I tipped over the table, with its coffee cups and dessert plates. I opened one of the cupboards: the wedding china. I shoved out an entire shelf. That made Marta cry out. But still it wasn't enough. It was never enough. I stormed outside, to be free of her, with her tears, her scolding, her complaints. I had to get outside, to get away from the place, to get away from women, with their incessant demands.

But no matter how many places I went, I couldn't get away from the girl. Not from her. Of course, I couldn't find her either. Until I closed my eyes at night. Then the girl was there. I called out to her, but she couldn't hear me. I reached for her, and my hand passed right through her.

Every night, it was the same: I called and called, but the ship she was on drifted further and further from the shore. Away from me. I waded into the dark water. Calling. My legs were so heavy, and the water was brutally cold. My clothes dragged me deeper and deeper into the rough waves. *The Dead Bodies That Line the Streets* fell from my hands into the water. *The Dead Bodies* swelled, and became a raft. I threw myself onto the raft, and paddled out toward the sea.

I kept calling. Calling. I waved my arms. The girl stared out from the deck. I was right there. But she never saw me. I was so tired. And the water was getting colder. Deeper. It kept splashing into my eyes. Blinding me. I must've lost consciousness for a while, there on *The Dead Bodies.* From exhaustion. When I opened my eyes again, the ship was gone. She was gone.

Every time I woke, I was alone. Or with Marta. If she touched me or told me it was just a dream, I pushed her away. She couldn't possibly understand. Whenever I closed my eyes, the waves went over my head. Sometimes I forced myself to stay up all night, to keep the dreams away, to keep *The Dead Bodies* from dragging me under with them. I kept looking for the girl until the end, but I never found her.

GIRL FOUND

The telegram shook in my hands. I pulled over a chair and sat down. I looked back at the slip of paper in my hands.

GIRL FOUND
RENTING HOUSE FOR SUMMER
ADDRESS BELOW
MAY BE ALONE
GOES BY NAME RACHEL SARAH LEVI
WHAT NEXT?

Chapter Seven

So I caught up with you at last," said a repulsive man as he stood beside my table in the diner. "You're one tough bird to keep up with."

"I beg your pardon."

"Let's cut the crap," he said, pushing aside my coffee cup as he seated himself. "I know who you are. Hey, Honey, another cup of coffee here. And bring a couple of doughnuts."

"I am not in the habit of dining with strangers," I said, folding my napkin and placing it on the table.

"Yeah, well, we both know what you're in the habit of, don't we?" he said.

His hand snapped out and pinned my wrist to the table. He moved his jacket aside, revealing a gun.

"Now, you be a good boy and sit there while I have my coffee and doughnuts," he said. "And we'll talk about the situation we got here. Man to man. Gentleman-like."

"Is this a separate check?" asked the waitress, staring at him.

"No. Put it on his tab. You're a nice-looking Honey-girl. What time do you get off?"

"Do you need anything else, sir?" she said to me, turning away from him.

"He needs lots of things, but you can't give them to him."

"No, thank you. Nothing else," I said.

She frowned at the man before she left.

"Now, here's the way I see it," he said, biting into the pastry, crumbs falling from his mouth to the table.

"No, here's the way *I* see it," I said. "We have not been introduced to each other and I have no wish to make your acquaintance. I have completed my meal, and I have no desire to hear anything you might have to say."

"Is that right, Mr. High-and-Mighty? Well, maybe you'd like me to blow a hole in your belly. Or maybe you'd like to hear about the reward out for you. Money. On your head. And you don't have to be alive for me to get it."

He smiled.

"I thought that might get you to sit back down," he said.

He emptied the sugar bowl into his coffee, and he slurped down the thickened liquid. When he bit the second pastry, its jam oozed onto his chin. His belly and the gun bulged beneath his jacket.

"What do you want?" I said.

"Now we're talking. What do you think I want?"

"I have no idea."

"Oh, come on, now, you're a smart man. A Commander and all. Guess."

"I am not in the habit of playing games. Tell me what you want."

"No, come on. Guess."

"Tell me."

"Come on, Commander. Guess," he said, smiling a gap-toothed smile.

"You want advice."

"Advice?"

"And that's fine because I have nothing for you except advice."

"Advice, he says. That's a good one. They didn't tell me you was funny, Commander."

"Don't call me that. Let me pass on something I learned..."

"Advice. That's a good one."

"Any lie told often enough becomes the truth."

"Truth?" he said, snorting with laughter, dribbling coffee onto his shirt. "This has nothing to do with truth."

He was wrong. It had everything to do with truth. There was nothing left in the world but the truth. And sometimes, I felt I'd been left behind to tell it.

"Do you want the truth?" said Dieter as we sat together in the back of my car, touring the Camp. "You're a better man than Owl-eyes."

"What? Better than Heinrich? What are you talking about?"

"He came out last week, I told you that, and he decided he wanted to see how the killing was done."

"How the killing was done? Why? Are you doing something special?"

"No," he said, gazing out the window at the rows of inmates standing at attention for head-count. "Just shooting. The same as always. But he ordered me and my men to line up a hundred prisoners. Men *and* women."

"Women?"

"Yes. He wanted us to execute them. Right then. Right there."

"But you were only shooting them. Why would he want to see that?"

Dieter shrugged as the car paused to allow a line of inmates to pass. After one of the inmates fell, a guard released his dog and the animal pounced on the prisoner. I motioned the driver to continue. The driver tapped the horn; the guards and the dogs herded the remaining inmates to the side so the car could proceed. When we turned at the corner of the Camp, Dieter rolled up his window.

"When the first shots were fired, and the victims collapsed, Heinrich got ill."

"No. Not Heinrich."

"He reeled."

"No."

"He almost fell to the ground before he pulled himself together."

"It was only a shooting."

"And then — listen to this — he screamed abuse at my firing squad."

"What?"

"Screamed at them. At me. For poor marksmanship."

"But you're the best there is. What did he mean, 'poor marksmanship'?"

"Some of the women were still alive. The bullets had merely wounded them."

"That's why he screamed at you?"

"As if we did it on purpose," said Dieter.

He was always telling us what was expected of us. How we should act, think, believe. How history would regard us as the Saviours of the German race. He said we were connected by more than our desires, by more than our hopes and our dreams. We were connected by blood.

"We will become the blood community. We are the bearers of the blood of the Aryan race. Pure blood runs in our veins, through our hearts. We must be swift like the greyhound. Tough like leather. Hard like Krupp steel. Tough. Hard. Pure. Only the purest of the pure can act without hesitation. Only the purest of the pure can see the truth. Only the pure can act on truth."

"We act on principle. We oppose your truth," said the leader of the dirty, blood-stained group.

There were seven of them, dressed in rags, filthy and bloody. One of them could hardly stand on his own. A young boy was with them. So was a woman with short hair. She spat at me when I stood before her. My adjutant slapped her with the back of his hand.

"Where did you find them?" I said.

"In the woods outside the Camp, Kommandant."

"Partisans," I said. "We can take care of partisans."

"They had weapons, sir. We lost a few of our men."

"How many?"

"At least three."

"No," said the dirty leader, in my language. "Four."

"Five," said the woman, and she raised her chin defiantly as she smiled.

"Did you find their hiding places?"

"Some."

"Weapons?"

"Only a few. But a lot of other supplies. Food. Bandages. Gasoline."

"Gasoline?"

"Yes, sir."

"Stolen from my Camp."

"Of course stolen from your Camp," said the leader. "From under your very nose."

"It was easy," said the boy.

"Too easy," said the woman.

Before she'd finished speaking, their dirty leader lunged forward, throwing himself onto me, his hands grabbing for my pistol, for my service dagger. The guards shouted as the force of his body threw me back against the desk. The woman shrieked when I bashed her leader's head, and again when my guards yanked him off me. My adjutant put his pistol against the partisan's head and pulled the trigger. The woman rushed forward, slapping at the two guards who tried to prevent her from taking the man in her arms. The other guards had their weapons trained on the remaining partisans. The boy clenched his fists, but no one else moved. I straightened my uniform. The woman looked up at me, the bloodied head of her leader held against her breasts.

"Our lives mean nothing unless we defeat you," she said.

"Then your lives mean nothing," said my adjutant.

"Shall I execute them, sir?" said the guard who'd brought them in.

"You get some rest."

"What about the prisoners, sir?"

"They'll be taken care of. You get some rest. You deserve it."

"Thank you, sir."

"Tomorrow you'll go out again. We'll rid the woods of these pests."

Two of the partisans picked up their slain leader, and the guards hurried them out of the office, into the Camp's yard.

"Kommandant?" said my adjutant.

"I'm fine."

He looked down at the pool of red on the floor.

"I'll get the housekeeper," he said.

"Tell her to get the blood in the bathroom, too."

"There's blood in the bathroom, Kommandant?"

"It looks like blood. On the floor, near the sink. And tell her to put dry towels in. Every time I've tried to use one of the towels this week, it's been wet."

"I'll take care of it myself, Kommandant."

"Thank you, Josef. I can always count on you."

He walked toward the door.

"Josef."

He turned around.

"Good work," I said.

He nodded, with a sharp click of his heels.

"Tonight, we'll all get some rest," I said. "We'll all sleep easy.

"Max, you've got to get some rest," said Marta.

I put the damp cloth on Ilse's forehead. I sponged her small body with cloths soaked in alcohol.

"You can't stay up all night, Max."

"You've been with her all day, Marta."

"You're exhausted, Max. You work all day. You haven't slept in three nights. You can't make yourself ill, too. I need you. Hans needs you."

"The fever's still high."

"I'll stay with her now. You sleep."

"Nothing's doing any good."

"Max, get some rest. I'll be with her."

"It's the same as..."

"No, it's not. Don't even say that, Max."

"She's going to die."

"No, the doctor said it wasn't the same."

"He wasn't there. He couldn't know absolutely. What'll we do if we lose her?"

"Stop it, Max. I won't let you say it. I won't. It's not the same as the fever that..."

"Then it's this Camp."

"What?" said Marta, taking the damp cloth from me. "What are you saying?"

"This Camp. It's the Camp. The Camp's made her ill."

"The Camp didn't make her ill."

"We'll have to go. Then she'll recover. We'll leave the Camp."

"This Camp is your life, Max."

"The polluted water. The fetid air. Those damned, diseased inmates. Coughing. Spitting. Dying everywhere. That's what it is."

"It's not the Camp, Max," she said. "If it were the Camp, we'd all be sick."

She put her arms around me and held me tightly. We both looked at Ilse: she was so pale, so small and helpless, lying there.

"She'll be all right, Max. We've got to believe that. And Hans won't get ill. You'll see. Pray, Max. God won't abandon us now."

"You pray for me, Marta. I don't know how."

Even if I had prayed, it wouldn't have made any difference. Nothing would have changed. I was alone. I was always alone, but sometimes it was worse than others. When Marta took the children and went to visit her sister in Hamburg, I was alone in the house. In the spring. I took the girl's arm and pulled her to the stairs. She looked wildly about. At each step she resisted, but I tugged her upward, into the house proper. We passed the kitchen and the dining room. Everything was quiet. Empty.

The hall clock was louder than our steps. The girl glanced around constantly as I led her to the main staircase. She stopped, putting her hand on the banister, holding tight. She looked at the front door, toward the living room, up the stairs. I pulled at her.

With each step, her body became heavier, dragging more and more against me. In the upstairs hall, I had to take hold of both of her wrists. She didn't even walk. Her feet slid on the polished wood floor. Though she was slight, my heart was pounding by the time we reached the bedroom. I opened the door.

She shook her head. I had to catch her wrist again to prevent her flight back down the stairs. I didn't even try to say anything: there was no translator. I just kept pulling at her until she was in the room.

How frail she looked. How grey and frail against the white curtains and bedspread. Her arms hugged themselves tightly to her body as she stood there, her head bent, looking at me like that. I closed the door and stood there, leaning against it. She kept looking at me, with her head bent. There was no need to lock the door. We were alone. She stepped back, until the bed stopped her. There was no one but us, and I wanted her heart to pound, like mine. I unbuckled my holster.

My heart was racing. I was alone in the house. Marta was gone. I couldn't find her anywhere. I went outside. Ilse was with Nanny in the garden. Ilse clapped her hands and bounced up and down when she saw me. I lifted her up and kissed her cheek. Nanny hadn't seen Marta. I spoke to our neighbor, Mrs. Green. I spoke to Mr. and Mrs. Stein. No one had seen her.

"Marta? Marta?"

I came back to the house. My heart pounded as I ran up the stairs. Bathroom: empty. Our bedroom: empty. Ilse's bedroom: empty. I found Marta in the nursery, sitting in the rocking chair. She didn't move when I came in.

"Marta, I've been so worried. I've been looking everywhere for you."

She held the christening gown in her hands: its lace had yellowed. When I touched her arm, she looked up at me. Her lashes and cheeks were wet.

"Marta, what is it?"

"I don't think I can go through this again, Max."

"Go through what? What's happened?"

"I'm not strong enough. I'm not as strong as you think I am."

"What are you talking about?"

"I'm pregnant."

I knelt and took both of her hands in mine. The lace of the christening gown covered our hands and wrists. When I leaned forward and kissed the backs of her hands, through the faded gown, she began to weep again.

"I don't know if I can go through it again."

I brushed the yellowed lace aside. I turned her hands over and kissed her palms. I buried my face in her lap. She bent over me, and her breasts pressed against the back of my head. Her tears were cool on my neck.

"I can't bear to disappoint you again."

I lifted my head. She looked tired. And fragile. The neck of her dress was open, and her pulse throbbed at the base of her throat. I stood. I pulled her up from the rocking chair. She seemed so frail, so beautiful. I held her face between my hands and wiped her tears away. I kissed her forehead, her cheeks, her eyes. She let the christening gown fall. She clutched my uniform lapels and leaned against my chest.

"Oh, Max, I can't bear to disappoint you again," she said.

I kissed her and held her until there were no more tears.

The disappointments in my life were my own fault: I'd always had expectations that were too high. I expected too much from the Party, from my marriage, from my entire life. At the end, after so much searching, I was even disappointed at how easily I found the girl's house. It was right up the hill, off the dirt road, just as the grocer had told me. Though the house was surrounded by shade trees, it was visible from the road. I parked the car under the cover of trees and sat there. There were no other houses, no cars, no animals, no people. I picked up my field-glasses from the seat beside me and looked at the house.

The front door was open. There was a screen-door. The porch swing drifted slightly in the breeze. Curtains fluttered at the upstairs windows. I saw no one. Not that day. I don't know what I expected. Yes, I do: I thought it would be easy, but I never got out of the car. No, my gun was in the trunk. Once, toward dusk, when I was looking at *The Dead Bodies* again, someone closed the curtains and turned on the lights. I snatched up my field-glasses and pressed them to my eyes until they gave me a headache. It didn't do any good. I saw no one.

I stayed until long after all the lights had been turned out. Once, I thought I saw the curtains in an upstairs window move aside, as if she'd seen, as if she were watching me, but it must've been my imagination. It should've been easy: I was the Kommandant. No, I couldn't even make myself open the door. I put the field-glasses back down on the seat. Then I drove away.

Some things are harder than anyone could imagine. Even I thought it would be easy. But I sat there for hours. For hours. Not moving. Just sitting. Staring. I could feel the metal of the bed frame through the cheap, thin mattress. My thigh ached from it. All the lights were on, as usual. The room was cool and slightly damp, but I was sweating.

My shirt was wet, and clinging to my skin. With my free hand, I pulled the fabric away, but it immediately slapped back. Whenever I heard movement in the hallway, I closed my fingers over my palm. I don't know how long I sat there. An hour? It might have been an hour. It might have been a day. I didn't eat. Or sleep. It may have been only a minute. One minute. No, it was longer than that. It was long enough to fill the room with the smell of my fear. Long enough to shame me. I opened my hand, and closed my eyes. There was no other way.

I put the cyanide capsule into my mouth.

I spit it back out.

It lay there, in my lap, taunting me. The story of my life: I disappoint even myself.

Marta's letter lay on the table. I didn't open it. I knew what it contained: taunts, questions, pleas, accusations, disappointment. The same as before. The same as always. I pushed her letter aside and picked up the children's.

I tore open Hans' letter and read the uneven block letters he had copied out.

Daddy I love you Hans

At the bottom, under the letters, there was a drawing: a tall stick figure with curls held the overly long stick arms of two small figures, one with curls, one without. All three of the figures had huge eyes. None was smiling. A dog with three legs and a bright red tongue stood beside a crooked yellow house. Its chimney belched out great clouds of smoke, darkening a misshapen sun.

I opened Ilse's letter.

Querido Papa,
That means Dear Daddy in the way we have to talk now.
I don't like it here. There's no one to play with.
Mommy is mean to me. So is Hans.
Why don't you come live with us?
Daddys are supposed to live with their children.
Why aren't you here? Don't you love us anymore?

Chapter Eight

Questions. Accusations. Lies. I'm sick of it all."

"Yes, sir," said my adjutant. "This..."

"Reinhard couldn't get anything on me. Ernst isn't going to do it. There's nothing for them to get."

"No, sir. They..."

"They envy my success, Josef, but they're not going to beat me. I'm loyal. No one can say I'm not loyal."

"No, sir. This also..."

"They've got no proof. No evidence. And they'll never have any."

My adjutant tried to hand me another paper as I paced in my office. Each time I put my full weight on my leg, the pain in my thigh forced me to stop until the pain subsided. An artillery shell exploded in the distance. My head was pounding. The pain in my thigh made me nauseous. My adjutant held out the paper. I brushed his arm aside.

"The Party is my life. I'd never betray the Party. Just because some Jews tried to..."

"This telegram also came for you, sir."

"From whom?"

"I didn't open it, sir."

I took it from him, and tore open the envelope.

ALL NEGOTIATIONS SUSPENDED
CAMPS LIBERATED BY ADVANCING FRONT
AHORA HABLO ESPAÑOL
THE FIGHTING DAYS WERE BEST
DIETER

I crushed the paper.

"Kommandant?"

"*Sieg heil,*" I said.

I tossed the telegram aside. Pain seared my thigh. Another shell shook the air.

"*Sieg heil.*"

"*Heil. Heil,*" said Hans as he marched about my bedroom.

"Say, '*Sieg heil*', Hans," I said.

"*Heil.*"

"Now raise your arm, Hans. Like this."

Hans marched back and forth in my room, then around in a circle, his right arm raised, my officer's cap falling over his eyes.

"*Heil. Heil.*"

"Come here, Hans."

I undid the leather belt holding my service dagger, fastened it on the last hole, and draped the leather band around Hans' body, over his shoulder. The dagger, in its sheath, hit the floor.

"*Ja,*" said Hans, nodding, reaching for the dagger's handle.

"Listen to Daddy, Hans. Say the oath. Say, 'I swear obedience and allegiance...'"

"*Ja.*"

"'...to the Saviour of this country, Adolf Hitler'."

"*Ja. Ja.*"

"'I am willing to give up my life for him, so help me God'."

"*Ja.*"

I went to the bureau and opened the top drawer. Hans held the handle of my service dagger tightly. Each time he looked down at the dagger, my cap fell over his eyes. I pulled out a long narrow box from the bureau drawer. I knelt in front of Hans and opened the box. I took out the dagger.

"When you get old enough, this Hitler Youth dagger will be yours," I said.

I held out the broad flat blade with its inscription: *Blut und Ehre.* Hans clapped and reached for it.

"See what this says: 'Blood and Honor.' And it'll be yours one day."

"Blood?" said Adolf, making a disdainful face as he sat there in the garden with us after one of his tours. "There's no blood on my hands."

"Does our beloved *Führer* know that?" said Dieter. "I thought he promoted you for your zealous…"

"I never killed a Jew," said Adolf.

We all looked at him. Marta glanced anxiously toward the children, but they were playing in the fallen leaves: they didn't hear. Ilse was picking up handfuls of brown leaves and tossing them onto Hans. He laughed, rolling back and forth in the pile. Ilse giggled and gathered more leaves.

"I never killed a non-Jew either," Adolf said.

He knocked his wineglass when he reached for it, spilling the wine on the tablecloth.

"I've never killed anybody," he said.

"Let me get it for you," said Marta, righting his glass.

Adolf held the wine bottle by its neck as Marta dabbed her napkin on the spill.

"I never ordered anybody to kill a Jew," he said.

When Dieter laughed, Adolf gave him a look.

"I never ordered anybody to kill a non-Jew either."

"No," said Dieter. "None of us did."

"Are you mocking me?"

"No, of course he's not. That's just the way Dieter is," said Marta.

She took the wine from Adolf and refilled his glass. She gave me a look, but I pretended I hadn't seen.

"Please, let's not talk about this in front of the children," she said.

Dieter leaned back in his chair to look at them.

"What are they going to hear," he said, "that they don't already know?"

"Did you ever kill a Jew, von Walther?"

"No."

"Ever kill anybody?"

"No."

Dieter laughed and poured himself more wine. Marta stacked the empty plates, and collected the silver. Ilse tried to pick up Hans, and the two of them fell, laughing, into the leaves. Hans kicked and laughed. Ilse buried him in the leaves until he squealed with joy.

"Ever order anybody else to kill?"

"No," I said. "Never."

I was no murderer. I didn't kill the girl. I protected her. She was a Jew. I never used my weapons on her. I unbuckled my holster and laid my weapons on the bureau. The girl stood motionless, grey against the bedroom's white, as I undid my uniform buttons. My fingers were cold. The clock on the bureau ticked loudly. The chimneys hadn't been burning for several days, so there was no scent of smoke in the breeze that moved the curtains. My boots thudded on the floor. My belt buckle clanked. The girl stood. Watching me. I started to say something, then shook my head. I was always forgetting. Though I pointed to the bed, she didn't move. The air chilled my bare skin. I got under the covers and tugged at her wrist. When she continued to stand, I pulled more firmly.

She sat on the edge of the bed. I slid the grey shift away and kissed her shoulder. She closed her eyes when the gown slipped off. She was so frail. So delicate. I was almost afraid to touch her. My hands seemed so large on her. I pulled her to me, to feel her skin next to mine. She was cold. I rubbed my hands all over her, to warm her. I got out of bed, pulled another blanket from the chest in the hallway, and spread the blanket over her, but still she shivered. I touched her face, turning it toward mine.

"*Sieh mich an*," I said, but I could see nothing behind her eyes.

I rubbed my cheek against her face and throat as I stretched my body along hers. I wrapped my arms around her and hugged her to me, my knee sliding between her legs. She closed her eyes. She always closed her eyes. I covered her face and throat with kisses. I held her breasts in my hands and I kissed them. Over and over, I kissed her breasts, the space between them, her ribs. This time when I moved my mouth to her belly, and lower, she didn't shove me away. She'd never let me put my mouth on her before, and it excited me so much that my hands trembled. Marta didn't like my kissing, or touching, but it was different with the girl. Every time her mouth and tongue pressed wet on me I felt strong. And hard. And good. Better than with anyone else. When my tongue touched her, she shuddered, and pressed her thigh against my cheek: I had to think of something else so it wouldn't be over too quickly. I tried to be gentle, and patient, but when she arched her back and tangled her fingers in my hair, I couldn't think of anything except how I wanted to be inside her.

I pressed her onto her back, and her thighs were soft on either side of mine. Her breasts brushed against my chest, her belly against mine. My hands stroked the flower-like scar on the inside of her thigh. I brushed the back of her thighs and lifted her hips. When her fingers dragged themselves down my back, I wanted to tell her things, things I'd done, things that were best forgotten. I clutched her short hair and pressed against her as hard as I could. When she breathed against my ear, I whispered her things. When she tightened her legs around me, I wished she spoke my language, and I was glad she couldn't understand me. When I moved deep in her, I wanted her to open her eyes, I wanted her to tangle her fingers in my hair, I wanted her to sigh my name against my chest and throat, I wanted her to move and thrust with me, I wanted to lose myself.

I was almost happy.

I must've slept afterward. When I woke, she was sitting in the chair by the window, with the white blanket wrapped around her, and the sun on her hair. My pistol was lying on the bureau, and she was sitting in the sunlight, wrapped in white, with my weapon, fully loaded, and my service dagger, lying there, in the same room where I slept, and she was sitting, surrounded by white and sunlight, sitting by the window, with her eyes closed. I never understood her.

"I don't understand," said my adjutant. "I've never done anything except what you told me to do."

I handed him more files to pack in the boxes.

"I'm no criminal," he said. "I was bound by my oath. To the Party. To you. We all were bound. By our duty. By our honor."

The smoke belched out of the chimneys, and lay in heavy palls over the Camp. The smoke rubbed itself upon the windows, clung to our hair and clothes, snarled itself around our ankles and heels. I urged more files into my adjutant's hands. The girl watched us.

"I only did what you ordered me to do," said my adjutant. "I took an oath."

"Words," I said, and I shoved more files at him. "Words."

"You gave your word," said Marta. "You promised."

"Give me a kiss."

"You swore, Max. You stink," said Marta, slapping my hands away. "You're drunk."

"I want to make love to you."

"No."

"You're my wife."

"I won't let you touch me. Not now that you've touched a Jew."

"Marta..."

"You even smell like sex. Don't. Stop it. If you're going to do it with Jews, you're not going to do it with me."

"I love you."

She hit my hands, and she dragged her nightgown back down over her legs.

"You said you'd get rid of her. Stop that. Stop."

"I love you."

"I can't stand it when you're drunk. You smell like liquor, and smoke, and worse. Let go. Stop kissing me. God knows where your mouth has been."

She turned her face away, her hands pushing at my chest.

"Let go. Stop it. I mean it. If you won't stop with that Jew, you're not going to touch me."

"You're my wife."

"When you treat me like a wife, I'll act like a wife."

She shoved the blanket at me and got out of the bed.

"What are you doing?" I said. "Where are you going?"

"Downstairs," said Marta. "To sleep on the sofa."

"You'd better be careful," I said. "Some women like me."

She liked me. She trusted me. I tried to show her the real me. So there'd be nothing dishonest between us. Nothing bad. Or ugly. I talked to her all the time, even though she couldn't understand me. And I tried to let her know in other ways. That's what the gifts were for, to make her see.

She stood hesitantly in the dining room, glancing toward the other rooms. I lit the candles in the center of the table and opened the champagne. I poured two glasses, drank one, and poured another before taking one of the glasses of champagne to the girl. The china and crystal sparkled. The silver gleamed. The odor of roast goose filled the room. As she stood there looking at it all, I brought the package to her.

She stared at it, and I had to lift her hands to put the box in them. She held the package. I undid the ribbon, lifted the lid, and folded back the tissue paper. Her expression didn't change, even after she looked down at the open box, but she must've been pleased: the silk was the color of her eyes.

I pulled the gown from the box. When I held it up to her body, she looked at me instead of at the dress. I motioned for her to slip off the prison uniform, but her fingers fumbled with the worn material. I helped her put on the silk dress. I did up the small buttons in the back. My hands brushed the material. I pulled my comb out of my pocket and offered it to her, but she merely stood there. I combed her short hair, smoothing it back. I took the pearl earrings from my breast pocket. I leaned close to put the pearls in her ears.

I took her hand and led her from the room. A mirror hung over the table in the entry hall. I stood the girl in front of it. At first, she wouldn't look up. I nudged her closer to the glass, my hands on her back.

She glanced up at the mirror.

She burst into tears.

There were no tears in the words that screamed out at me from that book. No tears. No tenderness. I felt as if I'd been smashed in the chest. I didn't hear Marta's words as I stumbled closer to the fallen book, as I knelt beside it, as I touched it. A voice was there but I didn't know it. I'd lost the words. I thought it was over, done with, finished. Yet here she was: in that country, in my home, after all that had happened. When I touched *The Dead Bodies That Line the Streets,* her words were louder than Marta's. Crueler. More vicious.

"You even told her private things," said Marta. "Things between you and me. How do you think that makes me feel?"

I opened the book.

"I don't understand you at all, Max," she said. "And I don't understand all the things she wrote about you. Who's this boy Klaus in 'Love Song for Klaus'? Why would you cry about his death?"

I turned to one of the poems.

"You never think of anyone but yourself," said Marta. "That's the only thing in the universe that exists for you: Max, only Max. Not even God. Just Max."

I started to read:

Cutthroat: A Player Who Plays for Himself

One finds a way out. The Kommandant keeps her
in his special place, gives her Cognac, champagne, caviar.
She says nothing when he grunts over her.
He does not mind her stillness. He falls asleep.
Afterward, she walks anywhere she pleases.
They won't speak to her. Some spit.
Soldiers call to her, but she only knows German in dreams.
She used to dream of grassy fields, towering sunflowers,

Jan's callused hands, sun-bleached hair, rough lips.
Now dreams dark bread, potatoes, bits of greasy butter,
his face, his smell, his panting sweating weight.

Howling, I tore the pages from the book. I shredded *The Dead Bodies* and stuffed the fragments into the fireplace. Marta became silent as I broke the book's spine and tore it in half, as I shoved it into the flames. After all I'd done for her: fed her, clothed her, kept her safe, warm. And this was what she did to me.

She betrayed me.

At the end, everyone betrayed me. Or deserted me. At the end, I was the only one left. I drank all the vodka in the house. All the champagne in the cellar. The shells were booming, rattling the walls. On my desk lay my pistol, readied for firing; my dagger, unsheathed; and the three cyanide capsules. The artillery pounded just outside the Camp.

"Kommandant," said my adjutant, rushing in. "Kommandant, the car's waiting."

The girl knelt on the floor in front of me, between my legs, her hands on my thighs. I turned over the girl's left hand. Her palm was scarred. The raised white lines seemed almost like a triangle atop an inverted triangle. I leaned forward and squinted at the scar more closely.

"Kommandant," said my adjutant as the phone on his desk rang. "We've got to get you out of here. Now, Kommandant."

He rushed back out to silence the phone. Each time he replaced its receiver, it rang again. Each time it rang, shells exploded. My finger traced the girl's scar, so I could see it better.

"Hurry, Kommandant, before it's too late."

"It ain't too late for you. 'Least not the way I see it," said the repulsive man, sitting across the table from me in the diner. "Here's the deal. You make it worth my time, I'll let you escape."

"You want money."

"They told me you was smart. I like a man comes right to the point. Honey, can we get a refill on this coffee here?"

"How much do you want?" I said.

"How much you got?"

"What makes you think I have any money at all?"

"I know who you are," he said to me.

The waitress filled his cup. She glared at him when he took my half-empty plate from her hand and set it in front of himself. He scooped the remainder of the eggs into his mouth. The waitress shook her head and frowned as she left. He looked at me.

"I know what you did," he said.

"There's nothing to know," I said. "Besides, you weren't even there."

"My partner was. He told me plenty."

"Your partner? And who might that be?"

"Listen, I ain't in no mood for games. I want the price on your head."

"Whatever it is, I don't have it," I said, opening my wallet and displaying the cash. "This is all I have."

"Sixty dollars?"

He soaked my toast in his coffee, then put the dripping crust into his mouth.

"Get the money from your wife. Her family's got it."

"Not since the war."

"You all say that. You got money all right. Now all you got to do is give me my part of it."

"Even if my wife did have money, which she does not, we're obviously separated. We don't live together. We're not even in the same..."

"I seen the letters. I know where she is, but I got you right here. And you're wanted dead or alive. Makes no difference to me how I get paid. Long as I get my money."

He snatched up a half-piece of bacon from my plate, and crammed it into his mouth.

"Get my meaning?"

"Yes," I said. "I do."

Chapter Nine

I should dock some of your salary, Josef," I said after my adjutant entered my office.

"Kommandant?"

"For general incompetence."

"What? What did I do?"

"It's what you didn't do. You neglected to remove the Safe-Conducts from the deportation and arrest orders."

"No, I did exactly as you instructed. I removed all the Safe-Conducts and..."

"What do you call this? And this?"

He accepted the documents from my hands and eyed them closely, frowning.

"These aren't the same as the other Safe-Conducts I removed."

"You didn't remove them. They're still there."

"These aren't like any of the Safe-Conducts I separated."

He pointed to the bottom of the papers, turning them so I could see the signature.

"I can't even read this signature," he said. "It doesn't..."

"What difference does it make if you can read the signature or not? I told you to remove them all, before I saw the deportation and arrest orders."

"I know that, sir."

"Now I have to deal with these Safe-Conducts. I told you I didn't want to see any of them."

"I did remove them all, sir. These are not the Safe-Conducts that came originally."

"What's that supposed to mean?"

"These are forgeries, sir."

"Forgeries?"

I took the documents back. After I looked at them closely, I laid them on my desk.

"How would we get forged Safe-Conducts? Who would forge Safe-Conducts?"

"Someone who wanted to save the Jews, sir."

"Who in this Camp?"

He looked at the girl. She lay on the cot, wrapped in a blanket. Her eyes were closed.

"You're not serious."

"She'd have access to the documents."

"She doesn't even speak German."

"She's in your office."

"The documents are locked in my desk."

"She's here. Alone."

"Where would she get the forms?"

"From someone in the Camp."

"Does she ever leave this office?"

"Not that I'm aware of, sir."

"Does anyone else come in, when I'm not here?"

"No, sir."

"But she gets blank Safe-Conducts from an inmate in the Camp, fills in the names, forges the signatures, unlocks my desk, probably with a forged key, and attaches these forged documents: is that what you expect me to believe?"

"Yes, Kommandant."

"Don't insult my intelligence."

"Sir?"

"And don't blame your lapses of duty on anyone else. Forgeries. The girl."

"She's a Jew."

"Are you being insolent?"

He stared over my head and said nothing, but the muscles of his jaw twitched beneath the skin.

"I'll let it pass this time. We all forget things," I said as I sat back down at my desk and picked up my pen. "In the future, I don't want to see any of these Safe-Conducts."

"Yes, Kommandant."

"And your attitude has been very poor of late, Josef. If your attitude doesn't change, your position will. Is that clear?"

"Very clear, Kommandant."

It wasn't the first time I'd had to reprimand my adjutant. Or another subordinate. It wasn't an isolated incident. Every day, it seemed, I had to instruct the men on the most basic procedures. On things they should have learned as privates. Like shooting. How to shoot a prisoner. You'd think they were still in primary school. You'd think they were still in short pants.

"We're ready, *Herr Sturmbannführer.*"

"Ready?" I said, looking over at the group of prisoners standing in the woods. "They're still dressed."

"You want them to undress, sir?"

"Do you want blood all over the clothes?" I said. "Of course they have to undress. Hurry, now, I want to be done by lunch."

"Yes, sir."

He scurried over to the prisoners and began shouting instructions. I pulled out a cigarette. A nasty habit, I know. I was always trying to quit. I did manage to quit smoking once I got to the Camp. I was always so busy that I didn't have the time for it. But I still smoked then. Sometimes nothing else would do. I blew smoke toward the trees. One of the women started wailing. That made the children cry. The men undressed in silence. If you could call them "men". At least they were better than Gypsies. Gypsies screamed, cried, threw themselves on the ground. Some Gypsies even jumped into the grave and pretended to be already dead. As if we were that stupid. But not the Jews. After they folded the clothes neatly and stacked them beside the shoes, they stood, shivering, in front of the gaping earth. The corporal motioned to me.

"Is this how you're going to do it?" I said.

"Sir?"

"With them looking at you?"

"I'm sorry, sir. This is my first time."

"You should've told me you were a virgin. I would've been more patient."

He blushed as he looked down at the ground. A few of the guards stared openly at one of the young girls. She tried vainly to hide herself with her hands. Some of the old men, naked except for their beards, rocked back and forth as they murmured under their breath. I tossed down my cigarette.

"To avoid unnecessary physical contact afterward, it would be appropriate for the candidates for shooting to kneel."

"To kneel. Yes, sir."

"Facing the pit. Not facing the men."

"Yes, sir."

After much confused movement and increased squalling from the babies, the Jews were kneeling.

"Your men should form two groups. About eight to ten yards back. Yes, there. That's fine. One group should aim at the deportees' heads. One, at their chests. They should fire simultaneously."

"Yes, sir."

"Simultaneously."

"Yes, sir."

"The doctor will give orders for mercy shots. You do have a doctor present, don't you?"

"Oh, yes, sir."

"Clothes and shoes will be handed over to the local military officer. Under no circumstances are personal effects to be handed out to the population."

"No, sir."

"Otherwise they'll be hanging about like crows during the special actions."

"Yes, sir."

"Ready?"

They nodded, gripping their rifles.

"Aim."

They were boys really. Some of their weapons trembled.

"Fire."

That's what made us hard. Forcing young boys to become men before their time. But we didn't talk about things like that. Even among ourselves.

"Among ourselves it should be mentioned quite frankly, and yet we will never speak of it publicly."

I had a fierce headache, and my leg was throbbing: that made it hard to concentrate on what Heinrich was saying.

"We will never be rough or heartless where it isn't necessary. That is clear."

"Do you have anything for pain?" I said.

"Do you have another headache?"

"We Germans, who are the only people in the world who have a decent attitude toward animals, will also adopt a decent attitude toward these human animals..."

"Do you have any..."

"No. Let me ask someone else."

No one around me had anything for the pain. I massaged my thigh. One of the others offered me a cigarette. I thanked him, but shook my head.

"Most of you know what it means to see a hundred corpses lying together. Five hundred. Or a thousand."

I rubbed my forehead, but the throbbing in my temples only worsened.

"To have stuck it out and at the same time to have remained decent fellows. Decent, loyal, honest. That is what has made us hard."

Hard. The pounding in my head was hard. As hard as bone. No, harder. The gun was hard against my head. But not as hard as it was going to be. When I straightened up and glimpsed myself in the mirror, with my pistol pressed against my temple, my stomach revolted.

A cold sweat accompanied the gagging. My free hand kept slipping on the bathroom sink. I gripped the cold porcelain tighter. I was glad I hadn't eaten. I shouldn't have looked in the mirror. That was the problem. Yes, that was it. I shouldn't look. I splashed cold water on my face, and pressed the metal to my temple again.

The girl said nothing when she came up behind me. She merely reached up and pushed the gun away. Just like that. One movement. Pure.

Clean. Honest. One movement, and the gun wasn't butting my head. It wasn't even in my hand. The gun clattered into the sink, and the girl folded me in her arms. She murmured something, but I didn't catch the words. When she dried my face with her gown, I wept.

"Don't start crying, Max," said Marta, "because it's not going to change my mind."

She crossed the room and sat on the end of the bed. Her eyes were red. The closet and bureau drawers were open. Suitcases stood by the doorway.

"I love you. You're my wife."

"You don't know what it is to love someone. It's taken me a long time to realize it."

"Marta."

"Crying isn't going to work for you this time. I want a divorce."

"But why?"

"Oh, Max," she said, shaking her head. "Can you be so blind?"

"What is it? What have I done? Tell me. I'll change it."

"We've been through this so many times."

"Tell me. I'll change. I swear it. I promise."

"Your drinking…"

"I'll stop. I'll never have another drink in my life."

"Your lying..."

"What have I lied about?"

"Max..."

"I didn't mean to. Whatever it was."

"Your women."

"Never again. I swear it."

"What about her?"

"It's over."

"Since when?"

"Since now. This minute."

"It's not going to work this time."

"I love you."

"You do this every time. You say you love me..."

"I do."

"...you say you can't live without me..."

"It's true."

"...you say you're sorry. You cry. You say you'll change..."

"I will change."

"But then you don't."

"I swear."

"You always swear. Get up."

"Not till you say you don't mean it."

"Please, don't degrade yourself. Get up off your knees."

"Not till you say you'll stay."

"I can't."

"Of course you can. You love me, don't you? I know you do. You love me."

"I can't stand living this way."

"It'll be different. Give me one more chance. It's the last time I'll ever ask. If I'm not different this time, you can leave. But I'll be different. I'll show you. I've changed. Let me prove it to you."

"Stop crying."

"I love you. I need you."

"Max..."

"They've never meant anything to me. You're the only one who's ever been important to me. I can't live without you. Without the children. You're the whole world to me."

"I don't believe it anymore."

"Give me one more chance. Say you'll stay. Just one more chance. Please. I won't look at another woman. I love you. I need you. Life means nothing without you and the children."

She looked at me. A cold look. A woman's look.

"You'll stop drinking?"

"Yes."

"You'll stop lying?"

"Absolutely."

"You'll stop with her?"

"I swear it."

"Get up, Max. Please. Wipe your face."

"You do still love me, don't you, Marta?"

She closed her eyes. I grasped her hands and covered them with kisses.

"You won't regret it, my Darling. I'll never even look at another woman."

She pulled her hands away.

"I'm looking for the girl who wrote this book," I said.

I laid the book on the counter. The grocer wiped his hands on his apron as he looked at *The Dead Bodies.*

"I was told she lives in this area," I said. "I have the address, but I can't seem to find the road."

As the grocer squinted at the book, a small boy came up to the counter and held out a crumpled note. The grocer took the wadded paper and flattened it out. Then he turned, note in hand, and gathered up several items. The boy stared silently up at me as the items on his list were piled on the counter: sugar, flour, cornmeal, lard. The boy drew several coins out of his pocket, and placed them beside the food. The grocer counted the coins, passed one back to the boy, and handed him a piece of hard candy before he carried the supplies outside and put them into the boy's wagon. He patted the boy on the head. The boy dragged the wagon away, turning once to wave. The man came back into his store. He picked up *The Dead Bodies.*

"You're not from around here," he said.

"No."

"Didn't think so."

"I'm trying to..."

"No name on this book," he said.

"I know. But she wrote it. Her name is..."

"How do you know who wrote it, if there's no name?"

"I know her. From... before the war. Her name's Rachel. Rachel Levi."

"This is Miss Levi's?"

"Yes."

"This is one of hers?"

"Yes."

"Why doesn't it have her name on it? Like her other books do?"

I said nothing. The sun streamed in the front windows, heating the store. My shirt grew damp as I waited for his answer. He pulled up the end of his apron and wiped his face with it.

"*The Dead Bodies That Line the Streets*," he said.

He shrugged as he put the book back down on the counter.

"Sounds like something she'd write. Did you read *No Man's Land*?"

"No."

"Did you read *The Kommandant* ?"

Sweat trickled cold down my ribs, and my head pounded. My throat felt wrapped with piano wire, tightening with each breath I took.

"*No Man's Land* gave me nightmares when I read it. It made my wife cry. Especially the ending."

Another shopper came in and greeted the grocer. He smiled and raised his hand in acknowledgment. The woman purchased some blue thread, a package of needles, and five pounds of flour. I stared at the book the whole time she was in the store. The grocer took a damp rag from beneath the counter and wiped off the dusting of flour that remained after the bag had been removed.

"All the children around here like Miss Levi," he said. "They're all the time bothering her, going up to her house, playing in her yard."

He stood there, the rag hanging from his hand, his arms crossed over his chest. He stared openly at me.

"She doesn't seem to mind the children hanging about," he said.

I picked up the book. He motioned me to follow as he walked over to the storefront windows.

"The road to her house is easy to miss if you don't know the area," he said. "There's a narrow road between two big oaks, just where the wider road turns toward the mountain. You want the narrow road. That's the one that leads to her place. It's a few miles up, after you turn."

I nodded.

"Tell her Mr. Godfrey says 'hello'."

"Yes."

I had missed the road. None of them were paved. The car strained on the incline, going slower and slower, until I thought it would stop. At the crest of the hill, white and surrounded by trees, was her house. After all this time. Thousands of miles behind me. A lifetime behind me.

I parked the car under the shade of the big trees at the end of the drive. I looked at *The Dead Bodies That Line the Streets.* Every day I read some of her words. Every day I vowed to find her. I thought about changing to my uniform. No, I had to go to her without the uniform, without ornaments.

"You're not wearing your uniform," said Marta when I came into the walled garden after dinner. "Why not?"

"I... I spilled something on it. At lunch."

"What did you spill?"

"Wine."

"Wine? Wine will leave a stain," she said, standing up. "I'd better try to get it out."

"The housekeeper's doing it."

"You gave your uniform to the housekeeper?"

"Yes. Don't look at me like that. She'll take care of it."

"She's an inmate."

"Don't worry about it."

"But it's your uniform."

"She'll do it, Marta."

"All right. Let's not fight. How's your headache?"

"The same."

"Is your leg any better?"

"No. Is there any more coffee?"

Marta poured some coffee into my cup: black, no sugar. When I accepted the cup from her, my sleeve moved up, over my wrist.

"Max, what happened to your watch?"

"I dropped it."

"Let me see," she said, reaching for my wrist. "It looks like the crystal is cracked."

"It's nothing."

"Take it off. I'll give it to the jeweler when I go to Berlin next week."

"I'll take care of it."

"It's no bother. I'm going there anyway."

"That's all right."

"I'd be happy to..."

"I'm really not in the mood for this."

She pressed her lips tightly together and stared at me while I drank the coffee. It was bitter. Cold. I put the cup down. Marta poured some coffee into her own cup.

"Maybe I'll just buy you a new watch for your birthday," she said.

"I don't need one."

"The crystal's broken."

"It's fine."

"I've never understood your attachment to that watch," said Marta. "What's so special about it?"

I turned my head to look at the children. Hans lay on his belly at the end of the walk, playing with wooden soldiers. He made little exploding sounds with his mouth and knocked them down as they shot each other. After they were all dead, he lined them up and started another war. Ilse jumped rope nearby. As the rope slapped the walk, Ilse chanted.

Never mind to whom he prays
The rotten mess is in the race.

"Ilse," I said. "I thought I told you to stop singing that song."

"It's not a song," said Ilse. "It's for jumping."

"Sing some other song."

"What's wrong with that one?" said Marta.

"It's not a song, Daddy. It's for jumping."

"Well, jump to something else. I told you I don't like it."

Marta looked at me, the pitcher of cream in her hand. Ilse stood at the edge of the walk, the rope dangling at her side.

"What's wrong with it?" said Marta.

"I don't like it. Isn't that enough?"

"Is it enough? Did you bring enough?" said the bounty hunter when he saw me.

He squeezed his bulk into the space between the table and the bench. His jacket bulged when he laid it on the seat beside him. The gun wasn't at his belt: it must've been in the pocket of the jacket. He licked his lips and rubbed his hands together.

"Do you have enough?"

"How much is enough?"

"Enough to save your life, Commander."

"Don't call me that."

"Where's the money?"

"In my car."

"Why didn't you bring it in with you?"

"Surely you don't expect me to carry that much money on my person."

"Oh. Yeah. I guess not. Well, go get it."

"It's in the trunk of my car. You'll have to come with me."

"Anything you say. You're the boss."

It was dark already. And chilly. He had left the jacket with the weapon behind, in the diner. He rubbed his hands up and down over his arms.

"Where's your car?"

"Around back."

"You ain't playing no games with me, are you?"

I stopped walking and turned around. He stepped back, ducking his head. I wouldn't have hit him: he wasn't worth hitting.

"Why don't you pull your car out here?" he said. "In front."

"I'm not going to give you money in the open, where someone might try to rob us. Come around back. Unless you don't want it."

"Now that's funny. You're a funny man, Commander."

"I told you not to call me that."

"Sure, Boss, anything you say. Wait. This isn't the same car you had yesterday."

"Yes, it is."

When I opened the trunk, he peered anxiously inside. It was too dark to see anything.

"Where is it? Never mind. I'll find it."

When he reached in, I pushed the lid down slightly, trapping his arm.

"What guarantee do I have that you won't still try to turn me in," I said, "or to kill me, to get the reward money as well?"

"Hey, what kind of man do you think I am?" he said. "We made a deal, Commander. You got my word."

"A gentlemen's agreement."

"Yeah. That's a nice way of putting it."

I let the trunk's lid open again.

"Where is it?"

"There. In the suitcase. Let me light a match so you can count it."

"Count it? I trust you. You ain't stupid."

He leaned over the trunk, his hands groping in the darkness.

"No," I said. "I'm no fool."

The electrical cord around his throat cut off his voice as it closed his windpipe. He was a big man, and he clutched at the wire. He tried to kick, but I have strong hands, strong arms, a strong will. I pressed myself against his back and leaned forward while I kept a tight hold on the wire. He clawed at the cord. To no avail. My strength was greater than his.

When he collapsed in the trunk, a foul odor assaulted me. He had soiled himself. I turned my face away as I lifted his legs and hips and twisted them into the trunk. I closed the lid. No, no one was around. No one saw. Money? There was never any money. I tossed the keys into one of the garbage pails behind the diner. Then I got into a second car, beside the first. The night was cold and clear as I drove away.

The night was cold. The torches weren't enough to warm us, but we didn't notice. Not that night. That night we would be granted entrance into his bodyguard. That night, we would become his. Heart, mind, body, soul.

"One thing is clear. Absolutely clear. We owe our salvation to our *Führer.*"

We nodded, anxious for his speech to be over, anxious to swear our loyalty, to become part of the brotherhood.

"Without our Saviour, Adolf Hitler, we won't survive. Without him, there is nothing. If you believe that, you can become one of us."

We did.

"If you believe in him, you may recite the oath."

No vow I ever took meant as much to me as that vow, at that moment. Except my wedding vows. I extended my right arm, in the salute. All around me, the best of Germany did the same. We didn't notice the cold then. We didn't see anything except him. We didn't see anything at all.

"We pledge to you loyalty and bravery. We swear obedience, even unto death, as God is our witness."

"I swear," I said.

"'As God is my witness'," said the soldier sitting with me in the small, dingy room.

"As God is my witness," I said.

"Is that it?" said the soldier.

"Yes."

"Everything?"

"Yes."

"You read it all?"

"Yes."

"Is there anything you want to change? Or clarify?"

"No."

"Are you sure? We want to make sure we have all the words right."

"Yes."

"We want you to change anything you don't agree with. We want to deal with you fairly."

"Yes."

"There's nothing you'd change?"

"No."

"All right then. Read this."

> I hereby certify that I have compared this transcript with the tape recording and corrected it with my own hand. I certify the accuracy and correctness of the reproduction with my signature.

"Sign it," he said.
I did.

Chapter Ten

Words. That's all he ever gave us. Words.

"We are the sword of the revolution," Heinrich said, and we believed him. "*Mehr sein als scheinen:* Be greater than you seem."

We believed that, too. We believed it all. But we were young then.

"What happens to the Russians or what happens to the Czechs is a matter of utter indifference to me," he told us, time after time. "But one principle must be absolute for us: we must be honest, decent, loyal, and comradely to members of our own blood. To our own blood. And to no one else."

Words. Words make more revolutions than swords. Words cut deeper than knives. Words cut more cleanly, and leave the victim alive. I watched *The Dead Bodies* curling in the flames, and I hated words. Words can't be trusted. Even mine: ask Marta.

But women's words are the worst. Their words slice you open. Women spit words out at you, words that cut to the bone. Women take any words you've given them and give those words to others. Your most private words, your most anguished words. And women complain about men's betrayals. They're nothing like the betrayals of women. I don't trust words. I don't believe in them anymore. No matter what words you try to say, people don't hear. They don't listen. They don't want to.

"Listen. Listen," I said. "No. enemy. No partisans."

"What's he saying, Doctor?" said Marta.

Her pregnant belly pressed against my arm as she leaned over me. She wiped the sweat from my face.

"It's the pain," said the doctor. "He doesn't know what he's saying."

I tried to push Marta away, so they could hear me better.

"Coordinates. Wrong."

"He's so distressed," said Marta. "Can't you do something?"

"I could give him more morphine," said the doctor, "but the *Oberstleutnant* 's coming to give him his medals. I thought he'd want to be awake."

"Friendly fire. No partisans. No enemy."

"Max, I don't understand."

"Maybe he should have just a bit more morphine, to ease the pain," said the doctor.

"Listen," I said, but I felt a prick in my arm, a rushing in my head.

"Shhh," said Marta, stroking my face. "It'll be all right, Max."

"Bad coordinates. My fault."

"What? What did you say?"

"Killed my own."

"I can't understand you, Max. What did you say?"

"It's the morphine," said the doctor. "And the pain. It's a bad wound. He's lucky he survived."

"But he seems upset about something," said Marta. "About something that happened."

"Don't try to make him talk. It'll wear him out."

"Max," said Marta. "Try to rest, Darling. I know you're in pain, but try to rest. We can talk later."

"My own men."

"Here's the *Oberstleutnant*, with his medals," said the doctor.

The nurses and the men in uniform gathered around the bed.

"For extraordinary bravery in the line of duty," said the *Oberstleutnant.*

He laid the Roll of Honor clasp, its gold laurel leaves encircling the broken-armed cross, on my chest. Next, he pinned on the silver Wound Badge.

"For devotion and loyalty to the Fatherland."

"No enemy," I said.

"No enemy here, son," said the *Oberstleutnant*, and he patted my shoulder.

"No partisans. Bad mistake."

"Yes, war's a bad thing, my boy, but we're proud of you."

"He's lucky he's alive," said the doctor.

"He and his men make it safe for our fighting boys," said the *Oberstleutnant.*

"You have a brave husband," said the *Oberstleutnant*'s adjutant.

"I'm so proud of him," said Marta, weeping and holding my hand.

"All Germany's proud of him."

"The *Führer* will be proud when he hears about this."

I caught hold of the *Oberstleutnant*'s sleeve, and tried to tell him.

"You're safe here, son," said the *Oberstleutnant.*

"Let me give him a bit more of this," said the doctor, "for the pain."

After the prick in my arm, the faces and the rest of the room slipped away from me. I closed my eyes.

"Don't close your eyes when you blow out your candles, Hans," said Marta, "or you won't get them all. Daddy, aren't you going to help Hans blow out his candles?"

"Why can't I help Hans blow out his candles?" said Ilse.

"Because it makes him scream, and you know it," said Marta. "Besides, it's his birthday."

"He blows out the candles on my birthday."

"That's because he's little."

"That's not fair."

"Daddy's going to help Hans."

"No, he's not. He's just sitting there."

"Ilse, don't argue. Max, help Hans. Max."

"It's not fair," said Ilse. "Hans gets to blow out the candles on my cake."

"Max, help Hans blow out his candles."

"What have I done?" I said.

"Max, what are you talking about now?"

"It's not fair," said Ilse.

"What have I done?" I said.

Marta sighed.

"What now, Max?"

"It's not fair," said Ilse.

Hans squealed as she pinched him.

"Ilse, stop that," said Marta. "I've had just about all I'm going to take from you."

Hans looked down at the red mark on his arm. He started to cry.

"What have I done," I said, "to deserve all this?"

"But what have I done?" said my adjutant. "I was doing my job. I was following orders."

"Take these, Josef," I said, shoving the box of files at him. "Take them out to the car. Put them in the trunk. Hurry."

The girl stayed out of my way. She sat on the cot in the corner, her legs drawn up. She wrapped her arms around her head each time another blast shook the walls. She was watching me, but it was too late for that to matter.

I lit the corner of the paper. I held the paper until the flames had securely caught. I dropped it into the wastebasket and lit another. I dropped it in. The flames devoured the documents, licked the sides of the metal container, flashed up from the top. I dropped in more. And more. Until there was nothing but a pile of black ash. Until the smoke stung my eyes and made me cough. Until the smoke blackened my skin. I had to do it. There was nothing else I could've done.

"There's nothing more to be done, now that the documents are signed."

"Except to have dinner."

"It's about time."

"You should've fed us beforehand. The negotiations would've gone quicker."

The others in the room laughed. I stood in the corner. Drinking. Servants in black coats and white vests opened the doors to the main dining room. The smell of hot food drifted in. The officers moved toward the laden tables.

"Actually, I have nothing against the Jews."

"Nor do I. I've met many fine and honorable people among them."

"Here they come: our eighty million good Germans. And each one has his 'decent Jew'."

"It's clear the others are swine..."

"...but this one is a 'first-class Jew'."

They laughed.

"I ask nothing of the Jews."

"Nor do I. Except that they should disappear from the face of the earth."

They laughed heartily. I poured more wine into me.

"You've been drinking again," said Marta.

"How astute of you, my Dear."

"You promised."

"Leave me alone. Or I'll sleep downstairs."

"I'm sorry," said Marta.

I got into bed. I yanked the covers over my shoulders as I turned on my side, away from her, and closed my eyes.

"Turn out the light."

"I know how hard it must be for you. How worried you are…"

"Good-night, Marta."

"If you lose everything, after all your hard work, after all your sacrifice..."

"You'd like me ruined."

"That's horrible. How can you say something like that?"

"You said it yourself: 'It would serve you right if somebody brought you down'."

"I didn't mean it. I was just angry."

"Turn out the light."

"You know I didn't mean it, don't you?"

"I want to sleep. Turn out the light."

"You're so tense. Let me massage your neck and back for you. You're so tight. Like rock. Did your headache ever go away?"

"No."

"Is your leg still bothering you?"

"What do you think?"

Her hands and fingers kneaded my neck and shoulders.

"How's that? Any better?"

"No," I said, "but it feels good."

I was too tired to fight. I was sick of fighting. I let Marta massage my shoulders till they felt more relaxed. She rubbed my neck till the throbbing in my head seemed to lessen. Her nightgown was cool against my skin.

"You have such a strong back, Max, and such strong arms."

She kissed the back of my neck. Her arms slipped under the blanket and around my chest. When she pressed her hips closer to mine, I moved my leg, so my thigh wouldn't get touched.

"You've always had a nice body. And you're still the handsomest man I've ever seen."

She pressed her body against mine, her cheek against the back of my neck, against my shoulder. She pushed the covers down to my waist, to my legs. Her hands rubbed my hips, and her breath warmed my skin.

"It's been a long time, Max."

I turned over on my back and put my arm around her.

"I love you, Max."

She wrapped her arms around me. She put her leg over mine, and I winced, but she didn't notice. I concentrated on the feel of her body: her thigh was soft. Her fingers brushed my belly, tangled themselves in my hair, stroked my thighs. Her tongue was wet on my skin. I closed my eyes and buried my face in her hair. It smelled clean.

"I love you so much. I'm sorry about all the fighting."

"I know. Let's not talk."

"I know you're under a lot of pressure. Especially now."

"Let's not talk anymore."

"I'll be a better wife."

"Yes."

"You'll see," she said, and her hand moved on me. "You won't need anyone else."

"Marta, not tonight."

"What's wrong?"

"I'm too tired."

"It'll make you feel better."

"I've got too much on my mind."

"It might make your headache go away."

"No."

"It doesn't matter if you can't," said Marta. "I'll do what we did when the children were due. You always liked that."

"Not tonight."

"It's been a long time."

"There's no one else, if that's what you're asking."

"That isn't what I meant."

"I'm sorry. I'm tired. Let me sleep."

"But I don't mind. I like it, too."

"Not tonight."

"Do you want me to hold you?"

"No."

I turned over on my side, my back to her. She lay very still. Very quiet.

"Good-night, Marta."

"I love you."

I knew that. But everything had changed. Nothing was the same anymore. No matter how much we wanted to believe it. No matter how much we pretended. I stripped off my uniform and stuffed it into the satchel. I forced myself into the clothes my adjutant had brought me. They were dirty. They were a peasant's clothes, but there was nothing else. It was too late to do anything different. The jacket was a little tight, but it would do.

I pulled the girl to her feet. She was pale, and her breathing was rapid. I forced my pistol into her hand, the butt toward me. I motioned for her to hit me with it. Her eyes widened.

"*Ja,*" I said.

I motioned again, to show her that I wanted her to hit me in the face with the gun. It had to be realistic: that's why I couldn't ask Josef. Or Marta.

"*Mach es,*" I said. "*Mach es.*"

She hit me.

She hit me hard. My ears roared, and there was blackness, but only for a moment. I blinked my eyes as I took back the gun. My cheek ached already. When I opened my mouth, the ache rushed to my jaw. Some blood dropped onto my sleeve. I wiped my mouth and nose with my handkerchief, then held the cloth against the bleeding.

"Kommandant," said my adjutant.

"Yes, Josef. I'm ready."

But I was never really ready. How could I be? No matter how many times one goes over it, when it happens, everything changes. I don't know how long I sat there before I got out of the car. The trunk made a tremendous noise when I slammed it, but there was no movement from the house.

The dust from the drive made clouds when I walked. I tried to relax my hands. I tried not to clench my teeth. The clothes pinched. The shoes hurt. My uniform had been so comfortable. My mouth was dry, as if I'd swallowed the dust I was stirring up. The steps creaked as I mounted them. Though the porch announced my arrival with each step, no one appeared. Of course, I thought about turning away. Anyone would. But I didn't turn away. I've never turned away from anything. *If I am to perish, then I shall perish.* I knocked on the door.

"He's here, Kommandant," said my adjutant, and the sleek black car slid up beside us.

My adjutant opened the door and Reinhard emerged from the shiny black womb, his long legs making him tower over almost everyone.

"Welcome," I said, and he laughed.

"They told me you had a sense of humor," he said.

As we toured the Camp, my adjutant and Reinhard's adjutant ran along behind us, taking down notes, scribbling out orders. I was glad that it hadn't rained for several days: the clay ground, though it was uneven to walk on, was hard and didn't soil his boots. When he took off his hat, to wipe his forehead with his handkerchief, his hair was almost white in the sun. Some of the inmates stumbled before him, but he didn't notice. I opened the ovens myself, so he wouldn't dirty his gloves. He nodded. We walked past the rows of inmates and barracks to the house.

"How would you like to join the *Gestapo*?" he said.

"The *Gestapo*? You want me?"

"I want hard men. Men who will ruthlessly ferret out enemies of the state. Men who will brutally stamp out opposition. And Jews."

"I'm flattered."

"I thought you would be. By the way, von Walther, I brought my violin," he said. "Perhaps, after dinner, your lovely wife could play the piano while I play my violin."

"She'll be very pleased."

"Good. It'll be a delightful duet."

We entered the walled garden.

"Before we have dinner, von Walther, I'd like to see your office."

"My office?"

"Yes," he said, smiling as he peeled off his gloves. "I want to see if the information in my file on you is accurate."

None of it was accurate. None of it was true. They didn't have me: not Reinhard, not Ernst, not Marta, not the girl. None of them had me. Every word in every file, every word in every letter, every word in *The Dead Bodies:* a lie. Every syllable in *Survivor:* lies, falsehoods, prevarications. I wasn't going to let any of them destroy what had taken me my whole life to build. *The Dead Bodies* had done the most damage: that was where I'd start. My hands and jaw were clenched when I knocked on the girl's door.

"Just a minute."

Sweat dampened my shirt, so I pressed my arms against my sides. She came into the hallway, drying her hands on a white dishtowel, humming for two kittens who bounded after her, racing her to the door. She smiled at them. Laughed. It was the first time I'd ever seen her smile.

Then she saw me.

The bright in her cheeks drained down her throat and hid behind her dress. The kittens rubbed their backs against her ankles. The towel trembled.

She flinched when I raised my right hand in front of me. My fingers shook slightly as I opened the slim volume to its first selection. Her brow furrowed. Though I knew the words, I was afraid I might forget, so I put on my reading glasses. To make sure I got the words right.

I said them very slowly, very carefully. She was silent the entire time. The fingers of one hand clenched the dishtowel. The fingers of the other hand hid her mouth. I read "In the Bedroom of the Kommandant."

But I didn't need my glasses after all. I didn't even need to turn the page. All the words that had been twisting inside me came pouring out. Even in her language, instead of in mine, the words swept everything from me and laid it at the girl's feet. My pronunciation was poor, and my tongue stumbled over the strange words, but I wanted her to understand. I had to make her see. That's why I used her words. Mine had already failed.

When I was emptied of words, I looked up at her, over the rim of my glasses. She was still. She'd unbraided her hair. She'd cut it: the ends brushed her shoulders. She was very pale, almost as pale as in the Camp. When I offered *The Dead Bodies* to her, my hand faltered. I cursed myself, but she didn't even breathe.

"*Ja*," I said.

I removed my glasses and slid them behind my lapel into my shirt pocket. My arm lowered, and the pages with her words closed around my thumb.

"*Ja*."

I bowed my head, with a great effort not to click my heels. The summer heat pressed down on me, and my shirt was wet under the jacket. She said nothing. I turned away, but still she didn't speak, and the screen door was like a shadow between us. I understood. I nodded. I laid *The Dead Bodies* on the wide porch rail. The sun blinded me as I stepped down.

The door creaked, and I turned around.

She came out onto the porch, the screen door held open with her thin body. The two kittens watched warily from her feet. Her white towel fluttered in the early morning breeze. The sun glowed on *The Dead Bodies,* lying there between us.

Part Two

There is no left or right
without remembering.

Gertrude Stein

Chapter One

Then I saw him. There he stood, in the midst of the black uniforms, taller than anyone else, the spotlights glinting on his silver buttons and medals. He stood, holding his baton in both hands, surveying the mass of guards, dogs, inmates, Jews, and he nodded as he watched it all. I got out of the boxcar and helped my parents down. People were shoving and shouting. Babies were crying. Dogs barked and snarled. But he stood, tall and unmoved, in the center of it all. Men with shaved heads and wearing striped uniforms scrambled up into the boxcars and threw out the luggage, into a pile.

"They'll mix up the suitcases," said my mother, clutching my arm. "Tell them to stop."

"Hush," I said to her.

Guards with gleaming weapons and growling dogs marched up to the boxcars, shouting and yelling.

Los! Los! aussteigen! aussteigen!

"What are they saying?" said my father.

"They're telling everyone to get out of the train," I said.

"Maybe you should talk to them," said my father.

"No," I said.

"But they've mixed up the luggage," said my mother, "and Papa has to have his medicine."

"No," I said.

The spotlights passed over the jumble of deportees and guards. The tall German turned. Over the heads of inmates and guards, across the mass of barking dogs and crying babies, he looked at me. Then he came toward us.

"Now be quiet," I said to my parents. "Don't say anything."

Raus! Raus!

"You shouldn't have come with us," said my father. "We shouldn't have let you. You should have stayed at the first..."

"Shhh."

"Hyman," said my mother, calling and waving to a young man from our village. "Samuel, look: it's Hyman."

"Mama, don't call attention to us."

"I'm not. I'm just calling Hyman."

But the German had arrived. He looked down at us. At me. Several guards followed him over. Hyman stood, clutching his cap, beside my mother.

"What's this, Josef?" said the tall one.

"A family reunion, Kommandant," said the one who had come over with him.

"What did he say?" said my father, leaning close to me, pulling at my sleeve.

"He looks important," said my mother. "Tell him about the luggage."

"We're from the same village," said Hyman, in their language.

"A Jew who speaks German," said the Kommandant, and he tapped Hyman on the shoulder with his baton. "How amusing."

"What are they saying? What did he say?" said my father.

"Tell them they've made a mistake," said my mother. "Tell them to fix it."

"Be quiet, Mama. Please."

"So, these are your parents?" said the Kommandant to Hyman before he brushed Hyman aside to step closer to me. "And this must be your beautiful wife."

"What? Oh, no," said Hyman, looking around at me. "No. My parents are dead. These are..."

"You have a most beautiful wife," said the Kommandant, staring at me.

"A very lovely wife," said one of the guards.

"For a Jew," said the one named Josef, standing next to the Kommandant.

"This isn't my wife," said Hyman.

"I beg your pardon. I must have misunderstood," said the Kommandant. "Your fiancée."

Hyman looked around uncomfortably, twisting his cap. One of the dogs growled, baring its teeth: sharp and white in the spotlight. The Kommandant kept staring at me. His guards smiled.

"Maybe we shouldn't bother him," said my mother.

"Be quiet, Hannah," said my father.

"You've made a mistake, sir," said Hyman as several other Germans turned to watch us.

"I don't make mistakes," said the Kommandant. "Did you wish to marry your fiancée before you die?"

"I'm... I'm already married," said Hyman. "My wife is... at home... in..."

"Shame on you," said the Kommandant.

Several of the guards wagged their heads and clicked their tongues.

"Does your girlfriend know you're already married?" said the Kommandant.

"He should make a decent woman out of her," said the one named Josef, "even if she is a Jew."

"Yes. He should marry her, Kommandant," said one of the guards.

"It's the only decent thing to do," said another.

The Kommandant motioned us forward, and guards grabbed our wrists, yanking Hyman and me together. I looked up at the Kommandant. The angles of his face were sharp, hard. As if he'd been formed out of the train's steel. His eyes, when he looked at me, were a German's eyes.

"I don't understand what you're talking about," said Hyman. "I've told you..."

"Do you take this woman to be your lawfully wedded wife?" said the Kommandant.

"But I told you, I'm already..."

The blow from the Kommandant's pistol interrupted Hyman's words, and split his lip. My mother began to cry, and my father mumbled to himself. Hyman staggered back a few steps, blinking, and holding his hand to his bleeding mouth. One of the guards pulled him roughly forward, next to me. I stared at the Kommandant. He smiled at me.

"Jew-boy, I believe the proper response to that question is 'Yes'," said the Kommandant.

"Yes," said Hyman. "Yes, sir."

"Good. By the authority vested in me, as officer of the Third Reich and as Kommandant of this Camp, I now pronounce you man and wife."

The Kommandant put his pistol to Hyman's forehead.

"You may now kiss the bride," said the one named Josef.

The Kommandant pulled the trigger. My mother screamed. Hyman fell against me, then down, onto the platform. Tears burst from my eyes, but I stood as still as possible. Behind me, holding my weeping mother, my father began to pray.

"My condolences," said the Kommandant as he roughly patted my face with his black-gloved hand. "Now you're a widow."

His subordinates guffawed.

"I love weddings," said Josef.

"Back to work," said the Kommandant.

"I just love your work," said an elderly woman in the bookstore, and she held out a book to me. "Would you sign it for me?"

"I'm afraid you've made a mistake," I said. "That's not one of mine."

"It's not?" she said. "But everyone told me it was."

"I'm sorry. It's not my book."

"You're not..."

"Rachel Levi. This is my book, this one here."

She glanced down at the table, at *No Man's Land,* but held the other book close to her breast. Another woman came to the table with a copy of my novel to be signed. After I signed it, she thanked me and showed it to her husband. He smiled, and the two of them walked slowly away, looking at my signature. The first woman stood there, looking at me.

"You can get a copy of this book, and I can sign it for you," I said.

She leaned closer, over *No Man's Land.*

"I was there," she said.

I looked at her in silence. Though she seemed old, I could see now that she wasn't really an old woman. Her eyes were very tired. The noise of the shoppers in the bookstore suddenly seemed far away, and there was only her voice.

"Oh, not in the same Camp as you, but in the Camps."

"I don't know what you mean," I said.

"You don't have to be ashamed," she said. "It wasn't our fault."

"I wasn't in any of the Camps," I said. "You've made a mistake."

"No one else could have written like this," she said.

She laid the book on the table.

"Please sign it for me. It would mean so much to me."

I pushed away *The Dead Bodies That Line the Streets.*

"I won't sign. I wasn't there."

"It's been signed. The law's been passed."

Our neighbor Tomás rushed into our apartment.

"It's true. They've done it," he said.

"Done what?" said my mother, wiping her hands on the front of her apron as she came from the kitchen.

"'All persons of alien blood — hence, especially Jews'," said Tomás, "'are automatically excluded from citizenship'."

"I knew it," I said.

My father sank into his chair, a dazed look on his face.

"What does it mean, 'excluded from citizenship'?" said my mother. "We were born here."

"It means we're undesirables," said Tomás, "now that Hitler's made us part of his family."

"We can leave," I said. "Let's go. All three of us."

"Where?"

"Hungary. Or Poland."

"You could go," said my mother slowly. "That family would take you. The papers are already drawn up."

"I'm not leaving you and Papa."

"I don't understand why they've taken away our citizenship," said my father. "We've done nothing to the Germans."

"The Germans are 'protecting us'," said Tomás.

"This is our country," said my father, "not theirs."

"We're Jews," I said. "We don't have a country."

My father frowned and shook his head. I knelt before his chair and took his hands in mine.

"I told you it was going to happen," I said. "Now the Germans will do to us what they've already done in Germany."

"Decent Germans were always un-political," said my father.

"Papa, you're living in a different world," I said. "We should go. Tonight."

"There are two types of Nazis," said my father, "the decent and the gutter types."

"Papa, there's only one type of Nazi."

"In the end, the decent ones will win out," he said.

"Papa..."

"Maybe we should listen to her, Samuel," said my mother.

My father touched my face.

"Don't be ridiculous. This is our home. Besides," he said, "where would we go?"

"Where would I go? What would I do without you?" said David after I opened my eyes.

I lay in a hospital bed, stitched and taped and bandaged. My wrists hurt. David sat beside the bed, clutching my right hand.

"Oh, Rachel," he said, "if I hadn't forgotten those papers and come home to get them..."

I closed my eyes. David kissed my hand repeatedly, and pressed it to his wet face. The nurses rustled back and forth. A cool hand touched my forehead, rearranged the sheet, plumped the pillow. Somewhere down the hall, in another room, a man cried out. The nurse slid away. David's voice was muffled by sobs.

"I love you, Rachel," he said. "I can't live without you. I don't know what I would've done if you'd... Oh, Rachel."

He buried his face against my body. I opened my eyes to look at him. His hair was mussed, and his clothes rumpled. He must've been here for days, probably without sleeping. I reached across with my left hand. The bandages on my wrist were white. Clean and white. I stroked the top of David's head.

"Shhh."

"Why would you do such a thing, Rachel?" he said, looking up at me.

The room was very clean, very white, and I wished I could stay there for a long time, maybe forever, with the starched white nurses and the stiff white sheets, with the sunlight streaming through the windows and warming my chilled bones, with David there, but not crying, not talking.

"You're free now, Rachel. We're both free."

"Shhh," I said, stroking his head as I closed my eyes. "Hush."

"Hush. Don't say anything," I said as the Kommandant strode over to us.

"But he might be able to help us," said my mother.

"I'll talk to him," said Hyman, a boy from our village.

"Yes, let Hyman talk to him," said my father.

But then Hyman was dead, and the Kommandant stood there, staring down at me.

"Are you a Jew ?" he said.

The spotlights glared in my eyes when I looked up at him. My mother pinched my arm. My father caught hold of my coat, tugging at me. I didn't move. The guards who'd been with the Kommandant drifted away, shouting at the other Jews who were descending from the train. All around us, dogs barked until they were hoarse. Or until they were released to chase one of us down.

"Josef," said the Kommandant. "Find out what language she speaks."

"Magyar," I said.

"Hungarian," said the Kommandant's adjutant.

"Are you a Jew?" said the Kommandant.

"She's a Jew."

"You can't be a Jew," said the Kommandant, lifting my chin with his baton. "You don't even look like a Jew."

"She says she's a Jew."

"Are both of your parents Jews?" said the Kommandant, his baton butting my lips.

"These are her parents. They're clearly Jews."

"Do you have any ancestors who weren't Jews?" said the Kommandant.

His gloved hand touched my cheek, my mouth. His thumb forced itself between my lips and teeth.

"All of her family is Jewish."

The Kommandant stared at me a moment longer before he waved his adjutant aside.

"What a pity," said the Kommandant.

"Pity you didn't have a flower or something pretty put on, instead of them numbers," said the fat man as he squinted at my forearm. "Never seen nobody do numbers before. *A-20093*. What do they mean?"

"Nothing," I said. "Can you..."

"How about a rose? You kinda look like a rose yourself."

"I don't want another tattoo," I said, easing my arm from his grip. "I want to know if you can take this tattoo off."

"Take it off?"

"Yes. Can you?"

"Well, now, ain't nobody never asked me to take one off before. 'Course I don't get many ladies in here neither. The ones that do come in like roses, though."

"Can you get rid of this one for me?"

He took my arm again and looked at it while he rubbed his chin with his free hand.

"Don't know," he said. "Don't know if it can be done."

A sailor came in the front door, with a woman clutching his arm. They were both drunk, and they swayed unsteadily. The red and green lights of the shop glared, and the sailor grinned.

"See? What'd I tell you?" said the sailor, nudging the woman.

"I don't know, Charlie," she said, leaning heavily against him. "I ain't never done nothing like this before."

I freed my arm and rolled down my sleeve.

"How about a rose?" said the fat man. "A rose would be nice. You'd like a flower."

"He's like a flower," someone said, in my language.

I turned around.

"And he likes the ladies."

It was one of the inmates taking care of the luggage.

"What did you say?"

He grabbed my arm, pulling me away from the boxcars, away from the spotlights, away from the guards and their dogs.

"Listen," he said.

"Have you seen my parents?" I said.

"Your parents?"

"We got separated. I can't find them."

He jerked his thumb over his shoulder.

"Your parents are gone."

"Gone? Gone where?"

He inhaled deeply, dramatically. The air was foul, and smelled of something burnt.

"Into the chimneys," he said. "They're smoke."

"What a horrible thing to say. Why are you saying that?"

"The only way to stay alive here is to face the truth," he said, roughly taking my arm. "It's too late for your parents. You have to think of yourself now."

"No," I said, trying to pull free of him. "No."

"You have to stay alive. We can't let them beat us. We have to survive so we can witness."

"I have to find my parents. My father's ill. He'll need his medication."

"There's only one way to survive in this Camp, and he was standing right in front of you. Give him lots of attention, he'll blossom," said the inmate. "Ignore him, or starve him, and he'll wither, but you'll die."

"Who? What are you talking about?"

"The Kommandant, the Kommandant," said the inmate.

He gripped my arm so tightly that I cried out.

"Listen to me. I'm trying to help you," he said. "You're the first one he's noticed in a long time. In ages. He's your only hope of survival."

"I don't know what you're talking about,"

"You've got to make sure he notices you again," said the inmate. "Take off your coat. You can't go to him with blood on you."

He yanked my coat off me and shoved another into my hands. It was ermine. When I just stood there, he tugged the fur coat around me and roughly fastened it.

"Yes. He'll like this," he said. "It emphasizes how blonde you are. How Aryan. It'll excite him."

"But I don't... what should I... how..."

"He'll teach you everything you need to know."

"You know we need you," said one of the inmates from the Camp.

Three of them huddled outside the Kommandant's office window, squatting in the wet clay. They were gaunt and dirty, and trembled in the damp air. They were with the Camp's Underground, and they came in the night, tapping at the glass until I opened the window. Or worse: they wrote cryptic messages on scraps of paper and shoved them between the window frame and the sill.

"Why won't you help us?"

"I can't help you," I said, glancing toward the office door. "I told you that, when you left the last message."

"You mean you won't help us," said their leader. She was called Rebekah.

"And you've got to stop leaving messages," I said. "This is his office. He's bound to find one of them."

"She's not going to help us," said the one standing next to Rebekah.

Her arms were folded over her chest. She was called Sharón, and I didn't like the way she looked at me. She spat at the ground.

"I can't help you," I said. "I can't even help myself. If I could, I wouldn't be here. Now, go away. He's been coming down in the night, when he can't sleep."

"What kind of Jew are you?" said Sharón, reaching in and digging her fingers into my forearm. "Don't you even think about the rest of us?"

"We don't want to damage his merchandise. Let her go. Let her go," said Rebekah, but the others mumbled. "One day, she'll need us."

"And in the meantime, she keeps on living her pampered life," said Sharón.

Rebekah looked at me, with a hard look. I rubbed my arm: I hoped there wouldn't be any bruises.

"One day, she'll need our help," said Rebekah, "but maybe we won't be there for her."

"I'm here, Rachel. I'm here with you," said David in the darkness.

He put his arms around me and pulled me closer to him in the bed. He smoothed my tangled hair back from my face.

"The dogs were barking. People were screaming," I said.

"I know," he said, "but it was just a dream. It's over. You're here. With me."

"I was trying to find you," I said, "but the smoke, the smoke from the chimneys, it was everywhere. I couldn't see. I couldn't find you."

"Shhh."

His face was against my hair, and his arms were tight around me. The room was dark, and the breeze from the open window blew across my sweaty skin.

"I was trying to reach you, before the train left. I was running, but the train was already pulling away from the station."

"It's over, Rachel."

"My legs were so heavy, and my feet were dragging. I ran as fast as I could, but you were already pulling into the Camp. I saw the sign at the entrance: *Arbeit macht frei.* Do you remember it, David?"

"I remember."

"Only this time, the train pulled right into the ovens. It didn't even stop at the platform. Right into the ovens, right into the chimneys. It didn't really happen like that, did it?"

"No, not like that. Not when I was there."

"This time the train went right into the ovens. And there was nothing I could do, but stand there, under *Arbeit macht frei.* When I reached out for you, there was nothing in my arms but smoke."

He rocked me in his arms. He murmured something, but I didn't catch the words. I closed my eyes, yet the words were still there. I opened my eyes again. The room was even darker.

"It'll never be over, David."

"I'll stay awake for you, Rachel."

He pulled the sheet and the thin blanket up around my shoulders.

"I'll watch over you while you're sleeping. I'll keep you safe."

When I pressed my face against his chest, I could hear his heart beating. His body was warm. The room was still dark, but his heartbeat was steady and strong.

Arbeit macht frei: work makes you free. The sign's letters towered above us, and the spotlights glared on the words. *Arbeit macht frei.* The Kommandant shoved me inside one of the guards' towers. No one else was inside. There were no lights except when the spotlights passed. As soon as the Kommandant kicked the door closed behind him, he grabbed me, between the legs.

He ripped aside the fur coat. His mouth, hot and wet, covered my face and neck. He stank of liquor, and he forced his tongue into my mouth. He dragged up my dress as he pushed me backward. One hand pushed aside my panties and the other groped my breasts. I bumped into a table. With one movement, he swept all the papers from the table, then forced me onto it. His breathing was loud as he shoved my legs apart. Dogs were barking, and guards shouted as they fired their weapons. I closed my eyes as the Kommandant yanked open his pants. He leaned over me, heavy and hot in the darkness, and forced himself between my thighs, his gloved fingers roughly guiding him.

When he thrust into me, my head hit the wall, and I cried out, but he didn't hear me. Babies were screaming outside, and their mothers were crying out to the guards. The Kommandant's face chafed mine as he moved roughly against me, and the buttons of his uniform gouged my belly. When I tried to move, he pushed harder. I put my hand up, between my head and the wall, but it didn't help. Even the dense fur coat couldn't ease the hardness of the table beneath me, or lessen his pounding.

He took my head in both his gloved hands and forced my face toward his. He opened his mouth on mine, and his tongue gagged me each time he pushed himself deeper. Then his shoulder jammed against my chin, my cheek. My head roared with the rattle of machine guns, with the barking of dogs. The smoke from the chimneys made my eyes water. His uniform covered my mouth and nose: I couldn't breathe. When he released my shoulders to grab my hips, to lift me so he could shove himself tighter deeper faster, I turned my face. Then I could breathe.

I stared out the grimy window. I clutched the sides of the table so my head wouldn't hit the wall as often, but his weight was too much for me. Spotlights slashed the darkness, the dogs growled, his buttons scraped, the guards shouted, the wool suffocated, his nails scratched, faster deeper harder. The weapons rattled, his gun bruised my ribs, his fingers burned my thighs, his medals cut, the babies wailed, the coat slid, faster deeper harder.

When the chimneys belched out their thick dark smoke, God turned his face away.

Arbeit macht frei.

Chapter Two

Would you like to see the work we do, while you lounge around in the Kommandant's office?" said one of the *Sonderkommando*.

His body was thin beneath the striped uniform, but his arms looked strong. He leaned near me, over the windowsill, his toothless mouth a black hole in his face. He smelled of smoke.

"Yes, let's take her to the Bakery," said Sharón, her eyes cold.

"You know I can't leave his office," I said.

But they gripped my wrists and arms, and pulled at me. The inmates dragged me out into the Camp's yard through his office window.

"What if he comes down?"

"He'll see his little bird has flown," said Rebekah.

"No. Let go. Let go of me."

They dragged me along in the darkness.

"Come on, little bird," said Rebekah. "We're going to give you a tour of the Bakery."

"Maybe we'll give you some bread, little bird," said Sharón, and the others laughed.

Their fingers dug into my skin. Each time I slipped in the wet clay of the Camp's yard, they roughly yanked me up. They scrambled alongside the barracks, just out of reach of the spotlights, dragging me behind. I pulled vainly against them.

"He's sure to come down. He'll kill me if I'm not there."

"No, he won't," said Rebekah. "He'll just send you on a visit to the Bakery."

"To make your acquaintance with the ovens," said Sharón, turning her head to laugh at me.

I tripped. There was a tremendous noise as I stumbled against one of the containers stacked behind the Red Cross trucks. The other inmates released me to prevent themselves from falling. I crashed to the wet, slippery ground and landed against the wheels of one of the trucks. I could hear the others breathing. Dogs barked on the other side of the Camp. The container rolled into the spotlights' path, and its skull and crossbones grinned up into the light.

ZYKLON B
POISON GAS
CYANOGEN COMPOUND

DANGER! POISON!
FOR PEST CONTROL ONLY

I scrambled to my feet.

"I won't go," I said.

I ran back toward his office.

"You can't make me go with you."

"Jewish whore," said Sharón, and she threw something at me.

"Fly, little bird," said Rebekah, "or we'll clip your wings and shove you into the gas."

"There's a problem with the gas, sir," said the Kommandant's adjutant.

"What is it, Josef?" said the Kommandant.

"It's not working well in the damp conditions."

It had been raining, almost constantly, for three weeks now. When it rained, the Kommandant didn't go out into the Camp as often, and he became irritable. When it rained, the trains didn't run punctually and the ovens didn't work. When it rained, the children couldn't go out to play in the garden and the Kommandant's wife yelled at him. When it rained, the Kommandant didn't sleep well and came down to his office in the middle of the night. I didn't like the rain. And it had been raining for three weeks. The Kommandant put down his pen, with an annoyed look on his face.

"Are they using the old gas?"

"No, sir. We exhausted that batch. This is the new gas."

"How new?"

"Only six weeks old."

"Damn. What's wrong with it?"

"It just doesn't work well in the damp," said the adjutant, and the Kommandant frowned.

"Are all the fans working?"

"Yes, sir."

"Are they using the fans?"

"As far as I know, sir."

"All right," said the Kommandant, picking up his pen. "I'll look into it tomorrow. Right now, I have to get this memo finished."

"There's also a problem with the ovens."

"Again?"

"Yes, sir. The firebricks of the inner lining are crumbling. The chimney might collapse."

"Are they overloading the ovens again?"

"I passed your instructions on to the *Kapos.*"

"What's the problem then?"

"The company representative says we need a new chimney if we're going to use it twenty-four hours a day."

"The ovens are crumbling?" said the Kommandant.

His adjutant nodded.

"Probably a Jew made it," said the Kommandant.

"Also, there's a man from the village council here."

"At this hour? What does he want?"

"The villagers are upset about the..."

"I can't do anything about the smell," said the Kommandant. "I've already told them that."

"About the stream Sola," said his adjutant. "It's their drinking water, and..."

"How do they know about the Sola?"

"Someone must've told them, sir."

"I can't believe they notice any difference in the water. We pulverize the bones first," said the Kommandant. "Tell him it's only a rumor. Spread by Jews."

"What if that doesn't satisfy him, sir?"

"That'll satisfy him. Now, I've got to get this memo finished in time for the dinner party," said the Kommandant, and he began writing furiously. "Otherwise, Marta will kill me."

"I'll kill you," the Kommandant's wife said to me when she came into his office.

The Kommandant looked up from his desk.

"Max, what's that filthy Jewess doing here?"

"I've asked you to knock before you come in, Marta," he said, returning his attention to his paperwork.

"And I asked you what that filthy Jew is doing here."

"This is my office, Marta. I'm working. I'm very busy."

"Busy doing what? Sleeping with Jews?"

"How dare you?" said the Kommandant.

He slammed down his pen and rose from his desk. His wife stepped back, but her face was flushed. I scooted more into the corner, pulling my legs against my chest, my head on my knees, my arms around the sides and back of my head. So I wouldn't get hurt too much. His wife clenched her hands into fists as she stepped toward me. The Kommandant came around his desk.

"It's not enough for you to be unfaithful," she said. "Now you have to sleep with Jews."

The Kommandant grabbed her arm and forced her away from me, toward the door.

"How dare you insult me in that way?" he said. "I'm a German officer."

"Dirty whore," his wife said. "Filthy, dirty Jewish whore."

She spat at me.

The Kommandant slapped her.

"What? You're coming out of your office?" said David as I came into the kitchen. "I thought you'd died in there."

I said nothing as I went over to the table. David put down his newspaper. I picked up my coffee.

"Like Beauty awakening from her hundred-years' sleep, she emerges from the tomb of her office."

"Not this morning, David," I said.

"Hark: she speaks."

"I'm not in the mood for it."

"You should be in a good mood, Rachel: you've been working all morning."

"I don't call it 'working' to write the same sentence over and over."

"If it's a good sentence, what does it matter how long it takes?"

I sighed. I picked up a piece of toast. My plate was already filled with eggs and slices of apple sprinkled with cinnamon. David's plate was empty. He'd eaten without me.

"Can we talk now?" he said.

"Not if it's going to be the same conversation we've been having for the past three days."

"We have to talk about it some time."

"I've got too much on my mind, and I have a terrible headache."

"You've been having a lot of headaches lately, Rachel."

"I don't want to argue."

"Neither do I," said David. "Having a headache whenever I want to talk isn't going to solve anything."

I picked up my fork. The scrambled eggs were done just the way I liked them. I chewed a spoonful. I spit them back out.

"The eggs are cold."

"Don't blame me. I called you for breakfast twenty minutes ago."

I stood up.

"I'll make more."

"There aren't any more eggs," said David.

"We're out of eggs?"

"You didn't go to the store yesterday. Like you said you would."

I picked up my cup, went to the stove, and poured myself some fresh coffee. I drank some of it. It was hot. Strong.

"Why won't you have a baby, Rachel?"

"Not again, David."

"We love each other."

"This has nothing to do with love," I said.

"I want you to have my child."

"This world is no place for a child. Especially a Jewish child."

"If everyone felt that way, then there'd be none of us left, and the Nazis would've won."

I came back to the table. I spread some jam on my toast and took a bite. I drank some of the coffee.

"I think a better revenge against the Nazis would be to have lots of children," said David.

When I said nothing, he leaned toward me, laying his hand on mine. His eyes were very bright. He looked very young. It was hard to believe that he'd been there. Harder to believe that he remembered.

"Think of it, Rachel. We'll have lots of children, and we'll raise them devout Jews. That's how we'll defeat the Nazis."

I closed my eyes. My head was pounding. Now my coffee was getting cold.

"I don't care if it's a son or a daughter," said David, "as long as it's ours."

"David, after the war..."

He released my hand and slumped back in his chair. He shoved his emptied plate away.

"I don't want to hear another war story."

"After the war, David, I went to a doctor."

He sat up straighter. He said nothing, but I hated the way he was looking at me. I got up from the table and dumped the coffee into the sink. I poured myself another cup and drank some of it. It was hot, bitter. I poured it out. David sat quietly at the table. I stared out the window over the sink. Most of the leaves had fallen from the trees, and the yard looked bare, cold. David stood up and came over to me. I could feel the heat of his body behind me, but I couldn't move: he was standing too close. A slight wind stirred the dried leaves, revealing the ground beneath them. The grass under the leaves was dead.

"Who did it?" he said.

"It wasn't in the Camp. It was afterward. Not in the Camp."

When he touched my arm, I pulled away.

"Don't," I said. "I hate pity."

"They pity us," said the Rabbi, and my parents nodded.

"No," I said, shaking my head. "They mock us."

"That's not true," said the Rabbi. "They wear the yellow roses in their lapels to show their solidarity with us."

"To mock us."

"To show their opposition to the Nazis," said the Rabbi.

"Opposition? What kind of opposition is that?"

I threw down my dishtowel and faced the Rabbi. His big belly had shrunk a little during the Occupation, but he was still rotund. Bits of cake were tangled in his sparse beard, and his nose and eyes were reddened. His black coat was patched and faded.

"Will they wear the yellow rose in the prison cells for us?" I said. "Or in the labor Camps?"

"To Rabbi Aharon you talk like this?" said my father. "Ask his forgiveness."

The Rabbi shrugged his shoulders.

"She's young. She's upset," he said.

"Don't dismiss me like that," I said.

"This is how we taught you? This is respect for your elders?" said my father. "You shame me."

"Papa, you worry so much about the most inconsequential things," I said. "And you do nothing about the important things, like opposing the Germans."

"Those people with the yellow roses do oppose the Nazis," said my mother. "I know the sister of one of the men who's wearing a yellow rose, and both of them..."

"If they oppose the Nazis, why do we have to live like this, crowded into a single room, sharing our house with five other families?"

"Jewish families," said the Rabbi.

"Shhh, they'll hear you. You'll hurt their feelings," said my mother.

She glanced anxiously at the doorway to the parlor.

"Samuel, tell her to calm herself."

"Apologize to the Rabbi."

"If there's so much opposition to the Nazis, why can't I go to school? Why can't Papa work?"

"My own daughter," said my father. "This is the way she talks, in my own house."

"Try to understand," said the Rabbi. "It's moral resistance."

"The Nazis will get tired," said my mother. "They'll leave us alone. That's the way it's always been. You'll see."

"It's moral opposition. That's important," said the Rabbi. "You'll see, when you get older."

"Moral opposition," I said. "How blind can you be? We're the ones who'll suffer from their so-called moral opposition."

"My own daughter, talking like this," said my father. "What's happened to her?"

"The Germans have already taken everything away from us," said my mother. "What else can they do?"

"Yes, what else can they do?" said the Rabbi. "Kill us all?"

"You're going to kill somebody with this thing," said David.

I looked up from the bed, where I was reading. David lifted the gun from the top bureau drawer.

"And it's loaded," he said. "Rachel."

He frowned at me. At the gun. I turned the page of my book. He marched over to the bed, holding the pistol out to me.

"This isn't the first time I've asked you to get rid of this thing."

I wrote some notes in the margin of the book.

"You know I don't like having it here."

David leaned closer.

"You say you want to forget everything that happened, but you keep a German pistol in the bureau drawer."

"I'll take care of it tomorrow," I said.

I turned the page. He thrust the gun forward, over the book.

"I said I'll get rid of it tomorrow."

"But you won't, will you?"

I looked up at him. He was pale. His face had a strange expression. I took off my reading glasses, and put down my book. When I held out my hand for the gun, he pulled it back.

"Now what?" I said.

"This was his, wasn't it?"

He threw it on the bed.

"That's why you keep it around. This was his gun."

He rubbed his hands roughly against his pants legs as he paced beside the bed.

"I won't have his gun in my house."

The gun lay there against the bedclothes. My fingers were very white as they slid down the long barrel.

"If you don't get rid of it, I will. If it's not out of this house, by tomorrow..."

David paced, his fingers combing repeatedly through his hair. I put the gun in my lap. I picked up my book and put on my reading glasses.

"Get rid of it."

"I'm not your prisoner," I said. "Don't tell me what to do."

"Get rid of that coat. Quick," said the woman prisoner in the sorting-hut in the Camp. "Unless you want to catch it bad."

"It's not mine," I said.

I let the ermine coat slide down my arms to the ground.

"Someone gave it to me," I said. "Even the coat I arrived in wasn't mine. Someone took my coat, days ago."

"Who cares? Get rid of it, before the *Kapo*... too late."

A brutal-looking woman shoved herself into the hut, through the crowd of newly arrived Jews. She wore a red triangle over her left breast: she was a political prisoner, not a Jew. She marched in, glaring at us. My head was pounding, and my body was aching. My legs were sticky and wet. I wiped my thighs with my slip.

"What are these prisoners doing still dressed?" said the *Kapo.*

She cracked one of the women near her with a whip.

"Get undressed, you filthy Jews."

She strode over to me, sneering at the coat. With her dirty boot, she kicked at its white fur.

"Whose is that? Yours?"

"No. Someone gave it to me."

She cracked me across the face with the handle of the whip. The skin burst, and blood trickled out. The *Kapo* passed on to her next victim.

"That was stupid," said the woman inmate who'd told me to remove the coat. "Why didn't you just keep your mouth shut?"

The *Kapo* marched around the hut, staring lasciviously at us while we undressed, striking indiscriminately with her whip. Whenever one of the women cried out, the *Kapo* lashed her harder. I wiped my bloody lip on the hem of my dress. I stood there, looking around the hut, holding the dress.

"Drop it. Go on," said the woman working in the hut as she began to gather up the discarded clothes.

The *Kapo* shouted us into the next room. Some of the women gasped, and fell back against the others who were entering the room. Great piles of hair littered the floor: curls, braids, waves; red, blonde, brunette. Stony-faced women grabbed us, and forced us onto hard benches. Several of the new arrivals protested when clumps of their hair began to fall to the floor, joining the great pile. The *Kapo* hit them. The women with the shears hit them. Some women said nothing: they only cried. They were hit. Some whimpered. They were also hit. They yanked hard on our hair, and the blades gouged our scalps, making them bleed. I didn't say anything and I didn't cry, but I got hit anyway.

We were pushed off the benches and into the next room. We stared, open-mouthed, at each other, at our new selves: naked and shorn. Some of the older women began to pray. Some of the younger ones held hands. I did neither.

In the next room, female inmates shoved clothes and shoes at us, without even glancing at us to see our sizes. I knew by looking at the shoes that they wouldn't fit. The grey dress I was given was so thin I could almost see through the material. It was the middle of February, with six inches of snow on the ground, and the dress was almost threadbare. There was a hole in the center of the yellow star stitched over its left breast. There was a brown stain around the hole. It wasn't dirt. My stomach heaved.

"This has blood on it," I said to the women passing out the clothes, "and these shoes..."

The *Kapo* bashed me so hard that I fell into the wall. I hadn't even seen her. The room spun. My ears roared, and my nose was bleeding. I hadn't even seen her. I dropped the shoes to pull myself to my feet. The other women stared in silence at me, clutching their garments to their bare chests. The *Kapo* kicked the shoes away from me. She hit me with the whip.

"See how you like going barefoot in the snow," she said, hitting me again. "Or naked."

I dragged the dress on before she could take it away from me, before she could hit me again. My hands were shaking, and I was unsteady. I put one hand against the wall so I wouldn't fall. I could taste blood as it ran from my nose to my mouth. The blood dropped onto the dress, beside the star.

"One more word out of you," said the *Kapo,* "and it's into the gas with you."

"Not one word. Not one word," I said to David as I put dinner on the table.

He put down his book to pour us some wine.

"Not anything? All day?"

"No. Nothing. Not even one word. I can't write anymore."

"You're trying too hard."

"I've lost it. I can't write."

"Oh, it's not that bad," said David, and he tore off a piece of bread. "It's only one day."

"It's not only one day," I said as he drank some of his wine. "It's a whole month of days. And not a single word."

"It's just a dry spell. It happens to all of us."

"I'll never be able to write again."

"Don't be silly."

"I can't write."

"You're a good writer. You know that."

"I can't write anymore."

"This, too, will pass. You'll see."

"You're making fun," I said. "You never listen."

David put down his silver, wiped his mouth with his napkin, and sat, looking at me.

"All right. I'm listening."

I picked at the hem of my napkin. My throat scratched. I took a sip of my water, of my wine.

"Well?" said David. "I'm listening, so tell me."

"I haven't written anything since the first book."

"You've been trying."

"It's been over a year."

I put the napkin in my lap. I drank some more wine. I looked at David.

"Write about the Camp," he said.

"What?"

"The Camp," said David. "Why don't you write about that?"

I sighed.

"I wasn't in any of the Camps," I said. "How many times do I have to tell you that?"

"They're sending us to one of those Camps, aren't they?" said my father, and he held my mother tightly as I opened the letter.

"You've been ordered to report for relocation," I said.

"When?"

"Day after tomorrow."

My father staggered to his chair, his face pale.

"This is the end of us," he said. "I knew it was coming."

"What will we do, Samuel?"

"What can we do?" said my father. "We'll do as we're ordered: report for relocation."

I put on my hat and coat. I folded the letter and put it into my pocket.

"Where are you going?" said my mother.

"To headquarters."

"It's after curfew."

"I know that."

"Don't be foolish," said my mother. "They don't mention you in the letter."

"It's too late to do anything anyway," said my father. "And what can you do? You're just a girl."

"Samuel, don't let her go down there."

"Do you think I'm going to let you be sent off alone, without me?" I said.

"We should've gone with Uncle Jacob," said my mother.

"You're right, Hannah," said my father. "She told us to go. We should've listened to her."

"It's too late to talk about that now," I said.

"The things that happen at *Gestapo* headquarters," said my mother. "The things we've heard. Samuel, don't let her go."

"As long as we're not separated, everything will be fine," I said.

Then I hugged them to me, as tightly as I could.

"She's separated from the rest of us," said Sharón. "She doesn't think she has to help us."

"She doesn't know what it's like for the rest of us in this Camp," said a man without teeth.

"She's living a good life, there in his office," said another.

"Maybe we should show her what the Camp's really like," said Sharón, grabbing for my arm.

"She knows," said Rebekah.

When she held out her hand to prevent Sharón from touching me, the others glared at me.

"She's not deaf. Or blind," said Rebekah. "She can smell. She knows what's happening to us. She doesn't care."

"That's not true," I said.

"You don't do anything for us," said Rebekah. "Not even the simplest thing."

"You don't even bring us any of your food," said Sharón, poking me in the chest with her finger.

"I don't get enough to eat myself," I said.

"You have an obligation to us," said Rebekah. "You're one of us."

"None of you has ever helped me," I said.

"Helped you what?"

"Eat all the food he gives you?"

"Stay warm in his office?"

"Wear his wife's clothes?"

"No, help her with the Kommandant," said Sharón.

She thrust her hips forward as she grabbed her own breasts, rocking her pelvis as she moaned and closed her eyes. She rolled her head back. She gasped and shuddered as her hands disappeared between her legs. The others made disgusting noises as they pinched my arms and legs, as they grabbed me. Some of the men slobbered against my throat and cheek as their hands groped for my breasts. I slapped at them. I dug my broken nails into their exposed skin until they cried out and released me.

"Oh, no, Kommandant," said Sharón breathlessly, her hips pounding. "Please don't torture me this way."

"You have a responsibility to us," said Rebekah. "We're not going to let you forget that."

"I have a responsibility to myself," I said. "No one watches out for me."

"You're worse than he is," said Rebekah. "At least the Kommandant has principles. You're just a whore."

"And if you leave one more message," I said, "maybe I'll just let him find it."

Chapter Three

"Did you find it?" I said to my father. "Is that the letter?"

"What does it say?" said my mother. "Is Jacob all right?"

My father looked up from the letter, his eyes glistening.

"They broke all the windows of his shop. Of all the shops owned by Jews."

"I thought they painted *Jude* on the windows," I said, "to keep people from buying their groceries there."

"They broke all the windows, of all of the shops."

"Is Jacob all right?" said my mother. "And Naomi?"

"They locked Jews in the synagogue, and they set fire to it."

Tears began to roll down my father's face, and my mother went to him, her hand on his arm.

"What about Jacob? And Naomi?"

"They shot the Rabbi," said my father, "when he tried to keep them from touching the Scrolls."

My mother took the letter from my father and read it herself. My father covered his face with his hands. He looked very small, and very old.

"Jacob and Naomi are safe," said my mother.

"They burned the synagogue," said my father, and his shoulders shook with his weeping. "They killed the Rabbi."

"Thank God we didn't emigrate with Uncle Jacob," said my mother.

I went over to them. I took their hands in mine.

"We're going to have to look out for ourselves now, and protect each other," I said. "No one else is going to do it."

"This is a Protective Custody letter," said the young man standing on the platform in front of one of the train's emptied boxcars. "Where's your Kommandant? Get me your Kommandant."

The sirens split the air, over and over. The guard waved to one of his comrades, and pointed in the direction of their commanding officer. The second guard marched over to the Kommandant, and pointed out the young man with the letter. The young man waved the paper. The Kommandant nodded to his guard, and moved through the crowd toward the boy. I moved toward the boy. I shoved my way through the mass of elbows and shoulders. I stumbled over the luggage. I pushed aside a woman with a screaming baby. I stood beside the boy with the letter.

"It means the German government protects me," said the boy.

He held the letter out so I could see it, but I was watching the Kommandant as he came toward us. The guard ignored the boy. The dogs barked, and people jostled us as we stood there. The boy gripped his letter.

The Kommandant arrived. I was sweating, but not from fear: the coat was very heavy. I unfastened it at the top, letting its collar fall open. I slid my right foot forward, just a few inches closer to the Kommandant. I'd lost my hat somewhere, and the cold air kept blowing my hair in my eyes, but I didn't brush it away. The coat was so hot and heavy, it made my heart pound. I unfastened it the rest of the way. The boy shoved his letter up at the Kommandant, but the Kommandant was looking at me.

"This is the second time I've seen you tonight," said the Kommandant.

His adjutant didn't translate.

"It must be fate," said the Kommandant.

His adjutant said nothing. He only frowned.

"This is a Protective Custody letter," said the boy.

"I know how to read," said the Kommandant.

"It certifies that I'm essential to the economy," said the boy.

"I certify who's essential in this Camp," said the Kommandant.

His baton pushed open the fur coat I was wearing. He nodded to himself.

"The country needs me," said the boy. "I'm an engineer."

"You're a Jew," said the Kommandant.

He shot the boy.

I stepped aside this time, so no blood sprayed the white coat. The protective letter lay on the ground beside the boy. Dogs barked, and they strained at their leashes, but no dog attacked the boy or his letter. Behind me, in one of the boxcars that had just been opened, new inmates stumbled down from the train, shielding their heads and faces with their hands, crying out for their family members. The Kommandant held open my coat with one gloved hand. His baton lifted the hem of my dress. I looked him in the face.

"She can't be a Jew," said the Kommandant to his adjutant. "Look at that face, Josef. At that coloring."

His adjutant stopped writing, an annoyed expression on his face.

"She must be a Jew," said his adjutant. "She's here."

The Kommandant stepped closer, and his baton moved up, between my legs, until it couldn't go any further. Then he slid it, front to back, and his breathing deepened.

"She's a Jew," said his adjutant. "Who else but a Jew would have a coat like that?"

The baton pressed more insistently upward, harder, faster. I pressed my legs together, trapping the baton between my thighs, stopping its movement.

"Have you ever seen so many Jews?" said the adjutant. "They're repulsive."

"Not this one," said the Kommandant.

His grip on the fur coat tightened as he stepped closer. I breathed through my open mouth, and I looked up at him as he eased his baton from between my legs.

"Plenty of Jews like her around," said the adjutant.

"Not that I've ever seen," said the Kommandant, and he dragged me away with him.

"Have you ever seen so many letters?" I said as David came into my office. "All to one person?"

"Never. I've never seen so many letters," said David, laughing. "Have you opened any of them yet?"

"Not yet," I said, sitting on the floor among the piles of letters. "I'm overwhelmed."

"Apparently, you have a great many devoted readers," said David, picking up some of the envelopes, "from all over the world."

"And they all write," I said. "Maybe I went into the wrong profession."

"You couldn't have done anything else," said David.

"Probably not," I said, and we both looked at all the letters.

"I hate to abandon you to all this, Rachel, but I have to go into town, before the library closes."

"Didn't you say you were going to help me answer all this mail?" I said, and he laughed again.

"Good luck, my Darling."

He leaned down to kiss me on the forehead.

"I'll be back in a couple of hours."

"If you can't find me, I'll be buried in this mound of paper."

"I'll send a search-party."

His laughter drifted after him as he left the room. After the front door slammed, I sighed at the mound of mail. I picked out an envelope. It had a foreign postmark. I opened it.

> *Dear Miss Levi, The way you describe No Man's Land is very powerful and moving... You must have suffered a very great deal to write so beautifully.*

I opened another.

```
You filthy dirty lying Jewish whore.
Too bad we didnt get you into the gas.
```

And this.

I sought you, but found you not.

I dropped the letter, and stood. The room was chilly, and I rubbed my hands on my arms. I went to the windows and closed them. It was just dusk. The yard around the house was quite empty. I drew the drapes. When I sat at my desk, I looked out at all the letters. The paper in my typewriter was blank. I picked up my coffee cup: it was empty. I returned to the pile of mail, and retrieved the third letter.

I sought you, but found you not.
I call, but you do not answer.

I crumpled the letter. It was nothing but words.

Words. Everywhere, on every scrap of paper on his desk: words, rules, orders. My heart was pounding as I sat at the Kommandant's desk. It was the middle of the night, and I had only the small desk lamp for light. There was no sound in the house. Even the dogs in the Camp were quiet. I wanted to see some of his words. I opened the top folder.

SPECIAL INSTRUCTIONS FOR THE
IMPLEMENTATION OF SHOOTINGS

> The shooting detachments should be officer-led, and the shootings should be carried out with rifles, from a distance of eight to ten yards, simultaneously aiming at head and chest. To avoid unnecessary touching of corpses, the candidates for shooting should stand at the end of the grave. In mass shootings, it would be appropriate to...

I shoved the paper away from me and pushed myself away from his desk. The words lay there, mocking me. I hit them, but they lay there, undisturbed. I hit them again. And again. And again. Until the heel of my hand was bruised. But not one letter of those words changed. Not one.

"Not one more minute," said the Kommandant's wife as she swept into his office. "Stop writing, Max. The guests are here."

"I have to draft this letter, Marta."

"People are already here."

"Everyone?"

"Not everyone, but..."

"Then I can finish this," said the Kommandant.

She put a small lamp with a decorated shade on his desk.

"Look at this," she said.

He continued writing.

"It's a house-warming present."

"That's nice," he said, without looking up.

"It's from *Frau* Koch."

"Good."

"What's her first name again?"

"Ilse."

"Oh, of course, how silly of me to forget something like that," she said.

She stroked the lamp's brass base, its patterned shade.

"Do you like it? Don't you think it's lovely?"

"Yes, it's fine," he said, writing away.

"Where do you think we should put it?"

"I don't know. I'm trying to finish this letter."

"Do you want the lamp down here on your desk?"

"That's fine. Now let me finish this letter."

"It's a shame that hardly anyone will get to see it down here," she said.

Her fingers brushed the black designs on its shade.

"Do you really think you need another lamp in here?"

"Put it wherever you like."

"The guest bedroom?"

"Yes. Wherever you like. Now let me finish this, or I'll never get up to the party."

"All right, Darling," she said.

Clutching the lamp to her breast, she went around the desk and kissed the Kommandant on the top of his head.

"But do hurry. Everyone's here."

"Is everyone here?" said the Deputy SS Chief, looking at the group of us, gathered in the courtyard.

"Yes, sir."

"All the women and children, too?"

"Yes, sir. Everyone in the Ghetto is here."

"Good," said the Deputy SS Chief.

He nodded as he paced in front of us, his baton held in both hands behind his back. When he frowned, the assembled Jews shifted uneasily. Some of the guards cocked their weapons and aimed them at us while a machine gun was set up at the edge of the courtyard. My mother clutched my father's hand. The Deputy Chief continued to pace. Some of the old people mumbled prayers: worthless words.

"In the outside mail that we intercepted yesterday, we found three letters from Jews," said the Deputy Chief. "Three letters from Jews in this Ghetto."

He stopped pacing and stared at us. I tried to look at him without betraying any emotion, without blinking.

"This is a most unfortunate situation," he said, shaking his head. "It makes me look very bad. Like I'm not doing my job properly."

One of the smallest children dropped a button he'd been holding. When he bent down to pick it up, a German soldier stepped on the button. The child pushed at the boot, and tried to lift it, but the German stood fast. When the child began to cry, his mother hurriedly swept him up into her arms. After the Deputy Chief looked over, the soldier moved his foot. The Deputy Chief looked down at the button, then smiled at the woman and her child. The mother didn't return his gaze. She bounced the little boy in her arms, trying to quiet him. The Deputy Chief walked toward the mother and child.

"I wish to know who wrote those letters," he said. "If the Jews who wrote these illegal letters come forward, they won't suffer."

He bent over and retrieved the fallen button.

"None of the Ghetto residents will suffer," he said. "You have my word."

After he handed the button to the little boy, he pinched the little boy's chin. The child held tightly to his button, pouting as he stared at the Deputy Chief. The German tickled the boy's belly. The little boy buried his face against his mother's neck and hair, the button clenched firmly in his fist. The Deputy Chief looked back at the rest of us.

"If the perpetrators don't come forward, I will be forced to take punitive action."

"We don't want to cause you any problems, *Herr Obersturmführer,*" said the Rabbi, stepping forward.

I closed my eyes. I wanted the ground to open up and swallow the old man. To swallow the Germans, too. To swallow all of us. Just so it would be over.

"I'm sure you found that the letters were merely personal ones," said the Rabbi, "to family members and loved ones, nothing political."

"Nevertheless," said the Deputy Chief, "it's against the rules."

"Of course, we understand that," said the Rabbi. "But, sometimes, the young, when they're in love, or lonely, they don't always remember all the rules. You're a young man yourself. You understand."

"If the writers don't come forward," said the Deputy Chief, "I will be forced to randomly deport ten Jews for each letter. You have three minutes."

He pushed up his sleeve to regard his wristwatch.

"The writers of the letters," said the Rabbi, "they won't suffer?"

"Two and a half minutes."

A young bearded man put his hand on the Rabbi's arm, pulling the Rabbi back. The young man stepped out from the group to face the German. When the Rabbi started to say something, the young man shook his head at him.

"Two minutes," said the Deputy Chief.

Another man, balding, clutching his cap, stepped forward and stood beside the first. The second man didn't look up at the German. There was movement in the rear of the group as another young man stepped forward. Then there were three.

At a signal from the Deputy SS Chief, the guards behind the young men gripped the Jews' shoulders and raised pistols to the napes of their necks. Before anyone could move, before even the Rabbi could utter another of his worthless syllables, they pulled the triggers. Simultaneously. The men fell. No one else moved.

"There's no one there, Ilse," said the Kommandant's adjutant as the office door opened. "Your daddy's out in the Camp."

"Can't we wait for him?" said Ilse. "We'll be good."

"I don't think you should wait for your daddy in his office."

"But we do it all the time," said Ilse.

"Yes, but that was before..."

"We'll be good," said Ilse.

The phone on the adjutant's desk rang. When he answered it, Ilse pulled Hans into the office. She closed the office door.

"Now we can play Kommandant," she said.

She ran over to the desk, scrambling into the desk chair and picking up her father's pen. She uncapped the pen and wrote on some of his papers.

"Yes. Yes," she said in a deep voice, and she nodded. "I'll take care of that tomorrow. What? Not again. Use the dogs. I'm busy. I can't worry about that right now."

Her brother stood at the door. He didn't suck his thumb any longer, but he still carried his blanket. He looked over at his sister. At me.

"Not now, Marta," said Ilse in the Kommandant's voice, waving the pen. "I'm busy. No, the children can't go play outside. There's a Jew-fever in the Camp."

Hans wandered over to me. The satin border of his blanket was coming off. He blinked at me. His eyes were very big.

"Do you know what she is, Hans?" said Ilse.

She put the pen down and slid from her father's chair. She came over and stood beside him.

"She's a Jew," said Ilse. "Jews are bad."

Hans stared at me. I didn't move.

"She's bad. Mommy told me," said Ilse.

She looked over to the opposite side of the office, to the corner, where the Kommandant had installed a military cot. She grabbed her brother's hand.

"Let's go play on the bed."

They raced over to the cot. Ilse lifted Hans onto the cot, then crawled onto it herself. They tried to jump, but it had no springs. There was no pillow. Ilse pulled up the blanket and put it over her head. She made noises and held out her hands, her fingers curved like claws.

"I'm the big, bad Jew," she said, "who eats little boys."

Hans squealed and hit her with his own blanket. Ilse tossed off her disguise and tickled Hans. The two of them rolled around on the cot, giggling and kicking, until they were breathless. Ilse sat up, brushing her hair away from her eyes, and she looked at me.

"Do you want to play with us?" she said.

"I want you to stop this game you're playing," said the Kommandant's wife. "I want you to stop with this girl."

She was in the kitchen, which was above the Kommandant's office, and I heard her voice through the heating vents. I pulled the thin blanket tighter around me. It didn't cover all of me, and I shivered.

"Stop with this girl," she said.

The Kommandant said something, but he wasn't yelling: I could hear the sound of his voice, but I couldn't understand his words.

"I don't care if I wake the children. I don't care if I wake the dead," said his wife. "I've had it with you and this girl. I want it to stop."

I couldn't lock the office door: he kept the key with him. I went to the Kommandant's desk. I pulled his chair around, and pushed it to the door, to keep me safe from her. I shoved the small table and the other two chairs in front of the door. I tried to move one of the cabinets, but it was too heavy. I went back to my corner, and pulled the blanket around me again. The Kommandant said something, and I heard his wife's footsteps rush across the floor.

"Don't you walk away from me. I have every right to tell you what to do. You gave me that right when you married me."

Water ran a moment in the sink. Then it stopped. I wrapped the blanket around my head, but it didn't drown out her voice.

"That's a nasty thing to say. You're being cruel. I didn't force you. If I could've forced you, we would've been married a lot sooner, and you know it."

A chair toppled to the floor as his wife's footsteps followed the Kommandant's. Her voice got louder, and it was mingled with harsh sobs.

"That's hateful. Hateful. And you know it's not true. I've never been with anyone but you. You're just trying to change the subject. That's what you always do when I find out you have a mistress."

A glass crashed to the floor.

"Don't insult me like that. Don't lie, then. I don't care if you are the Kommandant. I know you're sleeping with her. I know you are. I've smelled her on you. And she's worse than a whore. She's a Jew. It makes me sick to think you've been with a Jew. You send her to the gas, with the rest of them."

The Kommandant's boots thudded across the floor, out of the kitchen.

"Don't you tell me to be quiet. This is my house, too. I can be as loud as I want. And if you don't stop with this girl, I'll leave. I've put up with a lot of things from you, Max, but I won't put up with a Jew. I mean it this time. I'll leave you if you don't end it with her. I swear I'll leave you."

"You're not leaving," said David as he came into our bedroom. "Rachel, what are you doing?"

I shoved clothes into the suitcases. My books were already in a box, sitting at the foot of the bed. I picked up the loose papers from the bedside table.

"Not again."

I placed the loose papers on top of the clothes in the suitcase.

"Where was he this time?" said David, and I turned to look at him. "When did you see him: last night, in the middle of the night?"

"You don't have to come with me," I said.

I slammed one suitcase. The lock on the second suitcase wouldn't close properly. I rearranged some of the clothes and papers. I pushed down on the lid again. It resisted. David sat on the side of the bed.

"Why is it you always see him in the middle of the night?"

"What's that supposed to mean?"

"Nothing."

He sighed loudly as I wrestled with the second suitcase. He sat, staring at the opened bureau drawers, at the emptied closet, at the bulging suitcases.

"Are you coming with me or not?"

"Do I have a choice?" he said.

"Which will you choose? Are you going to go, or stay?" said Mrs. Greenbaum as she cut the meager potatoes.

"Please, not today," said my mother as she put pickles on the table. "Not on *Shabbas*."

"Why not on *Shabbas*?" said my father.

"It's too important not to discuss it," said Mr. Silverstein.

"It gets everyone so upset," said my mother. "I want to have a peaceful *Shabbas*. For once."

"It's living in this Ghetto that gets everyone so upset," I said, putting the plates on the table, "not talking about how to get out of this place."

"Talking about suicide would get anyone upset," said my mother. "Let's not talk about it during dinner."

"Suicide isn't the only way out, Hannah," said Mr. Silverstein, putting his cane on the floor beside his chair. "The Germans are letting some of us buy our way out."

"Who has enough money for that?" said my father.

"You do," said cousin Leo, who was only a boy of twelve.

Everyone looked at him.

"Well, he does," said Leo, "if he sells the furniture."

"Not enough for all three."

"Enough for one," said Leo.

"Enough for one, he says, when there's three of them."

"But one could get out," said Leo. "And I know which guard to ask. He's let two of us out already."

"And which of the three of us would go?" said my father.

"Who would choose?" said my mother.

"Your daughter should go," said Mrs. Chaim. "She's young."

"Too young," said my mother.

"She has her whole life to live. Better she should do it somewhere else."

"I'm not going anywhere without my parents," I said.

"But you could get out," said Leo. "I know you could. I could help you."

"I'm not leaving them."

"Everyone knows that," said Mrs. Greenbaum. "You're a good girl."

"Too good," said Mr. Silverstein.

My father cut the cold meat into almost transparent slices, so there would be enough for everyone. Mrs. Greenbaum passed the cooked potatoes. They were very small, and a little soft. There was some cabbage lying with them in the bowl. I cut the dark bread and put it in the center of the table. My mother lit the tiny candle.

"A feast," said Mr. Silverstein.

"Yes, a feast."

"There are other ways out," said Leo. "You could go Underground."

"Please, not on *Shabbas,*" said my mother.

"Go Underground?" I said. "That's the same as committing suicide. It just takes longer."

"It's almost like murder, going Underground," said Mrs. Greenbaum.

Everyone nodded.

"When they catch someone in the Underground, they round up his whole family," said my father.

"And shoot them all," said my mother.

"Killing the whole family, because of one," said Mr. Silverstein, shaking his head.

"They're killing whole families anyway," said Leo. "And for nothing."

"We're not dead yet," said my mother. "Thanks be to God."

"God has nothing to do with it," I said.

"Such a thing to say to your Mama," said my father.

"And on *Shabbas*," said Mrs. Greenbaum.

"So, what will you do?" said Mr. Silverstein.

Everyone stopped eating to look at me.

"Will you take your life or let yourself be evacuated?"

"I'll kill myself," I said, "before I suffer at the hands of the Germans."

Chapter Four

Suffering. They didn't know what suffering was. What were a few bits of food, a threadbare blanket, a cold stone floor? They didn't even try to understand what it was like for me. They were always ordering me to help them, threatening me, telling me to risk myself to save a few Jews I didn't even know. I tried to help in little ways, but it didn't do any good. They couldn't have done anything either, if they'd been in my position. They didn't know what it was like for me, and they didn't even try to understand.

I wedged the Kommandant's letter opener into the space between the desk and the center drawer. Of course it was locked. He always locked it. When I tried to force the lock, my hand slipped, then slammed into the desk. I listened for any sounds or movements from upstairs, then tried again. It slipped again. The third time, the letter opener bent. The drawer was still locked. I pulled the letter opener out, but it wouldn't straighten, and I couldn't let him find it.

Holding it in my hand, I roamed the office, seeking a hiding place. There was no place to put it in the small bathroom off his office. The file cabinets and the desk were too heavy for me to move. I shoved the window up and leaned out, still gripping the letter opener. I touched the ground just below the ledge. The clay was hard. Even if I threw the opener as far as I could, it would be too close to the office. It was sure to be found: it was gold, and inscribed with the Kommandant's initials. I couldn't just throw it out into the Camp's yard. I thought about giving it to one of the members of the Underground, to use for bribes, but I only considered that for an instant. I closed the window. I looked over at the bookcases.

I dragged his desk chair over to the bookcases, but even with that I wasn't tall enough to reach the top of them. There was a wide wooden cabinet, where he stored his liquor, on the same wall as the bookcases. It was too heavy to move. I pushed the chair over to the cabinet, climbed onto the chair, then onto the top of the cabinet. I put one hand on the wall, to steady myself, and leaned as close to the bookcases as I could. I tossed the letter opener onto the bookcases.

It lay, bent and gold, on the top of the center bookcase, near the wall. It made a small dull *cling* when it landed, but that was all. There was no noise from the house. I got back down from the cabinet. When I pushed his chair back to his desk, my hand hit one of the folders, knocking it to the floor. The papers scattered everywhere. I grabbed them up as quickly as I could, shoving them back into the folder. Some of them were upside down. I righted them. I laid the folder back on this desk, careful not to disturb anything else. I looked up at the bookcases. I couldn't see any hint of the gold letter opener. I stood by the window and looked: nothing. By the door: nothing. I sank down into my corner and closed my eyes.

"Gold. Silver. They want it all. You're not listening, Samuel," said Mr. Weinstein to my father as I came into the room.

"It makes no sense," said my father. "They're the ones who destroyed the shops."

"What are you talking about?" I said. "What's happened?"

"The Jews in Germany have been fined," said Mr. Weinstein, "for destruction of the shops and businesses."

"One billion marks," said Mrs. Weinstein.

"Thank God we didn't emigrate to Germany," said my mother.

"And Germans were ordered to eliminate Jews from the economy," said my father.

"Worse yet," said Mr. Weinstein.

"More?" I said, and Mr. Weinstein nodded.

"What else can they do to us?" said my mother. "Samuel can't teach. They've destroyed Jacob's grocery."

"They've taken away the property," said Mr. Weinstein.

"Business property?" I said.

"And personal property," said Mr. Weinstein.

"What will Jews do?" said my father. "How will we live?"

"They call it 'Aryanization'," said Mr. Weinstein.

"I call it 'theft'," I said. "Now will you listen to me, Papa? Now will you consider emigration?"

"But where would we go?" said my father.

"Poland," I said as my father pulled his handkerchief from his pocket to wipe his eyes.

"Poland?"

"Or Hungary. Neither is far," I said. "I already speak the languages."

"But we've never lived anywhere except home," said my father. "We're not so young anymore."

"Uncle Jacob and Aunt Naomi could come with us," I said. "They have nothing in Germany now."

My father looked at me, at my mother; then he nodded slowly.

"If we all go together," he said, "maybe it won't be so bad."

"How much worse could it be," said my mother, "than losing everything?"

"If we lose one more day building this road," said the *Kapo* as we trudged by, "I'll send all of you to the gas."

The rocks under our feet tripped us. They cut our heels and ankles. The rocks we were carrying stretched our arms down until our shoulders were rounded. Our skin was bruised from their weight, and our throats and eyes were red from their powdery dust. Inmates fell constantly and, despite the threats and blows from the *Kapos,* few of them rose again. The Germans were summoned to dispatch those who could no longer work. The *Kapos* slashed at our backs and heads. The rocks gouged our feet. The rocks dragged on our arms and shoulders. The dust choked us. Still, there was no respite. No reprieve. The road had to be paved. As the Kommandant ordered, so it was. The *Kapo* bashed me in the ribs.

"You there, Sleeping Beauty," she said. "Watch where you're going. And get a bigger rock next time. That one's too small."

I stepped around the dead inmate. His eyes stared up at the clear sky; his mouth was open. I deposited my rock next to those that had just been placed. I hurried to the quarry to get the next stone. The *Kapos* hit us with whips if we didn't run quickly enough. Sometimes, the Germans used their pistols. They kicked the bodies of the laggards into the quarry. I squatted and pulled another stone to my chest. When I lifted it and stood, my back throbbed with its weight. I trudged up the hill.

Then I saw the Kommandant's car.

It was shining and black in the sunlight, and it was moving slowly alongside the stone road: an inspection. I glanced back as the car glided toward us, and I stepped just slightly to my left. The *Kapo* didn't notice. I kept walking, but with every other step, I moved a bit more left of the line, until I was completely out of the line. About ten feet ahead of me, the *Kapo* yelled at one of the frailer women, hitting her with a club. The Kommandant's car slowed, almost stopping, just near me.

I turned to face his car.

I dropped my stone.

The *Kapo* heard the noise and turned around.

"You stupid bitch," she said.

She marched over to me.

"You would drop it now."

I threw myself down, on top of the rock. But I raised my face, and looked up at the Kommandant.

The car stopped.

"Get up, you whore," said the *Kapo,* and she kicked me. "You did that on purpose, to make me look bad. Don't think I'm going to forget this."

The car door opened.

"Get up. Get up," said the *Kapo,* kicking me and bashing me with her club.

The Kommandant emerged.

"Get up. Now. You filthy Jewish whore," said the *Kapo,* and she dug her nails into my arm.

The dress I wore was too big in the neck: I pulled the material down, so it hung low in the front, revealing the curve of my breasts. Then I stood, leaving the rock at my feet. The Kommandant came over. The *Kapo* snapped to attention. The Kommandant looked at the curve of my breasts. The sun was shining behind me: the Kommandant looked at the outline of my legs through the thin, sheer dress. He lifted my chin with his baton. He smiled.

"Yes, it is you. Now I know it's fate," he said in his language.

He looked down at my throat, at my bared skin. His baton brushed my collarbone, and he smiled more broadly.

"Josef," said the Kommandant.

His adjutant got out of the car.

"Yes, Kommandant?"

"Have this one cleaned up, and brought to my office."

"Yes, sir."

"And no more road-building for this one," said the Kommandant as he turned back toward the car.

"No, sir," said his adjutant, and he waved over one of the guards. "Take this one to the Kommandant's office. Wait for me there."

The guard saluted. The adjutant frowned at me before he returned to the car and got in. The door closed. The Kommandant looked at me a moment longer before he motioned the driver. The car glinted in the sun as it lurched away. When the guard took my arm, the *Kapo* bashed me. The other inmates stared at me. Some of them tugged their loose gowns. Some dropped their rocks, gazing after the Kommandant's car as it rolled up the hill. The *Kapo* hit me again, but I didn't feel it. I didn't feel anything.

"I don't feel anything," said my Aunt Miriam as she sat on the couch in our living room. "I'm numb."

"There's been a mistake," said my mother. "It can't be. They've misunderstood."

"No," said Aunt Miriam. Her eyes were red, but she wasn't weeping now. "They've arrested him."

"Arrested whom?" said my father.

"Boris," said my mother.

"Boris? Miriam's husband Boris?" said my father.

"He's not even Jewish," I said. "Why would they arrest him?"

"For being married to Miriam," said my mother, and my aunt nodded.

"What are you talking about?" said my father. "How could they arrest him for being married?"

"For being married to a Jew," said my mother.

"They said it was... they called it... *Rassenschande,* " said my aunt.

They looked over at me.

"'Race defilement'," I said. "For having sexual relations with a Jew."

Miriam began to weep again.

"Maybe if we talk to them," said my father. "Show them the marriage certificate."

"They've already seen it," said my aunt. "They declared it invalid."

"Have they already taken him?" I said.

"Yes. And they said I'm guilty, too."

"Of what?"

"Extramarital intercourse," she said. "They told me to report for re-education."

She cried louder, and my mother took her in her arms.

"What are we going to do, Samuel?" said my mother.

"What do you want me to do?" said my father. "One man can't do anything against all of them."

"She's my sister. We have to do something."

"Who ordered you to report for re-education?" I said.

My aunt wiped her eyes and nose. She opened up her purse, took out a piece of paper, and unfolded it.

"*Gruppenführer* Heydrich," she said. "But I'm supposed to report to someone named Müller."

"*Gestapo,*" I said.

"What should she do?" said my mother.

"What can she do?" said my father. "It's an order."

"I order you to come here," said the Kommandant, slamming his office door and looking around the room for me. "Where are you, Girl?"

He was drunk. I could smell the liquor on him as soon as he came near me. He grabbed my wrist.

"Come here. That's an order. I need you."

He yanked me to my feet. He held my wrist with one hand as he unbuttoned his uniform with the other. He pushed me toward his desk. There was a commotion outside in the Camp. The dogs were barking, and the machine guns had been rattling all morning.

The Kommandant tossed his jacket to the chair and eased off his suspenders. As he undid his pants, he leaned against me, his mouth open and wet and stinking of alcohol. He pressed me hard against the desk. When he pushed the paperwork off the desk, the folders spilled on the floor. He pushed against me until I was flat on the desk. When he got on top of me, I turned my head away, toward the windows.

Outside, in the Camp's yard, rows of men, women, and children stood, naked, waiting to go into the showers. The chimneys belched out the black smoke that had been their comrades, and the smoke hung in palls over the shivering Jews. They clung to each other for warmth, or used their hands to hide their nakedness from the soldiers who walked slowly back and forth, their rifles ready. The Kommandant's fingers dug into me as he thrust, and he rubbed his face against my cheek. He hadn't shaved. His shoulder jammed my chin. His lips and tongue moved wetly on my face, seeking my mouth. If I turned away when he put his mouth on mine, he would bite and leave bruises. I didn't turn my face away. He held my face between his hands as he kissed me.

But this time, he didn't put his tongue in my mouth. He dragged his lips and tongue back down my throat, across my collarbone, to my breasts. He bit me, but not hard enough for it to hurt. He wasn't in a bad mood today. He pulled at the thin material of my dress until my breasts were bared. He put his mouth on me. I didn't like it when he used his mouth or fingers: he would stop moving, and it would take longer. I didn't want him to hold my breasts and kiss them. I didn't want him to take a long time. He raised himself up from me, took my hand and placed it between us, laying his fingers on mine. He guided my fingers downward, but when he made my fingers touch myself, he became excited, and he moved, harder and faster, pulling me closer. Faster. Faster. His weight was on me again, and my fingers lay crushed beneath his belly. He groaned, and slowed his pounding. If I pushed up against him, he'd finish more quickly. If I moved my legs so that my thighs pressed against his hips, he'd finish almost before he'd started. If I said his name, he'd cry out and be done. But I could only say his name when he was very, very drunk.

The naked Jews outside moved slowly toward the brick building with its tall chimneys. A guard pulled one of the young girls from the line. She looked back toward the others as the guard took her around the corner of the building. Three other guards followed them. Several guards laughed as a dog tore at the flesh of an elderly Jew. Man and dog collapsed to the ground, and the guards shouted and cheered. The Kommandant slowed again, and he stroked my belly. He stroked the inside of my thigh. He touched me where he entered me: that excited him. His breathing was quick and shallow. He wet his fingers with his tongue, and moved my hand so he could touch me himself, but I didn't want him to touch me. Not ever. I caught hold of his shirt and dragged him forward, pushing my hips up against him, grinding bone against bone. I tightened my legs around him. I bit his shoulder, hard, hard enough to leave a mark. I said his name. And again, his name. He shoved himself deeper, and cried out. The smoke rolled down from the chimneys to the emptied yard. I closed my eyes. The Kommandant lay heavy and wet against me.

I closed my eyes when I saw *The Dead Bodies That Line the Streets.* I was passing a bookstore, and in the window: *The Dead Bodies.* I touched the pane: it was cold. One of the salesclerks came to the window with a customer. The clerk picked up *The Dead Bodies* and handed it to the man. He said something to the clerk. She shook her head. He nodded. She shook her head again. He pulled up his sleeve and held out his arm. The clerk's fingers covered her mouth as she looked down at the blue-black numbers tattooed on his inner left forearm. The man clutched *The Dead Bodies* tightly to his chest. I turned, and walked away.

"The dead bodies," said my father when I got home, "they're lying in the streets."

"What do you want me to do about it?" I said as I yanked out the few small potatoes hidden in the seams of my coat.

"They're not even burying them," said my father.

"Complain to the Germans," I said. "They're in charge here."

"What's gotten into you?" said my mother. "This is the way you talk to Papa now?"

"Where's the bread I brought home yesterday?" I said. "You didn't eat it all already, did you?"

"No, of course not," said my mother. "It's in the cupboard under the sink, wrapped in newspaper."

"Why are they letting the bodies lie around on the streets?" said my father.

"What are you doing with the bread?" said my mother.

"I need some of it," I said, cutting off a large hunk of it. "To trade for sugar."

"I covered some of their faces with the pages of my newspaper," said my father. "Out of respect."

"We don't need sugar," said my mother.

"We need Papa's medicine," I said. "And we need sugar to get that."

"Some of the dead were piled up on Karmelicka Street," said my father. "Right under the store windows."

"You're taking that much bread?" said my mother.

"Sugar's expensive."

"Dead bodies right under the store windows," said my father. "Under windows full of pastries and cold meats and marmalades."

"What will we eat," said my mother, "if you take all that bread?"

"I'm not taking all of it."

"At the funeral home," said my father, grabbing my arm. "All those naked corpses, piled on top of each other like... like cords of wood. It's disgraceful. With tags on their toes. And with nothing to cover their private parts or their faces..."

"They're dead, Papa. They're dead."

I threw the pieces of bread onto the floor, and the two of them looked at me.

"You worry more about the dead than the living," I said.

"Who told them they were going to die?" said the Kommandant. "One of the *Sonderkommando*?"

"Not this time, sir," said his adjutant. "It was one of the guards who made the remarks. And he didn't come right out and say the Jews were going to die."

"One of the guards?"

"Yes, sir."

"What kind of remarks did he make?"

"Something to the effect that the Jews would have jobs providing food for worms."

"Do you know which guard said it?"

"No, Kommandant. I heard it, but my back was turned."

"Memo," said the Kommandant.

His adjutant readied his pen over his note-book.

"To all Camp personnel."

The Kommandant buckled on his holster, and checked to see that his pistol was fully loaded.

"Jews are not to be confronted with disturbing remarks about the place and nature of their future utilization," said the Kommandant as his adjutant scribbled away. "Neither should they be presented with resistance-provoking indications or speculations about their intended quarters."

The Kommandant glanced around the office. The adjutant finished writing and looked up.

"Josef, have you seen my dagger?"

"No, sir."

"First my letter opener, now my dagger."

The Kommandant frowned as he put on his overcoat.

"I must have left the dagger upstairs: Hans was playing with it. How many guards did we lose?"

"Five dead. Two injured."

"And the Jews?"

"All in the gas, sir. Except the one who started it."

"Where's he?"

"In the interrogation cell."

"All right, Josef," said the Kommandant. "Let's take care of him."

"It's all right, David. I'll take care of it," I said. "You go back to sleep."

"What's wrong?"

David sat up in bed, rubbing his eyes.

"What are you doing?"

"I was just locking the doors," I said. "I'm sorry I woke you."

I went to the window and looked out. Moonlight glowed on the trees and the yard. I stared. There was a car parked by the far trees. I leaned closer to the window, my throat tight, my body cold. No. There was no car. It was just a shadow. There was nothing there. The curtains brushed against me when the breeze moved them.

"Didn't you lock the door before we went to bed?"

"I was just checking it again," I said, closing the window and sliding its latch. "I thought I heard something."

"I wish you wouldn't wake me every time you hear something in the night."

He lay back down, noisily rearranging the pillows and blankets. He sighed loudly and turned over several times. When I got back under the covers, he turned away, pushing the blanket between us.

"I wish you wouldn't wake me every time you hear a noise," he said. "Just once, I'd like to sleep the whole night through."

We were asleep, and the *Kapos* woke us. It was the middle of the night. We were cold: it was our first night without real clothes, or shoes, or hair. The *Kapos* hit us furiously as they pushed us out of the bunks and into another building. As we came in, we were each handed a picture postcard: lush trees surrounded a placid lake; snow-covered mountains rose into a cloudless blue sky; there were flowers, grass, trees: no people. I turned the postcard over.

From Waldsee:
We are doing very well here.
We have work and are well treated.
We await your arrival.
Love,

The *Kapo* bashed me on the shoulder with her baton.

"Sign it," she said.

I did.

Chapter Five

Most of them were signed, but not all of them. Some of the papers on the Kommandant's desk had his full signature: *Maximilian von Walther*. Some of them had only *Von Walther* scribbled at the bottom. His *V* and *W* were bold and large; he made them the same size. The other letters in his name were practically indistinguishable. Most of the papers on his desk, however, didn't have his name. They bore only a huge, jagged *K* at the bottom: *K* for Kommandant.

I sat at his desk, looking at the papers he'd left on top. Whenever he left the office, the Kommandant put unfinished work from the Camp in his desk drawers, and locked the desk. He put the handwritten papers in his center desk drawer. That was always locked. He kept the key on a chain in his pocket. Though I knew it was locked, I pulled gently on the center desk drawer as I was getting up from the chair.

The lock hadn't caught.

The drawer opened.

My heart pounded as I stood there, looking down. The drawer was filled with pages of the Kommandant's personal stationery, covered with his handwriting. Holding my breath, I reached out, and my fingers brushed the top page. I lifted the edge of the first sheet: "Love Song for Klaus." I dropped it.

I slammed the drawer closed, and rushed back to my corner.

"Don't drop them, Hannah," said my father as he came back to the house. "You'll get them dirty."

"I'll be careful," she said, and she unwrapped the package.

I slammed the door.

"I won't even look at them," I said. "Don't even try to make me."

"Look, it's not yellow," said my mother.

"I won't wear it," I said.

"You have to," said my father. "It's the law."

"Look, it's not even yellow," said my mother. "It's a white armband, with a blue star."

"I don't care what it is," I said. "I'm not wearing it. We came here to get away from the Germans."

"The Germans followed us," said my father.

"We should go with Uncle Jacob," I said.

I slapped my mother's hand away when she tried to put the armband on me.

"We should go to America," I said.

"America?" said my mother. "Even you don't speak their language."

"We're too old for that," said my father. "I couldn't take another trip like this one."

"It's only an armband," said my mother, when I pushed her away. "Why cause trouble?"

"You're in trouble," said cousin Leo as he dashed into the room. "They're coming for you."

"*Gestapo*?" I said, standing.

"I think so."

"Oh, my God," said my mother, clutching her hands together.

"I knew this would happen," said my father.

"We asked you to go with Uncle Jacob," said my mother. "We begged you to go without us."

I grabbed my plate and dumped its food onto my parents' plates. I wiped off my dish and my silver and stashed them in the cupboard. I shoved my arms into my coat.

"Where are you going?" said my father.

"What are you doing?" said my mother.

"You haven't seen me," I said, kissing them each on the cheek. "You don't have any idea where I am. You don't even know if I'm alive."

"Samuel," said my mother, and my father took her hand.

"What are you going to do?" he said.

"Don't worry," I said. "And remember: you haven't seen me."

Leo wrapped a black scarf around his face. He handed me a scarf, and I covered my hair, mouth, and nose with it. Leo opened the door. My mother wept, and reached out for me. My father called my name. I closed the door. I never looked back.

I didn't look back at the bed. I didn't look at the gun. I didn't need to look at the gun. I knew every inch of it. Every line. Every groove. But I wanted to feel it, to hold it in my hands. I sat on the bedroom floor in the dark, in front of the bureau. I reached into the bottom drawer, beneath the nightgowns, and lifted the gun out. David was in bed, asleep.

The gun was cool, and heavy. I straightened my arm, aiming the weapon at the darkness. I knew how to use it. I closed my eyes, and pressed the gun's barrel lengthwise to my cheek. I rubbed its elegant metal against my face. The gun was warm now. It was always loaded.

I laid it carefully back in the drawer and covered it with one of the nightgowns. I closed the drawer. I went back to the bed and crawled in beside David, careful not to let my body touch his. So I wouldn't wake him.

I pulled the blankets up to my chin. I was awake most of the night. David cried out once in sleep.

Everyone in the house was asleep. The Kommandant hadn't come down at night for weeks. Everything in the Camp was quiet. The ovens were working. The chimneys were solid. The trains were punctual. The guards and the *Sonderkommando* did their jobs without opening their mouths. The Kommandant's children played in the garden every day, and each morning, his wife sang as she made breakfast. She didn't keep him awake all night with her crying and her fighting. The Kommandant had stopped smoking again, and he'd cut back on his drinking. He would sleep the night through.

I turned on his desk lamp. I knelt on the floor, wedging a stolen spoon between the floorboards. Very carefully, I raised the edge of the board until I could get my fingers under it. I wiggled it free.

I reached in and pulled out a small bundle, wrapped in a scrap of cloth. I unrolled the cloth and removed the loose pages it held. I uncapped the Kommandant's pen.

I read the first page. I crossed out several lines. In small script, I wrote something above them. I reread the entire page. I changed a word. Another. I crossed out the title. "Bitter Herbs," I wrote in its place. I read the page again. I crossed out a word. Two. The next time I read the page, I changed nothing. I put "Bitter Herbs" on the bottom of the stack, and read the next.

"We have no bitter herbs," said my mother. "How can we have a *Seder* without bitter herbs?"

"The Germans don't allow us to have a *Seder* anyway," my father said, "so God won't mind if we don't have bitter herbs."

"But the children..."

"The children have bitter lives," I said. "They don't need anything to remind them of it. Papa, did you cover all the windows?"

"Yes, of course. Just like you told me."

"Mama, where did you put the bone?"

"What kind of bone was that?" said my mother. "Where did you find it?"

"Don't worry about it. Where is it?"

"On the plate. Next to the apple."

"You found an apple?" my father said.

"Without the bitter herbs," said my mother, "it won't be the same."

"Mama, please."

"Who are all these people who are coming?" said my father.

"You mean besides all the people who live here with us?" I said.

"They're friends of hers, Samuel," said my mother.

"They're the people who come here at all hours of the night, aren't they?" said my father.

"You don't know anything about that," I said, kissing him on the forehead.

"What are those packages you're always giving each other?" he said, standing up and following me around the room.

"Nothing, Papa, don't worry. Mama, is there any more candle left?"

"No, no more candle," said my mother.

"You're doing something dangerous," said my father.

"It's dangerous living in this Ghetto," I said, "shut off from the rest of the world."

"I can always tell when you're hiding something, ever since you were a little girl," he said. "You're doing something bad."

"What I'm doing puts food on the table," I said.

"It's something you're ashamed of. Something you don't want me or Mama to know," he said.

"Samuel, leave her alone."

"Hannah, she's going to be hurt. We should know what she's doing."

"She's a good girl, Samuel. Let her be."

"Tell me who these people are," said my father, and he gripped my arm.

"Are you *Gestapo* now?" I said.

He released my arm and stumbled back, his mouth opening soundlessly.

"What a terrible thing to say to Papa," said my mother.

"He's interrogating me."

"He's not interrogating you. He's worried."

"There's nothing to worry about."

"We're both worried," said my mother. "You're our only child. We love you."

"Don't worry about me. I can take care of myself."

"I need you to take care of Hans," said the Kommandant's wife as she came into his office. "I have to get dressed for the party."

She stood there, her arms full: baby, blanket, rattle, stuffed animal, bottle. The Kommandant frowned.

"You're not serious," he said.

"I have to get dressed. And do my hair."

"What am I supposed to do with the baby?" said the Kommandant. "I'm working."

"You don't have to do anything," she said. "Just keep an eye on him."

She leaned forward and placed a small blanket on the floor. After she straightened the blanket, she put the baby on it. The baby watched as she piled his things around him.

"He's been fed and changed, so he should be fine. But I brought some juice, in case he gets fussy."

"Where's Ilse?" said the Kommandant.

"She's with Cook, icing the cake."

"Can't Cook watch Hans, too?"

"I told you: she's doing the cake."

"I've got too much work to do."

"My God, Max, how many times do I ask you to do something for me? It's a birthday party for your best friend, not mine."

"All right. Leave Hans here."

"I've done everything else: the shopping, the cooking, the cleaning. How am I supposed to watch the children and get ready, too?"

"All right, Marta, all right. I said leave the baby here. Go get dressed."

She stood a moment, her hands on her hips. The Kommandant scowled at the papers on his desk. The baby lifted himself onto his hands and knees, swaying gently as he cooed to himself.

"I brought his toys down," she said. "And some juice. He'll be good."

"Yes, yes."

She stood there, looking at the Kommandant. He pushed aside some of the papers, signed one, wrote on another.

"I was going to wear my red dress. Unless you'd like me to wear a different one."

The Kommandant said nothing. He opened a folder and paged through its contents. The baby dropped back onto his belly, reaching for the rattle. He put it in his mouth.

"Let's not have an argument just before the party."

"The red dress is fine."

She smiled.

"The baby won't be any trouble, Darling."

"All right."

"Be good for Daddy, Hans. I'll come get him as soon as I'm dressed."

"Make sure Ilse stays upstairs," said the Kommandant. "I can't watch both of them."

"Ilse will stay with Cook," she said, and she closed the office door.

The Kommandant looked over his desk at the baby. Hans was rocking back and forth on his hands and knees, gurgling at the small stuffed bear lying in front of him on the blanket. When he groped for the bear, he fell onto his belly. He pulled the bear to his mouth, and chewed on its ear. The Kommandant returned his attention to the papers on his desk.

The baby released the bear and got back up on his knees. He rocked back and forth. After a few minutes, he began to crawl, away from the bear, off the blanket. I looked up at the Kommandant, but he was writing. The baby drooled on the wood floor. He let himself rest on his belly several times, his hand in his mouth. Each time he got up on his knees, he turned his head to gaze around the office. The Kommandant stood and opened one of his file cabinets. He pulled out several folders and flipped through them, his back turned. The baby crawled toward me.

I moved my legs out of his path. He shifted his direction, turning toward my new position. I pulled my legs up to my chest, so the baby wouldn't run into them. He crawled up to me. The Kommandant replaced the folders and bent over another file drawer. The baby smacked my bare foot. His hand was wet.

The Kommandant rummaged through the file drawer, muttering to himself. The baby arched his back to see me. His mouth opened in a sort of smile. When I touched his hand, he blinked at me. His wet fingers scratched my foot. I brushed his hand again. He was so soft and small. So beautiful. When I touched his cheek, he cooed at me.

"So soft, the life she's leading," said Sharón. "Such a soft life for such a selfish woman."

"For a whore," said one of the others.

"Take a few Safe-Conducts," said Rebekah, and she pressed some papers into my hands.

"The Germans don't honor them anymore," I said. "Besides, the Kommandant has his adjutant remove all the Safe-Conducts."

"You could try," said Rebekah. "If we could just get a few Safe-Conducts attached to the arrest orders."

"Where did you get these?" I said as I looked down at the papers in my hands.

"We made them," said Rebekah.

"Are you mad?" I said, dropping the papers.

The others scrambled to pick them up, before they got soiled.

"I couldn't even attach real ones, let alone forgeries."

"I told you she wouldn't help us," said Sharón. "She likes the Kommandant."

I pushed her away from me.

"You're disgusting," I said.

"I'd like him, too, if he led me such a soft life," she said.

"You want to see a soft life?" I said.

I hiked up my dress to display the bruises on my thighs. I pulled the dress off my shoulder to reveal the welts on my back.

"Such a soft life I'm leading," I said. "You want to take my place?"

"Could you get us something with his writing on it?" said Rebekah.

"She probably won't even do that," said Sharón.

I pushed my dress back over the bruises, over the welts.

"If you could just get us his signature, or if you could destroy some of the orders..."

"He'll notice if something's missing," I said. "And he locks his desk. Every night. He's very careful about those things."

"I told you," said Sharón.

"We ask for so little," said Rebekah, "and you won't even do that much."

It was too much. Everyone wanted too much from me: my parents, the inmates, him. When the Kommandant couldn't sleep, or when he had too much work to do, he came down to his office in the middle of the night. Sometimes he woke me. He always wanted something from me, just like the rest of them, only he never asked.

Sometimes he didn't seem to remember I was there. If I stayed very still, and very, very quiet, he could forget me for hours, for days. Once he forgot me for a month. He hardly came into his office then, and when he did, he was so preoccupied that he never even looked at me: he rubbed his thigh all the time, and his forehead. He'd lost weight, and he seemed to be limping. He frowned constantly and swallowed little white pills. But he remembered me again. He always remembered me eventually.

Often, he worked all night. The light kept me awake. I lay on the cot he'd brought down and watched him. When his pen stopped, he pulled off his ring. Not his wedding ring. He never took that off. The silver band with the death's head. He turned it over and over in his left hand. He touched the nib of his pen to the indentations in the ring. He held it up, so the skull on its crossed bones was looking at him. He imitated its grin. He slipped the ring back on, and wrote again. When he saw me watching, he stopped writing. He put down his pen. He pushed the papers into his center desk drawer and locked it. I closed my eyes and lay very still, but he came over to me anyway. I said nothing, but he touched me anyway. Nothing I'd said would've mattered.

There were no words. There was nothing.

Not a word.

I put another sheet of paper into the typewriter, and pulled my chair closer to the desk. I put my fingers on the keys. I closed my eyes. I tried to see a new place, with new faces and new lives. I tried to see children, laughing and splashing in pools formed by rain. A boy and a girl, both blond. No, two boys, blond and thin. No, three boys, one much smaller than the other two. Three boys, three brothers, their hair and clothes drenched with rain, their bare feet kicking at the puddles, their heads thrown back, their mouths open to catch the rain. I tried to hear their laughter, to feel the rain on their soft skin.

I tried to see a woman, sitting on a porch, sipping tea. She could hear the children laughing. She could see them. She would shake her head when the two bigger ones chased the smallest one into the house, their bare feet leaving puddles on the clean wood floor. I tried to feel the warmth of the cat that lay dozing in her lap, to feel its soft fur, to hear its contented purr. I opened my eyes.

The page in the typewriter was blank.

I left the office and went to the head of the stairs.

"David? David? Let's go for a walk," I said. "It's no good trying to work on a day like this."

I went into the parlor, into the kitchen, out onto the back porch. David wasn't there. I found a note on the table by the front door.

> Rachel,
> Went to the library to do more
> research on the book. Home soon.
> Love,

I went back up to my office. The house was too quiet. I couldn't write in this kind of quiet. I could hear my blood pulsing through my ears. I could hear my heart pounding. But I couldn't hear the children's laughter. I couldn't even see the woman's face, let alone hear her words. I couldn't see the cat. I couldn't even see David. I wanted the typewriter to break the silence, but nothing happened. No words appeared on the blank page.

There was only me. I hated it.

I hit one key, just to end the silence, to soil the white. I typed another letter. Another. Three more. The letters in my name.

I rolled the sheet up to read what I had typed.

Kazett

I shoved the typewriter off the desk.

Chapter Six

Kazett. Kazett. That's all I ever hear about," said David. "I don't want to talk about the Concentration Camp. I want to talk about a child."

"This is about a child. You know I can't have a baby," I said. "Because of the Camp."

I stepped out of the bath and wrapped a towel around me. I wrapped a second towel around my hair. David said nothing. When I sat at the small vanity, he came up behind me and loosened the towel around my hair. I closed my eyes as he dried my hair, as he put down the towel and picked up the comb. I leaned back against him as he gently combed out the tangles. He was always careful. He never rushed. He never tugged too hard on the comb, or made me cry out. He never hurt me. My hair lay wet against my shoulders and back. When David leaned forward to put the comb down, his cheek was warm next to mine.

"I love you so much, Rachel."

He put his arms around me, and I let my body curve into his. He kissed me on the ear, throat, shoulder. I didn't want any more words. I wanted him to hold me, the way he used to hold me. I touched his face.

"We can adopt," he said.

I opened my eyes. He released me to pick up a small folder.

"Look, I got these from an agency that..."

"We can't adopt."

"Why not?"

"We wouldn't know whose child it was."

"I'm reasonably sure that it won't be his, if that's what you're worried about."

"That's not funny, David. I don't want someone else's child."

I dragged the comb through my hair again. It was cold and heavy against my neck and back.

"We could adopt an orphan, a Jewish child who lost its parents in the war."

I looked at David in the mirror.

"You're serious."

"I want a child."

"And if I don't want one?"

"I lost my entire family in the Camps."

"So did I."

"I want a family."

"You have me."

"I want a child."

"Are you telling me that I don't have any choice in the matter?"

He threw down the papers.

"I'm telling you I'm not going to let the past destroy me."

He paced back and forth, his hands clenched. I wiped the steam off the mirror.

"I'm not going to live in the Camps all my life."

I turned around from the steamy glass, to look him in the face.

"I ran away when the Nazis put me in a Camp," he said. "I'm not going to let you keep me in one."

"You ran away from the Camp," I said, "and they killed your parents."

He looked at me, with a cold look. Then he bent down and picked up the papers, slowly, one by one. He stood up, straightening the papers into their folder.

"You didn't run away from the Camp," he said. "Where are your parents?"

"Where's your Mama?" I said. "What are you doing there, all by yourself?"

Hans kept crying. He was on the landing of the stairs that led from the Kommandant's office area to the house proper. He could stand now, and walk. He had come down half the stairs, but stood there, on the landing, crying in distress.

"Can't you get back upstairs?" I said, softly, so no one else would hear. "Is that what's wrong?"

The Kommandant and his adjutant were out in the Camp. I stood in the doorway of the Kommandant's office, looking up at Hans.

"What's the matter, Hans?" I said.

I moved cautiously to the foot of the stairs.

"Where's Mama?"

Hans continued to cry. Then I saw the reason: his bottle had rolled down the stairs. It lay on one of the steps, halfway between us. Upstairs, the Kommandant's wife called out for Hans, and I heard her footsteps going around the house. Hans cried louder.

"Here, Sweetheart," I said.

I crept up the stairs and retrieved the bottle. I held it out to him.

"Here, Baby."

His mouth poured forth great wails, and tears flooded from his eyes. The Kommandant's wife called again. And again. Her footsteps became quicker, more urgent.

"Here, Hans," I said.

I went up another step. And another.

"Here's your bottle, Hans."

When the nipple touched his arm, he looked down at it. His crying grew quieter, but didn't stop. His mother's calls became frantic, but they sounded very far away.

"Take the bottle. Here, Hans. Take it. Take it, Sweetheart."

He cried. I knelt on the landing beside him, offering the bottle.

"Here, Darling. Here it is."

Hans stopped crying. He leaned forward, over the bottle, his mouth open. I lifted the bottle until the nipple was in his mouth. I put his hands around the bottle, but he wouldn't take hold of it. He sucked on the nipple, but it was empty because of the bottle's angle. His brow wrinkled, and he opened his mouth to cry. I tilted the bottle so milk would pour into the nipple. As he sucked, Hans leaned against me.

Then he was in my arms.

As he drank, he gazed up at me. His lashes were clumped together with moisture, and his cheeks were streaked with tears. He gripped the front of my gown with one hand, and clutched the bottle with the other. I brushed the tears from his face. There was a movement on the stairs, and I looked up.

The Kommandant's wife shrieked.

There was a shriek near the tiny, grated window of the boxcar. Then another shriek. Then pushing and shoving and hitting and bodies surging toward the grating.

"Rain."

"Rain."

There had been no water for days, and the Jews crushed together with us in the boxcar took up the cry.

"Rain."

"Take my cup," said my father. "It's bigger than yours."

"Take both cups," said my mother.

"Let's not be greedy," said my father.

"But get enough for all of us," said my mother.

They pushed themselves along behind me. I held the cup high as I struggled through the crowd. I was pinched and jabbed as I tried to reach the grate. Someone bit my ankle when I crawled up onto the luggage, so I kicked. Yes, it was raining. I shoved the cup out through the bars of the grate. I had to slap and kick at those who were trying to drag me down. The cup grew heavy with the rain. Slowly I pulled the cup back in. The water trembled as I raised the cup. My mother slapped my knee.

"For shame," she said. "Give some to Papa. He needs it most."

Without taking a sip, I carefully began to lower the cup down to my parents. My father raised his hand. Someone bumped my arm, knocking the cup sideways.

All the water was lost.

"His Mama's lost," said my mother as I came into the kitchen.

"Whose mother's lost?" I said.

She indicated a small boy standing beside her. I didn't know his name. There were so many of them, and they all looked exactly the same: bulging dark eyes, hollowed cheeks, running noses, cracked and bleeding lips. They were dying. The small boy shook his head. He tugged at the hem of my mother's dress.

"No, she's not lost anymore. I found her," he said. "Come with me. I found her."

We hurried out of the crowded apartment, following the child into the hallway.

"Where is she? Where's your Mama?"

"Up here," he said, climbing the narrow stairs to the attic.

"She must be suffocating from the heat up there," said my mother.

"Why would anyone go up there?" said cousin Leo.

"Probably she went up there to have a bit of space," said Mr. Silverstein.

"Or some privacy," said Mrs. Greenbaum.

"I found her. I found her," said the boy as he crawled into the attic. "Here she is. Mama. Mama."

We stopped. Some of us closed our eyes. Some of the others wept. I did neither. Yes, he'd found her. She was hanging from the rafters, a stout piece of rope wrapped tightly around her neck. Her eyes stared. Her tongue protruded. Her shoes brushed the edge of the milking stool, overturned beneath. Her little boy pulled at her ankle, making her body sway gently.

"Mama, wake up," he said. "Mama."

"How horrible," said my mother.

One of the women went to the boy and took his hand. My father and one of the other old men went to the body.

"How terrible."

"Poor woman."

"How selfish," I said. "How absolutely selfish."

"You're being selfish," said the Kommandant into the telephone.

He was frowning.

"I told you not to call me anymore. You agreed. I didn't say you were happy about it. I said you agreed. I know it's my office, but it might as well be the house. No, Marta's not here. I'm alone. Yes, I just said so. What's so important? You need more money?"

The Kommandant pulled his chair closer to the desk, and he continued looking through his paperwork, even as he listened to the voice on the telephone.

"Yes, yes, what about him?"

He stopped shuffling through the papers.

"When? How?"

His frown deepened to a scowl. His voice grew louder.

"Why didn't you call me? Right away, not three days later. Of course I'd want to know something like that. I don't want to argue about that now. What did the doctor say? Is he going to be all right?"

The Kommandant grew very still, very pale. His pen fell from his hand to the desk. He stared straight ahead. His voice wasn't loud now.

"Why did you think I wouldn't come? I know it's been a long time, but if you'd told me, if only I'd known. The war? What does the war matter? No, not the Camp either. When is the... Yesterday?"

He was very quiet. I almost couldn't hear him.

"You should've told me, no matter what happened between us. When I think of you there, all alone. You're not? You what? When did you do that? Why didn't you tell me? I know. I know what I said, but something that important... Don't cry. Please, don't cry."

He closed his eyes, and covered them with his hand.

"I know you did. Yes, it was a long time. You were very patient. Very good. I know you couldn't wait any longer. You need someone. You deserve someone. Please, don't cry. Please, don't."

He sat a long time, without saying anything, without uncovering his eyes.

"Yes, of course it was right to tell me. No, it's not your fault. Yes, I know. I'm sorry, too."

The Kommandant uncovered his eyes. He replaced the receiver. He sat there, staring. Then he looked down at his desk. He picked up his pen. He put it back down. He stood, turning toward the windows. He paced back and forth in front of the glass. His fingers combed agitatedly through his hair. His breath was loud and irregular. Suddenly he stopped pacing. He stared out the window, his back to me. Without a word, he put his fist through the pane.

When he drew back his hand and looked at it, there was blood. He looked back at the window. The winter air rushed in. He punched out another pane of glass. He punched another. Without looking at his hand, he hit again and again. Until there were cuts and blood all over the back of his hand, until there were glass fragments all over the floor at his feet, until he knelt in the glittering mess. Snow blew in through the broken windows and landed on his bent head. He looked at his cut and bleeding hand. He wept.

"Daddy?" said Ilse. "Daddy?"

But the Kommandant wasn't in his office. Ilse strolled into the room, brushing her hair. After each stroke of the brush, she smoothed her hair with her other hand. She closed the office door and walked over to me.

"Where's my daddy?"

I said nothing. Still brushing, she looked down at me.

"That's Mommy's dress," she said.

Her hair crackled under the brush. Her hair spread over her shoulders like pale fire: electric and alive.

"This is Mommy's brush, but she said I could use it."

She stepped closer. The toe of her shoe touched my leg. I didn't move. She sighed loudly.

"Your hair's awful messy. It's all tangly," she said. "Here, let me brush it for you."

She leaned forward, smelling of soap, her starched dress rustling, and I felt the brush touch my scalp.

"Are you going to let your hair grow longer?" she said.

The brush moved across my head, from front to back. Slow and rhythmic. Front to back. I closed my eyes.

"You're a girl, you know," said Ilse. "Girls are supposed to have long hair."

Front to back. Top and sides. Front to back. With her little hand following each even, measured stroke.

"Now, you look pretty," she said.

I slowly raised my hand. I touched my hair.

"It's pretty," said Ilse.

She held out the brush.

"Do you want to do mine?"

"Ilse," said the Kommandant, calling from the stairs. "Are you down in my office?"

She dropped the hairbrush, and ran.

There was running everywhere: old people, Germans, dogs, children, prisoners. I told my parents to stay close to me, but I had to keep grabbing onto their coats to keep from losing them. It was worse than it had been on the train. So many people, so much pushing, shoving, crying, screaming. And the Germans with their guns and their dogs. And the chimneys, coughing out that foul, black smoke. I dug my fingers into my parents' arms.

"You're hurting," said my father, trying to pry free my fingers.

"Stay with me," I said.

"Let go," said my mother. "That hurts."

"I'm afraid you'll get lost."

"No, we won't. We'll stay right with you."

"I'm not taking any chances," I said. "I'm not letting go of either of you."

But then we were at the head of the line. A medical officer barely glanced at us. He pointed us in separate directions.

"Right," he said. "Left."

My parents were on one side. I was on the other. I didn't know which was the better side: left or right. No one knew. Left or right. There were many elderly people on the other side, with my parents, but there were also children.

Left or right. A young woman was standing next to my parents. She was holding a baby, and she seemed my age. My mother and father held hands, their eyes on me as the doctor continued to direct the new arrivals into two groups. Left. Right.

Left. Right. As more and more people separated us, my mother began to weep. My father smiled bravely.

Left. Right. I stepped toward my parents, but then the Kommandant strode down the center of the two groups. When he glanced over, and saw me, he stopped. Left. Right.

He looked over at the other group, then back at me. He nodded, and passed on. Left. Right.

I stayed where I was.

"You want to change sides now?" said Sharón. "You're worse than a whore."

"Why should we let you?" said one of her comrades. "We don't care what happens to you."

"What's going on?" said Rebekah.

She came to the fence behind the crematoria. Several other inmates were with her. They huddled by her, misshapen shadows in the half-light cast by the passing spotlights. The wind blew ashes in my eyes. I stepped closer to them.

"What do you want?" said Rebekah.

"She wants our help," said one of the inmates.

"Let her rot," said Sharón.

Rebekah smiled.

"You want us to help you?" she said.

"I'm pregnant."

They looked at me. They were gaunt and pale. Their clothes were wet, from all the rain, and the material clung to their bones.

"You must be getting enough to eat," said Rebekah.

I grabbed Rebekah's arm, and the others moved closer around her. She roughly shook my hand off.

"I'll kill myself before I have his baby."

"You won't kill yourself," said Rebekah.

"Please. You've got to help me. I can't do it on my own. I'll do anything you want."

"Don't help her," said Sharón.

"You know I can't have this baby. I'll do whatever you want."

"Don't listen to her," said Sharón.

"You'll do anything?" said Rebekah.

"Tell me," I said. "I'll do it."

Sharón pushed herself between the two of us.

"How can you do this, Rebekah? After all the times she's refused us?"

"He'll send her to the gas if she's pregnant," said one of the others.

"So?" said Sharón.

"What are we going to do?" said one of them.

Rebekah crossed her arms over her chest.

"It'll hurt," she said.

"I know."

"You'll have bad cramps, for days."

"It doesn't matter."

"There'll be blood," said Rebekah. "How will you hide it from him?"

"I'll worry about that."

She nodded slowly. The hollows around her eyes and under her cheekbones formed great shadows: when she grinned at me, she looked like the skull on the Kommandant's silver ring.

"So," she said, "you need us now."

"What's she going to do?" said Ilse.

She sat in the Kommandant's lap in his office chair, and she gazed up at him.

"What's she going to do, Daddy?"

"I don't know," said the Kommandant. "I can't turn the page. You turn it for me."

> The little old woman, although she was kind,
> was really a wicked old witch...

"Oh, no," said Ilse.

She clutched the Kommandant's lapels and hid her face against his jacket. She peeked out at the open book from behind her fingers.

> She'd built the pretty little gingerbread house
> on purpose, to lure little children inside.
> Once they were inside her little house,
> she cooked them, and then she ate them.

"Oh, no," said Ilse.

> The old witch's eyes were red, like fire or blood,
> so she couldn't see very far, but she had a keen scent,
> like the beasts, so she knew that Hansel and Gretel were near.

"You wouldn't let a witch eat me, would you, Daddy?" said Ilse.

"No, never."

"Would you let a witch eat Hans?"

"Oh, no," said the Kommandant.

He looked down at the little boy who lay sleeping in the crook of his other arm. He kissed Hans on the top of his head.

"I'd never let a witch eat either one of you."

"Would you let a witch eat Mommy?"

"No."

"But witches only eat little boys and girls, right? When they get lost?"

"Not my little boy and girl."

The Kommandant hugged them tightly, his face against their hair.

"I'd never lose my children," he said.

"I lost my parents, too," said David. "You're not the only one who suffered during the war."

"I never said I was. Do we have to go through this again? Now?"

"Yes."

"Why does it have to be now?"

"Because I'm tired of running away."

David took his folded shirts from the suitcase and returned them to the bureau drawer. He closed it. He took his suit from my hand and placed it back in the closet.

"What are you doing?"

"Not this time, Rachel."

"What do you mean, 'not this time'?"

"I'm not going to spend my whole life running away. I want to settle down. I want a family."

"Don't you care what I want?"

"I think I should be the one asking you that question."

"And if I go?" I said. "If I have to go?"

He looked at me. His eyes were tired. His face was thin, drawn. He rested his hand against the doorframe.

"I love you, Rachel, but I'm not going."

"You're my husband."

He sighed.

"You promised."

He said nothing.

"You said you'd never leave me. You swore."

He looked at me, but his eyes were a stranger's eyes. He shook his head. I shoved the suitcase off the bed. It hit the bedside table and knocked over the lamp. David closed his eyes.

"You promised," I said. "You gave your word."

Chapter Seven

"You promised."

"I said I'd try."

"No, you said you'd help us."

"I knew we couldn't trust her," said Sharón.

"It's not as easy as you think," I said.

"You lied to us," said Rebekah.

"No, I didn't," I said. "But surely you don't expect me to risk myself unless there's some chance of success. Those documents you gave me..."

Someone hit me, from behind, and my knees buckled. My knees and hands slammed against the wet clay, and my ears were ringing. The next blow, across my back, pitched me to the ground. My cheek smacked the clay. They kicked me in the ribs, the stomach, the head. Though I curled myself forward, hiding my head and drawing my knees up, I couldn't protect myself from them. I heard a crack, and felt a tremendous rush of pain in my side. My head roared, but I didn't lose consciousness.

"That's enough," said Rebekah.

The others moved away, forming a circle around me. Rebekah bent down and grabbed my hair, yanking my head up and back so I was forced to look at her. The pain ripped hotly in my side.

"You owe us," she said. "Don't think we'll forget it."

"We don't owe them anything," I said.

My father just stood there, hanging his head, a loaf of dark bread held tightly to his chest. The stranger stood near the doorway, in the dark. His hands were full of paper money.

"He's a Jew, just like us," said my father.

"He's a U-boat: he's in hiding. The only Jews in hiding are the rich ones. That means he's not like us," I said.

"Just let him have this bread," said my father.

"No Jew can afford to stay in hiding unless he's one of the wealthy ones. Let him get his food somewhere else."

"It isn't much," said my father.

"I have money," said the U-boat. "I'll pay you for it."

"We don't need money. Money's worthless," I said. "But we need to eat."

"It's only bread," said my father, trying to offer the man the loaf.

"Do you know what I had to do to get that much bread?" I said, standing between them. "And you want to give it away."

"I'm not asking you to give it away. I have money," said the U-boat. "Plenty of money."

"If we had to go into hiding," said my father, "we'd want people to help us."

"I have a wife," said the U-boat. "And a three-year-old child."

I yanked the loaf of bread from my father's hands, and tore the loaf into uneven portions. My father smiled. I gave the U-boat the smaller of the two portions.

"Give him the larger piece," said my father. "He has a wife and child."

"He's lucky to get any of it," I said.

The U-boat snatched the bread. He tried to press the money into my hands, but I wouldn't take it.

"Get out," I said. "And don't ever come back here."

The U-boat scrambled out the back door and down the alley. I threw the bolt on the door.

"How can you be so heartless?" said my father. "We have to take care of our own."

"How can you be so foolish?" I said. "We have to take care of ourselves."

"Shall I take care of the partisans, sir?" said the Kommandant's adjutant.

"No, Josef," said the Kommandant, pulling out his pistol. "I'll take care of them myself."

The partisans moved uneasily as they glanced at each other, at the Kommandant. The woman, dressed in men's clothes, stopped dabbing at her bleeding lip. She looked at her comrade, then slipped her hand into his. He squeezed it tightly. One of the older men started to weep, and the young boy patted his arm, to comfort him.

"Take them out to the courtyard," said the Kommandant.

The guards herded the partisans out of the office. The Kommandant followed.

I rushed into the bathroom adjoining the office. I climbed unsteadily onto the bathtub's rim, and pushed open the tiny window near the ceiling. I forced my fingers through the grating and pulled myself up, on my toes, until I could see into the courtyard.

Most of the partisans clung to one another. The woman and the man who were the leaders didn't slouch or tremble. They lifted their chins: they looked right at the Kommandant. The young boy cursed Germans, and spat at the ground. The soldiers gripped their weapons. The Kommandant raised his pistol. The woman threw her arms around her companion, her face against his. The Kommandant fired. Twice. They fell. The Kommandant fired again.

My body was trembling, but not from the cold. I got down from the tub. My legs were still weak, and I stumbled. Outside, the gun fired. One of the partisans cried out. Another shot was fired. I huddled in the corner, against the cold tile. Another shot. I put my hands over my ears to muffle the sound of the gun, to drown out the cries of the dying. It didn't help me. And it didn't help the dead.

"She's dead?" said David. "The woman in the Camp is dead?"

"Yes," I said. "She died there."

David stood in front of my desk. He shrugged.

"I forgot," he said. "You weren't in any of the Camps. But, somehow, you know that the woman who was there is dead, is that right?"

"You're not very attractive when you're like this."

He leaned over my desk to look at the sheet of paper in the typewriter. I covered the blank sheet of paper with both hands.

"Why can't you write about the woman who was in the Camp? Because she's dead?"

"Because I don't want to write about her."

"You don't seem to want to write about anything. It's been almost a year and a half."

"Are you my publisher now, or just a critic?"

"I'm a concerned husband."

"I pay half the bills."

"Because you insist on it. Besides, this has nothing to do with money."

He walked over to the bookcases. On a small table in front of the shelves lay *The Dead Bodies That Line the Streets.* He picked it up.

"Where'd you get this?"

"Someone sent it to me, with a letter."

He replaced the book, without opening it. He stood a few minutes in front of the fireplace, staring at the glowing logs. Ice pelted the windows.

"You're hell to live with when you're not writing."

"That's kind of you to say."

"It's time for you to start writing again."

"I'm trying.

"Write about the Camp."

"I can't."

"You dream the Camp. You talk the Camp. You eat, sleep, breathe the Camp."

I turned away and stared out the window. Outside, everything was as white and blank as the paper in my typewriter. Everything was brittle with ice. I shivered. From the cold.

"Write the Camp, Rachel," said David. "What are you so afraid of?"

"I'm not afraid of him," said the inmate as the guard strode by. "He's nothing but a fat pig."

"A fat pig with a gun," said another inmate from the quarry.

"And a baton, which he loves to use."

"And a temper."

"I'm not afraid of him either," I said. "I just like to stay out of his way."

The others nodded in agreement as I accepted my piece of the rock-hard bread from one of the inmate-cooks. Our tin bowls were slopped full of soup made with grass and rusty water. At least, we hoped it was rust in the water.

"He's too stupid to be afraid of," said the first inmate.

"Who's stupid?" said the fat guard, and he loomed up behind us.

The other inmates scattered. I couldn't move: another guard stood right behind me. The fat guard pushed himself between me and the first inmate, knocking my bowl and spilling some of the discolored liquid onto my arm.

"Who's stupid?"

"Are you talking to me, *Herr Rottenführer*?" said the inmate.

"What do you think, Jew-cur?"

The fat guard hit the inmate across the jaw, and the inmate's head jerked back, his mouth opening with the force of the blow. The inmate put his hand up, over his mouth, but not quickly enough.

"Hey, what's that in your mouth?" said the fat guard.

The second guard stepped around me to be closer to the inmate. The fat guard grabbed for the inmate, but the inmate ducked his head. He tried to reach for his dropped bowl.

"I don't have anything in my mouth, *Herr Rottenführer*."

"It looks like gold," said the fat guard.

He jerked the inmate's head up and back. He forced his gloved fingers into the inmate's mouth. The second guard craned his neck to see into the mouth. He shoved me aside so he could get closer. The remainder of my soup splashed onto my dress.

"It is. It's a gold tooth. You stinking Jew. Give it to me."

"I need it," said the inmate, "for eating."

"You don't hear good, Jew," said the fat guard. "I want that gold tooth."

"What will you give me for it?"

"Here's what I'll give you for it, Jew."

With a tremendous blow, the fat guard flattened the inmate. He bashed the inmate with his truncheon, and with his boots. The other guard helped. The louder the inmate cried, the harder they hit. Several other guards stopped what they were doing in order to watch. The fat guard and his comrade beat the inmate until he didn't make any more noise. Until he lay motionless on the rocks. Until his mouth gaped, revealing the golden tooth.

"Stupid Jew," said the fat guard.

He turned to the second guard, who stood there, smiling an open-mouthed smile and breathing heavily.

"Go get some pliers."

The second guard ran off, toward the trucks, and the fat guard gave the inmate one last kick. When the fat guard turned around, his hands on his hips, he practically knocked me down. He glared at me.

"I don't have any gold teeth," I said.

"Who asked you, Jew-whore?" he said, and he hit me.

"Did you hear what I asked you?" I said, from where I stood at the window.

He turned the page of the newspaper.

"David?"

"There's nothing there. I don't have to look to tell you that."

"It's different this time. That car's been parked by the trees all day. There's someone in it."

He turned another page.

"It's probably someone from the Camp," he said.

"That's not funny."

He looked at me over the top of the paper.

"It isn't my imagination this time."

He looked back down at the paper. After a few moments, he turned the page.

"You're not listening."

"When you start seeing the things that are there, I'll listen."

"Listen. You're not listening, Max," said the Kommandant's friend.

He and the Kommandant sat at the small table in his office, eating lunch. They'd been drinking since morning, after they toured the Camp. After the last transport had been dispatched, the Kommandant opened the champagne. Now they were on their eighth bottle. My eyes were burning from all the smoke. Each time my throat began to tickle, I pressed my face against my shoulder and arm, to muffle the cough.

"I'm still trying to picture her," said the Kommandant, "in a dress with no..."

"She said, 'Where did you get this tie'?"

"She didn't," said the Kommandant. "You're lying, Dieter."

"I swear," he said, holding up his right hand. "On my oath as an officer."

"'Where did you get this tie'?" said the Kommandant, and his friend laughed.

He laughed so hard he spilled his champagne. The Kommandant grabbed the glass and set it right. He poured champagne into it until it ran out over the sides. They laughed at that, too.

"She took hold of my collar..."

"Weren't you wearing your uniform?" said the Kommandant.

"Of course, I was wearing my uniform. I always wear my uniform when I want to impress the ladies. They like uniforms."

"And she asked you where you got your tie? She must've been drunk. How can you take advantage of them when they're drunk, Dieter?"

The Kommandant's friend scooped up some caviar with his fingers and crammed it into his mouth. The Kommandant pushed aside the rind of the cheese to reach the goose carcass. His fingers glistened as he raised one of the bones to his mouth and chewed at its shreds of meat. My eyes watered, and I coughed against my arm.

"She wasn't drunk. She was satisfied, to the point of incoherence."

"You're that good?"

"Better."

The Kommandant laughed and dropped the bone. His friend reached over and slapped him on the back. They both laughed harder.

"I must've been good because I got it again."

"Twice? With the same girl?"

"And once with her girlfriend. But she wasn't any fun."

"You, Dog, you."

"The first time, we did it standing up."

"Standing up?"

"Against the door, with her legs wrapped around my waist."

"I don't believe it."

"You would've killed for her."

"Tell me her name again. Next time I'm in Berlin, I'll look her up," said the Kommandant. "Even I've never done it standing up."

"Don't tell Marta if you do it standing up."

"She'll think it's one of my perversions."

"She won't take it as well as Katarina."

"You didn't tell Katarina?"

"Are you crazy, or just drunk?"

The two of them leaned over the table, laughing. Clouds lay heavy and black in the sky. Raindrops tapped erratically on the glass.

"Katarina just assumes I do it with every woman on the face of the earth."

"With every woman on the face of the earth?"

"With every woman in Germany, Poland, Czechoslovakia..."

The Kommandant shuddered violently.

"Even the ugly ones, Dieter? And the fat ones?"

"Even the Jews," he said, pointing his knife at him. "Even the Jews, Max."

"You'd have to be a desperate man," said the Kommandant, "to do a Jew."

"Not desperate. Just drunk."

"Very drunk."

"Very, very drunk."

The two of them laughed again as the rain began to pound insistently on the windows. The room grew darker. The Kommandant stumbled over to his desk and turned on the small lamp.

"Where did you get all this wonderful food?"

"I'm the Kommandant."

"You're a lucky bastard."

"You're the lucky bastard. You did it standing up."

"We're both lucky bastards. Let's have a toast."

The Kommandant's friend raised his glass, and stood. He lost his balance. When he put his hand down on the table to steady himself, his hand landed in the pâté. The Kommandant fumbled in his pocket for his handkerchief. His friend blinked a few times at the pâté on his hand before he put his fingers in his mouth. The Kommandant offered his handkerchief, and his friend stared at it. After the Kommandant knocked his glass off the table, he leaned close to the table top, squinting and touching things: no glass. He picked up the champagne bottle. When he stood, his chair toppled backward. Both men swayed on their feet. The Kommandant drank from the bottle.

"Wait. We have to make a toast first."

"Yes, a toast. To..."

"To our friendship."

"To us."

"And another toast. To... to..."

"To the wealth of the Jews," said the Kommandant.

The sky opened, and the rain poured down.

"To the Jews," said the Kommandant.

He was sitting on the cot, his clothes disheveled, and he raised his glass to me.

"To the Jews," he said, over and over.

He hadn't touched me. He'd been drinking the whole night. His wristwatch was lying on his desk, and I looked at it. 4:17. And still he wouldn't go to bed. I thought about going to him myself, to get it over with, but he was acting strangely. All that alcohol, and he hadn't touched me.

When he went to the cabinet for the third bottle, he was very steady. Very quiet. And he hadn't touched me. He sat on the cot, his uniform unbuttoned, drinking, first from the glass, then from the bottle, looking right at me and fondling his gun, but he hadn't touched me.

He stroked his gun, over and over. Then he stood up. Finally, it would be done with. He'd go back upstairs afterward, and I'd be able to sleep. He didn't come over to his desk, though. He went into the bathroom, taking the gun and the bottle with him. I heard water running. He must've finally made himself sick. The water stopped, then went on again. I picked up his watch and leaned back in the desk chair, the blanket around my shoulders, I turned the watch over. There was an inscription.

To my Darling, Max, forever and...

The Kommandant staggered out of the bathroom.

I dropped the watch.

The Kommandant held his gun to his head.

He came over to me, the pistol at his temple. He sank to his knees in front of the chair, his body pressed against my legs. I leaned back in the chair as far as I could. With his free hand, he clutched the front of my dress. The gun pressed harder against his flesh. Harder against the bone. The Kommandant pulled at my dress, dragging me forward. The gun fell to the floor.

The Kommandant buried his face in my lap, his hands clutching at me.

He wept.

I didn't move.

The Kommandant didn't move when I slipped out from beneath his arm. I inched further away. He snored softly. After I lifted the blanket and slid out of the bed, I stood, very still, holding the edge of the blanket, watching him. His service dagger and pistol were on the bureau. The Kommandant slept.

With my eyes on him, I crept across the bedroom to the bureau. My feet slid over the polished floor, onto the cotton rug, back onto the floor. The Kommandant turned over. I stopped, but his eyes didn't open. My arm bumped the bureau.

Yes, there they were: pistol and dagger, in holster and sheath. The same every day. First the weapons. Then the uniform. Then scars on naked skin. Then groping. Then wet, open-mouthed kisses. Then thrusting and, finally, sleep. With the pistol and the service dagger lying side by side in the same room.

My fingers trembled as I unbuckled the dagger's sheath, separating it from the rest. I had rehearsed this in my mind, every afternoon, every night, since he'd first brought me to his bedroom. Holding the dagger tightly, I went to the door. The Kommandant turned over, snoring into the pillow. I held my breath. I opened the door.

It was too risky to go all the way down to his office: it would take too much time. He might wake. He hadn't been drinking since his wife went away, or not as much, and not during the day. I'd have to get the dagger down to the office later, when he slept for the night. There was a cedar chest in the hallway, under the window. He'd taken a blanket from that chest. I slid the dagger behind the back of it, between the chest and the wall. The Kommandant stirred.

I rushed back into the room. I grabbed the extra blanket from the bed and wrapped it around me. I threw myself into the chair by the window and closed my eyes. The Kommandant didn't move. I stayed very still, with my eyes closed, in case he was awake, watching me. But nothing happened. Gradually, my heart slowed its pounding. The Kommandant didn't get out of bed to come to me again. He didn't call me to come to him. The sun glowed through the windows. The blanket was soft and warm around me. The Kommandant's breathing slowed and deepened. The Camp drifted away.

"I'm going away," said David, after supper. "For the summer."

"What are you talking about?"

We were sitting on the porch, in the swing, and David turned his head away from me, to look out across the yard.

"I've been offered a teaching post," he said. "For the summer. In Paris."

"This is already the first of June," I said as I poured more iced tea into my glass. "I'll have a rough time packing on such short notice."

"You don't have to pack. I'm going alone."

I looked at him, but he stared out at the yard. The glass in my hand was so cold that it burned. I put the glass down. My hand was wet, from the condensation. I wiped my palm on my skirt. When I touched his arm, he pulled away.

"You're leaving me."

"Not leaving. Just going away for a while."

"Without me?"

"I need to be by myself. To think about things."

"What things?"

"Us."

"What about us?"

He looked at me. He seemed so tired. So old. Aged beyond his endurance. The breeze ruffled his hair. He closed his eyes. My heart was pounding. I could hardly breathe. I wanted to touch him, to pull him close to me, but his hands were clenched and my own hands lay still in my lap.

"Why did you marry me?"

His voice was quiet. He didn't look at me. I didn't know what he wanted me to say. He smiled faintly, nodding. He leaned forward, his elbows resting on his thighs. His hands clutched each other so tightly that his knuckles were white.

"It's my own fault," he said. "I thought you would learn to love me."

"I do love you."

"Not the way I want you to love me."

"You're my husband."

"Oh, Rachel."

"Tell me what it is you want."

"You can't give me what I want."

"Tell me."

"I don't want to keep living this way: jumping at every noise, arguing all the time, running from my own shadow..."

"You want a divorce."

He looked out at the yard. He twisted his hands against each other. He said nothing.

"You're never coming back."

He frowned and shook his head. He leaned back in the swing, and put his hand on mine.

"I'd never do that to you. No matter what I decide, I'll come back."

My throat felt as if he were tightening a rope around it. I moved my hand from under his.

"You'll come back to tell me that you want a divorce."

"This is what I want, Rachel: for you to love me."

"I do."

"I don't want to compete anymore."

His voice wasn't loud. The wind rustling in the trees around the porch muffled his words and made them sound strange. I didn't know what to say. I didn't know what he wanted to hear. He stood, his fists jammed into his pockets, his back to me. My hands were cold. My sweater had fallen from my shoulders, and the wind on my bare arms made me shiver. My voice was trapped in my throat.

"It's taken me a long time to realize the truth. I didn't want to believe it. I didn't believe it in the beginning. I thought my love was enough for both of us. But I can't hide from it anymore."

He turned around and looked at me. I wanted to take him in my arms, to make the look on his face go away, but I couldn't move. David went to the edge of the porch and put his hands on the railing. The wind blew his hair away from his face and made him narrow his eyes. I clasped my hands together in my lap, to keep them from trembling.

"You have to choose."

"Don't do this."

"You have to choose who you're going to spend the rest of your life with."

"Take me with you."

He closed his eyes. There was so much I wanted to tell him, so many words were dashing around my head, banging around in my chest, trying to get out, but when I opened my mouth, the wrong words came out.

"When are you going?"

"It wasn't an easy decision."

"When?"

"Tomorrow morning."

I looked up at him, but his face was turned toward the yard.

"I'll be back in September. I promise."

All the things I wanted to tell him were caught in my chest, in my throat, choking me. When I spoke, I said the wrong thing. I always said the wrong thing. But this time, I wouldn't be able to take my words back. I'd never be able to make things right. The breeze chilled me. I closed my eyes.

"Will you write?"

"Of course."

"Will you call?"

"I haven't stopped loving you."

When I said nothing, David turned back toward me. He looked old. I wanted to cast away all the words that kept us from each other, but I didn't move.

"Do you know what hurts the most?"

I shook my head.

"You never cry," he said. "You never even cry."

Chapter Eight

I never cried. Except once. In the Camp. The Kommandant was so drunk he kept falling into the wall as we went up the stairs. He hadn't been drinking for several weeks, so the alcohol must've affected him more than usual. Or else he'd been drinking more. I'd never seen him like that. He was frowning, and his grip was hurting my wrist as he dragged me up after him. I tried to pull his fingers off my arm. He stumbled, but he held tight.

In the dining room, he'd laid out a table: china, silver, candles, champagne, food. I was faint from hunger, and I longed for it all. He poured champagne, drinking most of it himself before he offered me a glass. I wanted the food. The Kommandant wasn't ready to eat: first he had something to show me. He was so drunk that I could barely understand what he was saying. He wasn't wearing his uniform jacket, but he still smelled of smoke. As carefully as he could, swaying, shaking his head periodically to clear it, he rolled his left sleeve up until it was above the elbow. He caught hold of me, to keep himself from falling, and he held his arm out to me.

There, on his inner left forearm, in black ink: a Jewish, six-pointed star.

"Now I'm a Jew," he said.

I felt a coldness in me, like nothing I'd ever known before. I hated them all, but I hated him more than all the others. How dare he mock me. I'd show him what it was like to be branded for life. I'd show him what it was like to be a Jew. I put my hand on his service dagger.

He looked down, but didn't stop me when I lifted the dagger out of its sheath. I took his hand, and led the Kommandant to a chair. I sat down, pulling on his hand, pushing on his shoulder till he knelt beside me. His left arm lay across my thighs. He put the bottle of champagne down on the floor and watched me intently. I touched the tip of the dagger to the top of the star, on the black outline he had drawn. As the Kommandant looked at it, I pressed down.

There was resistance. It wasn't as easy to cut through skin as I'd thought it would be. I pressed harder. The dagger pierced the skin. The Kommandant drew his breath in sharply. With his mouth open, he looked up at me, but I looked down at the star.

Very carefully, very slowly, with steady pressure, I cut the six-pointed star on his inner left forearm. He didn't cry out, though I cut deep, deep and slow. I gouged out the skin: I wanted it to be a thick, raised scar. The

Kommandant clenched his teeth. That pleased me. Blood chased the knife's glittering path. I made the lines very straight, the angles sharp. I made it last a long time. The Kommandant turned pale. Sweat beaded on his upper lip, at his hairline. I felt happy. It was a big star: over an inch from tip to tip. Beside the star, almost the same size, I made three more cuts, so he'd never be free: *K* for *Kommandant.*

I smiled. I leaned over and retrieved the champagne bottle. I drank some of it. I poured the rest over the cuttings. That made the Kommandant cry out. My cheeks were flushed. My heart was racing.

"Now you're a Jew," I said, in his language.

Then I slapped him. As hard as I could. I liked the way my palm felt. I liked the look on his face. I liked the red across his cheek, and the red on his arm. I wanted to slap him again. Even harder. I wanted to cut him, on his chest, on his back, on his thighs. I wanted to put the dagger between his legs. I wanted him to writhe and cry out. I wanted to be with him, right then, there, on the floor. I wanted him to touch me for once, with his hands, with his mouth, with his tongue, until I was wet, until I closed my eyes and arched toward him, until I shuddered and relaxed my thighs. And I wanted him inside me. Not fast and hard, the way he liked it, but deep and slow, with him on his back instead, and for a long, long time. When I pulled him to me and kissed him, when I put my tongue in his mouth, the Kommandant moaned, and clutched me desperately to him.

Then the shame flooded me. I pushed him away. I pushed him so hard that his head banged on the table. The chair toppled behind me, and the dagger fell to the floor. The room was spinning. I couldn't breathe. I rushed out, down the stairs, back into the Kommandant's office. I slammed the door. I ran into the bathroom and crouched in the corner. My face was hot, and the tiles couldn't cool it. There was blood on my hands, on my dress. I grabbed the cloths and scrubbed at my stained hands, but I couldn't get all the blood off. That's when I cried. That was the only time. And even then, it didn't make any difference.

"It won't make any difference," said one of them. "She won't do it."

"Yes, she will."

They held me in a chair. They'd already cut my hand. With one of their daggers, in my palm: a six-pointed star. The cut was still throbbing, but most of the blood had stopped. They thought the cutting would do me in. They were wrong. I didn't lose consciousness. I didn't talk. They didn't like that. Now they were going to play a new game. The tall one nodded. He motioned them, and they pulled my dress up, over my thighs, to my waist. Two others grabbed my ankles and knees, forcing my legs apart. He bent his tall, thin body and leaned close to me, blowing smoke in my face.

"She won't change her mind," said one.

The tall one smiled. I knew about him: this was his favorite game. He took his cigarette and lowered it until it was between my legs, close to my thigh. I could feel its heat. I struggled against the hands that held me.

"Yes," they said. "Do it."

I stared at the scar on his face, and imagined that I'd put it there. When he touched the tip of the cigarette to the inside of my thigh, I bit my lip so I wouldn't cry out. That didn't help the third time.

"This is too slow," said someone from behind me.

The tall one put the cigarette back in his mouth and nodded. He grabbed my panties, slicing them from me with his service dagger. The two holding my knees reached out their hands to touch me, but he pushed them away. One holding my shoulder put his hand down between my legs and grabbed my hair, pulling roughly upward. The two holding my knees spread my legs further apart. One of them rubbed himself against my calf in his excitement. The other drooled on my thigh. Another one from behind put his arm around me, shoving his hand down into my brassiere. They were all breathing heavily, panting, pressing their heavy bodies against me. The tall one knelt and took the cigarette from his mouth. He put it between my legs. He was smiling. The one holding me by the hair pulled harder. One of them moaned at the sight of me. The glowing tip of the cigarette moved closer. Closer. I felt its heat.

I didn't need the touch of the cigarette to tell them everything they wanted to know.

And more.

"What do you want to know?" said the Kommandant, putting down his pen and turning his chair.

Ilse stood beside him, wearing her nightgown, holding her doll by the arm. She leaned on the arm of the Kommandant's chair. Hans stood nearby, taking small bites from a cookie. He looked around the office as he chewed. He looked over at the Kommandant. Ilse sagged against the chair. Hans came over to me.

"What kind of party is it?" said Ilse.

"A dinner party," said the Kommandant.

"A birthday dinner party?" said Ilse.

"No."

"Why can't children come?"

"Because it's only for grownups."

The Kommandant looked in my direction.

"Hans, come away from there."

Hans bit the arm of the gingerbread woman he was holding. He stood right in front of me. As he chewed, he held out the remaining cookie. I didn't move.

"I'm a big girl," said Ilse. "I'm bigger than Hans. Why can't I come to the dinner party?"

"Hans, come away from there," said the Kommandant.

Hans looked over at the Kommandant, then turned back to me. He took his gingerbread woman in both hands. He broke her head away from the rest of her body.

"I'm not sleepy," said Ilse. "I'm not a baby like Hans."

"It's a grownup party, Ilse, and you're not a grownup."

Hans held out the gingerbread woman's head. I looked at him.

"Hans," said the Kommandant.

I snatched the offering.

The Kommandant got up from his desk. Hans took another bite of the gingerbread woman's body. I put the broken piece down the front of my dress. Ilse whined as she followed the Kommandant across the room. The Kommandant picked up Hans.

"But why can't I come to the party?"

"Tell Mommy that Daddy's too busy to play."

"But she said we're in the way of the party," said Ilse. "Let me stay up for the party. I'm not sleepy."

The Kommandant took Ilse's hand and walked toward the door. Her doll scraped along on the floor behind them. Hans looked over the Kommandant's shoulder at me. Ilse started to cry as the Kommandant opened the office door. He set Hans beside Ilse.

"It's not fair," she said.

The Kommandant put Hans' hand in hers.

"You're a mean Daddy," said Ilse.

"Daddy has too much work to play," said the Kommandant as he guided them out.

Ilse began to cry. The Kommandant closed the door. He returned to his desk. Crying loudly, Ilse stomped up the stairs. Hans began to cry as well. The Kommandant picked up his pen. I touched my hand to my breast: there, beneath the thin dress, the gingerbread woman's head was still warm.

"What do you have under your clothes?" said the *SS-Mann* to us as I came down the street, with an elderly woman and a young boy close beside me.

A *Gestapo,* leaning on his black car, glanced at us. He was very tall. He threw down his cigarette and strolled over. Several guards followed him.

"What's under your clothes?" said the first guard.

The three of us stopped walking. The guard was looking at the young boy, not at me or at the other woman. The *Gestapo* arrived. He lit another cigarette. He was always smoking. He had a scar on the side of his face. One of the guards poked the boy with his rifle.

"I don't have anything under my clothes," said the older woman, and the guard scowled at her.

"Who asked you?" he said, turning back to the boy.

I said nothing.

"Open your coat," said the tall *Gestapo* with the scar and the cigarette.

The boy didn't move.

"You heard him," said the *SS-Mann,* shoving the boy. "Take off your coat."

The boy stared straight ahead. The guards yanked him closer, roughly pulling open his coat and shirt. His body was laden with food: small bags of flour, smaller bags of sugar, apples.

"Oh, ho, a smuggler," said the *Gestapo.*

The boy tried not to tremble as the guards relieved him of his burdens. The *Gestapo* drew heavily on his cigarette and eyed the boy closely. He leaned forward to lift the boy's pants leg.

"What's this?" he said.

A small bottle of milk was tied to the boy's leg. The guards frowned.

"It's for his baby sister," said the older woman.

I said nothing.

The *Gestapo* pulled out his pistol. He shot the boy. The old woman looked up at him. He shot her. He didn't look at me. The guards carried the food back to their *Kübelwagen.* One of the bags of sugar fell, ripping open as it hit the ground, spilling its sweet crystals. The German cursed and kicked at it. The *Gestapo* lit another cigarette and put it between his lips. The bodies lay, open-mouthed, in the street. I walked away from them.

"Don't you walk away from me," said the Kommandant.

Without getting up from his chair, he grabbed my wrist and yanked me back.

"You have to earn your keep."

I turned my face away as he forced me to my knees, as he pulled me to him. His mouth was greasy from his lunch, and his uniform smelled of smoke. I looked at the table. There were bits of chicken still clinging to the bones, and the marmalade jar wasn't completely empty. There were breadcrumbs on the tablecloth next to his plate, and some butter glistened on his knife. After he fell asleep, I could feast on what he'd left on the table. The Kommandant wrapped his fingers in my hair and turned my face from the table, toward him. He spread his legs apart, dragged me close, and hooked his legs around me. He unfastened his pants.

I made my neck rigid, staring past his shoulder at the wall behind him. He put more pressure on the back of my head. An opera record was playing on the phonograph in the corner.

Ah, della traviata sorridi al desio,
A lei deh perdona, tu accoglila, o Dio.

(Ah, pity the fallen one, and send her consolation,
pardon her transgressions, and send her salvation, O God!)

The Kommandant thrust his hips upward as he forced my head down.

Ah, tutto, tutto fini, oh, tutto, tutto fini.

(Ah, it all, it all ends, oh, it all, it all ends.)

The opera's music flooded the room, but my mouth couldn't form the words.

"What did you say?" said Josef as he turned toward the guard standing beside him.

"She is beautiful," said the guard, his fingers gripping his rifle. "Just like they said."

The adjutant shrugged.

"I've heard about her," said the guard, "but this is the first time I've ever seen her. Josef, don't you think she's beautiful?"

"Maybe," he said, "for a Jew. Now, here's what I want you to do, Karl. These documents came from the Camp..."

"Are you sure I'm allowed in here?" said the guard, glancing around. "Where's the Kommandant?"

"He's gone for the day," said the adjutant. "Look, Karl, I know these documents are forgeries. What I don't know is who's making them. Can you find out?"

"Sure," he said, slipping the documents into an inside pocket. "Anything for you."

"Don't worry. I'll pay you."

"You're my cousin. You wouldn't cheat me," he said, and he looked back at me. "I wish I were the Kommandant, just for an hour, just so I could do her."

"She's a whore," said the adjutant. "And a Jew."

"But a pretty one. I'd give anything to do her, Josef, wouldn't you?"

"If I did her," he said, "she'd know what a real German is like."

"You'd take care of her all right," said his cousin, laughing. "She wouldn't survive you."

"Wait till he gets tired of her," said the adjutant. "Then she'll get what she deserves."

"You'll show her what's what, eh?"

"I know how to take care of Jewish whores."

"You'll take care of her, huh?"

"She'll wish she'd never been born."

"The Kommandant's gone for the day?" said the cousin. "The whole day?"

They both looked at me, but the adjutant had a cold look. I pressed my body harder against the wall.

"What do you think?"

"You're not doing her unless I do," said the adjutant.

He pulled up his jacket to undo his pants. His cousin dropped his rifle and ripped open his own uniform. The adjutant grabbed my arm.

"But let me go first, or there'll be nothing left," said the cousin. "Let me go first."

"First, tell me, how you're going to take care of the girl," said the Kommandant's friend as he emptied the bottle of champagne.

"How did Rudi do his?" said the Kommandant.

"Sent her to the gas. No, wait. Maybe he shot her. I'll ask around. What are you going to do?"

"I don't know," said the Kommandant, pouring himself Cognac. "I'm not finished with her yet."

"Such an extraordinary face," said his friend. "Even now."

"Yes," said the Kommandant.

"I could get you some cyanide tablets," said his friend. "From my cousin. Three should be enough."

"I'll just shoot her," said the Kommandant. "It'll be quicker."

"It'll be quicker, *Herr Major,* to look at the list of foods that we are allowed to have," said the man standing in line in front of me. "Since there's nothing under 'permitted foods', it'll take less time."

"Coffee's not on the list of forbidden foods," said the man behind me.

His body brushed my shoulder as he leaned around to address the German.

"We can have coffee," he said.

"Jews aren't entitled to coffee," said the German. "You should know that."

"It's not on the list."

The German pointed at me. The men turned to look at me.

"Only non-Jews, like her, can have coffee," said the German. "Now get on with you. Both of you. No coffee for Jews."

"I want my coffee," said the man in the front of the line.

"It's not on the list," said the man behind me. "It's not forbidden."

"I'm putting it on the list," said the German. "And I'm fining you for disturbing the public order."

He scribbled something down, then looked up at me, a smile on his face.

"Can I help you, *Fräulein*?"

"Coffee's not forbidden," said the first man, pushing me aside. "Give us our coffee."

"We have our rights," said the second. "Even under your laws."

Two guards came up behind the protesters. The crowd moved uneasily as the men were shuffled out of line, as they were shoved around the side of the building. The crowd grew quiet. After two shots were fired, the guards returned. Alone. The officer smiled at me as he took my ration coupons.

"Now, *Fräulein*," he said, "what can I do for you?"

"What can I do for you, Dieter?" said the Kommandant.

"Never mind."

"You're my best friend. Name it: it's yours."

The Kommandant's friend stumbled, into the table. He was looking at me. His foot knocked the Kommandant's fallen glass, and it rolled across the floor. Neither man paid attention to it. The Kommandant, moving unsteadily, followed his friend.

"Tell me, Dieter. What is it you want for your birthday?"

"What I want, what I really want," he said, standing in front of me, "is one time with her."

"The girl?"

"After you're done with her."

"You want the girl?"

"Just once, and only after you're through with her."

The Kommandant sat on the floor in front of me. His friend did the same, taking my hand in his. He gazed at me as he stroked the back of my hand. The Kommandant frowned.

"I didn't know you wanted a Jew, Dieter."

"Only this Jew. Just once, before you send her to the gas."

"Maybe I'm not going to send her to the gas," said the Kommandant. "Maybe I'm going to shoot her."

"Just once before you shoot her. She's so beautiful. I've never had a Jew like her."

When the Kommandant gripped his friend's shoulder, his friend dropped my hand. I pulled it tight against my body. The Kommandant nodded. He looked at me, at his friend. The Kommandant leaned closer, closer, between the two of us.

"I would never take anything of yours."

"I know that."

"I love you like a brother."

"I love you like I love myself," said the Kommandant.

"I wasn't trying to insult you."

"You've never insulted me."

"You asked me what I wanted for my birthday."

"And you told me. You want the girl."

"But she's yours."

"What's mine is yours."

"Max, do you mean it?"

"But only once. Only one time. Because it's your birthday. And because I love you."

"Max," said the other, grasping the Kommandant's hand. "Max."

"But only once," said the Kommandant.

"Isn't once enough?" said the voice on the telephone. "How many times a day are you going to call?"

The phone was pressed hard against my ear, and the line made crackling sounds. I hadn't turned on the lights, so it was dark, except for the faint glimmer of moonlight that came in through the windows. The house creaked and groaned in the darkness around me.

"Does that mean that David's not there?" I said.

"David's not here. He's working."

"It's the middle of the night."

"It's not the middle of the night here."

"Oh, I forgot. Do you know when David will be back?"

"When he's done working."

"When will that be?"

"I don't know. I told you that the first time you called."

"Could you give him a message?"

"I already did."

"You told him I called?"

"I told him this morning. And yesterday morning. And the day before that. But I'll tell him again."

"I'm sorry for disturbing you."

The line was broken when she hung up the phone. I replaced the receiver and stood in the hall. In the dark. Now it was quiet, and I didn't hear the noise that had woken me. I went to the front door: yes, it was locked. I moved the curtains.

The car was there again.

I raced upstairs, my heart pounding. I yanked open the bottom bureau drawer and grabbed the pistol. It was already loaded. It was always loaded. I readied it for firing as I rushed back down the stairs, to the window beside the front door. Breathing heavily, I pushed the curtains aside.

The car was gone.

After an hour I went upstairs, pulled a blanket from the cupboard, and returned to my post by the front door. I sat there, my face next to the glass, my hands tense around the gun.

The car didn't come back that night.

The gun and I didn't sleep.

Chapter Nine

I didn't sleep. I was only waiting for the Kommandant to begin to snore. As soon as he was dreaming, I slipped out of the bed and retrieved the dagger from behind the chest. I didn't need the light as I crept down the stairs to the Kommandant's office, his service dagger pressed close to my breast. The clock in the main hall ticked too slowly: someone must've forgotten to wind it. My bare feet slipped across the wooden floors. The house was empty. The Kommandant slept.

I opened the door to his office. I went to the bathroom, to the sink. I freed some folded papers from their hiding place behind the mirror. I went over to the desk. I shoved the dagger into the space between the drawer and the lock. The thick blade unlatched it and the drawer opened. The knife easily managed the other drawers as well.

The arrest and deportation orders were in the top left-hand drawer. I laid the knife on the desk. I unfolded the hidden papers and attached one of them to an order. I attached the second to another order, further down in the stack. I rubbed my hand over the papers, trying to flatten out the creases. I slipped all the pages back into the desk drawer, then I gently pushed it closed.

Another dagger lay on the desk, taunting me. *Blut und Ehre:* Blood and honor. I picked up the dagger. *Blut und Ehre.* It sliced cleanly across the palm of my hand. I shoved the dagger under the latch, yanked the drawer back open, and tore the papers from the arrest orders.

They were stained with my blood.

```
Blut und Ehre
Meine Ehre heisst treue
Kazett
```

No matter what I tried to write, the same words appeared every time I sat at the typewriter.

```
Kazett
Kazett
Kazett
```

I stared at the letters, stark against the white sheet, but they didn't change into some other letters, to some other words. Always the same.

Kazett

I opened the packet of cigarettes I'd bought. I put a cigarette between my lips. Though I scraped match after match into flames, my hand shook so much that I couldn't light the cigarette. I took it out of my mouth, put it down on the desk, and looked at the typewriter again.

Kazett

I crossed the room and turned on the phonograph. When the music poured into the room, I sat in the chair beside the fireplace, my arms hugging myself, my eyes closed.

Così alla misera, ch'è un dì caduta,
Di più risorgere speranza è muta.
Se pur benefico le indulga Iddio
L'uomo implacabile per lei sarà.

(Thus, to the wretched, who falls, frail and erring,
when she would rise once again, hope is silent.
Though Heaven's indulgent, conferring its pardon,
Man will be unforgiving to her.)

I left the music on while I returned to the typewriter, but even the music couldn't shove those other words away. I don't know how long I sat there, trapped between the words on the record and the words on the page in the typewriter. The breeze from the open windows was warm on my skin. When the phone rang, it was David.

"I was worried when I didn't hear from you," I said.

"I did call, twice. There was no answer."

"You sound tired."

"Yes, I've been working hard."

"Is the teaching going well?"

"Yes."

"And the book?"

"Yes. Everything's fine. How's your writing?"

"You know I can't write when you're not here."

"You haven't been writing with me there," he said.

Morro — Morro la mia memoria Non fia ch'ei maledica
Se le mie pene orribili Vi sia chi almen gli dica.

(I die — I die, let my memory not be dirtied by him,
but let my woes and dark trials all be related to him.)

"Have you had enough time alone yet?"

"Have you had enough time to write yet?" said David.

"Why can't they just leave us alone?" I said.

The *Kapos* shoved us out into the Camp's yard, shouting and hitting. At tables outside, several women were giving fellow inmates tattoos, on our inner left forearms. As the inmates who were already marked stumbled away, they held out their arms, displaying the grotesque letters and numbers, permanently scrawled in jagged lines.

"Come over here," said a young inmate named Anna, and she pulled on my arm. "She does the best. Over here."

"How can one tattoo be better than another?" I said.

But I let her guide me to a different line. She worked on the rocks with me. She had a gentleness about her that made me forget the things around us.

"Moishe's covers his whole forearm," said one of the women.

"And Aharon's, it's even on the back of his forearm."

"How hideous of them, to do this to us," I said.

Anna tugged at me.

"Here, look at mine," said Anna.

She held out her arm. There, on her inner left forearm, very dainty, in carefully formed letters and numbers, her tattoo. She pulled me toward the furthest table.

"This girl does the smallest, and in the straightest line. I looked them all over yesterday before I picked her to do mine."

"You already have one," I said. "Why do you have to get another?"

Anna shrugged.

"They told us the numbers were wrong," said Anna. "I want her to do the second one, too. She does it best. If you compliment her work, she'll be very careful."

I frowned at her.

"How can you act so happy? They're mutilating us," I said. "Have you gone mad?"

"Even the Germans wouldn't be stupid enough to go through all this trouble and then kill us," said Anna.

And with a smile, she held out her arm to the needle.

I stretched out my hand and touched the papers on the Kommandant's desk. The Kommandant was in the Camp. So was his adjutant. There was a great commotion from the arrival of the latest transport. Guards and dogs and inmates scurried everywhere. The noise from the Camp battered the windows of the office. I was alone.

I sat in the Kommandant's chair, at his desk. The folder lay before me. I opened it.

> The assault sweep detachments dispatched today also had only minor success. Twenty-nine (29) new bunkers were discovered, but some of them no longer had occupants. Many bunkers can only be discovered when their locations are betrayed by other Jews.

Outside, the dogs were barking ferociously, but the house was quiet. The Kommandant's wife wasn't home. She'd taken the children with her. I turned the page.

> If Jews are ordered to leave bunkers voluntarily, they almost never obey. In a skirmish that developed around noon, the bandits again resisted, using Molotov cocktails, pistols, and homemade hand grenades.

There was shouting, cursing, the rattle of machine guns. The dogs were frantic. I looked out the window, but saw only a mass of black uniforms occasionally interrupted by huddled, naked bodies. I turned back to the documents on the Kommandant's desk.

> As soon as some of the inhabitants were about to be searched, one of the females — as so often happens — put her hand under her skirt, pulled out an oval hand grenade from her underpants, pulled the safety pin, threw the grenade into the group of men conducting the search, and herself jumped for cover.

As I was reading, the door opened.

"You have to obey me. I'm the Kommandant."

He pulled his chair around to the side of the desk where I sat and slipped his pistol out of its holster. He held the gun out to me.

"I order you to do it."

When I didn't move, he put the gun in my lap.

"You have to do it," he said. "I can't."

He opened the third bottle of champagne. My glass was full. He urged it into my hand, up to my mouth. I took a sip, then returned the glass to the desk. The Kommandant drank from the bottle. The gun was warm and heavy in my lap.

"Take it," he said.

He nudged the gun farther up my thighs.

"Free me."

He put the champagne bottle down and picked up the gun. He snapped the two circles on its top up and back: it was readied for firing. He pointed the gun at his chest, took my hand and placed it on the gun. I kept my hand limp. He stood, pulling me up with him, his palms crushing my fingers around the warm metal. He yanked the gun toward him until my arm was rigid, my elbow locked. The muzzle butted his chest. He straightened his shoulders, took a deep breath, and raised his chin.

"Free me," he said. "Fire."

He released my hand. I lowered the weapon.

"No, no. Fire."

The gun hit the floor. The Kommandant shook his head as he looked down at it.

I stood, absolutely still.

The gun lay there, between us.

I lay there, absolutely still, only sometimes turning my face away so his breath wouldn't hit me. He didn't use his hands to touch me anywhere. He gripped the edge of the cot. The steel frame pinched my shoulders and back with each hard movement. With each of his thrusts, his sweat dampened my dress. His uniform scratched. His hair, when he pushed against me, got into my mouth. I turned my face away, but I said nothing. I did nothing. When I closed my eyes, he was nothing. All of it was nothing.

The other stood nearby, watching, and I could hear his breathing: short and fast. His hands moved on himself. I could hear both of them: both moved in a fierce and furious rhythm, but only one moved on me. The smell of them made my throat tighten: alcohol, smoke, sweat, man. That made it come back to me. I closed my eyes again, and held my breath, to lose myself.

He finished. He drooled a moment against my neck. As he shoved himself away, the other approached.

"One more time?" he said.

"As often as you can: this is the only time."

"I'll just do it this one time, Mama," I said. "Don't worry."

"You can't. You can't go there," said my mother.

I put on my coat.

"He's the worst of the Germans," she said.

"Mama, didn't you hear the order?"

"Samuel, don't let her go to that man. You know what they say about him."

I yanked the paper from my father's hand and read it aloud.

> This is to inform you that you are to join this transport. You are to report on Sunday 18 June from 7:00 a.m. but no later than 6:00 p.m. to the transport staging area.

"Samuel, we can't just stand here and let her go to that man. You know what they say he does."

> You are to proceed immediately after receipt of this order to prepare your baggage: two (2) pieces of hand baggage — total weight thirty (30) kilograms. This weight isn't to be exceeded as there will be no help to assist during baggage collection for this transport.

"Samuel, what are you going to do?" said my mother.

"What can we do?" said my father. "This is the end."

"You don't know that," I said.

"They told us to bring luggage," said my father. "You know the ones who take luggage are the ones who never come back."

I shoved the order into my pocket. I rummaged through my mother's purse until I found an old tube of lipstick: red. That was good, but it was almost gone. I scooped some of the color out of the tube and smoothed it over my lips. I pinched my cheeks, to bring the blood to the surface. As I put my hand on the doorknob, my mother grasped my arm.

"Samuel, don't just stand there."

"What can I do, Hannah? You know how strong-willed she is."

"But he might send her with us," said my mother, tugging at me.

"What can we do?" said my father.

I slammed the door.

"What can we do?" I said. "What can any of us do? We're only prisoners."

Rebekah stood there, looking at me, as the other inmates relieved me of the bread-crusts and potato-bits I carried. They shoved the scraps of food into their mouths and choked them down. Sharón spat at me when I offered her a rind of hardened cheese: another inmate snatched it from my hand.

"Is that all you brought?" said Rebekah.

"Probably," said Sharón.

"No," I said. "I told you I'd do it, and I did."

I pulled the small package from inside my dress. Rebekah opened the box, and she nodded.

"That's not enough for all of us," said Sharón.

"That's all I could get," I said. "He keeps his gun with him all the time."

"It'll do," said Rebekah.

"It's not enough," said Sharón. "She did it on purpose, to foil us."

"It'll never work anyway," I said.

"It'll work," said one of the men.

"We have grenades," said Sharón. "And guns."

"All we need is to get the Kommandant alone," said Rebekah.

"The Kommandant? But you said..."

"Or with his adjutant," said Sharón.

"Yes," said Rebekah, counting out the bullets among them. "We could handle the two of them."

When I put my hand on Rebekah's arm, she looked up at me.

"You said it was for the guards, at the Bakery."

"Maybe we changed our minds," said Rebekah.

"Maybe we lied," said Sharón, and she laughed.

"You can't do it," I said. "They'll raze the entire Camp if you hurt him."

"It's better than waiting for him to kill us," said Rebekah.

They scratched and dug at the wet earth until they had created a hollow deep enough for the weapons and ammunition. They wrapped them in scraps of cloth and placed them in the shallow hole. Then they pushed the damp dirt over them.

"You don't stand a chance," I said.

"We'll do the best we can," said Rebekah. "After all, you wouldn't get us the pistols."

"The cabinet's locked. I told you that."

"You tell us a lot of things," said Sharón. "It doesn't make them true."

"When is he going to town again?" said Rebekah.

"It's a mistake to ask her," said Sharón.

"She's the only one with access to him," said Rebekah.

"She'll warn him," said Sharón.

"I doubt it," said Rebekah.

"It'll never work," I said.

"Two Czechs blew up Heydrich," said Sharón. "If they can do that, we can do the Kommandant."

"Two Czechs blew up Heydrich, and the Germans already executed over 150 Jews in Berlin for it," I said, "and all the Jews in Lidice..."

"You needn't say anymore," said Rebekah. "I think we understand each other."

"I'm trying to help you," I said.

"We don't listen to the Kommandant's whore," said Sharón.

And they all turned away from me.

"Don't turn away," said the inmate as he yanked on my arm. "Don't you understand? You're free. They're gone."

"Who's gone?"

"The Germans. The officers. The Kommandant."

Bombs screamed through the sky and hit the ground just beyond the Camp with tremendous explosions. The building groaned and shook with each blast. Artillery fire sounded almost constantly, and the cries and shouts of inmates filled the air between the whining bombs and their fierce explosions.

"They've abandoned the Camp," said the inmate, pulling at me again.

"Abandoned the Camp? The Kommandant?"

"There are only a few guards left, and they're running away now."

"I heard Hans crying, just this morning."

"The Kommandant's gone. He left in the middle of the night."

"I heard the Kommandant's wife, calling for Ilse."

"They're gone, I tell you. Now there's only a few guards left."

"He's gone?"

"They're all gone. We're free."

More inmates rushed into the office, their arms loaded with weapons and food. They were dirty and haggard, and their eyes burned with a strange light. A few of them wore German jackets, or caps. One of them, limping and shouting in a language I didn't know, shot out the glass in the weapons cabinet. One broke open the liquor cabinet and the others rushed to it, grabbing the bottles and pouring the liquor into their gaping mouths. Another sat himself in the Kommandant's chair and shot out the windowpanes. Another gouged the wood of the Kommandant's desk with an ax. They were all screaming and yelling and pushing and tearing at everything around them. The first inmate caught me by the shoulders and shook me so hard that my head rocked on my neck.

"We're free. Don't you understand? We're free."

I didn't move.

Uncle Jacob and my father didn't move, even though I called to them.

"Uncle Jacob? Papa?"

The university students dragged the books from the carts and trucks. They tossed the books onto the bonfire burning in the middle of the square. The windows of the Opera House glowed with the reflected flames.

"No more cultural decadence," said the students.

More books sailed into the flames.

"No more false ideas of freedom."

The pile of burning books grew larger.

"Maybe you shouldn't emigrate right now, Samuel," said Uncle Jacob. "Wait till things calm down."

"Papa. Uncle Jacob," I said, pulling at their coats.

"My God, what are you doing here?" said Uncle Jacob after he turned around.

"Mama's worried," I said. "And so is Aunt Naomi. They want you to come home."

"How did you even find us?" said Uncle Jacob. "You're just a child."

"Come home," I said. "Papa."

"How did Naomi let you come out?" said Uncle Jacob. "She should know better. This was a bad time for you to come visit us."

A diminutive German, smartly dressed but with a crippled foot, limped over to one of the trucks. The students gripped his arms and legs and raised him until he stood above them, on the back of the vehicle.

"We must stop the Jewish penetration of the professions," he said.

His fists beat the night air. The students gazed up at him, applauding and cheering. The fire snapped and hissed.

"The Jewish hordes must be considered unconditionally exterminable."

The crowd roared. The flames spat. Book after book sailed through the darkness and landed in the fire. Their pages curled and blackened. Smoke and heat filled the air.

"Papa."

I tugged at him. Uncle Jacob took my father's other arm and we dragged him through the crowd. When my father stumbled over a fallen book, I saw that his face was wet with tears. The German on the truck raised his arms to the night sky, and the students cheered as his voice cut the darkness around the flames.

"When we depart," he said, "let the earth tremble."

Chapter Ten

I was trembling, from the cold water. When my skin was completely wet, the *Kapo* shoved soap and a soiled rag at me.

"Make sure you get all the filth off, you dirty Jew," she said.

The smell of the harsh soap stung my nostrils. The rag was stained brown, but not by dirt. Wherever there was a scratch, the soap burned. I rubbed and scraped, until my skin was red. I slipped once, cracking my elbow and shoulder against the stone-wall: there would be a bruise. The *Kapo* sneered. She smoked cigarettes and stared at me as I scrubbed the Camp off my skin.

"Don't forget your hair," she said. "I mean, your head."

I washed my scalp vigorously, tilting my head back to keep the lather from dripping. It didn't help. The soap slid down my face and burned my eyes. The *Kapo* reached in, yanked away the soap, and flipped on the cold water. Its icy spray felt like needles. The soap and the cold pricked my skin raw. After the *Kapo* turned off the water, I stood there shivering. She motioned me to turn around. Above the door, in red letters, was a sign: *Unreine Seite.* Unclean Side. The *Kapo* smashed me with her baton, then threw the soap at me.

"It's the Kommandant, you stupid Jew, not one of your boyfriends," she said. "You'd better do it again."

"They've done it again," said the adjutant, rushing into the Kommandant's office, without knocking.

It was dark. The Kommandant sat up on the cot. The empty bottle fell off the cot, onto the floor, but it didn't break. The Camp's siren began to wail. The Kommandant groaned and covered his eyes when the adjutant turned on the lights.

"What is it, Josef? What time is it? Is it another escape?"

The adjutant glared at me as the Kommandant reached for his uniform jacket, lying on the floor. The Kommandant was wearing his shirt and pants.

"Worse than an escape," said the adjutant. "They've blown up the ovens."

"What?"

The Kommandant's body instantly straightened, though he winced when he put his weight on his leg, and his face lost its dazed expression.

"And they set Crematorium Four on fire."

The Kommandant shoved his arms into his jacket. As he buttoned it, the adjutant grabbed the Kommandant's boots from under the cot.

"Are the guards getting..."

"The machine guns. Yes, sir."

"And the dogs."

"Yes, sir. They've surrounded the yard."

The adjutant held the boots steady. The Kommandant forced his feet into them while he was buckling on his holster with its weapons. I gathered up the blankets and wrapped them around me. Lying on the cot, I pulled my legs up, close to my chest. I pressed my shoulders and back against the wall. The Kommandant unlocked his weapons cabinet for more ammunition. After he loaded his pistol, he closed the case.

"How much damage?" he said.

"The flames were coming through the roof in several places, but we can't tell any more until morning."

"Why not? What's wrong with the spotlights?"

"Too much smoke," said the adjutant.

The Kommandant picked up his field-glasses and went to the windows. His adjutant pressed close behind him. Already, without the glasses, even I could see the glow of the fire on the horizon: red and fierce against the black of night, with the smell of smoke creeping in between the windows and their frames. The Kommandant hit the field-glasses against his thigh, then dropped them into his chair. He turned and strode toward the door. Fire, in his Camp. Fire, glowing on the horizon, burning in his own Camp. Fire, disrupting his work and his sleep, its glow mocking him, in his very own Camp.

"Damned Jews," he said.

The glow of the burning candles was in every window. I pressed my face against the glass and saw the glowing points in other windows. I smiled.

"What are you doing?" said my father. "What's happening?"

"The Germans executed some of our young men this morning, for no reason," I said. "We're protesting the German action."

"Are all the Jews putting candles in their windows?" said my mother.

She wrung her hands as she followed me to the front door. She hovered by me as I slipped my shoes on.

"Is it safe?" she said. "Maybe we should blow out some of the candles. We might need them. One would be enough, wouldn't it?"

I rushed out into the street, without a coat. The cold air slapped my skin, but I didn't notice. My mother stood in the open doorway, and my father came up behind her. They called to me. In the middle of the street, I turned around and around. In every window, up and down the street, candles burned. Their flames formed a line of white against the darkness, a line of fire in the night, on either side, in every window. I hugged myself, but it wasn't to keep off the chill. Those candles warmed me. But the air was so cold, it brought tears to my eyes.

"Samuel, make her come in," said my mother from the doorway, "before somebody sees her."

"Come in," said David.

He was on the front porch: I heard his voice through the open window. I stopped typing and rushed to the head of the stairs. David set down the luggage, beside the door. The little girl was with him.

"It's all right," said David. "This is where we live. Rachel? We're here."

He took her hand and eased her into the house. As I came down the stairs, she gripped his hand tightly. She hid her face behind his arm. David saw me, and he looked down at the girl.

"This is Althea," he said.

She was so tiny, so frail. Her fingers were leaving indentations in the back of David's hand.

"She lost both her parents, and her grandparents, in the war," he said. "In the Camps."

When I knelt before her, she clung to him.

"This is Rachel," he said. "I told you about her. Remember?"

She peeked out at me from behind his sleeve. She was very thin. Her eyes looked too large for her head, and there were sores and scars on her face and neck. Her cheeks were sunken. She seemed nothing but bones. I tried to say something, but the words got caught in my throat. I didn't even know her language. I reached out my hand, but I was afraid to touch her. I sat on my heels before her, my hands in my lap, and she stared at me. She held onto David, her cheek pressed against his leg, and she stared at me with those eyes.

"Althea," I said.

She looked up at David.

"She has no one, Rachel," he said. "No one at all."

"No one, and I mean *no one* has gone into that office more than once," said the *Kapo.*

The two of us slipped and slid across the Camp's yard. She swung her baton with each step.

"No one's been with him more than once," she said. "So don't think you're anything special, Jew-cow."

I was wearing a clean dress, with no tears or patches, and no bloodstains. A red scarf covered my shaved head. I had shoes to walk in. He had sent for me. There were no clouds in the sky. The sun was shining, and little birds fluttered down from the clear, cloudless sky. He had sent for me. I was going to him. When the *Kapo* hit me on the arm with the baton, I looked at her.

"Jewish pig," she said.

The little birds chirped and sang. The *Kapo* hit me again.

"He'll tire of you as quickly as the others," she said.

The *Kapo* and I walked beside the electric fence. The *Kapo* spat at those who had gone into the wire. They were the young ones. Their hands still clung to the steel mesh, and their faces gazed up at the empty sky. I stepped very carefully in the uneven clay. I didn't want to soil myself. Not now.

The Kommandant's adjutant was standing on the other side of the yard, talking to one of the guards. They looked at us when we approached. The *Kapo* saluted, but the adjutant frowned at her. At me. After he'd dismissed her and the *Kapo* had gone, the adjutant's sneer revealed his teeth.

"Filthy Jewish whore," he said, in his language.

The guard beside him nodded.

"There's no end to them."

There was no end to the words. They gushed from me, all day, all night. In the end I abandoned sleep, and the typewriter, and wrote by hand. It was faster. But still I couldn't keep up with the words. They tore the white sheets, staining them. The pages darkened under the weight of the words, and the stack of paper beside the typewriter grew. Still the words came. I found more ink in David's office. More paper. The pen scratched on into the night. Every night. The words burst from me.

"Burst?" said the Kommandant. "Out of the ground?"

"Yes, sir," said his adjutant.

"The bodies in the Birch Grove burst out of the ground?"

"Yes, Kommandant."

"Didn't you put lime on them?"

"Of course, we did," said the adjutant.

"Then why are they coming out of the ground?"

"From the heat, sir. And from decomposing."

"God damn it," said the Kommandant. "The stench is going to be intolerable."

"It already is, sir."

"Re-bury them," said the Kommandant.

"We already tried that, sir."

"And?"

"The bodies came up again."

The Dead Bodies That Line the Streets lay beside me in the bed when David came up to the bedroom. He opened the door but didn't come in. I put the loose pages of the new manuscript in my lap. I took off my glasses and laid them beside *Survivor: One Who Survives.*

"You're awake," David said.

"Yes."

He closed the door and leaned against it.

"She's finally asleep," he said. "On the floor, with two blankets and a pillow, by the front door."

"Will she be warm enough?"

"I think so."

David walked slowly to the bed.

"New places frighten her."

He picked up *Survivor,* then put it down again, beside the loose pages. When he touched the manuscript, picking up one of its pages, I put my hand on his.

"Not yet," I said.

He nodded. He pushed aside *The Dead Bodies* and *Survivor* to sit on the edge of the bed. I put my glasses on the bedside table. I gathered up the loose pages. David took them from my hands and placed them carefully beside my glasses. I laid my pen on top of the pile.

"You look tired."

"You cut your hair," he said.

My cheeks felt flushed as I looked down. *The Dead Bodies* bumped into my leg as David leaned nearer, as he touched my hair.

"You told me you were never going to cut it again."

His hand brushed the length of my hair. He touched the strap of my nightgown, my bare shoulder, the swell of my breast. I caught his hand and kissed it. I held his hand tightly. I kicked away *The Dead Bodies* and *One Who Survives.* I moved closer to David and placed my fingers against his face. Now the words were there. Now, at last, I might finally tell him everything, so he'd understand, so the words wouldn't be between us anymore, so things could be the way he wanted them to be. I leaned close, till he could feel my breath, so he could hear the words better, and he put his arms around me.

"David," I said.

But he stopped my words with the kisses of his mouth.

My mouth was dry. The stack of paper was heavy in my lap. The bathroom tiles were cold on my legs. A bottle of the Kommandant's liquor sat beside me: he was so drunk most of the time, he wouldn't notice if any of the liquor was missing. The house was very quiet. We were alone, and he was upstairs, asleep. I'd let him kiss me, everywhere. I'd stroked his face and kissed him. I'd put my tongue in his mouth. I'd wrapped my legs around him and breathed his name against his throat. I'd trembled and sighed, as if he'd touched me. He'd cried out, and wept against my breast. He'd sleep a long time.

I looked down at the papers in my lap. I lifted a corner of the first page. I tore off a small piece.

I put it in my mouth.

I swallowed.

I took a drink of his liquor, to wash the words down. It burned my throat and made my eyes water, but it made my mouth less dry. It took only a moment to get the words down. It took forever.

I tore off another piece.

I put his words in my mouth.

"Just a moment," I said after I heard the knock on the door.

The kittens jumped off the kitchen table. I rinsed the flour from my hands. There was another knock: louder, more insistent.

"Just a minute," I said.

I took the towel with me, drying my hands as I went. The kittens rushed into the hallway. There was a man at the door. The sun was bright: I couldn't tell who he was standing at the door, this man, this tall man. He was shadowed, because the sun was so bright behind him. He was very tall. The kittens fell over each other in their race. That made me laugh.

Then I saw who it was.

Then I saw him.

He'd found me.

My heart started to pound. I stood in the hallway, with only the screen door between us. His right hand was behind his back. Without taking his eyes from me, he moved his hand to the front. My fingers tightened on the towel. He was holding a small book. The kittens cried as they rubbed themselves against my ankles. He looked at me a long time before he opened the book, before he started to read. My fingers covered my mouth.

He'd brought *The Dead Bodies* to me.

I didn't need his words to recognize him, even without his uniform. He was greyer than I remembered. His face seemed more lined, craggier, tired: but there was no doubt about who he was. He was the Kommandant. I knew that body, even without the uniform. I knew that voice, even in English. I knew every scent, every scar, every word of him.

I should've known that he'd find me. Perhaps I'd always known it. All the months of hiding, all the years of running away, all the miles I'd put between us: none of it mattered. There was no escape. Not from him. Yes, I knew that. I'd always known it, deep inside. No matter what else I said or did in my life, I knew the Kommandant would find me.

He'd said he would.

He'd said, "No matter what you do, you'll never be free of me."

He'd said, "No matter where you go, I'll be there."

He was the Kommandant.

As the Kommandant ordered, so it was.

The Kommandant stood in the shadows of the front porch. When I saw him, I remembered everything. When I heard his voice, I lost my own. When I was with him, I felt cold.

But I was ready for him.

Before he'd finished his words, I'd taken the pistol from beneath the towel. His left eyelid began to twitch. He said something, but I couldn't understand it. I frowned. He kept talking: it was his language, but they weren't his words. I knew the words that came out of his mouth. They were my words: they were spelled with my skin, my blood, my bones. I knew those words he was giving to me. They were the Kommandant's words, but they were forged with my skin, my blood, my bones. The Kommandant opened his mouth, and *The Dead Bodies* poured out of him.

I readied the gun for firing: *snap, click.*

He closed the book. He took off his reading glasses and slid them into his breast pocket. He nodded, clicked his heels together, and stood straight. He always was a proud man.

"*Ja,*" he said.

He wouldn't close his eyes.

"*Ja.*"

Without opening the screen door, I fired.

I didn't miss.

The Kommandant was flung, in slowed motion, backward, and the book was thrown from his hand. I kept firing. The Kommandant's head cracked on the bottom step. I fired again. Every bullet hit him. Every one, but he never cried out. He wouldn't.

The acrid powder stung my nostrils, and the gun tugged me forward. When I opened the screen door, the kittens ran out. I went down the steps. I stood there, beside him, but not too close. I looked down at him. When he said my name, I fired again. I didn't need him to bring *The Dead Bodies* back to me. I didn't want him to say my name. I fired, again and again, until the gun was empty.

He wouldn't close his eyes. Blood was on his lips, and when he coughed, little bubbles formed in the red. His hand reached out, toward my leg, toward the hem of my dress, but I stepped aside, and he grasped at the air. His mouth moved, but I wouldn't listen to his words. I wouldn't kneel beside him, I wouldn't lean close, I wouldn't feel his hands or his breath on my skin: I didn't want any more of his words. I'd had enough of words. I had enough words to last the rest of my life. I stood there, looking down at him, but I wouldn't listen.

I said nothing. When his eyes became fixed and opaque, I dropped the gun. The weapon lay there, beside *The Dead Bodies,* which had fallen with him. The sun glowed on the pages of the open book. The kittens sniffed warily at him. They cried plaintively as they pressed themselves against my legs. My hair blew across my eyes, but I didn't brush it away.

The Kommandant didn't move.

In my hand, the white towel fluttered in the early morning breeze.

Part Three

The dead know nothing.

Ecclesiastes 9:5

Maximilian Ernst von Walther
(1909-1947)

Descendant of an old Prussian military family, Maximilian Ernst von Walther was born outside Berlin on 28 October 1909. An imaginative and intense student, von Walther displayed considerable powers of leadership and personal magnetism, even at an early age. During his undergraduate years, he acquired a reputation as having a violent temper, but this was generally overlooked by his devoted following, and did not seem to affect his studies. He was awarded his baccalaureate in Germanic literature in 1931. He then went on to study literature at Heidelberg and Berlin. Though he completed the course work for a *Doktorat* in Germanic literature and successfully passed his comprehensive examinations in 1939, von Walther failed to complete his dissertation.

In his youth, von Walther was a prolific writer of poetry, and the poems in his dissertation manuscript show his interest in folklore, German peasantry, *völkisch* and National Socialist ideology, as well as a marked adolescent romanticism. His writings often portray idealized German heroes and unrealistic heroines. His poems are rank with racism, anti-Semitism, and the *völkisch* cult of the peasant. Though he seems never to have attempted to have any of his work published, in 1937 he became a member of the National Socialist Writers' Association (*Reichsschrifttumskammer*).

Well over six feet tall, powerfully built, and considered exceedingly physically attractive, von Walther married only reluctantly. On 12 October 1936, he wed Marta Ottilie Kramer. The only child of a prominent, formerly wealthy German family, she was, by all accounts, fanatically devoted to her husband. By her, von Walther fathered two surviving children: Ilse (born February 1938) and Hans (born January 1942). Three other sons died in infancy: Albert (born January 1937, died April 1937), and twins Karl and Wilhelm (born September 1939, died February and March, respectively, 1940). Each of the three died after contracting a fever of indeterminate origin.

A paternity suit against von Walther was filed by Suzanne Reining in the summer of 1939, but the charges were dropped by the plaintiff later in the year. By his longtime mistress, Dianne Braun, who lived in a Nazi-sponsored *Lebensborn* maternity home, von Walther fathered a son Klaus (born October 1940) who died from injuries suffered in an air raid in February 1944. Von Walther did not attend his son's funeral.

An outspoken nationalist, von Walther was a dynamic and ambitious member of the National Socialist German Workers' Party (*Nationalsozialistische Deutsche Arbeiterpartei,* NSDAP, or, more familiarly, the Nazi Party), which he joined in 1932, and he quickly acquired his colleagues' respect. An expert marksman, he participated in the Blood Purge on 30 June 1934, which came to be known as the Night of the Long Knives, during which twenty-seven leading Nazis, including Ernst Rohm, Chief of Staff of the Storm Troopers or "BrownShirts" (*Sturmabteilungen,* SA), and at least one hundred others were massacred. In 1936, in a simultaneously cunning and brutal move, von Walther publicly denounced Ludwig Beck, the only German general to consistently oppose Hitler. Von Walther denounced Beck again in 1938, just prior to Beck's resignation.

In 1938, von Walther attained the rank of *SS-Hauptsturmführer,* and from this time, the diligent, adaptable, and clever von Walther began his rise, acquiring a mastery of bureaucratic mechanism as well as his superiors' trust. His self-discipline and imposing personality brought him to the attention of Heinrich Himmler, *Reichsführer-SS,* head of the Secret State Police *(Geheime Staatspolizei,* Gestapo), head of the black-uniformed Guard Squadrons (*Schutzstaffeln*, SS; originally, Hitler's personal bodyguards), and second most powerful man in Nazi Germany. Von Walther was promoted to *SS-Sturmbannführer* in 1940. An able and courageous fighter, von Walther was twice severely wounded in battle with partisans and Russians. He was awarded the Iron Cross, First Class, in 1940; the silver Wound Badge and the Roll of Honor Clasp in 1941.

The severity of his injuries the second time prompted Himmler to request von Walther's transfer from the Eastern Front. Once established in the bureaucracy, von Walther evidenced a single-minded dedication to his work and an incredible devotion to the Party. Obviously impressed, Himmler sought to reward von Walther with a position of prominence and real power. It was on Himmler's orders that von Walther first visited Auschwitz in 1941.

As early as 1941, Reinhard Heydrich, the Head of the Security Service of the SS (*Sicherheitsdienst,* SD) had compiled an extensive file on von Walther and was urging an investigation into von Walther's lapses of National Socialist behavior. After Heydrich's assassination (by Czech free agents) in 1942, the investigation of von Walther was relentlessly pursued by Heydrich's successor, Ernst Kaltenbrunner, who openly despised and denigrated von Walther.

The minutes kept by Adolf Eichmann show that von Walther attended the Wannsee Conference on 20 January 1942 (at *Am Grossen Wannsee No. 56),* over which Heydrich presided. The purpose of this conference was to "Solve the Jewish Problem in Europe": in other words, to discuss methods and means of extermination. Von Walther was given the task of researching the lethal dose of hydrogen cyanide, known as Zyklon B; he reported this to conference members as one milligram per kilogram of body weight. Von Walther also reported that the only drawback of Zyklon B was its deterioration in the container within three months, so it could not be stockpiled. Von Walther's conscientious notes were discovered in his files after the war.

His participation in the Wannsee Conference, his participation in the drive against "forest Jews" (comprised of individual escapees, members of the Soviet partisan movement, and members of Jewish resistance units who hid in, and attacked Germans from, the forests) which was launched early in 1942, and his distinguished participation in the Mobile Killing Units *(Einsatzkommandos)* on the Eastern Front garnered for von Walther the respect and admiration of Himmler. In 1942 von Walther was promoted to *SS-Obersturmbannführer* and made Kommandant of his own Concentration Camp *(Konzentrationslager,* or, in the contemporaneous slang, *Kazett:* the German pronunciation of the letters *K-Z).*

As Kommandant, under direct supervision of Richard Glücks, von Walther's unbounded ambition and latent sadism blossomed. Renowned for his innovation and efficiency in the extermination and destruction process, von Walther won both admirers and enemies. Blinded, perhaps, by his own sense of superiority, by his overconfidence in his innate abilities, or by his trust in his superiors' protection, von Walther chose to ignore his enemies, to his own political demise. By 1943, with Kaltenbrunner's approval, von Walther's enemies were openly scheming to secure his downfall.

Von Walther survived two assassination attempts in the Camp by members of the Resistance, though he was injured in the second attack: wounded in the leg by shrapnel from a grenade, von Walther was left with a permanent limp. Because his superiors regarded these assassination attempts, albeit unsuccessful, as an indication of von Walther's loss of control, von Walther tightened his already relentless grip on the Camp's personnel and inmates. It was to no avail, however, since by that time his conflicts with Party members and personal problems had seriously affected his ability to run the Camp and outmaneuver his opponents. By the end of the war, even Himmler, who had been von Walther's most ardent supporter, had abandoned him. Von Walther's closest friend and age-mate, Dieter Hoffmann, was killed in action on 31 December 1944. Thus, by the end of the war, von Walther had few personal supporters and virtually no political ones.

By the time the Allies liberated the Camp, von Walther had already fled. His home and office, however, located on the Camp's grounds, were virtually intact, and a great many incriminating documents were recovered. Among these were two complete manuscripts of verse, discovered under the floorboards of his office. Though the poems in these manuscripts are filled with intimate details of von Walther's personal and professional life, the handwriting of these manuscripts does not exactly match that on the other documents alleged to have been written by von Walther, so it is highly unlikely that the poems were written by him. In addition, the poems in these manuscripts portray Jews sympathetically, an attitude of which von Walther would not have been capable. Up to his death, von Walther steadfastly denied any knowledge of these manuscripts. Nevertheless, many of his detractors denounced von Walther for his betrayal of Nazi principles, insisting that he had composed the manuscripts in their entirety.

As he was one of the most intensely sought war criminals, rumors of von Walther's fate abounded at the close of the war: some claimed he had committed suicide, some that he had escaped (with American help) via Rome to South America, some that he had eluded his captors and fled to the United States. In reality, however, von Walther was captured in Poland after the war. With his typical egotism, he had not even bothered to change his name or to disguise himself. He was charged with war crimes and put on trial at Nuremberg.

During his trial, he was alternately charming and bitter, revealing his incredible egocentrism and powerful charisma. His semantic facility won him the respect of many but exasperated his accusers. At one point, the prosecutor lost his temper and shouted at von Walther: it was the prosecutor who was admonished for unprofessional behavior. Indeed, throughout the trial, despite the graphic revelations and undeniable allegations concerning him, von Walther nevertheless managed to increase his number of admirers and supporters.

Despite his charm and cleverness, von Walther was found guilty of crimes against peace, war crimes, and crimes against humanity committed in the Concentration Camps. In his final statement, von Walther once again displayed the quick intelligence and impressive personality that had contributed to his success in the Nazi Party. No mitigating circumstances were found, however: von Walther was sentenced to death.

Despite appeals, his sentence was not commuted. Von Walther asked permission to be shot rather than hanged, the latter of which was considered shameful for a man in his position. This request was denied. The day before the execution, to the amazement and consternation of his American captors, von Walther handed over to the guards two cyanide capsules which he had until then concealed in his prison cell. On 23 October 1947, unrepentant and proud still, Maximilian Ernst von Walther was executed by hanging at the Concentration Camp where he had served.

Leah Sarah Abramson

(1920-1945?)

A renowned beauty from an early age, Leah Sarah Abramson was born on 18 June 1920 in a small village near Prague, Czechoslovakia. She was the only child, born late, of the accomplished pianist Hannah Sarah Silber and the brilliant mathematician Samuel Isaac Abramson. Between 1934 and 1935, fearing Hitler's spreading influence and to protect their daughter, the Abramsons tried to get Leah adopted by a Christian family. With her fair skin and coloring, Leah could, indeed, have passed as the adoptive family's daughter. The adoption papers were drawn up, but Leah refused to remain with the Gentile family and returned home.

After the Abramsons' elderly, non-Jewish housekeeper was forced to quit their employment, under the Law for Protection of German Blood and Honor (*Gesetz zum Schutze des deutschen Blutes und der deutschen Ehre*, 1935; which actually only forbade Jews from employing German servants under the age of 45), Leah maintained a loving and frequent correspondence with her. Because their former housekeeper was unable to find employment, no doubt due to her advanced age, the Abramson family sent her food and clothing. This continued until, depressed and in ill health, the housekeeper committed suicide. Her death greatly affected Leah, who had considered her part of the family: Leah was despondent for several months afterward.

Her maternal aunt, Miriam, and Miriam's non-Jewish husband Boris were arrested for Race Defilement (*Rassenschande).* Miriam and Boris were forced to endure public scorn and ridicule by standing in the village square wearing placards: on Boris' were the words, "I am a swine who has sexual relations with Jews," while Miriam's read, "I am a Jew. I can get any man into my bedroom." Miriam died after a brutal interrogation by members of the Secret State Police (*Geheime Staatspolizei,* Gestapo), while her husband Boris disappeared in the maze of Concentration Camps.

Leah's paternal uncle, Jacob Abramson, had emigrated with his wife Naomi to Germany in 1925, and Jacob urged Leah's family to join him in Germany. After Czechoslovakia ceded the Sudetenland to Hitler on 1 October 1938, Samuel Abramson was deprived of his university post. On 9/10 November 1938, the small grocery that Jacob had established was destroyed during the Nazi-induced night of violence which came to be known as the Night of the Broken Glass (*Reichskristallnacht*). Along with Jacob and Naomi, the entire Abramson family emigrated to Poland in March

1939, just days before Czechoslovakia agreed to German "protection" of the provinces of Bohemia and Moravia. Later, Jacob, then widowed, emigrated again: first to Hungary and then to America.An accomplished linguist, fluent in several languages (including Czech, Polish, Hungarian, French, Hebrew, Yiddish, and German), Leah excelled in academics. She studied modern languages, history, and philosophy. Under the Law Against Overcrowding of German Schools and Universities (*Gesetz gegen die Überfüllung deutscher Schulen und Hochschulen,* 1933), she was among the final Jewish students expelled. Though she was awarded a university scholarship to study in Poland during the summer of 1939, she was forced to relinquish even her private studies, with Hitler's 1 September invasion of Poland and the start of World War II. By her late teens, however, Leah had already begun writing the poetic works for which she is now famous.

In 1938, she published her first collection of poems: *Cain's Lament,* a series of striking dramatic monologues by Old Testament characters. By 1939, when her second volume of poems, *Ahab's Wife and Other Women,* was published, she had already established herself as a major talent. Incredibly, she continued to write even after the upheavals of emigration and war. In 1942, her last documented book appeared: *Little Birds,* a long poem comprised of several voices and dealing with the Nazi-Jewish conflict. Even at this early age, Leah Abramson was arguably one of the most innovative poets in the European community. By the time of *Little Birds,* she was considered an influential and powerful poet, one whose career was cut short by the Nazis and by World War II.

As openly political in private life as she was in her art, Leah Abramson advocated the establishment of a Jewish state in Palestine, with a Jewish army and unrestricted Jewish immigration. She opposed the total assimilation of Jews into the national community and supported Zionism. Because of her vocal opposition to the Nazis, she was arrested and briefly imprisoned several times, but her prominence as an artist seems to have protected her from German retaliation in the early years.

In 1939, after suffering a series of minor heart attacks, Samuel Abramson rapidly deteriorated, both mentally and physically. His wife, Hannah, who had never been robust, became more frequently ill, leaving Leah not only to fend for herself but to care for them as well. As long as she was able to find employment, Leah worked several part-time jobs in order to help support her ailing parents. Eventually, as the Nazi sphere of influence increased, Leah was forced into smuggling and other Black Market activities in order to get the medications and food the family so desperately needed.

Once the family was forced into the Warsaw Ghetto, Leah's smuggling activities increased, though her own health was beginning to be affected. No longer protected by her reputation as an artist, Leah was under Nazi surveillance. She survived two interrogations by the Secret State Police (*Geheime Staatspolizei,* Gestapo), who suspected her of being a member of the Resistance. The second time, she was imprisoned and tortured by the sadistic Ernst Kaltenbrunner, who later succeeded Reinhard Heydrich as the head of the *Gestapo.* Though her confession, which was obviously obtained under duress and at great physical and emotional cost to her, could not possibly have implicated fellow Resistance members who had been arrested the same night, Leah blamed herself for their capture and subsequent execution. After her experience with Kaltenbrunner, Leah became extremely withdrawn and circumspect. Indeed, members of the Jewish community and members of the *Gestapo* came to believe that she was no longer politically active.

Nevertheless, in 1942, Leah was arrested and charged with smuggling pistols into the Warsaw Ghetto. Out of pettiness and perhaps out of a sense of wounded pride, Kaltenbrunner had Leah's parents deported with her. After their arrival at Treblinka, upon learning that her elderly parents were to be immediately transferred to another Camp, Leah bribed Camp and train guards to allow her on the second transport, with her parents.

Not much is known with certainty of her experiences in the Concentration Camps, though it is clear that she ultimately ended up in the Concentration Camp of Kommandant Maximilian von Walther, one of the most notoriously vicious of the officers. It is also known that her parents, due to their advanced age, were sent to the gas chambers upon arrival. Then fact and rumor converge. There are tales that Leah was a member of the Camp's Underground, tales that she perished in the quarries or of one of the virulent and deadly fevers prevalent in the Camps.

The most persistent rumor, however, is that she became Kommandant von Walther's mistress. Given her nature and her violent and unceasing opposition to the Nazis, this seems quite improbable. Other stories abound, but nothing definitive is known of this period in her life except that, miraculously, she seems to have continued her writing.

Though published anonymously, the two collections of poems discovered in Kommandant von Walther's residence are generally believed to have been authored by Leah Abramson.

The poems in *The Dead Bodies That Line the Streets* and in *Survivor: One Who Survives* are highly controversial. They contain a curious blend of romanticized Germanic heroes and folklore on the one hand, and biting irony and naked violence on the other. The poems in these two volumes, though stylistically different and much more complex than her earlier work, continue the techniques and trademarks for which Abramson is famous. Most notably, her sympathetic portrayal of unsympathetic characters (and vice versa) continues the method she employed in *Cain's Lament* and in *Ahab's Wife and Other Women.*

The poems in *The Dead Bodies* and *Survivor* demonstrate impressive emotional weight, fierce directness, and an exceptionally fine craft. These two works are often likened to Rachel Levi's postwar novel *No Man's Land.* Indeed, that novel does portray a society modeled after the Third Reich and does show a Holocaust, but Levi's work, though compelling and powerful, lacks the tenderness and range of emotion for which Abramson is emulated.

Several postwar sightings of Leah were reported, including some in America, but none were ever substantiated. Her only surviving family member, Jacob Abramson, suffered a stroke and was unable to communicate for many years before his death. Several rewards were offered, both in the European community and in America, by artists' associations and publishers, for information concerning Leah's whereabouts or fate, but no one was able to claim any of the awards, not being able to adequately document what happened to her after she entered the Camp. Apparently Leah Sarah Abramson did not survive the Concentration Camps.

Chapter-by-Chapter Scene Index

Scenes are indicated by Part: Chapter: Scene: Page Number [1:1:1:4 = Part One: Chapter One: Scene 1: Page 4]. Because the e-book version does not have page numbers, and the Scene Index is hyperlinked back to the novel's text, I have retained the scene numbers here so that if people in a book group or class are using different versions of the novel, they can still find the scenes under discussion.

Each Part of the novel has 10 chapters, each chapter has ten scenes (except as noted below): I was attempting to imitate the arbitrary rigidity of the Nazi Concentration Camps in the structure of the novel. (In Part One, chapters One and Six each have 11 scenes rather than the intended 10: either I miscounted or the artist in me was being subconsciously "arbitrary".)

Spoiler Alert: This Index is intended for readers **after** they have completed the book for reference/discussion purposes. If you read this before reading the novel, please be aware that it reveals plot elements by describing scene events. Please do not feel morally obligated to read this section of the Revised Edition if you only want to read the novel itself.

Part One: Max

Chapter One

[1:1:1:3] Max sees girl in grocery

[1:1:2:3] Max has girl brought to office

[1:1:3:4] Himmler's Nuremburg rally: "Save your Country"

[1:1:4:4] Max's suicide attempt

[1:1:5:5] Ilse & Jew-gas

[1:1:6:6] Max & Dieter office luncheon

[1:1:7:8] Marta shows Max book *Dead Bodies*

[1:1:8:10] Max questions girl's Jewish ethnicity

[1:1:9:11] Boy accosts Max in hotel dining room

[1:1:10:12] Dieter tells of evening w/ Hitler

[1:1:11:13] Max's arrest warrant issued

Chapter Two

[1:2:1:14] Wannsee Conference: Eichmann & Heydrich

[1:2:2:15] Max tries to get girl to shoot him

[1:2:3:16] Max & Red Cross Worker & refugees

[1:2:4:17] Marta & Max argue about living in Camp

[1:2:5:19] Chimneys crumbling

[1:2:6:19] Ilse reads storybook to Hans

[1:2:7:20] Marta finds girl in Max's office

[1:2:8:21] Dieter's brother's-in-law expelled from Party

[1:2:9:22] Max's private papers missing

[1:2:10:22] Letters from Max's family (in hotel safe)

Chapter Three

[1:3:1:25] Max's promotion celebration

[1:3:2:28] Himmler's Nuremberg rally "Purest of the Pure"

[1:3:3:28] Jew-pure execution

[1:3:4:29] Dieter on their personal & collective guilt

[1:3:5:31] Max sees girl among refugees

[1:3:6:31] At breakfast, Marta orders Max to stop w/ girl

[1:3:7:33] Max, girl, & boy w/ Protective Custody Letter

[1:3:8:34] In hotel room, Max kills boy searching for him

[1:3:9:37] Max asks Dieter for cyanide capsules

[1:3:10:38] Ilse & Jew-soap

Chapter Four

[1:4:1:40] Bounty-hunter searching for Max at hotel

[1:4:2:41] Max & Dieter in Camp garden w/ Marta & children

[1:4:3:42] Max disciplines guards fraternizing w/ Camp inmates

[1:4:4:43] Max destroys unsigned Order to execute girl

[1:4:5:45] Max distracted while Ilse reading (injured hand)

[1:4:6:46] Max packing, not going w/ Marta & children

[1:4:7:47] Erotic scene in Max's office

[1:4:8:48] Eichmann at Max's dinner party in Camp

[1:4:9:49] Max gives girl cyanide capsules, flees Camp

[1:4:10:50] Bounty-hunter finds Max in motel

Chapter Five

[1:5:1:51] Wannsee Conference: "Final Solution"

[1:5:2:52] Max's six-pointed star

[1:5:3:52] Max meets Himmler

[1:5:4:53] Max writing poetry in office

[1:5:5:54] Ilse plays escaped-Jews w/ paper-dolls

[1:5:6:56] Max's papers scattered in office
[1:5:7:57] Max gets publisher's letter
[1:5:8:57] Josef & Max's missing letters
[1:5:9:59] Ilse's baby-doll "missing/lost"
[1:5:10:60] Max hires man to find girl

Chapter Six

[1:6:1:62] Max sworn into Party as SS
[1:6:2:63] Max & Marta & "firstborn"
[1:6:3:63] Goebbels' speech: *Ein Volk, Ein Reich, Ein Führer*
[1:6:4:64] Night of the Long Knives: BrownShirts' execution
[1:6:5:65] Max & Dieter discuss Ghetto-clearing
[1:6:6:65] Marta sends children to Max's office
[1:6:7:66] Girl watches Max write poetry
[1:6:8:67] Max tells Dieter mistress got married
[1:6:9:67] Max finds Marta's hairbrush & girl beaten
[1:6:10:68] Max dreams of *Dead Bodies*
[1:6:11:68] Telegram: GIRL FOUND

Chapter Seven

[1:7:1:70] Bounty-hunter catches Max at breakfast
[1:7:2:71] Himmler's reaction to shootings
[1:7:3:73] Hitler's "Pure/Tough/Hard" speech
[1:7:4:73] Captured partisans from woods executed
[1:7:5:75] Ilse's fever
[1:7:6:76] Max takes girl to bedroom
[1:7:7:76] Marta weeps over pregnancy
[1:7:8:77] Max in car outside girl's house
[1:7:9:78] Max spits out secreted cyanide capsules
[1:7:10:79] Ilse's & Hans' letters from South America

Chapter Eight

[1:8:1:80] Dieter's telegram: CAMPS LIBERATED
[1:8:2:81] Max shows Hans Hitler Youth dagger
[1:8:3:82] Eichmann, in Camp garden, denies killing Jews
[1:8:4:83] Erotic scene w/ girl in Max's bedroom
[1:8:5:84] Max burns evidence in office

[1:8:6:84] In bedroom, Max & Marta fight over girl
[1:8:7:85] Max gives girl "gifts"
[1:8:8:86] Max reads "Cutthroat"
[1:8:9:87] Max w/ girl before fleeing Camp
[1:8:10:88] Bounty-hunter demands money

Chapter Nine

[1:9:1:90] Max & Josef argue about Safe-Conducts
[1:9:2:92] Max instructs men in forest how to shoot prisoners
[1:9:3:93] Max's headache/leg pain during Himmler speech
[1:9:4:94] Girl takes gun from Max during suicide attempt
[1:9:5:94] Marta wants divorce
[1:9:6:96] Max shows grocer *Dead Bodies*
[1:9:7:98] Max, Marta, children in garden: Ilse's jump-rope song
[1:9:8:100] Max kills Bounty-hunter
[1:9:9:102] Max swears SS-oath of loyalty to Hitler
[1:9:10:102] Max signs transcription-verification document

Chapter Ten

[1:10:1:104] Max complains "words can't be trusted"
[1:10:2:104] Max's Wound medals
[1:10:3:106] Hans' birthday
[1:10:4:107] Max destroys evidence as girl watches
[1:10:5:107] "Negotiations" to destroy Jews
[1:10:6:108] Max impotent w/ Marta
[1:10:7:110] Girl hits Max w/ his pistol
[1:10:8:110] Max walks up path to girl's house
[1:10:9:111] Heydrich (Head of *Gestapo*) visits Max in Camp
[1:10:10:112] Max at girl's house w/ *Dead Bodies*

Part Two: Rachel

Chapter One

[2:1:1:117] Rachel arrives at Camp: Wedding Game
[2:1:2:120] Rachel denies being in Camps to survivor
[2:1:3:121] Jews excluded from citizenship: law passed
[2:1:4:122] Rachel's post-war suicide attempt
[2:1:5:123] Hyman talks to Kommandant

[2:1:6:123] Rachel attempts to get Camp tattoo removed

[2:1:7:124] *Sonderkommando* tells Rachel: get Kommandant's attention

[2:1:8:125] Camp's Underground requests Rachel's help

[2:1:9:126] Rachel's nightmare about trains & Camp

[2:1:10:127] *Arbeit Macht Frei*: Max rapes Rachel

Chapter Two

[2:2:1:129] Camp's Underground & Zyklon B gas

[2:2:2:130] Problems w/ gas not working "in damp"

[2:2:3:132] Marta finds Rachel in Kommandant's office

[2:2:4:132] Rachel tells David story about doctor after war

[2:2:5:134] Yellow roses in lapels "as opposition"

[2:2:6:136] David finds gun

[2:2:7:136] *Kapo* beats Rachel: clothes & shoes taken, head shaved

[2:2:8:138] Rachel tells David she wasn't in Camps

[2:2:9:139] Rachel's parents' Relocation Order

[2:2:10:140] Camp's Underground & Rachel threaten each other

Chapter Three

[2:3:1:142] Night of Broken Glass

[2:3:2:143] Boy at Camp w/ Protective Custody Letter

[2:3:3:144] Letters to Rachel

[2:3:4:146] Rachel finds "Special Instructions for Shootings"

[2:3:5:146] Guests arrive for dinner-party (tattoo-lamp-shade gift)

[2:3:6:147] Ghetto letters found/executions

[2:3:7:149] Ilse & Hans play in Kommandant's office

[2:3:8:150] In kitchen, above office, Max & Marta argue about girl

[2:3:9:152] Rachel leaving: David accompanies her

[2:3:10:152] Ghetto *Shabbas*

Chapter Four

[2:4:1:155] Rachel hides Kommandant's letter-opener

[2:4:2:156] Jews fined for Night of Broken Glass damage

[2:4:3:157] Kommandant inspecting road-building: Rachel drops rock

[2:4:4:159] Rachel's Aunt & Uncle arrested for "mixed marriage"

[2:4:5:160] Kommandant rapes Rachel during gassing of new arrivals

[2:4:6:162] Rachel sees *Dead Bodies* in bookstore window

[2:4:7:162] Rachel's father complains about dead bodies in Ghetto
[2:4:8:163] Arriving Jews riot / Camp-guard's remark: "worm-food"
[2:4:9:164] David annoyed at Rachel's waking him
[2:4:10:165] *Waldsee* postcard

Chapter Five

[2:5:1:166] Rachel opens desk drawer w/ Max's private papers
[2:5:2:166] Star of David armbands
[2:5:3:167] *Gestapo* coming for Rachel in Ghetto
[2:5:4:168] Rachel w/ gun in bedroom as David sleeps
[2:5:5:168] Rachel writing/hiding poems in Kommandant's office
[2:5:6:169] Ghetto *Seder* (Passover)
[2:5:7:170] Baby Hans in Kommandant's office
[2:5:8:172] Rachel shows Underground her bruises
[2:5:9:173] Rachel watches Kommandant writing at night
[2:5:10:174] Rachel types *Kazett*

Chapter Six

[2:6:1:176] David & Rachel fight over adoption
[2:6:2:177] Hans drops bottle on stairs to Kommandant's office
[2:6:3:179] Rachel & parents on train to Camp
[2:6:4:179] Ghetto mother commits suicide by hanging
[2:6:5:180] Kommandant's phone call: breaks windows afterward
[2:6:6:181] Ilse brushes Rachel's hair
[2:6:7:182] Rachel separated from parents in Camp: Left/Right
[2:6:8:183] Rachel wants abortion from Underground
[2:6:9:184] Kommandant reading "Hansel & Gretel" to children
[2:6:10:186] Rachel leaving: David refuses to go

Chapter Seven

[2:7:1:188] Underground beats Rachel
[2:7:2:188] U-Boat (rich Jews in hiding) wants bread
[2:7:3:189] Partisans executed in Camp
[2:7:4:190] David tells Rachel "write the Camp"
[2:7:5:191] Jewish inmate w/ gold tooth
[2:7:6:193] David ignores Rachel's claim about car outside
[2:7:7:193] Dieter brags about sexual conquests

[2:7:8:196] Max drops gun from head, weeps in Rachel's lap

[2:7:9:197] Rachel hides dagger behind chest upstairs

[2:7:10:198] David leaves Rachel for summer

Chapter Eight

[2:8:1:201] Rachel cuts six-pointed star into Max's forearm

[2:8:2:203] Rachel tortured by *Gestapo* (Kaltenbrunner)

[2:8:3:204] Hans gives Rachel part of gingerbread cookie

[2:8:4:205] Ghetto-boy w/ food executed by *Gestapo* (Kaltenbrunner)

[2:8:5:206] Max forces Rachel to perform sex-act (opera)

[2:8:6:207] Josef & cousin rape Rachel

[2:8:7:208] Max & Dieter discuss getting rid of Rachel

[2:8:8:209] Coffee not on "Forbidden Foods List"

[2:8:9:209] Max gives Dieter Rachel as birthday gift

[2:8:10:211] David in Paris, car outside house

Chapter Nine

[2:9:1:212] Rachel attaches then removes Safe-Conducts

[2:9:2:213] Rachel tries to write about Camp (opera)

[2:9:3:214] Rachel & Anna get tattoos in Camp

[2:9:4:215] Office door opens when Rachel reading papers

[2:9:5:216] Kommandant orders Rachel to shoot him

[2:9:6:217] Rachel being raped: 2 men present

[2:9:7:217] Rachel's parents receive Transport Orders

[2:9:8:218] Rachel gives Underground food/ammunition

[2:9:9:220] Inmates tell Rachel Kommandant's gone

[2:9:10:221] Goebbels' book-burning

Chapter Ten

[2:10:1:223] Rachel showers, to go to Kommandant (in office)

[2:10:2:223] Jews blow up crematoria

[2:10:3:225] Candles in window to protest Nazi executions

[2:10:4:225] David returns w/ Althea

[2:10:5:226] *Kapo* takes Rachel to Kommandant's office

[2:10:6:227] Rachel writes "Camp"

[2:10:7:227] Bodies burst from ground in Camp

[2:10:8:227] David & Rachel re-unite: book finished

[2:10:9:228] Rachel eats Kommandant's papers
[2:10:10:229] Kommandant comes to Rachel's house w/ *Dead Bodies*

Part Three: Biographical Encyclopedia Entries

[Max: 235] Maximilian Ernst von Walther
[Rachel: 241] Leah Sarah Abramson

Discussion Questions for *The Kommandant's Mistress*

Author's Note: Parts One & Two, Max's & Rachel's, respectively, were to contain 10 chapters with 10 scenes each. I was attempting to imitate the arbitrary, rigid, "rules" of the Nazi Con- centration Camps in the construction of the novel. Two chapters have eleven scenes each, however (Chapters 1 and 6 in Part One, Max's Part); either I miscounted, or the artist in me was being "arbitrary".

Quotes from the e-book version of the novel in Discussion Questions include Part, Chapter, & Scene references (for the e-book or non-American English versions), noted in the following manner [Part: Chapter: Scene], i.e., [1:3:10 = Part 1: Chapter 3: Scene 10]. Questions are hyperlinked back to scenes in the e-book.

The print book includes page numbers as well [Part: Chapter: Scene: Page] so that people using different versions of the book in groups and classes may refer to the scenes easily.

Discussion Question Topics

The Characters & Their Relationships 212
Epigraphs 213
Max's Six-Pointed Star 213
The Three Different Endings 214
  Max's Ending 214
  Rachel's Ending 215
  Additional Questions on Max's and Rachel's Endings 215
The Biographies of Part Three 216
  The Endings of Part Three 217
  The Biographer of Part Three 218
  Additional Questions Concerning the Three Endings 219
Rachel as the Kommandant's "Mistress" 220
The Theme of Parents & Their Children 221
Rachel & The Underground 224

Spoiler Alert: The Index & Discussion Questions are intended for readers after they have completed the book, for reference/discussion purposes. If you read these before reading the novel, please be aware that they reveal plot elements by describing scene events, as well as in the questions themselves. Please do not feel morally obligated to read this section of the Revised Edition if you only want to read the novel itself.

The Characters & their Relationships

Rachel frequently denies having been in any of the Concentration Camps, even to her husband David — Part Two, Chapter 1, Scene Two, Page 99 [2:1:2:99]; Part Two, Chapter 2, Scene Eight, Page 115 [2:2:8:115]; Part Two, Chapter 7, Scene Four, Page 158 [2:7:4:158]), who tells her, "You dream the Camp. You talk the Camp. You eat, sleep, breathe the Camp" [2:7:4:158]. Why does Rachel deny being in one of the Camps? Does she feel guilty? Ashamed? What does her husband mean when he says that she "eats, sleeps, breathes the Camp"?

Max also denies having been in the Camps — Part One, Chapter 1, Scene Eleven, Page 11 [1:1:11:11]; Part One, Chapter Three, Scene Eight, Page 28 [1:3:8:28]; Part One, Chapter Eight, Scene Ten, Page 72 [1:8:10:72]; Part One, Chapter Nine, Scene Eight, Page 82 [1:9:8:82]. Is there any significance to the fact that both Max and Rachel deny having been there? If so, what? If not, why not?

Though Max and Rachel share the same experience in the Concentration Camp, their stories of what happened differ significantly. Are Max and Rachel reliable narrators, that is, can you trust that what they tell you is the truth? If they're reliable narrators, are they equally reliable? If so, what evidence can you provide from the novel to support that? If not, why not? Which of the two is more reliable, Max or Rachel? Why? Which of the stories is more plausible, Max's or Rachel's? Why? Why is it that we get different versions of the same story when these two are telling it?

What are Max's feelings for Rachel? Does Max love Rachel? If so, why? If not, why not? What would Max think/do/say if someone said Max loved Rachel? Why? What is Max's definition of "love"? Does Max love Marta? If so, why? If not, why not? Why does Marta think Max loves Rachel? Does Max love his children? If so, why? If not, why not?

What are Rachel's feelings for Max in the Camp? What are her feelings for him after the War? What do the members of the Underground think Rachel feels for Max? Do Rachel's feelings for Max change after she is no longer in the Concentration Camp? If so, how? If not, why not? Does Rachel love Max? If so, why? If not, why not? What would Rachel think/do/say if someone said that Rachel loved Max? Why? Why does David think Rachel loves Max?

Epigraphs

Epigraphs are designed to guide readers in an interpretation of the work. This novel has three epigraphs, one for each section.

The epigraph for Max's section [Part One: page 1] is from the *Hebrew Bible*, also known as the *Old Testament:* "For who can make straight that which He hath made crooked?" (*Ecclesiastes* 7:13) How is this epigraph related to Max's part of the story? Does it change your interpretation of Max? The "He" in the epigraph is capitalized, which conventionally means that it is referring to God. What does that mean in relation to the novel? Does it change your view of Max? What does it say about free will? About Max's behavior and the events that led to the Holocaust? Is there anyone else in the story to whom this epigraph could apply? How? Why?

The epigraph for Rachel's section of the novel [Part Two: page 93] is from American writer Gertrude Stein: "There is no left or right without remembering." What does this epigraph mean? What does this epigraph have to do with Rachel and her story? Is there anyone else in the story to whom this epigraph could apply? How? Why?

The epigraph for the Biographical Encyclopedia Entries [Part Three: page 193] of the novel is from the *Hebrew Bible*, also known as the *Old Testament:* "The dead know nothing." (*Ecclesiastes* 9:5). What does this mean? Who in the novel is "dead"? In what ways are they "dead"? Can this epigraph apply to anyone besides the major protagonists? If so, to whom? How? Why? Why is it that the "dead" know nothing?

Max's Six-Pointed Star

In his part of the novel, Max tells us that he cut a six-pointed star on his forearm and that when he showed it to Rachel, telling her, *Jetzt bin ich ein Jude*, she slapped him [1:5:2:43]. Why has Max called the six-pointed star "her name" [1:5:2:43]? What was Max trying to do? Why does he speak to her in German? Does he really believe that this Star of David on his forearm will make the two of them closer? If so, how would it make them closer? If not, why not?

In Rachel's version of this story, she claims that Max drew the six-pointed star on his forearm in black ink and that she cut this star with his service dagger [2:8:1:167]. She also claims to have cut the capital letter *K* beside the star "so he would never be free: *K for Kommandant* " [2:8:1:168]. We learn that when Max said, *"Jetzt bin ich ein Jude,"* he was saying "Now I'm a Jew." Rachel says, "Now you're a Jew," — in German — and slaps him [2:8:1:168]. Why does Rachel cut the Star of David in his forearm? Why does she say, "Now you're a Jew" in German after she's gone through all the trouble of making him think that she doesn't understand that language?

Why does Rachel get sexually excited about cutting Max's arm? Is she interpreting the excitement she feels about having power over him as sexual excitement? If not, why is she excited? Does Max interpret his power over Rachel and over the inmates in the Camp sexually? If not, why does he always want sex with her when Actions or Selections are going on?

In this scene, where Rachel physically tortures and hurts Max, is this the closest Rachel ever gets to understanding him and his behavior? If not, does she ever understand Max? If not in this scene, can you point out another in which you think Rachel understands Max better? Are Max and Rachel alike? If so, in what ways? If not, why not?

Why does Rachel feel shame when she's excited after cutting the star on his arm? Why does she run away from him back to the office? Why does she first tell us, at the beginning of that scene, that she "never cried" and then immediately contradict herself by admitting that she did cry "once" (after she gets sexually aroused by hurting Max when she cuts the star into his forearm)? (She either "never cried" or she did cry, even if it was only "once".) Why does she insist that was the only time she ever cried? Do you believe that that was the only time she ever cried, in other words, is she a reliable narrator? Why did she cry then? Why does she say, after admitting that she cried, that, "even then, it didn't make any difference" [2:8:1:168]? What does she mean?

The Three Different Endings

There are three different endings to the novel, and all three of the endings are true at the same time. These questions will help you understand on a conscious level and discuss the importance of the different endings.

Max's Ending

In Max's version [1:10:10:92], he claims that he found Rachel and went to her home, bringing her a copy of the poetry collection titled *The Dead Bodies That Line the Street.* He reads a poem called "In the Bedroom of the Kommandant," in which it is implied that the Kommandant has told the Jewish inmate that he loves her [1:1:7:7-8]. (When Marta confronts Max with the poetry book, she mentions the poem, saying, "You didn't tell her that you loved her, did you, Max?" and "Even you couldn't love a Jew, could you, Max?" [1:1:7:7-8]) Why does Max claim that he went to find Rachel? What is it that he wants her to understand? Why does he use "her words" instead of his own, and what, exactly, does he mean by that statement? What is the symbolic meaning of the last sentence of Max's version: "The sun glowed on

The Dead Bodies, lying there between us" [1:10:10:93]? Why are the dead bodies still between them and what is the significance of the sun's glowing on them?

Rachel's Ending

In Rachel's version of the story [2:10:10:191], she claims that she shot the Kommandant when he "brought *The Dead Bodies*" to her. The last sentence of her section is this: "In my hand, the white towel fluttered in the early morning breeze" [2:10:10:192]. What is the symbolic significance of the difference between the last sentence in Max's version and the last sentence in Rachel's version? What is the symbolic significance of the white towel? Is someone surrendering? Seeking a truce? A cease-fire? What?

If Max went to Rachel seeking forgiveness, why is it that *his* story ends with *The Dead Bodies* between them, while *hers* ends with the white towel? If Max is telling the truth, then shouldn't Rachel's version have ended with *The Dead Bodies* between them, and the white towel at the end of *his* version?

Is Rachel the one who's surrendered, ceased fire, found peace? Has she, indeed, found peace? If not, what evidence can you present to show that she has not? If so, what evidence from the novel illustrates this? Has Rachel found forgiveness? If so, who has been forgiven: Rachel? Leah? Max? All the Nazis?

Additional Questions on Max's and Rachel's Endings

Max claims that he went to find Rachel after the War, that he saw her several times [1:1:1:3], [1:3:5:26]; then that he found her and read "In the Bedroom of the Kommandant" to her, which he had memorized [1:10:10:92]. Did Max really go to find Rachel? If so, why? If not, why not? If not, why did he claim that he did? What was he expecting from her?

Rachel constantly claims to see a car outside the house [2:7:6:160], [2:8:10:175], and is running away because she thinks she's seen Max [2:3:9:126], [2:4:9:136], [2:6:10:154]. Has she seen him? If she hasn't, why does she think she does?

Does Max actually come to her house? If so, why? If not, why not? Did Rachel really shoot and kill Max at her home? Rachel's ending is true, i.e., she is telling the "truth" as she sees it, so why are the two endings different? Is she lying? If so, why? To whom? Is he lying? If so, why? To whom?

If Max is also telling the truth as he sees it, then why is his ending so dramatically different from hers? Why is Max's family not with him after the War [1:2:10:19], [1:4:6:39], [1:4:10:42], [1:7:10:65]? What does Max's version of their post-War encounter reveal about his character, nature, and personality? What does Rachel's version of their post-War encounter reveal about her character, nature, and personality?

Is it symbolic that Rachel finally "confronts" Max [2:10:10:191] *after* she's completed writing her book about her experiences in the Camp (i.e., Part Two of *The Kommandant's Mistress*) [2:10:6:189], [2:10:8:189]? If so, how? Why? What is the significance of the fact that David does not return home with Althea until after Rachel has completed her book about the Camp [2:10:8:189]?

The Biographies of Part Three

Note: The "biographies" of Part Three are entirely fictional. Over the years, many scholars and reviewers have written that I "fictionalized" — in Parts One & Two — the "real people" whose "biographies comprise Part Three". I thank those writers most sincerely for the compliment on my writing style in that third section as I apparently succeeded in imitating the countless number of biographical encyclopedia entries on in/famous or historical persons that I read to learn the style of such entries. Closer examination, however, reveals that Part 3 must be fictional since no single person, Nazi or Jew, could possibly have done everything I wrote that Max and Rachel did.

Max

I didn't want Max to represent only one Nazi but, rather, all the Nazis, so I could show all the atrocities they committed against the Jews. Thus, he's at virtually every Nuremburg rally where Hitler, Himmler, or Goebbels spoke [1:1:3:3], [1:3:2:23], [1:6:3:53], etc. Max participates in the Night of the Broken Glass [1:3:3:23]; in the Night of the Long Knives (the purge of the BrownShirts, also known as Storm-Troopers, or SA; whose members were the precursors and competitors of the *Schutzstaffeln*, SS, who wore black uniforms) [1:6:4:53]; and in the *Wannsee* Conference, where the "Final Solution to the Jewish Problem" — killing them "more efficiently" with cyanide gas rather than with the carbon monoxide trucks which had been in use [1:5:1:43]. Max heads a Mobile Killing Squad (*Einsatzkommando*) and instructs the soldiers on the correct way to shoot prisoners in the forest [1:9:2:75]. He serves alongside the Army — as a member of the SS — at the Eastern Front, where he's wounded by German fire after he mistakes fellow soldiers for partisans [1:10:2:86]; he meets Himmler [1:5:3:44] and is promoted through the ranks of the SS until he becomes Kommandant of a Concentration Camp [1:3:1:21], [Part Three: page 197].

No one Nazi could have done all that. Though Max is a "real person" as a literary character, he is a representative, symbolic Nazi; his career and life reflect everything the Nazis did to the Jews in Germany and in the other conquered territories.

Rachel

Likewise, Rachel is not modeled after any single Jewish person from that period, though I did interview many survivors. I also read memoirs, diaries, letters, autobiographies, and biographies of Camp inmates who survived and of those who perished. Rachel is symbolic of what all the Jews in Europe experienced (hence, her family's moving from country to country in an attempt to escape the encroaching Nazi destruction and persecution).

Rachel is at the Goebbels'-organized Book Burning with her father and uncle [2:9:10:184]; she and her family are in Czechoslovakia when Jews are deprived of their citizenship [2:1:3:100]; she passes as a non-Jew ("Aryan") in order to get food for her family [2:8:8:173]; she is in the Warsaw Ghetto [2:3:6:122], [2:3:10:126], [2:4:7:135], [2:5:6:140]. Rachel has encounters with the *Gestapo* [2:8:2:168], [2:8:4:170]; with the Camp's Underground [2:1:8:104], [2:2:1:107], [2:2:10:116], etc. She is in the Camp proper [2:7:5:159]; builds roads with the labor crew supervised by the Camp's *Kapo* and Nazi guards [2:4:3:130]; is in a "Selection" upon her arrival at the Camp, where Jews are cursorily inspected by a Doctor (the most infamous being Josef Mengele at Auschwitz-Birkenau) and arbitrarily assigned to go to the "Left" or to the "Right", one group of which will immediately be gassed, while the other will remain as laborers in the Camp [2:6:7:151]. (I have intentionally not indicated which "side" — Left or Right — went to the gas, since the Jews themselves didn't know what the sides meant during the Selections.)

Just as no single Nazi could have possibly done everything that Max does in the novel, no individual Jew could have experienced everything that Rachel does. She, too — despite being a "real person" in literary terms — is representative and symbolic of all the Jews persecuted, enslaved, imprisoned, tortured, killed, and systematically exterminated by the Nazis.

Questions about the Endings in the Biographies of Part Three

In the third section of the novel, the ostensible biographical encyclopedia entries — which are entirely fictional — it states that Max was "executed by hanging at the Concentration Camp where he had served" [Part Three, "Maximilian von Walther", last lines: page 198] and that Rachel, who is called Leah, "apparently did not survive the Concentration Camps" [Part Three, "Leah Sarah Abramson", last lines: page 202]. If all three of the endings in this novel are all true at the same time, then why are all the endings different? What do the different endings say about how human beings who apparently participate in the same events experience them in various ways? What do the three different endings say about our understanding of history itself and supposedly objective history books?

The "Biographer" of Part Three

The "biographer" of Part Three (whom I've always thought of as a man) does not seem very objective. For example, he consistently calls Max by his last name, yet calls Rachel/Leah by her first name? Why does he do this? Is it sexism? Is it something else? If something else, what is it?

The biographer presents statements of fact about Max in a more negative light by not providing any interpretation of Max's actions. For example, he writes, "Though [von Walther] completed the course work for a *Doktorat* in Germanic literature and successfully passed his comprehensive examinations in 1939, von Walther failed to complete his dissertation" [dissertation, Part Three, Max: page 195]. Why didn't Max complete his doctoral dissertation? Did it have anything to do with the start of the War? Why does the biographer imply that Max didn't complete his dissertation for some reason other than the start of the War?

The biographer also provides the following information about Max: "By his longtime mistress, Dianne Braun, who lived in the Nazi-sponsored *Lebensborn* maternity home, von Walther fathered a son Klaus (born October 1940) who died from injuries suffered in an air raid in February 1944. Von Walther did not attend his son's funeral" [funeral, Part Three, Max: page 195]. In Rachel's version of the story, however, we hear a one-sided telephone conversation where Max's former mistress, the mother of the son killed in the air raid, apparently tells Max about the boy's death and funeral only *after* they have taken place [2:6:5:149-150]. Therefore, Max could not have attended his own son's funeral.

Did the biographer not know this piece of information or did he intentionally leave it out? If the former, how could he not have known if he'd exhaustively and professionally researched Max's life to the extent that he knew about the mistress, the son, and that Max did not attend his son's funeral? If the latter, and the biographer intentionally left out the fact that Max didn't know about his son's death and funeral until after they had taken place, why did the biographer leave out that vital information? Is the biographer trying to influence his readers' opinions of Max? If so, how? If not, why do you think he wrote the biography in this manner?

The biographer also presents information about Rachel in a more positive light than others might have seen it either during or after the War. In fact, the biographer of Leah Sarah Abramson does not even seem to know that she did, indeed, survive the Camp, and changed her name to Rachel. Instead, he writes, "Apparently Leah Sarah Abramson did not survive the Concentration Camps" [last lines, Part Three, Rachel: page 202].

Why did the biographer say this? Did he really not know that Rachel and Leah are the same person? Does the biographer even know anything about Rachel/Leah after the War? If he did know they were the same person, and also knew about what happened to Rachel after the War, then why didn't he include that information in his Biography of Rachel/Leah? Was he trying to protect Rachel? If so, from whom or what? If not, why did he omit this information? Was there some other reason he ended his biography of her in the manner he did? If so, what might it be?

Additional Questions Concerning the Three Different Endings

To whom is Max speaking when he says things like, "No, I wasn't afraid. I wasn't strong enough" [last lines 1.1.4:4], "I've always told the truth" [1.3.2:23], and "No, that wasn't running away. That was saving myself" [last lines 1.3.8:31]? Look at the last scene in Part 1, Chapter 9, when Max is with a soldier who is ordering Max to sign something [1.9.10:84-85]. Is the soldier German? Is he a Nazi? What document is Max signing? Is it a confession? If so, how is Max portraying himself and his actions? If it's not a confession, what might it be? Is Max, as the soldier asks, leaving anything important out of his version of events? If so, what? If so, why? If not, why not?

Are the statements listed in this paragraph ("I wasn't afraid: I wasn't strong enough", "I've always told the truth", "That wasn't running away: that was saving myself") related in any way to the document Max is told to sign? If so, how? If not, why not? Can you find other examples, like these, when Max is specifically addressing someone who is not named in the story? What do all these examples tell you about Max's character, his nature, his personality?

Did Max really go to find Rachel as he claims, or didn't he? If Max didn't go to find Rachel and was, instead, captured, imprisoned, and executed (as it indicates at the end of Part Three: page 198), then why and to whom did he claim that he had found her? Does Max really believe that Rachel would have forgiven him had he gone to her after the War? If so, why? If not, why does he imply it?

Did Rachel really shoot Max or did she only shoot him symbolically? Even if she shoots him only symbolically, why does she have to imagine such a violent ending to their relationship? Why does Rachel continually tell everyone, even her husband David, that she was never in any of the Camps [2:1:2:99], [2:2:8:115]?

Why did Rachel change her name from Leah (which means "weary") to Rachel (which means "lamb") [Part Three: page 199]? Does Rachel view herself as a sacrifice? If so, when was she a sacrifice: in the Ghetto, in the Camp, after the War, all of the aforementioned times, some other time(s)? If so, for whom or for what reason(s) was she a sacrifice?

Why did she try to commit suicide after the War, when she was free [2:1:4:101];? While in the Ghetto, celebrating *Shabbas,* Rachel claims that she'd kill herself before she'd let herself suffer at the hands of the Germans

[2:3:10:128], but she does not attempt to commit suicide in the Camps: why not?

Rachel as the Kommandant's "Mistress"

Note on novel's title: The title of this novel was originally *The Kommandant,* since I viewed it as three different versions of Max. One of the Vice-Presidents at HarperCollins, which originally published the novel, wanted to put the novel's focus more on Rachel, and suggested the new title, *The Kommandant's Mistress,* based on the "most persistent rumor" of what happened to Rachel/Leah in the Camp, and modeling the title after John Fowles' classic *The French Lieutenant's Woman,* where the "woman" of that title, though considered a whore and virtually a prostitute by everyone else in the novel, is actually a virgin who never had intimate relations of any kind with the French Lieutenant, with whom she was in love, who had promised to marry her, and whom she discovered to be unfaithful to her before she slept with him.

Historical note: Like Rachel in this novel, many of the Jewish women who were raped, whether in the Camps or not, and inmates (male or female) who were forced into prostitution or unwilling sexual servitude in the Nazi Concentration Camps were considered "collaborators" by their fellow inmates and treated brutally after the liberation. (In fact, one inconsiderate borrower of a library's copy of *The Kommandant's Mistress* crossed out the word "Mistress" on the title page and wrote "Whore, more like it" in ink beside the title; that reader was behaving exactly as did the inmates who judged and condemned, then punished, tortured, or killed any fellow inmates who were raped or forced into sexual situations/prostitution by the Nazis.)

Rudolf Höss, the Kommandant of Auschwitz, for example, who lived with his family on the Concentration Camp's grounds, had a "mistress" who bore him a son. The day before SS-Head Heinrich Himmler was to "visit" the Camp to investigate the allegations, the "mistress," the son, and the guard who'd reported it all disappeared. I can only assume that, since such behavior went against Nazi principles and would have resulted in more than a mere reprimand for Kommandant Höss, the three were all sent to the gas-chambers.

Questions about Rachel as "Mistress"

The biographer of Part Three admits that nothing definitive is known about Rachel/Leah's experiences once she was deported except that she ended up in the Concentration Camp of Maximilian von Walther. The biographer reports several rumors of Rachel's activities in the Camps, stating that the "most persistent rumor" was that she became von Walther's "mistress", which he declares "highly improbable" [Mistress, Part Three, Rachel: page 201].

However, Max's wife Marta certainly considers Rachel/Leah to be Max's "mistress" because Marta assumes that Max is in love with "the girl". The members of the Underground consider Rachel/Leah to be in a "consensual sexual relationship" despite the fact that she is just as much a Camp inmate as they themselves are. Even Rachel's husband David, at times, expresses his suspicions that Rachel was in love with Max and was willingly his "mistress" [2:7:10:164-166], saying that he doesn't want to "compete" with Max any longer.

Though Max always portrays Rachel as a willing participant in their sexual activities [1:4:7:40], [1:7:6:62], [1:8:4:68], [1:8:7:70]; Rachel always describes them as rapes and forced sexual encounters [2:1:10:106], [2:4:5:133], [2:5:8:142], [2:8:5:171], [2:9:6:181]. Are any of these interpretations of the "relationship" between Max and Rachel reliable? Is any more reliable than the others? If so, which? If so, why? If not, why not? Do you think Rachel was a willing participant in the sexual relationship with the Kommandant of the Nazi Concentration Camp in which she was interred? If so, why? If not, why not?

Do you think that Marta was correct in her assumption that Max loved Rachel? If so, why? If not, why not? Is David's belief that Rachel loved (and perhaps still loves) Max justified? If so, why? If not, why not?

Was Rachel a "mistress" in the sense that she loved Max and wanted to be with him sexually? If so, what scenes from Rachel's section indicate this? If not, what scenes from Max's section indicate that she was not a willing participant? Who is the more reliable interpreter of the sexual relationship between Max and Rachel: Max, Rachel, the Biographer, Marta, David, the Members of the Underground? If none of these, why not? If someone else, who, and why? Present scenes from the novel to support your interpretation.

The Theme of Parents & their Children

Max & His Children

The theme of parents and their children is an important one in the novel. Ilse and Hans, Max's children, are obviously affected by living in a house on the grounds of the Concentration Camp. Ilse complains about smelling the "Jew-gas" [1:1:5:4], she worries about taking a bath with "Jew-soap" [1:3:10:31], she plays "escaped Jews" with her dolls before she throws them into the fire, saying "Into the gas with you" [1:5:5:45], and she tells Hans, "See what you did, Hans? You bad boy. Daddy should send you to the gas" [1:5:9:49]. Ilse also "plays Kommandant" in his office when he's out in the Camp [2:3:7:124]. Does Max notice how his children are being affected by the Concentration Camp? If he does notice, why does he react the way he does? If not, why not? Does Marta notice? If so, how does she react? If not, why not?

Dieter mentions that Max has been paying child-support for his son by his mistress [1:6:8:56], Max weeps when he learns this son has been killed in an air-raid [2:6:5:149], Max apparently writes a poem to this son called "Love Song for Klaus", to which Marta alludes [1:8:8:71] and which Rachel sees in his desk drawer [2:5:1:138]. Max lets Ilse play with her dolls while he's trying to read the newspaper, even though the dolls keep bumping into the paper and making him lose his place [1:5:5:45], he reads "Hansel and Gretel" to his children in his office [2:6:9:153], he keeps his family with him at the Concentration Camp rather than be separated from them.

Is Max a good father? If so, how? If not, why not? Does he think he's a good father? Does Marta think Max is a good father? If he is a good father, then why does he only directly refer to his firstborn son once [1:6:2:52], and allude to him (and his other dead children) once: when Ilse is sick with fever [1:7:5:62]? Why do we have to learn about all of Max's children from the Biographer of Part Three [Children, Part Three, Max: page 195]?

Marta & Her Children

Marta takes care of the house, the cooking, the children; she is protective of Ilse and Hans even before they live on the grounds of the Concentration Camp [1:3:1:21], worries about leaks from the stove at the Camp's house that might hurt them [1:1:5:4], doesn't like the (non-Jewish) inmates who are servants in the house to be around the children [1:3:10:31], makes paper dolls for Ilse to play with [1:5:5:45], and makes sure Max and Ilse are affectionate to Hans [1:5:5:45]. Is Marta a good mother? If so, how? If not, why not? Does she think she's a good mother? If so, why? If not, why not? Does Max think Marta is a good mother? If so, why? If not, why not?

Rachel, Ilse, & Hans

The children are also affected by Rachel's presence in their father's office. When the children are "playing Kommandant" alone in the office, Ilse chases Hans, saying "I'm the big, bad Jew who eats little boys"; she tells Hans that Rachel is "a Jew" and that "Jews are bad" but then asks Rachel if she wants to play with her and Hans [2:3:7:124-125]. Why does she want Rachel to play with them [2:3:7:125]? Ilse brushes Rachel's hair and tells her "Now, you look pretty" [2:6:6:151]. Does Ilse's attitude toward Rachel change in the novel? If so, how? If so, why? If not, why not? In the scene where Ilse is brushing Rachel's hair, why does Ilse run away when her father calls for her [2:6:6:151]?

Hans also is aware of Rachel and has several interactions with her. He crawls toward her and coos at her when she touches his cheek [2:5:7:141]: Why does Rachel try to avoid Hans when he's crawling across the floor toward her? Why does Rachel touch his cheek? How does she feel when he coos at her? Why? On the stairs between the house proper and Max's office, Hans stops crying when he's lost his bottle and Rachel holds him [2:6:2:147-148]: Why does Rachel pick him up? Why does Marta shriek when she sees Rachel holding Hans?

When Max is watching Ilse and Hans while Marta is getting ready for the dinner party, why does he keep telling Hans to "get away from there [from Rachel]" [1:6:6:54-55], [2:8:3:169-170]? At one point in Max's office, Hans offers Rachel a bite of his gingerbread woman cookie, and then breaks off the head and gives it to her [2:8:3:169-170]: How does Hans feel toward Rachel? What does he think of her? Does he understand that she's a Jew? If so, what does that mean to him? If not, why not? What is the significance of Hans' offering Rachel a bite of this cookie? What is the significance of Hans' breaking apart his cookie and giving some of it to her when she doesn't take the bite he offers? What is the symbolic significance of Hans' breaking the cookie's head away from the body and giving Rachel the "head" of the cookie?

Rachel, David, the Abortion, & Althea

David repeatedly asks Rachel to have a child with him but she tells him she can't [2:2:4:110]. Instead of telling him about the pregnancy and abortion [2:6:8:152] in the Camp, she claims to have gone to a doctor after the war [2:2:4:110]. Why does Rachel tell David this story? Why doesn't she tell him about getting pregnant with Max's child? How does she feel about getting pregnant in the Camp? How do the members of the Underground feel about her pregnancy? How does Rachel feel about the abortion? Why?

Why doesn't Rachel want to adopt a child when David asks her to do so [2:6:1:146]? Why do they say such cruel things to each other about losing their own parents in the Camps [2:6:1:147]? Why is it important to David that he and Rachel adopt a child whose parents were killed in the Concentration Camps [2:2:4:110]?

How does Rachel feel when David brings Althea home [2:10:4:188]? Why is Rachel afraid to touch Althea? Althea's name means "healing." What is the significance of her name? Will Althea help Rachel heal? If so, how? If not, why not? Will Althea help heal David's and Rachel's marriage? If so, how? If not, why not? Will Rachel be a good mother to Althea? If so, why? If not, why not?

Rachel & The Underground

Historical Note: There were Underground Resistance members in many of the Camps and, in the case of Auschwitz-Birkenau, in the woods surrounding the Camp; members of the *Sonderkommando* did blow up the crematoria in Auschwitz-Birkenau, after which the Camp in this novel is most closely modeled. The Underground in Auschwitz-Birkenau, however, did not move about as freely as they did in some of the other Camps. I've used artistic license in this instance, giving them more freedom of movement so they could interact with Rachel, and so readers would be aware that there were Resistance movements inside and outside the actual Camps.

Questions about Rachel & The Underground

The members of the Underground in the Concentration Camp seem to hate Rachel. They often claim that she has a soft and pampered life [2:1:8:104, 2:2:1:107, 2:2:10:116, 2:5:8:142]. They also call her a whore [2:5:8:142, 2:6:8:152] and beat her when she doesn't do what they've asked her to do [2:7:1:156]. Compared to the other inmates at the Camp, does Rachel have a "soft and pampered life"? If so, how? If not, why not? Why do the members of the Camp's Underground seem to hate Rachel? How does Rachel feel about them? Why?

Why won't Rachel do as the Underground asks? Doesn't Rachel have loyalty to the other Jews? Should she use her position in the Kommandant's office to help other Jews in the Camp? Why or why not? Are the members of the Underground justified in their feelings toward Rachel? Is Rachel being selfish? If so, how? If not, why not? Is she being wise? If so, how? If not, why not?

For her part, Rachel believes that the members of the Underground don't understand her position. "They didn't even know what suffering was... I tried to help in little ways, but it didn't do any good. They couldn't have done anything either, if they'd been in my position. They didn't know what it was like for me, and they didn't even try to understand" [2:4:1:129]. Does Rachel try to help, as she claims? If so, what are the "little ways" in which Rachel tries to help? If not, why not? Is Rachel's position in the Camp better than that of the members of the Underground? If so, how? If not, why not? How does Rachel feel about her own position in the Camp? How does Rachel feel about the members of the Underground? Why? When Rachel claims that she did finally help the members of the Camp's Underground, she says she brought them food and weapons, but that they claimed it wasn't enough for everyone [2:9:8:182]. They believe that she did it intentionally. Did she? If so, why? If not, why not?

Rachel gets distressed when the Underground reveals its plans to kill the Kommandant, mentioning Reinhard Heydrich's assassination [2:9:8:183], and Rachel lies to them, telling them that the Nazis executed Jews in Lidice *and in Berlin* after that assassination (the Nazis *did* raze Lidice and kill all its occupants in retaliation for Heydrich's assassination, but didn't kill any Jews in Berlin over it). Why does Rachel tell them that lie [2:9:8:183]? Why doesn't she want the members of the Underground to kill Max [2:9:8:182-183]? What would happen to Rachel if Max got killed? Why?

Author's Note on Select Sources

This work, though fiction, contains historical figures, including Hitler, Himmler, Heydrich, and Eichmann, whose words and deeds have been well documented. Many of the quotes attributed both directly and indirectly to these figures appear in this novel. I have, however, used artistic license by putting this material into contexts in which it didn't originally appear.

Quoted material attributed to the historical figures who appear in my novel was taken from the following books (which are intentionally listed by title first, rather than in a more scholarly fashion, for the general reader, who'd look for titles rather than for authors' last names):

• *The Destruction of the European Jews (in Three Volumes, Revised and Definitive Edition),* by Raul Hilberg (New York: Holmes & Meier, 1985).
• *Eichmann Interrogated: Transcripts from the Archives of the Israeli Police,* edited by Jochen von Lang (New York: Farrar, Straus & Giroux, 1983).
• *Inside the Third Reich*, by Albert Speer (New York: Avon, 1971).
• *Kommandant of Auschwitz,* by Rudolf Höss, translated by Constantine FitzGibbon (London: Weidenfeld & Nicolson, 1959).
• *The Rise and Fall of the Third Reich: A History of Nazi Germany,* by William Shirer (New York: Simon & Schuster, 1960).
• *The SS* (Alexandria VA: Time-Life Books, 1988).
• *The SS: Alibi of a Nation, 1922—1945,* by Gerald Reitlinger (London: Arms & Armour Press, 1981).

Acknowledgment is also made to the following books, which provided some of the details of the Holocaust that appear in this novel; for example, many of Max's orders, memos, letters, and instructions include the actual wording of Nazi documents recovered by the Allies after the War. (Again, sources are intentionally listed by title first, rather than in a more academic fashion, for the general reader, who'd look for titles rather than for authors' last names):

• *Adolf Hitler,* by John Toland (New York: Ballantine, 1976).
• *The Auschwitz Album: A Book Based Upon an Album Discovered by a Concentration Camp Survivor, Lili Meier* (New York: Random House, 1981).
• *The Black Corps: The Structure and Power Struggles of the Nazi SS,* by Robert Lewis Koehl (Madison: University of Wisconsin Press, 1983).
• *The Book of Alfred Kantor* (New York: McGraw Hill, 1971).

• *Eyewitness Auschwitz: Three Years in the Gas Chambers,* by Filip Müller (New York: Stein & Day, 1984).
• *The Ghetto Anthology: A Comprehensive Chronicle of the Extermination of Jewry in Nazi Death Camps and Ghettos in Poland,* edited by Roman Mogilanski (Los Angeles: American Congress of Jews from Poland and Survivors of Concentration Camps, 1985).
• *The Goebbels Diaries, 1939—1941,* translated and edited by Fred Taylor (New York: Putnam's, 1983).
• *Hitler's Death Camps: The Sanity of Madness,* by Konnilyn G. Feig (New York: Holmes & Meier, 1981).
• *The Holocaust: A History of the Jews in Europe during the Second World War,* by Martin Gilbert (New York: Holt, Rinehart & Winston, 1985).
• *Nuremberg Diary,* by G. M. Gilbert (New York: NAL [New American Library], 1961).
• *The Nuremberg Trial,* by Ann Tusa and John Tusa (New York: Atheneum, 1984).
• *Shoah: An Oral History of the Holocaust, the Complete Text of the Film,* edited by Claude Lanzmann (New York: Pantheon, 1985).
• *Spandau: The Secret Diaries,* by Albert Speer (New York: Pocket Books, 1977).
• *Spiritual Resistance: Art from Concentration Camps, 1940—1945* (Philadelphia: Jewish Publication Society, 1981).
• *The Stroop Report: A Facsimile Edition and Translation of the Official Nazi Report on the Destruction of the Warsaw Ghetto,* translated by Sybil Milton (New York: Pantheon, 1979).
• *The Warsaw Ghetto in Photographs: 206 Views Made in 1941,* edited by Ulrich Keller (New York: Dover, 1984).
• *Who's Who in Nazi Germany,* by Robert Wistrich (New York: Bonanza, 1982).

Author's Note to Revised & Expanded, 20th Anniversary Edition of *The Kommandant's Mistress*

My Start as a Poet 228
Writing my First Novel 229
Publishing *The Kommandant's Mistress* 235
On My Name 238
Special Notes to Readers about *The Kommandant's Mistress* 239
    On the Three Different Endings 239
    On Rachel as the Kommandant's "Mistress" 241
    On Rachel's Poems & Books 242
    On the Camp's Underground 243
Additions to the 20th Anniversary Edition 243
Revisions to the 20th Anniversary Edition 245

Spoiler Alert: If you read this before reading the novel, please be aware that it reveals plot elements when answering questions posed by readers since the novel's publication. Please do not feel morally obligated to read this section of the Revised Edition if you only want to read the novel itself.

My Start as a Poet

I began my serious writing career as a poet when I was in college, and had modest critical success with my poetry. My work appeared regularly in University and literary journals; it was awarded some prestigious prizes, including the Elliston Poetry Prize (several times) as well as the Isabel and Mary Neff Fellowship for Creative Writing; my dissertation was comprised of original poetry, all of which had been published or accepted for publication by the time of my defense (about 1/3 of the poems in my dissertation were on the Holocaust).

I'd had dreams of being in the Nazi Concentration Camps, and of dying there, since before I was five-years-old. Though my great-grandparents acknowledged, when I was 8, that our family was, indeed, Jewish, I was cautioned to tell no one, and, if asked, to reply that "I was baptized and went Catholic schools", which I dutifully did my entire life. While I was working on my creative writing dissertation, the dreams of dying in a Concentration Camp became so frequent and so vivid that they began waking me up. I decided that I was supposed to write *a poem* on the Concentration Camps.

Yes, "a poem". One poem. On the entire, systematic program of Nazi-perpetrated violence against the Jews of Europe which has come to be known as the Holocaust.

Of course, as soon as I made this decision, I realized that I knew nothing about the Holocaust, as it had never been spoken of openly in our family, and I had never learned anything about it in schools. Thus began my seven-year-journey of research on the Holocaust. I began with books, then moved to interviewing survivors when I couldn't find answers to some of my questions in books.

My poems usually began with moral questions for which I had no answers. My first Holocaust poem, "Cutthroat: A Player Who Plays for Himself", attempted to deal with the fact that women who were raped in the Camps were considered "collaborators" by their fellow survivors after the war and dealt with harshly. This seemed very unfair, so I wrote a poem exploring the situation from the perspective of a woman raped in the Camps.

Later, other questions arose: What if you were a Nazi, but truly believed that what you were doing was good for your country? What if you were the wife of a Nazi? (You could get a divorce, I suppose, though they were much rarer and more difficult to get during that time period than they are now.) What if you were a child of a Nazi: you can't "divorce" your parents; you can't even leave them when you're young.

More challenging moral questions arose about the Jewish inmates themselves, most notably this one, which served as the basis of *The Kommandant's Mistress*: If you were an inmate in a Nazi Concentration Camp and the ultimate "good" was for you to survive, then is anything you did to survive also "good"? Would it have been permissible, for example, to steal food from another starving inmate if it meant that you yourself would have a greater chance of surviving? Would it have been "good" to kill another inmate if it meant that you yourself would survive?

The only way I know how to explore answers to these questions in any meaningful way is to create worlds in which the characters themselves struggle, consciously or not, with those moral dilemmas.

Writing My First Novel

From Poems to Novel

With each question came another poem, long after my dissertation had been completed and my degree awarded. My Holocaust poems, now gathered in the collection *Where Lightning Strikes,* got increasingly longer, including multiple characters, perspectives, and even dialogue. The editors of journals began to scribble notes on the bottom of rejection slips, asking,

"Are you sure you're not writing fiction?" Finally, one day, I wondered that myself.

I thought, "Maybe I should try to write a novel." As soon as that thought came, I heard the voice of the male protagonist of a poem I'd written called "The Kommandant" say, "Tell my story." Simultaneously, I heard the female protagonist's voice say, "You can't tell his story without telling mine."

Indeed.

I also saw the structure of the novel, with all three parts, including the controversial third part, the ostensible biographical encyclopedia entries on the two major protagonists. (Note the word "ostensible" as many reviewers, scholars, and readers have remarked that I merely fictionalized, in Parts One and Two, the "true stories" of "real people." I always thank them most politely since Part Three is as fictional as the rest of the novel and was, in fact, one of the most difficult sections to write as I had to write it in chronological order: something I do not do naturally, I'm afraid.)

Readers, other creative writers, and attendees at conferences often ask how I "see" a novel in a glance. I don't know: it just happens. This is what it feels like, though: it's as if I'm in a strange room in the dark. For a brief instant, a lightning strike illuminates the room. In that moment, I see everything there and know something, but not all, about it, including the people. The vision is actually the easy part of the process as I don't have to do anything: it just appears. Unbidden, briefly, and only once.

The difficult part is re-creating, with words, what I've "seen" in that room and what I learn about its inhabitants as I'm writing. (I've often wished I were a film-maker or director, imagining that it would be easier to re-create my vision in film, but since I've never made a film, I may be quite severely mistaken on this point.) Once, when I was writing *The Kommandant's Mistress,* someone asked how long I'd been writing on a particular day.

> *"Six hours," I said.*
> *"And how many words did you get written?"*
> *"One paragraph."*
> *"One paragraph? You wrote for six hours today and only got one little paragraph written?"*
> *"Yes," I said, "but it's a really good paragraph."*

Writing the Novel

Of course, I did all the research into how to write a novel, learning only what I already knew: that I had to have plot, characters, dialogue, etc.; all of which I'd already been putting into my poems. So, I learned how to write a novel as all novelists must learn to write one: by sitting down and writing it.

The first and most important decision I made was to write a book that I myself would like to read, more than once (good thing, too, since I've had to read it so many times: proofreading, copyediting, at signings, conferences, bookstores; for book clubs, discussion groups, high school classes, college classes, students; etc. My advice for anyone who wants to write a novel? Make sure you write the kind of novel you want to read over and over and over again.)

Next, I decided on the structure itself. I'd already seen the vision of it in Three Parts, with the final part consisting of the ostensible encyclopedia entries. I chose to have ten chapters with ten scenes each for Parts One and Two. An arbitrary decision. Just as the Holocaust poems' lines were broken according to arbitrary syllabic-count, I divided the chapters and scenes into a rigid, arbitrary structure to symbolically mimic the Nazi Concentration Camps. (Yes, Chapters One and Six of Part One, Max's section, do have eleven scenes each. I either miscounted or the artist in me was being more arbitrary than rigid, which symbolically fits the subject matter. It occurred to me as I was writing this Note that the extra scenes ended up in Max's part of the book, i.e., in the Nazi's part. The artist is not, I assure you, always conscious of what is going on at every level of what s/he writes.)

Having never written a novel before, I felt morally obligated to make an outline, which I dutifully did. For Part One, since I intended to write the Kommandant's part first, I wrote the first chapter over and over until I thought it was perfect. Then I showed it to select readers, swearing them to honesty in case it was the most frightful thing they'd ever read, and in case they couldn't understand what I was doing with all the time-shifting (without typographical warnings, like asterisks or extra space between scenes).

One of my readers suggested that instead of using Unlimited Point of View as I had in the original story and poem, I use 1st person, getting us inside the Kommandant's head. "Otherwise," she said, "he won't be a real human being that we care about: he'll just be a Nazi that we're observing."

I was stunned. How was I supposed to do a man's voice? A Nazi's voice? I had no idea. While I was trying to figure it out, however, I read Hemingway. His Voice seemed appropriate for the Kommandant, so, though I'd read all his novels and short stories already, I re-read them. Many times. In fact, besides the non-fiction, scholarly books or survivor memoirs of the Holocaust that I was re-reading while preparing for the novel, Hemingway's were the only other books I read. I was so terrified of losing my vision for the novel — having never written one — that I didn't want to be influenced by other authors' Voices, so I limited my book selection while writing.

It took approximately nine months from the time I determined to write Parts One and Two in 1st person POV to the day I actually "heard" Max's voice. The breakthrough came when I realized that (1) Max didn't think he'd done anything wrong, (2) he believed he was doing his job and that he was good at it, and (3) he was just a regular man: he wasn't criminally insane, and he wasn't, technically, committing any crimes since he was acting according to laws implemented by the Nazi Party against the Jews.

Suddenly, his voice came: "Then I saw her. There she stood…"

And so it began.

After I rewrote the first chapter until I thought it was ready for readers, I showed it to them. They unanimously raved over its success, all of them saying they thought I "was on to something" and that I should continue in that vein.

I soon realized, though, that I simply could not teach full-time and also write a novel the way I'd written my poems for years: on the weekends and during breaks from University. I felt like every time I wrote the novel, I was diving into a pool of water, a very deep murky pool. Every time I taught, graded papers, prepared lessons, attended committee meetings, and spent any significant time away from the novel, I found myself standing on the shore of that murky pool, having to dive in and start at the beginning again, i.e., re-read everything I'd already written, review the outline (which kept changing so often — when my characters did something unexpected — that I eventually abandoned it, writing a scene index afterward for purposes of revision). The hardest part was always finding Max's voice again. I soon came to believe that I simply couldn't write the novel and work at the same time. I had to find a way to write full-time.

My Brilliant Plan to Write Full-Time

I came up with what I believed was a brilliant plan: I'd take out a loan from the bank and ask for a year off work to write the novel (after all, I was a well-established, award-winning, published writer, with a Ph.D. in Creative Writing as well as a Ph.D. in English and Comparative Literatures; I was a tenured University Professor who'd taught for about 12 years). So, gathering my list of what I thought were pretty impressive publications, I headed to the bank.

Under "Reason for Loan", I wrote "novel".

To my surprise, an hour later, the bank manager invited me into his office. With my résumé in one hand and the loan application in the other, he looked up at me across his desk.

"So," he said, "let's hear your 'novel' reason for the loan."

"Oh, not 'novel' like that," I said. "I want to write a novel."

"You want to write a novel?"

"I've got it outlined and a good part of it written, but I simply can't do it while working full-time. I'd like to take a year off work and write full-time."

He stared at me for so long, I was convinced a third eye had sprouted in the middle of my forehead. He glanced down at the loan application. He turned the pages of the Vita, which listed all my publications. He looked at me again.

"Could you get me a letter from your employer stating that you'll have a job to return to at the end of the year?"

"I have tenure, but I'm sure they'd write that letter for you."

"Get me the letter," he said, with an actual smile, "and I'll get you the loan."

The smile on my own face was in *rigor mortis* as I shook his hand, left his office, drove home, went into the house, and promptly threw up. Then I started crying, asking myself what in God's name I'd just done. Had I actually asked to borrow $18,000 (my annual salary at the time) at 17 & 7/8% in order to take a year off work to write a novel when I'd never written one before? Had the bank manager just tentatively said "Yes"?

I calmed myself down by convincing myself that the University would never write me such a letter, that the Administration would think it ludicrous for anyone to borrow money to take a year off work (without pay, of course) to write a novel. Therefore, my problems were solved. Without the letter, I couldn't get the loan. Without the loan, it would take me years and years and years to complete the novel.

My chairman told me I had to ask the Dean of the College for the letter, but that he himself would write a memo recommending it. The Dean told me I had to ask the Vice-President of the Faculty for the letter, but that he would write a second memo asking that I be permitted to take the year off to write the novel and be guaranteed to have my job back, forwarding his memo with my Chairman's memo and my Vita of publications. The Vice-President of the Faculty advised me that he'd have to ask the Provost of the University for such a letter, but that he'd write his own memo and send it on with all the other paperwork.

The Provost, whom I'd actually never met, wrote the letter.

With one *proviso:* that after my novel got published, she receive a signed copy of it.

Letter in hand, I returned to the bank. Two hours later, with the monies deposited in my account, and the current school quarter ending in three days, I was ready to begin my year's "sabbatical" to write my novel.

I went home and promptly threw up again.

My Year of Writing Full-Time

After a week of crying, an entire month of "thinking" about writing the entire book, I realized that it had just cost me $2,000 at 17 & 7/8% to "think" for a month. My best friend suggested that I consider "thinking" with a pen in my hand, poised over a sheet of paper at the desk in my home office. (I did not, even for a second, regard her advice as sarcastic.)

> *"Act like it's your job," she said, "because for the next eleven months, it is. Be at your desk every day by a certain time. Showered, dressed, and with your hair and make-up done. Just as if you were going to the University. Sit down at your desk and work. Take a break. Work. Eat lunch. Work some more. Just like when you teach. Only now your full-time job is writing your novel."*

I forever bless her for that advice.

The very next morning, I got up and did what she'd suggested.

For the first few weeks, I could only write 2-3 hours a day, though I spent all day at my desk: doing the outline, reading research, making notes. But, no matter how long I actually wrote on the novel, I was at that desk five days a week, at least 8 hours a day.

By the six-month-point, I was writing 8-10 hours a day; by the start of the ninth month, I was working 12-14 hours a day, and forgetting to eat. I had to set alarms to remind myself to take breaks for lunch or dinner. By the tenth month, I was writing almost 18 hours a day, seven days a week.

It was the hardest work I'd ever done in my life.

I was the happiest I'd ever been.

At the end of the year, after 39 typed revisions (the computer kept track, and I hadn't typed in the first draft until I'd revised the written one at least a dozen times), I felt I had something to give to my readers, all of whom were anxiously awaiting it.

Of course, I was terrified to show it to anyone, and remember being nauseous the entire time I was waiting for them to get back to me. After they finished reading it, they told me they loved it. Their comments on the manuscript copies were eerily identical: virtually all my readers got confused at the same minor things; all of them praised the exact same sections. That had never happened before, not even with my poems. I dismissed their unanimous cries of "success", however, telling myself that they were my friends and they loved me: of course, they loved the novel, too. I'd love their novels if any of them had written one. That's what I told myself, despite my success with my poetry, simply not believing that I'd written a novel that could be considered "good" by anyone except me and my closest friends.

Publishing the Novel

Getting an Agent

Next came the part of a writing career that I hate as much as most writers because it always involves rejection: selling the book. I was used to queries and rejections (and acceptances) for my poems, but it's a lot harder to get rejections (photocopied rejections, at that) for something you've spent an entire year writing, up to 12-18 hours/day, and borrowed money to take time off from work to do it. The greater the emotional, psychological, and time investment, the greater the disappointment and psychic pain with the rejections, I suppose.

However, four months and 39 queries later (all sent out at the same time, to targeted agents who were accepting new clients and, more important, who represented literary fiction), seven New York agents called me (I'm not counting the ones who sent me letters saying I could send the entire novel). Seven real New York-based agents actually called me and asked to read the whole novel (I'd sent the first 3 chapters with the query, in which I pretended I was writing the back-copy of the novel, "selling" it to potential readers).

One agent asked if I could "over-night the manuscript". I agreed, dreading the horrendous cost involved ($39.50, twenty years ago). She received it on a Friday by 10 a.m. On Monday, I got home from school to a message from her, asking me to return the call, and giving me both her office and home phone numbers. She wasn't at the office. I called her at home, flattered that she'd trusted me enough to give me her home number.

She wanted to represent me.

I was wary. I'd read a book called *How to Be Your Own Literary Agent,* and decided that I didn't want to represent myself. Fortunately, the book had provided a list of questions for an author to ask a potential agent. I asked. She answered them all correctly. (Had she also read the book? I wondered.) I asked her if I could think about her offer and call her back in an hour. With a slight laugh, she agreed. I immediately called all my friends, who were shouting congratulations until I told them that I'd said I'd call the agent back with my answer.

> *"When?" they said. "In five minutes?"*
> *"In an hour."*
> *"Are you crazy?" they all said. "Get off the phone with us and call her back right now, you idiot."*

"Idiot."

You can always count on your friends to keep your feet securely on the ground.

I called the agent back in less than fifteen minutes. As soon as she answered, before I'd even said anything (and this was before the days of Caller-ID), she said my name and that she was so glad I'd returned her call. She told me she was very, very happy. I was so happy, I was probably incoherent. I don't remember a single thing I said.

New York, New York

Two months later, she said she was 99.99% sure that my novel was going to be sold to HarperCollins. She told me to expect an Advance of between $5,000 and $7,500, but she'd try her hardest to talk them up to $10,000 (warning me not to expect any more than $5,000 because it was my first novel and because I wrote literary fiction. "The only thing harder to sell than literary fiction," she said, "is poetry.")

I jumped into a rented car the next day (mine had 180,000 miles on it, and I didn't think it would survive the trip), drove to New York with my agent's approval, stayed at the recommended (i.e., cheapest) hotel in the Village, where my agent's office was located, to meet my agent and editor.

(One famous, relatively wealthy author I met years later made fun of me, to my face, for having done that. Apparently, having grown up in New York, she thought I was "innocent and naïve" for driving all the way to Manhattan just to meet my agent and editor. I've never understood her reaction. After all, she'd met her agent and editor. I didn't feel "innocent and naïve" when I went to New York after having sold my first novel, and remember it as one of the happiest times of my life. I loved New York. Still do. In fact, I'd recommend that any author who has a book accepted by a NY house go to the Big Apple to personally meet his agent and editor.)

As I was on my way, the sale was confirmed. The book sold late on a Thursday afternoon, and I was in a motel room in Pennsylvania when I got the news. It was raining, the motel room was gloomy even with the curtains open, the weather was chilly despite its being almost the end of July.

When my agent called me back (she'd been getting the final contract details when I'd arrived at the motel and called her office), the first words out of her mouth were, "Congratulations, my dear. You're an author."

I dropped onto the bed, crying.

"When you're finished crying," she said, "I'll tell you the rest of the good news."

"There's more?"

"Don't you want to know how much you got?"

(I would've given the book to HarperCollins just to have them publish it, and I'd told my agent that when she'd told me they were

definitely interested. She'd laughed and said it was a good thing I had an agent.)

After I stopped crying, she filled me in on the rest of the contract details.

"You got 25," she said.

"25?"

"25 thousand."

"Dollars?" I said.

"You were expecting something else?" she said, laughing.

I began sobbing again.

"They want to sell the foreign rights, too."

"What does that mean?"

"It means, the Vice-President and Director of Foreign Rights loves the book as much as your editor, and she thinks she can sell it overseas. They'll get 50% of every sale they make."

"Is that okay?"

"It is with me," said my agent. "They'll be doing all the work to sell your first novel to foreign publishers, and we'll be making 50% of anything they make. That's a pretty good deal for a first novel in literary fiction. Hey, why are you still crying?"

"It's HarperCollins..."

"And?"

"You told me only to expect $5,000."

"So," she said, "be five times happier."

I had just turned 36, sold my first novel to one of the most prestigious publishers in the world, and gotten enough money from the Advance (after my agent's commission; Federal, State, Local, and Social Security Self-Employment taxes) to pay off almost the entire remaining balance of the loan I'd taken out to write the novel in the first place (I netted approximately 49¢ on each dollar, so I got about $12,000 out of the Advance, divided into two payments: the first half of the Advance about 4-5 months after the book was sold, the second half approximately 3-4 months after the book was published).

It had taken me 7 years to research the Holocaust, 9 months to figure out Max's Voice in order to begin working on the novel, 1 year (off work, living on the bank loan) to write the novel full-time, 7 months to sell it, and another year before it was published: all that time to net roughly $12,000 while paying commission and taxes on the entire amount. You can do the math to figure out my "annual income" as a writer for my first novel.

The next morning, I would arrive in New York, where I'd always wanted to live.

That was twenty years ago.

I was the happiest person in the world.

The fact that I was crying the entire sixteen hours it took me to drive from Ohio to Manhattan did not mean I wasn't happy, trust me.

On My Name

My parents didn't name me "Alexandria Constantinova." They wouldn't have known how to spell it. They named me something I hated, and when I went to high school, I started using the nickname "Sherri" because I didn't like my given first name. When I was 17, after I read Lawrence Durrell's *The Alexandria Quartet,* I fell in love with the name "Alexandria" and immediately wanted to change mine to that. I felt I deserved a more exotic name. After all, I'd wanted to be a writer since I was 6-years-old, and writers had more interesting names than either the one I'd been given or than my high-school nickname.

My family not only vehemently disagreed, they obstinately insisted that only criminals changed their names, were insulted that I disliked the name they'd given me, and wondered who I thought I was wanting a weird-o name like Alexandria. They'd never even addressed me as "Sherri" so there was certainly no chance that they'd ever call me "Alexandria". (They also didn't understand why I wanted to be a writer, and throughout my life, did everything in their power to discourage, insult, and prevent me from writing.)

Still, "Alexandria" is the only name that I ever felt fit me, so I did change it common-law once I decided to ignore anyone who didn't like it, and legally once I thought of a middle name to go with it.

On Why I was Originally Published as "Sherri" Szeman

Because my first editor said my name wouldn't fit on the cover of the book. It's as simple and stupid as that. The editor also said she wanted an "easy" first name to go with my "hard" last name, so she balked at publishing *The Kommandant's Mistress* under Alexandria Szeman. My agent didn't say anything to contradict her. I was too naïve to realize that any name can fit on any book cover, too happy to be published by HarperCollins to feel anything but disappointment about my name, and too inexperienced to insist that the book be published under the name I wanted.

When I got my next agent, for my second novel, and my next publisher, I asked to have *Only with the Heart* published under Alexandria Szeman. My agent and publisher were horrified. It seems they were terrified that they'd "lose the name recognition of *The Kommandant's Mistress.*" Same thing with the third book, *Mastering Point of View: How to Control Point of View to Create Conflict, Depth, & Suspense.* That editor and publisher also didn't want to lose the "name recognition of *The Kommandant's Mistress*". Stuck again with "Sherri". I was not pleased, to say the least.

When my two poetry collections were accepted, at the same time, by UKA Press, I asked the publisher about the name issue. She laughed, saying that, of course, we could publish *Love in the Time of Dinosaurs* and *Where Lightning Strikes* under my name: we'd just add "formerly writing as Sherri". She also reminded me that authors write under different names all the time, and everybody knows it. Thank God for Andrea Lowne of UKA Press.

Revised, updated, and expanded Anniversary Editions of my first three books are re-published under my name, Alexandria Constantinova Szeman, with the *caveat* "formerly writing as Sherri" so readers understand that it's the same person, and my new books are being published under my real name.

I'm so much happier.

Special Notes to Readers

Spoiler Alert: If you read this before reading the novel, please be aware that it reveals plot elements when answering questions posed by readers since the novel's publication. Please do not feel morally obligated to read this section of the Revised Edition if you only want to read the novel itself.

On the Three Different Endings

There are three different endings to the novel, and all three of the endings are true at the same time. (Trust me on this: I wouldn't have written a novel with three different endings only to then tell you to ignore two of them.) Also, on a subconscious level, you probably already know how all three endings can be true all at the same time.

Often readers express disappointment that Part 3 is fictional: I'm not sure why; none has ever told me. The situation in the novel, unfortunately, is not "fictional" *per se*: Many women and men were forced into sexual servitude in the Camps, either as prostitutes for the guards or as individual "slaves" for the SS Officers.

The "biographies" of Part Three are entirely fictional. Over the years, many scholars and reviewers have written that I "fictionalized" — in Parts One & Two — the "real people" whose "biographies comprise Part Three". I thank those writers most sincerely for the compliment on my writing style in that third section as I apparently succeeded in imitating the countless number of biographical encyclopedia entries on in/famous or historical persons that I read to learn the style of such entries.

In the third section of the novel, the ostensible biographical encyclopedia entries — which, again, are entirely fictional — the "biographer" (whom I've always thought of as a man) does not seem very objective. For example, he consistently calls Max by his last name, yet calls Rachel/Leah by her first name. The biographer presents statements of fact about Max in a more negative light by not providing any interpretation of Max's actions. For examples, see Discussion Questions on The Three Endings (pages 214-216, 217, 219-220). The biographer presents information about Rachel in a more positive light than others might have seen it either during or after the War. In fact, the biographer of Leah Sarah Abramson does not even seem to know that she did, indeed, survive the Camp, and changed her name to Rachel.

Closer examination of Part Three, which serves as a commentary on history and historians in general, reveals that these entries must be fictional since no single person, Nazi or Jew, could possibly have done everything I say that Max and Rachel did.

Max

I didn't want Max to represent only one Nazi but, rather, all the Nazis, so I could show all the atrocities they committed against the Jews. Thus, he's at virtually every Nuremburg rally where Hitler, Himmler, or Goebbels spoke [1:1:3:3], [1:3:2:23], [1:6:3:53], etc. Max participates in the Night of the Broken Glass [1:3:3:23]; in the Night of the Long Knives (the purge of the BrownShirts, also known as Storm-Troopers, or SA; whose members were the precursors and competitors of the *Schutzstaffeln*, SS, who wore black uniforms) [1:6:4:53]; and in the *Wannsee* Conference, where the "Final Solution to the Jewish Problem" — killing them "more efficiently" with cyanide gas rather than with the carbon monoxide trucks which had been in use [1:5:1:43]. Max heads a Mobile Killing Squad (*Einsatzkommando*) and instructs the soldiers on the correct way to shoot prisoners in the forest [1:9:2:75]. He serves alongside the Army — as a member of the SS — at the Eastern Front, where he's wounded by German fire after he mistakes fellow soldiers for partisans [1:10:2:86]; he meets Himmler [1:5:3:44] and is promoted through the ranks of the SS until he becomes Kommandant of a Concentration Camp [1:3:1:21], [Part Three: page 197].

No one Nazi could have done all that. Though Max is a "real person" as a literary character, he is a representative, symbolic Nazi; his career and life reflect everything the Nazis did to the Jews in Germany and in the other conquered territories.

Rachel

Likewise, Rachel is not modeled after any single Jewish person from that period, though I did interview many survivors. I also read memoirs, diaries, letters, autobiographies, and biographies of Camp inmates who survived and of those who perished. Rachel is symbolic of what all the Jews in Europe experienced (hence, her family's moving from country to country in an attempt to escape the encroaching Nazi destruction and persecution).

Rachel is at the Goebbels'-organized Book Burning with her father and uncle [2:9:10:184]; she and her family are in Czechoslovakia when Jews are deprived of their citizenship [2:1:3:100]; she passes as a non-Jew ("Aryan") in order to get food for her family [2:8:8:173]; she is in the Warsaw Ghetto [2:3:6:122], [2:3:10:126], [2:4:7:135], [2:5:6:140]. Rachel has encounters with the *Gestapo* [2:8:2:168], [2:8:4:170]; with the Camp's Underground [2:1:8:104], [2:2:1:107], [2:2:10:116], etc. She is in the Camp proper [2:7:5:159]; builds roads with the labor crew supervised by the Camp's *Kapo* and Nazi guards [2:4:3:130]; is in a "Selection" upon her arrival at the Camp, where Jews are cursorily inspected by a Doctor (the most infamous being Josef Mengele at Auschwitz-Birkenau) and arbitrarily assigned to go to the "Left" or to the "Right", one group of which will immediately be gassed, while the other will remain as laborers in the Camp [2:6:7:151]. (I have intentionally not indicated which "side" — Left or Right — went to the gas, since the Jews themselves didn't know what the sides meant during the Selections.)

Just as no single Nazi could have possibly done everything that Max does in the novel, no individual Jew could have experienced everything that Rachel does. She, too — despite being a "real person" in literary terms — is representative and symbolic of all the Jews persecuted, enslaved, imprisoned, tortured, killed, and systematically exterminated by the Nazis.

On Rachel as the Kommandant's "Mistress"

Note on novel's title: The title of this novel was originally *The Kommandant,* since I viewed it as three different versions of Max. One of the Vice-Presidents at HarperCollins, which originally published the novel, wanted to put the novel's focus more on Rachel, and suggested the new title, *The Kommandant's Mistress,* based on the "most persistent rumor" of what happened to Rachel/Leah in the Camp, and modeling the title after John Fowles' classic *The French Lieutenant's Woman,* where the "woman" of that title, though considered a whore and virtually a prostitute by everyone else in the novel, is actually a virgin who never had intimate relations of any kind with the French Lieutenant, with whom she was in love, who had promised to marry her, and whom she discovered to be unfaithful to her before she slept with him.

Historical note: Like Rachel in this novel, many of the Jewish women who were raped, whether in the Camps or not, and inmates (male or female) who were forced into prostitution or unwilling sexual servitude in the Nazi Concentration Camps were considered "collaborators" by their fellow inmates and treated brutally after the liberation.

(In fact, one inconsiderate borrower of a library's copy of *The Kommandant's Mistress* crossed out the word "Mistress" on the title page and wrote "Whore, more like it" in ink beside the title; that reader was behaving exactly as did the inmates who judged and condemned, then punished, tortured, or killed any fellow inmates who were raped or forced into sexual situations/prostitution by the Nazis.)

Rudolf Höss, the Kommandant of Auschwitz, for example, who lived with his family on the Concentration Camp's grounds, had a "mistress" who bore him a son. The day before SS-Head Heinrich Himmler was to "visit" the Camp to investigate the allegations, the "mistress," the son, and the guard who'd reported it all disappeared. I can only assume that, since such behavior went against Nazi principles and would have resulted in more than a mere reprimand for Kommandant Höss, the three were all sent to the gas-chambers.

(For Discussion Questions concerning the relationship between Max and Rachel in the Camp, see Rachel as the Kommandant's "Mistress" pages 220-221.)

On Rachel's Poems & Books

Many people over the years have contacted me, looking for Rachel's books and poems. They do not exist, unless they are my own poems, dissertation, etc. *The Dead Bodies That Line the Streets* is the name of one of the poems in my Holocaust collection *Where Lightning Strikes,* while *Survivor: One Who Survives* is not only a poem in that volume, but also the title of my dissertation. "First Day of German Class", from which Marta reads aloud [1:1:7:7 = Part 1: Chapter 1: Scene 7: Page 7]; "Cutthroat: A Player who Plays for Himself", a portion of which is excerpted in the novel and which Max reads [1:8:8:71]; and "Little Birds" are also in my collection of Holocaust poetry, *Where Lightning Strikes.*

Rachel's poem "In the Bedroom of the Kommandant" does not exist, though the scenes upon which the poem was supposedly based do, in the novel itself [1:7:6:62], [1:8:4:68], [2:7:9:163]. Her poem "Bitter Herbs", which she is shown revising in the Kommandant's office [2:5:5:140], does not exist but is based on the Ghetto *Seder* (Passover) [2:5:6:140]. (Max's poem "Love Song for Klaus", about the death of his illegitimate son by his mistress Dianne Braun [Part Three: Max: funeral: page 195], to which Marta alludes

[1:8:8:71] and Rachel sees in his middle desk drawer [2:5:1:138], also does not exist.)

Her book *The Kommandant,* mentioned by the grocer when Max claims he searched for the girl [1:9:6:79], is the book she's writing about the Camp during David's absence [2:10:6:189] and which she tells him not to read yet, after his return with Althea [2:10:8:189]; it is, in fact, Part Two of *The Kommandant's Mistress.* (Max's version of the story, Part One, is the document alluded to when he is asked to sign the transcript-verification document [1:9:10:84].) Some of my non-Holocaust poems, "Cain's Lament" and "Ahab's Wife", which appear in my poetry collection *Love in the Time of Dinosaurs,* serve as the titles of Rachel's pre-War poetry books which are mentioned in Part Three [Rachel/Leah: page 199].

On the Camp's Underground

There were Underground Resistance members in many of the Camps and, in the case of Auschwitz-Birkenau, in the woods surrounding the Camp; members of the *Sonderkommando* did blow up the crematoria in Auschwitz-Birkenau, after which the Camp in this novel is most closely modeled.

The Underground in Auschwitz-Birkenau, however, did not move about as freely as they did in some of the other Camps. I've used artistic license in this instance, giving them more freedom of movement so they could interact with Rachel, and so readers would be aware that there were Resistance movements inside and outside the actual Camps.

Additions to the 20th Anniversary Edition

Before I published the first novel and actually did readings, I never realized that so many people would be interested in how I got my ideas; why I wrote the book the way I did; whether I wrote the book in chronological order, cut the scenes apart, threw them up in the air, then randomly put them together (yes, that was an actual question and one that's been asked several times, and, no, I wrote them as they came to me, which is the order in which they appear in the novel); whether I like writing poems, stories, or novels "better" (I like them all, but novels, because they involve the artistic psyche so completely for such an extended period of time, have become my "drug of choice"); why my name is different now, etc. I've tried to include all that information in this Note.

Chapter-by-Chapter Scene Index (pages 203-210)

Another addition came as a result of how the book is written. Since it imitates memory and how the mind works, it moves from scene to scene apparently without warning, but actually triggered by something in the previous scene. (People often ask if I wrote the novel in chronological order, cut the scenes apart, then threw them up in the air and picked them up randomly. No, this is how it came out. This is how my brain works. In fact, Part Three was one of the more challenging sections to write because I had to do it in chronological order, and apparently, the artist in me doesn't work well that way. The book as it appears is how the scenes came to me and how I wrote it.)

Once, during a commercial break in a radio interview, the host asked if I would read a scene from the book. I turned to the opening, being accustomed to reading from chapter one. The host then asked me to specifically read the scene where Max instructs the soldiers how to shoot prisoners [1:9:2:75 = Part 1: Chapter 9: Scene 2: Page 75].

> *"Where is it?" I said.*
> *"What do you mean, 'where is it'?" the host said. "You're the one who wrote it."*
> *"You've read the book; you know how it's written," I said. "I don't know where that scene is."*

Fortunately, one of the assistants outside the booth had a copy of the book, and had read it as well. He volunteered to look for the scene while we continued our on-air discussion, saying I could read that scene after the next commercial break. He found it, I read it, and the radio station was immediately flooded with calls for the name of the book and author. "Max at work, from his perspective," as I've come to refer to that scene [1:9:2:75], has become a standard part of my readings & performances since then (always followed by "Max at work, from Rachel's perspective: the Wedding Game" [2:1:1:97].

After my University students begged me for four years to allow them to read my novel "for credit" in the senior level "The Novel" course, to which I assigned a different theme every year, I realized that they wouldn't be able to either lead discussions themselves, which I required them to do, or adequately discuss the book and their interpretations of it if they were unable to find the scenes to which they wished to refer. I made a scene index for them, and they referred to it constantly. Many teachers and book groups, having heard that story, have requested that Chapter-by-Chapter Scene Index [pages 203-210] for their own use, so I've included that index in this edition as well.

Discussion Questions (pages 211-225)

Since so many book clubs, book groups, classes (eighth grade, high school, and college) have used the novel in all sorts of courses, from

Holocaust Studies to Women's Studies, from Political Science to Creative Writing, I've often been asked for Discussion Questions for use by leaders, teachers, and students. I've long had them on my web-site, but have included those, as well as some additional ones, in the book for the first time (some of the new questions not on the site deal with sections of the book that people have always asked about most, such as the three different endings).

The Original Story [pages 253-258] **& Poem** [pages 259-265] **for the novel, "The Kommandant"**

Also, at several readings in Cincinnati, where I'd earned my PhDs, some people had actually taken the time to look up the original poem, "The Kommandant", which appeared in my dissertation *Survivor: One Who Survives* (1986), stored in the University of Cincinnati Library, and asked questions about it. At one reading, a creative writing student actually had a copy of it, and several audience members asked to see it, so he passed it around. He wanted to talk about the changes between the poem and the novel, but since not everyone there had read both, we had to talk about it afterward. I included the poem because of the interest that many creative writers expressed about it.

That student asked about the original story "The Kommandant" as well. At the time, and for many years afterward, I didn't have a copy of the story, having destroyed it after I wrote what I considered a successful poem. He seemed sincerely disappointed at not being able to read that story.

It was only years after the novel was published (after my second novel was published, in fact) that one of my friends, Evelyn Schott, found her copy of the original story and sent it to me. Though it is absolutely dreadful — I'm not kidding about this — I've included it for anyone interested in the creative writing process itself, and as proof that even the worst writer can improve if s/he spends enough time on the craft, reads other good works constantly, and consciously attempts to become a better writer. (I hope the UC creative writing student who brought the poem to the reading and asked about the original story gets a copy of this; I also hope he doesn't laugh himself silly after reading the original story and regret ever asking to see it in the first place.)

Revisions to the 20th Anniversary Edition

The HarperCollins editor didn't want anything in the book changed. However, after reading the book countless times over the years, I decided that I did want two major things (and a few minor ones) changed for the Revised, 20th Anniversary edition.

First of all, I didn't use any contractions when I wrote the novel (except in dialogue) because I thought I had to be "formal". Then, at bookstores, whenever I did readings or, later, performances, of the novel, I found that not using contractions felt unnatural, so I read them as contractions. Sometimes, members of the audience who'd already read the book and had it with them came up to me afterward and asked why I'd read it differently from the way it was written: I told them the truth. They were not pleased with me. They felt that I should've read it exactly the way I'd written it. In this revised version, I've put the contractions in, except in places where the character is intentionally not using a contraction for the purpose of emphasis, e.g., "I did not have sex with a Jew" or "I would never rape a woman". We think in contractions, and since the narration of Parts One and Two is imitating memory and how our minds work, I put the contractions in. It's more natural that way. If I'd read the entire book aloud when I was writing it, instead of just doing the dialogue aloud, I would've used contractions from the very start.

The second major change in this edition is the arrangement of the last two scenes in Chapter Two of Part One, Max's section (pages 19-20). I'd originally written the final two scenes like this:

> "I need those papers, Josef," I said. "They're private."
>
> "What papers?" said my adjutant.
>
> "My private papers."
>
> My adjutant only looked at me.
>
> "There were papers on my desk, Josef."
>
> He glanced down at the cluttered desktop, covered with documents, files, and folders.
>
> "What kind of papers, Kommandant?"
>
> "Personal papers."
>
> "Personal papers?"
>
> "Handwritten papers. On my personal stationery."
>
> As I shuffled through the mound of documents on my desk, my adjutant glanced at the girl. She sat in her usual corner, arms wrapped around her legs, head against the wall, staring at nothing. Upstairs in the house, Hans was crying. Marta was in the garden, calling Ilse to lunch. I lifted some of the folders and papers on my desk, sifting through them. Hans continued crying. I dropped the papers I was holding back onto the desk. My adjutant blinked at me.
>
> "Josef, where are those papers?"
>
> "I'd be happy to help you find them, sir, if you'll tell me what I'm looking for."
>
> "I am looking for my personal papers. They were right here on the desk."
>
> "Perhaps you should lock up your personal papers, sir," he said, glancing again at the girl, "to keep them safe when you're not here."
>
> "I put some papers for you in the safe," said the hotel clerk as I passed the desk on my way to the elevator.

"Papers?" I said. "What papers?"

The hotel clerk glanced around at the lobby; then he leaned toward me.

"Some letters came for you," said the clerk in a hushed voice. "The postmark made me think you'd like them..."

"Like them what?"

"Kept safe," he said. "Private. Just a moment. Let me get them for you."

One of the bellboys helped an elderly gentleman to the front doors. A young woman in a fur coat straightened the collar on the coat of her small son. Her husband stood near, scanning the train schedule. I looked at my watch. The clerk was taking a long time. I looked through some of the papers on the front desk.

"*Herr* Hoffmann? *Herr* Hoffmann?"

I released the papers. The clerk had returned. He had a small bundle: three letters, their stamps and postmarks foreign. He held them out to me, a hesitant smile on his face.

"Oh, yes," I said. "My letters."

"Did I do the right thing?" he said, his hands clutched together, his eyes blinking. "Putting them in the safe, was that all right?"

"Yes," I said, reaching into my pocket, then placing my hand, palm down, on the desk. "Thank you."

"Oh, thank you, sir," he said, smiling and swiping his hand over the money. "Thank you. Any time. I'll be happy to look out for you. Always happy to look out after one of our own. Always..."

The elevator doors slid shut. A young couple surreptitiously held hands, blushing and smiling. I closed my eyes, folding the letters. The couple whispered to each other. Giggled. The elevator opened. In my room, I tossed aside Marta's letters, and read the other.

Dear Daddy,

We miss you and wish you were here.

Mommy cries and Hans is a bad boy all the time.

He won't eat his vegetables and he won't learn Spanish.

Why don't you come live with us in our new house?

Can't Uncle Ricardo get a new name for you too?

One of my friends convinced me that I'd written those two scenes wrong, and that they should be rearranged into three scenes, like this (I've put the first scene in bold, and separated it from the other scene, to show you where my reader thought it should go, and where it, in fact, did go, in the first two print editions of the novel):

"I put some papers for you in the safe," said the hotel clerk as I passed the desk on my way to the elevator.

"Papers?" I said. "What papers?"

The hotel clerk glanced around at the lobby; then he leaned toward me.

"Some letters came for you," said the clerk in a hushed voice. "The postmark made me think you'd like them..."

"Like them what?"

"Kept safe," he said. "Private. Just a moment. Let me get them for you."

One of the bellboys helped an elderly gentleman to the front doors. A young woman in a fur coat straightened the collar on the coat of her small son. Her husband stood near, scanning the train schedule. I looked at my watch. The clerk was taking a long time. I looked through some of the papers on the front desk.

"I need those papers, Josef," I said. "They're private."

"What papers?" said my adjutant.

"My private papers."

My adjutant only looked at me.

"There were papers on my desk, Josef."

He glanced down at the cluttered desktop, covered with documents, files, and folders.

"What kind of papers, Kommandant?"

"Personal papers."

"Personal papers?"

"Handwritten papers. On my personal stationery."

As I shuffled through the mound of documents on my desk, my adjutant glanced at the girl. She sat in her usual corner, arms wrapped around her legs, head against the wall, staring at nothing. Upstairs in the house, Hans was crying. Marta was in the garden, calling Ilse to lunch. I lifted some of the folders and papers on my desk, sifting through them. Hans continued crying. I dropped the papers I was holding back onto the desk. My adjutant blinked at me.

"Josef, where are those papers?"

"I'd be happy to help you find them, sir, if you'll tell me what I'm looking for."

"I am looking for my personal papers. They were right here on the desk."

"Perhaps you should lock up your personal papers, sir," he said, glancing again at the girl, "to keep them safe when you're not here."

"*Herr* Hoffmann? *Herr* Hoffmann?"

I released the papers on the front desk. The clerk had returned. He had a small bundle: three letters, their stamps and postmarks foreign. He held them out to me, a hesitant smile on his face.

"Oh, yes," I said. "My letters."

"Did I do the right thing?" he said, his hands clutched together, his eyes blinking. "Putting them in the safe, was that all right?"

"Yes," I said, reaching into my pocket, then placing my hand, palm down, on the desk. "Thank you."

"Oh, thank you, sir," he said, smiling and swiping his hand over the money. "Thank you. Any time. I'll be happy to look out for you. Always happy to look out after one of our own. Always..."

The elevator doors slid shut. A young couple surreptitiously held hands, blushing and smiling. I closed my eyes, folding the letters. The couple whispered to each other. Giggled. The elevator opened. In my room, I tossed aside Marta's letters, and read the other.

Dear Daddy,

We miss you and wish you were here.

Mommy cries and Hans is a bad boy all the time.

He won't eat his vegetables and he won't learn Spanish.

Why don't you come live with us in our new house?

Can't Uncle Ricardo get a new name for you too?

In effect, the first scene was moved, interrupting the second scene and dividing the final scene into two parts. I don't know why my editor-friend was so insistent that the scenes be presented that way. Despite my misgivings, I re-arranged the scenes as my friend suggested. After all, she was a professional editor, a literature major herself, and was absolutely convinced that I'd written it wrong, putting the scenes in the incorrect order. It was my first novel, I'd never even done a book before, and… In short, what did I know?

Yet, every time I've read the book since it was published, I've known that the arrangement was, quite simply, not "right". (For my friend, I'm sure that it was, but not for me.) It should've been done the way I'd originally had it. I have no explanation for this feeling: just a gut-reaction to those two scenes every time I've read the novel since it was published. An unwavering conviction that it should've remained the way I'd written it in the first place, and that it was, categorically and incontrovertibly, "wrong" in the published order that my friend had insisted upon and to which I, lacking confidence in my artistic intuition, had agreed.

In this version, I've restored the original order of the scenes. I feel much better about it now. You can decide which version you like best.

Besides the contractions and the arrangement of those two scenes, I changed a few minor things. I never liked the transition between [2:9:4:179] and [2:9:5:179], so I fixed that. In some of the dialogue, I deleted the repetitious direct address, especially if there were only two people in the scene. I corrected the couple of times the Bounty-Hunter addressed Max as "Commandant" rather than as "Commander"; I changed the Nazi Colonel's title to *Oberstleutnant,* and the American Jeep to the German *Kübelwagen,* which the Nazis would have had; I corrected any typos I missed when it was first accepted (the second edition was scanned from the first & I wasn't permitted to make the corrections, though I was allowed to insert the translations to Verdi's opera only because it didn't change the page numbers, and because I explained, very firmly, that audience members were always asking me which opera it was, and what the lines meant).

Another minor change I made was to Rachel's tattooed number. Because I could find nothing about the arbitrary, meaningless numbers with which the Nazis further humiliated, degraded, dehumanized, and mocked the Jewish inmates, I simply made up a number to be tattooed on Rachel's inner left arm. Since then, however, I discovered that the Nazis pretended that they had a system, and, as shown in the novel with Rachel and Anna in the tattoo scene (page 179), the Jews believed that they were being registered and identified; they believed that because they were being tattooed, they would not be killed.

The tattooing practice began in Auschwitz, an Extermination rather than a Concentration Camp, but then spread to the others. Even in Auschwitz, however, though the Nazis claimed that the numbers had a purpose, the numbers followed no logic and were completely meaningless. For example, Anna Brunn Ornstein, in Auschwitz at age 16, and whose story I used in the novel when she fictionally interacts with Rachel, has two numbers: *B-71* and *A-200,* with the *B* crossed out on the second day she was tattooed. She was told her number was then *A-20071.* The *A* and *B* were supposedly for the Barracks in which the inmates were housed. However, Anna was in B Barracks, and remained there after both tattoos, so altering the *B* to an *A* — ostensibly for the Barracks — was illogical and pointless since Anna did not change Barracks. Her numbers, in fact, look like this:

200
A-B-71

Since Rachel gets her tattoo on the day that Anna is getting her first tattoo "corrected," I changed the previously random number to one that was more in line with Anna's tattooed numbers, though, in fact, all the numbers were meaningless and were not recorded anywhere.

Other than the changes I've mentioned, the book remains as it was first published. I've resisted any stylistic changes which would've been the result of my maturation as a writer. I used to throw away all early versions of my poems once I had a copy with which I was satisfied. When I told my therapist that, she was horrified. She patiently explained to me that I was robbing myself of the opportunity to see myself improve as a writer.

James Joyce, whom I revere as an artist and (most of) whose work I respect, constantly revised his books throughout his life, always republishing it afterward so that the original versions were lost. I'm afraid that, except for the revisions noted here, I'm still relatively happy with *The Kommandant's Mistress* as I wrote it over two decades ago, and, in order not to "rob myself of the opportunity" to see how I've improved as a writer, have not made any substantive stylistic changes.

Happy, happy 20th Anniversary, my dear Readers.

Original Story & Poem "The Kommandant"
for *The Kommandant's Mistress*

I admit that, when I wrote it, I was very proud of the original poem, "The Kommandant", which formed the basis of this novel and is similar in structure & endings. It was rejected hundreds of times before being accepted by three different journals in the same week (all three eventually published it, with each waiting in turn according to their postmarked acceptance).

The story which preceded the poem, however, was absolutely dreadful. It was my first attempt at fiction since the age of 12, and was probably worse in quality than the stories I wrote when I was in seventh grade (which I attempted to sell, for 25¢ each, by designing my own covers & stapling the stories into "books"; unfortunately, there were no buyers. Fortunately for my artistic ego, I didn't let these early rejections stop me from my intended writing career).

Therefore, bear in mind that the story and poem are included here because so many readers of the first 2 editions of *The Kommandant's Mistress* have asked to see them. Not having had a computer in grad school, I actually did not have the original story: one of my friends discovered it over 20 years after it was written when she was doing spring-cleaning, and kindly sent me a copy. In an attempt to prevent blackmail should I ever become remotely famous, I am publishing it here myself.

Caveat Reader: it is terrible.

I shuddered when I re-read it. But I laughed, too, realizing how much I'd improved since then. I hope you are kind enough to laugh when you read it, too. (By the way, the paragraphing in the story, though gruesomely incorrect at times, is how I originally wrote it, so I forced myself to leave it as is/was.)

The original poem, which won a prize, follows the story, and (I hope) won't make you laugh quite as heartily. (Then again, maybe it will.)

Spoiler Alert: If you read this before reading the novel, please be aware that both the original story & poem reveal plot elements contained in the novel itself, even if changed slightly since they were written.

The Kommandant

(the original story)

For who can make straight
that which He hath made crooked?

He saw her for the first time after several years in the general store just beyond the village. Immediately he jumped back, his shoulder knocking a box of cornflakes from the shelf. He replaced it, glanced around the edge of the aisle toward her. His hand went, out of habit, to his hip, seeking the weight of his gun.

There she stood, even frailer than she had seemed in the yard, the large faded dress hanging loosely from thinned shoulders, more colour in the bandana on her head than in her cheeks. Though she was tall for a woman, her head only came to below his chin. He waved his adjutant outside and strode over to her.

He spoke.

She did not look up.

"Hmmm?" He raised her chin with his baton, looked into eyes bluer than his own.

She did not look away.

His arm dropped, brushing the gun on his hip.

He took off his holster, laid it on his desk. As was his custom of late, he poured champagne.

She obediently sipped some.

He drank more.

The cork on their third bottle exploded; pale liquid foamed down the sides. He urged her to drain her glass, refilled his own, hauled his chair to the side of the desk where she sat, moving until their knees collided, his monologue more earnest than usual.

She drank sparingly, her eyes tracing the design on the silver oval badge pinned over his left breast: two swords crossed behind an army steel helmet.

Leather hissed as he slipped his pistol from the holster. He leaned forward, displaying the gun.

She stared at his badge.

"*Freiheit.*"

She never gave any sign that she understood what he was saying.

Snap!

He pulled the two small circles on the gun up and back.

She looked at the cool dark of the weapon.

"*Freiheit.*"

The glass in her hand shuddered.

He held out the gun to her.

She did not move.

He took the champagne from her, set the glass on the desk. She let her hand fall to her lap.

"*Nein, nein,*" urging the butt toward her hand.

She stared.

He gripped her wrist, stood, tugging her to her feet along with him. He slammed the warm metal into her hand, crushed her limp fingers around its form, fixing her hand with both his rough palms. "*Du, Freiheit*," yanking gun and hands until the barrel butted his chest, her elbow rigid. "*Feuer.*"

Hard steel. His hands hot on hers.

"*Feuer.*"

Her eyes turned less opaque.

"*Ja.*"

She looked up into his eyes, at the colour of the weapon.

He swallowed, squared his wide shoulders, lifted his chin, took his hands from hers.

Her arm dropped to her side.

"*Nein. Feuer.*"

The piece thudded to her feet.

He stared down at her.

Her eyes turned inward, leaving him there.

The gun lay on the floor between them.

He had forgotten that he no longer wore it; his empty hand slid down his hip and leg as he watched her pay the shopkeeper for her items, her long pale braid down the center of her back. Morning sun glowed on her hair as she opened the door and stepped out, calling a goodbye to the store owner.

The German gazed after her.

"Help you wi' somethin'?" the old man was asking him.

"Cigarettes," he fumbled for the change.

"I knowed you wasn't from 'round here," the clerk grinned triumphantly. "Where you from?"

"Europe," he answered, trying to see her car's path.

"Always wanted to go there. Couldn't 'cause o' the war 'n all. Still, maybe the missus 'n I'll get there…"

"Does she live around here?" he interrupted, indicating with a nod of his head the woman who had left.

The older man turned suspicious. "You a fan o' hers?"

"I greatly admire her writing."

From the bookstore window, her face lashed out at him. He leaned, gasping, against the glass. Fuller cheeks, hair, bright eyes — but her. He dragged himself into the shop, forced the slim volume into his hands.

Survivor: One Who Survives. Poems by Esther Rebekah Levi.

Esther.

The publisher supplied him an address. She had moved by the time he reached the place, though it was easy enough to discover her new destination.

So it went.

This time, she was here.

"…lives up the mountain a ways in th'old McCormick place. Bought it couple o' years after old widder McCormick died. Didn't have no kin to speak of, so Sheriff Willoughby said we oughter auction…"

"Does she live alone?" reaching for the cigarettes still tight in the clerk's hand.

"You a friend o' hers?" he eyed him nervously.

"Esther and I have known each other many years."

The old clerk visibly relaxed at his use of her first name, releasing the cigarettes. "Jus' take that path to the left…"

The engine started almost too eagerly, jerking the car up onto the narrow road. After countless German, French, Italian villages, he found her in this mountain town in West Virginia. He wished he were wearing his uniform. He shook his head: He must go to her without ornaments.

The road twisted through the summer trees; an already-warm breeze whispered in his just-greying hair. He decided he would park far from the house and approach on foot. He didn't want her to have too much warning; she might call someone or, worse, she might disappear again.

All the lines he had been practicing for years scrambled away. He worried if he should address her in English or in his own language. He was still so uncomfortable in English, and his thick accent made him, he knew, difficult to understand.

"*Verdammt nochmal!*" He slammed the car to a stop, jerking the wheel to the side toward the trees. The house was in view, in a clearing. He turned off the engine, gripped the wheel.

His knees were weak when he closed the car-door. He leaned against the hood. Never had he been in this position. Why, during the war… the war was over. Now he was merely a man, as any other.

She wouldn't want to see him again. Maybe she had her own gun by now. His fingers touched the door handle. He should forget he had found her.

But the look in her eyes, the taste of her, the smell of her: there was no escape.

He made a great show of examining the numbers on her forearm: *S-34291*. She tried to slow her breathing, glanced down, her dark lashes long on her cheeks. He kneaded her shoulder and ribs through the threadbare material. Her hipbones jutted awkwardly beneath the skin.

He rubbed her cheek with the back of his long fingers, murmured something, pushed the scarf from her head, ran his hand across the light stubble. He circled her several times, nodding his head. "*Ja.*"

Marta guessed almost from the beginning. At first, she said nothing, assuming it would pass as quickly as all the others. Then she began making snide remarks, which he ignored. In the spring, she confronted him with it.

"Stop with this girl!"

He looked at her over his paper.

"There's only so much I can be expected to ignore!"

He sipped his coffee.

"I have my position to think of!"

He went back to reading his newspaper.

Marta pushed the paper down onto the table. "I'll complain to someone if this doesn't stop!"

He pulled the paper from under her hand.

"My uncle! He still has some power!"

He turned the page.

Marta locked herself in their room the rest of the day.

He had this things moved into the guest bedroom across the hall. Marta occupied herself with the children.

His civilian clothes pinched in all sorts of places — his uniform had always been so comfortable. He went to the trunk of the car, dug something out of the luggage. Thousands of miles of searching behind, her house less than an eighth of a mile ahead. He pushed his hair from his forehead, hoped she wouldn't see him walking up to the porch.

In the summer, Marta left for two weeks to visit her sister in Hamburg. He brought the girl to his room: he wanted to be with her in a bed.

He fussed about with things, chattering, as she undressed. His fingers trembled on his shirt buttons. He took her in his arms, his skin against hers. He whispered her all sorts of things, though he had tried to teach her German in the past without success. He loved her.

He told her.

Afterward, he fell asleep. He still shuddered to think what he would have done to the Kommandant had he been her, with his service dagger and pistol by the bowl of fruit on the bureau.

She did nothing.

"In the Bedroom of the Kommandant." The first poem in her book. His throat tightened. He began to read.

"*Verdammte Scheisse!*" She understood German!

He bellowed to see himself on the page: she was well-fed — had Cognac, champagne, caviare; well-dressed — wore one of Marta's old gowns; warm — slept with blankets in the corner of his office. Except for the time he was inspecting the Camp and Marta bashed the girl with the wooden back of her hairbrush, the girl was not beaten after he took her in.

"*Schmutzige Hure!*" The first blow smashed into the girl's cheekbone; others landed on her arms, shoulders, neck. That night after dinner, he found her huddled in the corner: swelling and bruises.

He roared into the kitchen, the abandoned brush clenched in his fist. Marta jumped, clutching the dishtowel to her breast. He hurled the wood through the window over the sink, the falling glass soundless beneath his rage. Then he stalked outside. Marta collapsed at the table, her white knuckles twisting, untwisting, twisting the towel. The booming of his gun lasted almost an hour.

He posted a guard at his office door, permitted no one entrance unless he were in: not his adjutant, not his children, not ever his wife.

He protected the girl, fed her, clothed her. And he never forced himself on her: she did not resist. True, he did things with her he did not do with Marta; his wife did not enjoy being touched or kissed there. But his girlfriends before the war had told him he was gentle, and good; some had fallen in love with him. Toward the end, he did not touch the girl at all, except sometimes to caress her face with calloused fingers, or to kiss her scarred palm and hold it against his lined face.

Howling, he shredded her book, burned the pages in the middle of the hotel room floor, stamped the flames and ashes.

Six months later, he purchased another copy, but turned cold when he tried to open it.

Every day he vowed he would see her one more time, for that time.

"It's her, isn't it?" Marta demanded.

He said nothing.

"You'll never see the children again!"

Nothing.

"I'll make them hate you!"

"Yes."

"*She* hates you!"

He knew that.

He looked back at the car in the shadows. His right hand tightened on its object. The porch resounded hollowly under his boots. He cleared his throat, knocked on the wood of the screen-door: *and if I perish, I perish.*

Silence.

He knocked again.

"Just a minute," floated from somewhere inside. Cold sweat dampened his shirt. He pressed his arms against his body, bent his right arm so that his hand was behind.

She came from the kitchen, drying her hands on a white dishtowel, talking to two grey kittens who bounded after her, racing her to the door. She smiled at them, laughed. It was the first time he had seen her smile.

Then she saw him.

Morning sunlight from the windows in the office haloed his head and shoulders. He was writing furiously and did not look up until his adjutant coughed politely. The Kommandant snapped his head up, frowning, pushed back the dark hair that had fallen over his forehead. The scowl faded.

He strode over to her, dismissing the other. He paced around and around, nodding. "*Ja.*" Taking her arm, he led her to a door beyond his desk: a small bathroom. He pointed at the towels and washcloths, unwrapped a sweet-smelling soap.

She did not move.

He guided her toward the basin, turned on the water.

She was still.

He began to pull the shift from her.

She turned her face away.

He closed the door, left her alone there.

She stood a long time without moving. The water gurgled in the sink. She folded a warm, wet cloth over her closed eyes, then began to wash. She left the water running while she blotted the moisture from her skin. She did not look at herself in the small mirror over the sink.

He knocked and opened the door simultaneously.

She jumped, holding the towel to her.

He stared.

The buttons of his jacket were undone.

He turned off the water.

Kicked the door closed.

She swallowed.

He stood before her, smelling of smoke, took the towel.

She vowed to make no sound.

He knelt before her, wrapped his arms around, pulled her rigid form to him.

Her eyelids clamped down, black cloth smooth on her buttocks and thighs.

The kittens meowed solemnly and rubbed their thin backs against her ankles. The bright in her cheeks drained down her long throat and his behind her blue-grey dress.

"May I come in?"

She recognized his voice even in English. A slight snort escaped her flaring nostrils, a hiss from beneath the towel.

He knew then that she had seen him in the store, had expected that he would follow.

She drew the heavy German pistol from beneath the cloth.

His left eyelid began to twitch. He nodded his head slightly, clicked his heels together. Her eyes were bluer than anything he had ever seen. He stood straight.

Snap!

She readied the gun.

He would not close his eyes.

She emptied the chambers into his chest without opening the screen door.

He felt himself pounded, flung, in slowed motion, backward; he heard the cats snarl, felt the acrid powder sting his nostrils. His head cracked on the bottom step. He hoped he hadn't cried out.

The kittens mewed, wrapping themselves around her ankles.

"Esth…" he cleared his throat. "Esther, may I come in?"

She almost didn't recognize his voice in English. He was slighter without the uniform, greying, craggier — but him. Her hands shook; her heart thudded behind her small breasts. She felt hot. Cold. She flinched as he moved his right hand to the front.

He opened the slim volume to the first selection.

Her brow furrowed.

He put on his reading glasses and in a wavering voice read "In the Bedroom of the Kommandant." Though the poem covered two pages, all the stanzas poured from him without his turning the page.

Her fingers pressed against her lips.

His hand faltered slightly as he held out the book to her, looked over the rim of his spectacles at her.

She did not move.

He removed his glasses, slid them behind his lapel into his shirt pocket, looked down.

Silence.

His arm lowered. "*Ja.*" He bowed his head, making a great effort not to click his heels together. He turned, stepped down.

Something creaked behind him.

He looked back at her.

She stepped out onto the porch, holding open the screen door. The kittens peered warily from her feet. The white towel fluttered in the early breeze.

To imitate the great actor Christopher Walken when he's doing comedy, saying, "Wowie-wow-wow-wow," let me say, about this story, "Owie-ow-ow-ow!" All the exclamation points! Marta uses them every time she speaks! Okay, we get it! She's yelling!

And all the single-sentence paragraphs!

What's that all about?

I've no idea!

Are you done laughing yet?

It's obvious that I probably knew as much about writing fiction when I first wrote "The Kommandant" as I did when I was 12. Fortunately, my dissertation advisor, Michael Atkinson, was kind enough to tell me the truth ("You'd probably better stick to poetry").

Months afterward, I dreamt that I saw "The Kommandant", arranged in stanzas, like a poem, rising out of a deep pool of water. I awoke, went to my office, and immediately began changing the story into a poem.

I present it here for you, so those of you who've asked to read it don't have to keep looking up my dissertation in the University of Cincinnati library, or searching for the journals in which it was published, in order to see it. Except for capitalizing things where appropriate (I used to write my poems in lower-case, though I didn't even like e.e. cummings' work), I've forced myself to leave everything else as it was in the original.

Line-breaks are based, as all my Holocaust poems are, on syllabic-breaks: imitating the arbitrary rigidity of the Nazis and the Concentration Camps. Some of my Holocaust poems had 10 syllables per line, one had 15, this one has 12. If I miscounted any of the syllables in the lines, please don't tell me as there's nothing I can do about it now. The poem's already been published in too many places for me to change it, and it'll just remind me why I was a literature major and not a math major.

Spoiler Alert: If you read this before reading the novel, please be aware that it reveals plot elements contained in the novel, even if slightly changed.

The Kommandant
(the original poem)

For who can make straight
that which He hath made crooked?

He saw her again, after years, in the village
store. He leapt back, his hand seeking the weight of his
gun. There she stood: frailer than in the yard, faded
dress hanging loosely from thinned shoulders, more colour

in the scarf on her head than in her cheeks. He barked
his adjutant outside, strode to her, forced her chin
up with his baton, found eyes bluer than his own.
She did not look away. His arm dropped, brushing the

gun on his hip. He unbuckled his holster, laid
it on his desk. The cork on their third bottle of
champagne exploded; he gulped the pale liquid, hauled
his chair to her side of the desk, scooting until

their knees collided, his monologue more earnest
than usual. She sipped, concentrating on the
silver oval pinned over his left breast: two swords
crossed behind an army steel helmet. Leather hissed

as he slipped pistol from holster; he leaned forward,
displaying the cool dark of the weapon. *Freiheit.*
He snapped the two small circles: up and back, urging
the butt toward her hand. Her glass shuddered. She stayed still.

He gripped her wrist, tugging her to her feet along
with him, slammed the warm metal into her hand, crushed
her limp fingers around its form, fixing her hand
there with both of his rough palms: *Du — Freiheit,* yanking

gun and hands until the barrel butted his chest,
her elbow rigid. *Feuer.* Her eyes became less
opaque. *Ja.* He swallowed, squared his shoulders, lifted
his chin, released her hands. Her arm lowered. *Nein, nein,*

Feuer. The piece thudded to her feet. He stared at
her; her eyes dulled, leaving him there. The gun lay on
the floor between them. He had forgotten that he
no longer wore it; his empty hand slid down his

hip and leg as he watched her pay for her items,
her long braid pale down the center of her back. Sun
glowed on her hair as she opened the shop-door and
stepped out, calling a goodbye to the owner. *She*

writes books, a squinting wife standing near him in the
aisle confided as the German gazed after her.
From the bookstore window, her face lashed out at him.
He leaned, gasping, against the glass. Fuller cheeks, hair,

bright eyes — but her. He dragged himself into the shop,
forced the slim volume into his hands. *Survivor:*
One who Survives. Poems by Esther Rebekah
Levi. Esther. The publisher supplied him an

address. She had moved by the time he reached the place,
though it was easy enough to discover her
new destination. So it went. This time, she was
here. The engine started almost too eagerly.

After countless European villages, he
found her in this mountain town. He wished now he were
wearing his uniform. He shook his head: he must
go to her without ornaments. The road twisted

through singing summer green, warmed by morning. He would
park far from the house, approach on foot. He practiced
the words in English. *Verdammt nochmal!* He slammed the
car stopped, jerking the wheel toward the flanking trees: her house.

The car door banged; he leaned on the hood. She would not
want to see him again; perhaps she had her own
gun by now. He should forget he had found her. His
fingers sought the door handle, but the look in her

eyes, the taste of her, the smell of her: he made a
great show of examining the numbers on her
forearm: *S-34291*. She glanced down, dark
lashes long on her cheeks. He kneaded her shoulders,

ribs through the threadbare material. Her hipbones
jutted awkwardly beneath the skin. He rubbed her
cheek with the back of his long fingers, murmured, pushed
the scarf from her head, ran his hand across the light

stubble; he circled her several times, nodding: *Ja.*
Marta guessed almost from the beginning. At first
she said nothing, assuming it would pass as all
the others. Then: sniping, chiding, remonstrative

silences. In spring she confronted him: *Stop with*
this girl. He looked up from his morning paper. *There's*
only so much I can ignore; I must think of
my position. He buttered his toast, scanned the print.

Marta pushed the paper down onto the table.
I'll complain to someone if this doesn't stop: my
aunt's husband still has influence. The wrench on her
wrist freed the paper. He snapped it straight, turned the page,

sipped his coffee. Marta locked herself in their room
the rest of the day. A week later he had his
things moved into the guest bedroom across the hall.
In summer Marta took the children to visit

her sister in Hamburg for two weeks. He brought the
girl to his room: to be with her in a bed. His
back to her, he unhooked his weapons, fumbled with
buttons. The sheets slid cool, crisp on his thighs. He pulled

her to him, his skin against hers; though he had been
unable to teach her German, he whispered her
all sorts of things: he told her he loved her. After,
he slept. He shuddered to think what he would have done

to the Kommandant had he been the girl, with his
service dagger and pistol by the bowl of fruit
on the bureau. She did nothing. *In the Bedroom*
of the Kommandant: the first poem in her book. His

throat tightened. *Verdammte Scheisse!* She understood
German! He bellowed to see himself on the page:
she had Cognac, champagne, caviar; wore one of
Marta's gowns; slept with blankets in the corner of

his office. The girl was not beaten after he
took her in, except once, when he was inspecting
the Camp and Marta bashed her with the wooden back
of a hairbrush: *Schmutzige Hure!* The first blows

smashed into the girl's cheekbone; others landed on
her arms, shoulders, neck. That night, after dinner, he
found her, huddled into the corner: swelling, bruises.
He roared into the kitchen, abandoned brush clenched

in fist. His wife started, clutched the dishtowel to her
breast. He hurled the wood through the window over the
sink, the falling glass soundless beneath his rage. Then
he stalked outside. Marta collapsed at the table,

white knuckles twisting, untwisting, twisting the cloth.
The thundering of his gun lasted almost an
hour. He posted a guard at his office door,
permitted no one entrance unless he were in:

not his adjutant, not his children, not ever
his wife. He protected the girl, fed her, clothed her.
And he never forced himself on her: she did not
resist. True, he did things with her he did not with

Marta; his wife disliked his touching, kissing. But
his girlfriends before the war had told him he was
gentle, good; some had even fallen in love with
him. Toward the end, he did not touch the girl at all,

except sometimes to caress her face with calloused
fingers, or to kiss her scarred palm and hold it to
his lined face. Howling, he shredded her book, burned its
pages in the middle of the hotel room floor,

stamped the flames, ashes. Six months later, he purchased
another copy, but turned cold when he tried to
open it. Every day he vowed he would see her
one more time, for that time. He went to the trunk of

the car, dug the small parcel from the luggage. His
civilian clothes pinched in all sorts of places — his
uniform had been so comfortable. Thousands of
miles of searching behind, her house less than an eighth

of a mile ahead. He pushed greying hair back from
his forehead, hoped she wouldn't see him walking up
to the porch. *It's her, isn't it?* Marta asked. *You'll
never see the children again.* He said nothing.

I'll make them hate you. Yes. *She hates you.* He knew that.
He glanced back at the shadowed car; his right hand strained
on its object. The porch resounded hollowly
under his boots. He swallowed, knocked on the wood of

the screen door: *and if I perish, I perish.* He
knocked again. *Just a minute,* floated from inside.
Sweat dampened his shirt; he pressed his arms against his
body, bent his right arm so it was behind. She

came from the kitchen, drying her hands on a white
dishtowel, humming for two grey kittens who bounded
after her, racing her to the door. She smiled at
them, laughed. It was the first time he had seen her smile.

Then she saw him. Morning sun from windows in the
office haloed his head, shoulders. He was writing
furiously, did not stop scribbling until his
adjutant coughed. The Kommandant snapped his head up,

scowling, shoved back the dark hair fallen over his
forehead. He strode to her, dismissing the other.
He paced around her, nodding: *Ja.* Gripping her arm,
he led her to a small bathroom beyond his desk.

He pointed out towel, washcloth, unwrapped a sweet soap.
When she did not move, he prodded her toward the sink,
turned on water. She was still. He began to drag
the shift from her. She closed her eyes. Water gurgled

in the basin. He closed the door, leaving her there.
He jerked open a cabinet on the far wall, poured
a whiskey, quaffed it, splashed out another, smoked
an Italian cigarette, loosed his collar, glanced

at his watch. He opened the door. She jumped, holding
the towel to her. He stopped the water, flattened his
cigarette, kicked the door closed. She swallowed. He forced
her chin in his palm, roughed his lips on hers, yanked free

the towel. She made no sound. He knelt, wound his arms
about, forced her rigid form to him. The kittens
meowed solemnly, rubbed their thin backs against her
ankles. The bright in her cheeks drained down her long throat

and hid behind her blue-grey dress. *May I come in?*
She recognized his voice even in English. A
slight snort escaped her flaring nostrils, a hiss from
under the towel. He knew then that she had seen him

in the store, had expected he would follow. She
drew the heavy German pistol from beneath the
cloth. His left eyelid began to twitch. He nodded,
clicked his heels together. Her eyes were bluer than

anything he had ever seen. She stood straight. She
readied the gun: *snap!* He would not close his eyes. She
emptied the chambers into his chest through the screen.
He felt himself pounded, flung, in slowed motion, back;

he heard the cats snarl, felt acrid powder sting his
nostrils. His head cracked on the bottom step. He hoped
he hadn't cried out. The kittens mewed, wrapped themselves
around her ankles. *Esth...* he coughed. *Esther, may I*

come in? She almost didn't recognize his voice
in English. He was slighter without uniform,
greying, craggier — but him. Her hands shook; she flinched
as his right hand swung around to the front: the slim volume

opened to its first selection. Her brow furrowed.
He put on reading glasses and in wavering
voice read *In the Bedroom of the Kommandant.* Though
the poem spanned two pages, all its stanzas poured from

him without his turning the page. Her fingers hid
her mouth. His hand faltered as he offered the book
to her, looked over the rim of his spectacles
at her. She did not even breathe. He removed his

glasses, slid them behind his lapel into shirt
pocket; his arm lowered. *Ja.* He bowed his head, with
a great effort not to click his heels. He laid the
open book on the wide porch-rail, stepped down. Something

creaked behind him. He turned. She came out onto the
porch, holding wide the screen-door. The two grey kittens
peered warily from her feet. The thin towel, her
book's pages fluttered in the early morning breeze.

Did I really say I was proud of that poem at the time I wrote it? Now, about 30 years later, I'm wondering things like, "What's with all the colons & semi-colons?" and "I actually used exclamation points! More than once!" and "No wonder it got rejected so many times before it got accepted!" Seriously, though, you can see that the basic structure of the novel is there, in the poem, with its shifting scenes, different perspectives, and double endings.

Hope you enjoyed the original story and poem, if only for a laugh & as examples of what not to do when writing either stories or poems, and are as glad as I am that I finally learned how to really write, with my first novel, *The Kommandant's Mistress.*

Author BIO, Photo, Amazon Page, Web-site, Twitter, Blog, & Contact Information

Alexandria Constantinova Szeman

Critically acclaimed & award-winning author, Alexandria Constantinova Szeman (formerly writing as "Sherri" Szeman because her 1st editor told her that her name "wouldn't fit on the book cover," & wanted an "easy" first name to go with her "hard" last name) began as a poet before she started writing novels, short fiction, and creative writing books.

Szeman has Ph.D.'s in Creative Writing and in English & Comparative World Literatures. Her dissertation, *Survivor: One Who Survives* (University of Cincinnati, 1986) was a collection of original poetry, all of which were accepted or published by university & literary journals before her dissertation defense. While in graduate school, her poetry was awarded numerous prizes, including The Elliston Poetry Prize (several times) & The Isabel and Mary Neff Creative Writing Fellowship.

Her first novel, *The Kommandant's Mistress*, on the Holocaust from multiple points of view and perspectives, was chosen as one of *The New York Times Book Review*'s "Top 100 Books of the Year" (1993). It was also awarded the University of Rochester's (NY) prestigious Kafka Prize "for the outstanding book of prose fiction by an American woman" (1994), and Central State University's (OH) Talmadge McKinney Research Award (1993).

Originally published by HarperCollins (1993) & HarperPerennial (1994), the novel has been sold to publishers in 10 foreign countries and translated into French, Spanish, Russian, Lithuanian, Danish, Swedish, Norwegian, among others. It was republished by Arcade (2000) & was optioned for film (though funded, it was never made).

Her second novel, *Only with the Heart,* on the devastating effects of Alzheimer's on a family, is on the recommended reading lists of Alzheimer's Associations nationwide. Originally published by Arcade (2000), the Revised & Expanded, 12th Anniversary Edition contains new scenes with updated medical treatment/medications for Alzheimer's, as well as new legal definitions and statutes regarding assisted suicide.

Her third novel, *No Feet in Heaven,* about two brothers and their female cousin who decide to attain fame by hunting down a notorious serial killer themselves, won praise from several NY editors before it was accepted by a New York Trade House; unfortunately, that House was purchased by a larger NY Trade House: the editor was then laid off, and the book "rejected."

The titular story in her award-winning collection of short stories, *Naked, with Glasses,* won Third Prize in *Story Magazine*'s "Seven Deadly Sins Contest" (1995), and the manuscript won the Grand Prize in the UKA Press [United Kingdom Authors Press] 2007 Annual International Writing Competition.

Her two poetry collections, *Love in the Time of Dinosaurs* and *Where Lightning Strikes: Poems on the Holocaust,* both contain critically acclaimed & award-winning poems. Each volume includes several poems from her dissertation, *Survivor: One Who Survives* (University of Cincinnati, 1986). The poems have won several prizes, including University of Cincinnati's Elliston Prize (anonymous competition; 1983, 1984, 1985), an Honorable Mention in the Chester H. Jones Poetry Foundation National Poetry Competition (1985), Michigan State University's *The Centennial Review* Michael Miller Award for Poetry (1985), an Honorable Mention in *Writer's Digest* National Writing Competition (1980), and The Isabel & Mary Neff Fellowship for Creative Writing (1984-85). Both volumes were unanimously accepted for publication by all outside readers of UKA Press [United Kingdom Authors Press] in 2004.

Szeman is currently completing her latest novel, as well as revising her memoir (about growing up with a mother who practiced Munchausen's by Proxy), and is about to publish several creative writing exercise books, including an updated version of her classic *Mastering Point of View* (originally published by Story Press, 2001).

Alexandria's Amazon Author Central Page
Amazon.com/author/alexandriaszeman

Alexandria's Web-Site
AlexandriaConstantinovaSzeman.com

Read excerpts from all her books:
AlexandriaConstantinovaSzeman.com/Books.php

Alexandria's Blog: The Alexandria Papers
TheAlexandriaPapers.com
AlexandriaConstantinovaSzeman.com/Blog.php

Alexandria's Twitter @Alexandria_SZ
Twitter.com/Alexandria_SZ
AlexandriaConstantinovaSzeman.com/Twitter.html

Contact Alexandria
AlexandriaConstantinovaSzeman.com/Contact.php